DARK SECRETS OF THE BAYOU

KIM CARTER

RAVEN SOUTH PUBLISHING

Published by Raven South Publishing
Atlanta, Georgia 30324, USA

Copyright © 2020 by Kim Carter

Edited by Evil Eye Editing

Cover Design by www.mariondesigns.com

ACKNOWLEDGMENTS

Once again, I find myself eternally grateful for those who gave freely of their time and knowledge to make this book possible. I cannot possibly thank them enough, but I will certainly give it a shot.

First and foremost, I give thanks to the true love of my life, Julius Herron, the man who always sought out the best in me and encouraged me to continue writing despite my shortcomings. This book has been my biggest challenge, not only because it was my first attempt at a historical mystery, but because Julius was also facing many health challenges. On March 15, 2020 he went to his heavenly home before this book made it to print, but he did see it to its completion, and for that, I am immensely grateful. I pray this novel makes you proud. You will forever be the other half of my heart. Forever and always....

This book wouldn't have been completed without the tireless efforts of my dear friend, Julia Simpson. Her ideas and hard work certainly made it far better than I ever could have without her. There were many times when we worked so late into the night that we became delirious, but I wouldn't trade anything for those memories! So exhausting, yet empowering, entertaining, and comical. It was during those times when I learned that the answer to everything is chocolate and a good friend! I love you so much, Juli. Cheers!

As always, research remains my favorite part of writing because it inevitably requires a road trip with friends. This novel has been no exception. Thanks to Bryce Michel, owner of Topwater Charters, LLC, in Chavin, Louisiana, who took us on an amazing tour of the bayou. His fishing lodge was quite impressive, and I'd highly recommend it to anyone looking for great fishing, unbelievable food, and knowledgeable guides.

Many thanks to Reese Johnson who shared hours and hours of knowledge about his home state of Louisiana. Your input was certainly key in getting even the smallest detail right. Philia Agape.

To my besties and road dogs, Kelly Keylon, Gudy Greg Headrick, and Lisa Mobley – I have more love for you guys than words could ever express.

To my cover designer and dear friend – Keith Saunders of Marion Designs – as usual, you once again knocked it out of the park. Thanks for bringing my visions to life.

Many thanks to Tierney James, one of my favorite authors, who graciously read an unedited copy and agreed to write a blurb. What a tremendous honor!!!

Thanks to the following who also agreed to be beta readers and read an extremely unedited manuscript without judgement: J.R. Keylon – you will forever be missed – hug my Jules for me; Jimmy Britton – old friend – much love to you; Keith 'Rumper' Cowart – always a willing proofreader, many thanks; and the Luthersville book club, 'Four Women and a Book' – I appreciated your input.

I certainly can't slight Ken Towry, synopsis supervisor, therapist extraordinaire, and awesome contractor for this crazy Mrs. Winchester.

I can't express how hard my editor, Holly Atkinson, worked on this project. It was the first time we'd worked together, and I'm sure many times she wondered what she'd gotten herself into. But she was a trooper and worked diligently until the end. I look forward to many more 'fun-filled' messes together. LOL...

A sincerely heartfelt thank-you to Dr. R. Bruce Prince, who has, for decades now, encouraged me to write without abandon. This book certainly made it to completion because of your insistence. A huge thank you to my friend, Joyce Prince, who never fails, despite my circumstances, to make me laugh. Without laughter, what a dreadful place our world would be!

To David Pitts – who unselfishly, and without hesitation, gave me the keys to his beautiful mountain estate so that I could find the peace and tranquility needed to finish this project and offer the inspiration for my next one. I also want to thank you for being someone to talk to when I lost Julius. Unfortunately – we were both inducted into a club we wanted nothing to do with. You have talked me off a ledge more times than I care to admit, and I will forever be grateful to you. Keep 'delivering dreams daily', for it is truly what you do best.

To Bo Pitts – many thanks for taking my calls about everything from skeleton keys to haunted attics. I so enjoyed touring your beautiful Savannah home. #jealous

And finally, thanks to my son, D Low Demetrius Whitfield, and my Sissy, Pamela Carter Youngblood, who read and re-read this manuscript in hopes of making it better. I love you both!

It's all I have to bring to-day,
    This, and my heart beside,
    This, and my heart, and all the fields
    And all the meadows wide.

— EMILY DICKINSON

For Austin...my first miracle...the golden child, as you've so often been dubbed. I'm so grateful you share my love of the written word for its truly the one thing that spans the generations and binds us all together.

Once you learn to read,
    You will forever be free.

— Frederick Douglass

PART I

BEFORE

1

KANE, LOUISIANA, 1859

EMMANUEL SINCLAIR STOOD BACK and surveyed the sprawling plantation that had encompassed his life for the past two years. He nodded with pleasure as if someone were there awaiting his approval.

Placed perfectly amidst rows of river oaks, magnolias, and sycamores, the estate was breathtakingly beautiful. The well-designed landscape surrounding the home contrasted sharply with the bald cypress and coastal willows rising prominently from the waters in the bayou.

Emmanuel had no doubt Lucretia, his soon-to-be bride, would be delighted with her stately new home. Within the next twenty-four hours, she was scheduled to go by train from Baltimore to the Ohio River. Lucretia would then travel by steamboat via the Ohio and the Mississippi to New Orleans, where Emmanuel would be waiting for her.

Lucretia's trip would be grueling, but she'd experienced many challenges over her eighteen years. Her grandparents had been part of the Expulsion of 1755 when the British ejected all French-Acadians refusing to pledge allegiance to the King of England. Originally settling in Maine, her family relocated to New York before putting down permanent stakes in Baltimore. Young Lucretia longed for consistency and it had been Emmanuel's stability that'd won her over.

By the age of thirty-five, he'd already made his fortune in the cotton business. His father had died seven years earlier, leaving Emmanuel a sizeable concession of land and a fledgling cotton crop which, at best, kept the plantation self-sufficient. But it was the combination of Emmanuel's business savvy, the increase of cotton production, and Louisiana's strategic ports that'd quickly increased his wealth.

As Emmanuel had been steadily building a prosperous empire, Thaddeus Jackson had been constructing a flourishing kingdom of his own, on an equally expansive plantation a few miles away. Thaddeus had his father, Mathias, to thank for being born a free man of color. He had caught the eye of Andrew Jackson as a standout on the battlefield during the War of 1812. His grueling work ethic and leadership skills had been pivotal in the construction of breastworks, later referred to as *Line Jackson*. Thaddeus had quickly tired of the story, even as a young boy, and considered his father nothing more than a yes-man who'd covered cotton bales with logs and mud to protect the white army. However, Andrew Jackson had been quite impressed— enough so, in fact, that he'd facilitated Mathias's freedom. Not one to take any blessing for granted, Mathias had chosen to acquire Jackson's surname out of gratitude.

Thaddeus had found much to dislike about his father, but he'd inherited many of his most admirable traits. He was a powerful leader, and quick learner with a sense of adventure. These characteristics had led to his success as a Mississippi River privateer. His tall frame and good looks didn't hinder him either. Both his appearance and self-confidence had also captured Fatima Lambert's attention.

Fatima came with quite the story of her own. With a shortage of white women in the state of Louisiana and laws forbidding interracial marriage, the institution of plaçage enabled her to be a mistress to the very wealthy, and incredibly old, William Lambert. She'd been merely a teenager when he'd spotted her working his fields and had quickly arranged for her to be a kept woman. Accustomed to hard labor and the unrelenting heat, she hadn't objected to being at his beck and call, and his bed, when he'd insisted.

Fortunately for Fatima, she'd only had to suffer through a few sessions of his sexual desires before he'd dropped dead of a heart attack at the ripe age of seventy-eight. With William being a childless widower and having no other heirs with whom to split his fortune, Fatima had become the proud owner of not only his cotton plantation, but his slaves as well.

It wasn't her attractiveness as a mulatto that'd lured Thaddeus to pursue Fatima, it'd been her property and the glorious cotton fields that promised a lifetime of financial security. Once he'd set his sights on her, there was little Fatima could do but concede to his advances. After all, who wouldn't want a bright, handsome husband to take care of things?

A RABBIT SCURRIED beneath some underbrush, drawing Emmanuel's attention to the cool, damp breeze and dark clouds promising an impending storm. He walked to the front porch, paused long enough to grab his oil lamp, and made his way inside.

Emmanuel hesitated briefly to take in the magnificence of the grand staircase winding its way, like an ornate ribbon, up to the second and third floors. One of his slaves, who'd been trained as a blacksmith, had spent the past few months creating it, and he hadn't disappointed. It would surely take Lucretia's breath away.

Aside from a bed and some office necessities, the remaining furnishings would be left to Lucretia's desires. Yet *another* of Emmanuel's wedding gifts to her.

Although it was midday, and the many windows gave way to ample light, thunder clouds had begun to darken the home's interior. Emmanuel made his way up the stairs, down the corridor leading to the west wing, and entered his office. He slid the mantel a smidgen to the left. This released the mechanism holding the entire faux fireplace intact, enabling him to unlock the steel door leading to an array of complex tunnels, and ultimately, his concealed vault.

THIS WAS where the lives of two greedy and shrewd businessmen merged. This was the beginning of a tale older than time, filled with greed, lust, superstition, and murderous secrets they'd both take to their graves.

It was a story meant to be locked away forever.

2

KANE, LOUISIANA, 1849

FATIMA HADN'T BEEN in love with William Lambert, but she'd missed him terribly after his death. In his own way, he'd genuinely cared for her, even though his feelings had initially been based solely on appearance.

Mr. Lambert had lost his wife of forty-two years after decades of struggling to produce an heir, and had been terribly lonely when he'd spotted Fatima working his fields. Her hair had been pulled up carelessly in a bun, but long tendrils of curls had managed to escape and cascade around her beautiful face. The inevitable perspiration from the brutal Louisianan sun had glistened like diamonds on her thin arms.

After the death of both parents, she'd been shuttled from one slave family to the next, never knowing where she'd lay her head at night. It'd become even more difficult as she'd blossomed into a young woman and the women grew concerned about their husbands' wandering eyes.

The only friend she'd made among the slave community had been Prudence, a kind midwife, five years her elder. Prudence had filled her mind with stories of working inside the huge estate. Fatima had reveled in Prudence's tales of washing fine china shipped from

Europe and of women wearing vibrantly colored silk dresses with something called crinolines underneath.

Fatima had pleaded with Prudence not to spare any details. When the days had lengthened, and the sun became unbearable, Fatima would envision what life was like in the world she'd never know.

WILLIAM LAMBERT HAD BEEN as enthralled with Fatima as she'd been with the detailed stories of life in his mansion. He'd had Prudence summon her from the fields and prepare a warm bath for her while Sara, a skilled seamstress, tailored a dress from the most expensive silk he could get his hands on.

The two women had washed the dirt and sweat from Fatima's long hair and pulled it back with a cloisonné barrette his wife had never worn. The pale pink dress, as simple as it'd been with such little time to stitch it, had been more beautiful on her than one purchased from the big city.

William had been waiting for her in the dining room when she came down to greet him. She'd taken his breath away just as she had the day he'd spotted her in the fields, filthy from hours of tedious labor.

Fatima couldn't keep her hands off the soft silk and subconsciously smoothed the dress around her thin hips. Had she known what a princess was, she would've surely felt like one. Without any decent shoes to fit Fatima, Sara had made the dress a little long to cover her small, bare feet.

"You look lovely," the older man had said. "Please, have a seat. There's no need to be frightened; I have no intention of harming you. My name is William."

"I know who you are, Master Lambert," Fatima had answered so softly he wasn't sure if he'd heard her. "I've seen you before from the fields. I was sorry about your wife."

"Yes, I was too. Please, Fatima... Are you comfortable with me calling you Fatima?"

"Yes."

"Please, call me William."

Their conversation was interrupted by two women who placed several bowls and crystal goblets on the table. The older woman used a silver ladle to pour thick stew into china bowls and placed a large rectangle of golden cornbread on each bread plate. William picked up his spoon and pointed it at hers. "Please, help yourself. Beef stew is one of my favorites. I hope you'll like it."

Meat was a rarity in the slave quarters and when they'd had any, it was mostly dispersed among the older men. Women and children were only given a taste, unless there were any leftovers. No one had ever shown concern if Fatima had eaten at all, and not being an aggressive person, she'd often gone without dinner.

The aroma coming from the stew was intoxicating. Fatima had shoved several quick bites in before she'd noticed the older man watching her. The thought of having such a large amount of food entirely for her was almost too much to comprehend. Fatima had lowered her head in humiliation, slowly swallowing what remained in her mouth.

"Don't be ashamed. I'm glad you like it. Continue to eat, for this is only the beginning, Fatima. Only the beginning of all the goodness I have in store for you."

3

KANE, LOUISIANA, 1857

ALTHOUGH BORN a free man of color, Thaddeus Jackson hadn't been born into money. His war hero father, Mathias, gauged success by one's integrity and good name, not by money or material wealth. Thaddeus had found him foolish and unambitious, which had driven him as far from his father's legend as he could have gotten.

By all legalities, Thaddeus was a privateer. But by most people's standards, he was simply a pirate, a robber of any vessel with valuable cargo daring to travel the wide berth of the mighty Mississippi or the open seas.

Thaddeus was a natural leader and used it to his advantage. His height, good looks, and intelligence drew people in, persuading them to trust him, even when their conscience tried to convince them otherwise.

By the time he hit his early twenties, Thaddeus had countless bands of men stationed along the river, not only gathering intel but invading ships for any valuables that could easily be sold on the black market.

It was an exciting life and he reveled in the glory of being not only respected, but feared. It was a greater high than the rotgut moonshine his men brought him every time they'd gotten their hands on some.

But then Thaddeus had received word of something that intrigued him a little more than life on the river. It was about a lovely mulatto woman who'd just inherited her plaçage husband's cotton plantation along with twenty slaves.

Louisiana was somewhat different from other established colonies. It was truly a melting pot of cultures, races, and religions. But the prospect of him, a free black man, becoming both the title-holder of a cotton plantation and his own slaves, was more than Thaddeus could've imagined.

IT'D BEEN Prudence who'd greeted Thaddeus Jackson the day he came calling in his newly tailored suit. Her heart had skipped a beat at the sight of him, for a man of color to be so impeccably polished was uncommon. He certainly wasn't a field worker, Prudence concluded, his nails were too clean.

After several seconds of looking him over, she finally spoke. "How may I help you?"

"The name is Jackson, Thaddeus Jackson. I've come to call on Ms. Fatima."

"Is *Ms. Lambert* expecting you?"

"No, ma'am, she isn't," he answered kindly. "But I've heard tell she's the most beautiful woman in the state, and I'd hate to continue on with my travels without ever having had the pleasure of meeting her myself."

"Ms. Lambert is still in mourning. She's a widow, but I'm sure you've heard *tell* of that, too."

"Yes, and what a tragedy. I was told it's been over a year. I'd never have considered stopping by had that not been the case."

"Oh, I'm sure you wouldn't," Prudence commented. She could already sense his cunning manipulation and the last thing she wanted was to let him anywhere near Fatima. But Prudence knew her place. It wasn't up to her to screen visitors. "You can take a seat on the porch," she said, nodding to several rockers. "I'll see if Ms. Lambert is available."

Thaddeus bowed to her, which made her want to throw up, but she smiled sweetly and closed the door in his face.

IT WAS NEARLY an hour later when Prudence returned, but Thaddeus was waiting patiently on the porch, just as she'd expected.

"Mr. Jackson, Ms. Lambert will see you now."

He postured a bow once again and followed behind her into the front parlor.

Fatima was seated in a large armchair that almost swallowed her whole, giving her the appearance of a small child. She was indeed as beautiful as Thaddeus had been told, and looked quite vulnerable, which was exactly what he'd hoped. She was still mourning the passing of the man who'd taught her how to be socially acceptable among the elite, yet not strong enough to stand up to anyone who was more worldly.

Fatima was a dream come true and all it took was one of his warm smiles to seal the fate of their future together. They were married on the plantation two months later in 1857.

4

1830

CLAUDE SINCLAIR, Emmanuel's father, had been the proverbial opposite of what the northern colonists envisioned as the typical plantation owner. He was the first one in the fields before the sun rose in
the east and back to his small four-room home after the sun had set.
He'd eaten his dinners alone, long after his wife and son had enjoyed
their warm meals and was often too exhausted to even wash the day's
filth from his worn body at day's end. There was never a profit and
they celebrated whenever the cotton harvest covered their markers
and they were considered self-sufficient.

Emmanuel had been a young boy when he'd begun to sit back
and study the many occupational errors his father had made. It
hadn't taken him long to realize no amount of hard, tedious work
could rival a savvy business mind. He vowed then he'd much rather
use his brain than his muscles.

Claude's first mistake had been to fall for Eli Whitney's cotton gin
plan. He'd been one of the few plantation owners who'd caved into
the entrepreneur's offer to install the new machine on his property at
no up-front cost, in exchange for a portion of his cotton production.
Claude had considered it a genius move with no out-of-pocket

money. He could always grow more cotton; it was removing the seeds that was time consuming.

What he hadn't accounted for was the many loopholes in the patenting process. Most cotton growers would quickly pirate Whitney's idea and make even better cotton gins of their own. He'd never been a risk-taker and believed hard work and determination would always provide enough for his family to survive.

Emmanuel wanted much more than to survive—he wanted to live.

5

1853

WITH ELI WHITNEY and his parents deceased, Emmanuel was quick to institute changes. He'd begun with little more than a handful of slaves and what was left of an aging cotton gin. More than willing to gamble his acreage as collateral against a loan, he'd upgraded his equipment and begun making connections to get his cotton crop sold to higher bidders.

Emmanuel's father had been so busy working himself to the bone that he'd failed to see New Orleans was the most strategic transfer point for all American and foreign goods. Products traveled up and down the Mississippi and its tributaries by steamboats, keelboats, and flatbeds to New Orleans where they were offloaded and stored in warehouses. Some products were immediately offloaded and transferred to oceangoing vessels and shipped to the Caribbean and Europe. Yet another untapped business connection was the railroads, which were now linked to the northeast and northwest.

Claude had sold his cotton at rock-bottom prices, to a company that'd transported his merchandise to various ports. Emmanuel dismissed such foolishness. With his cotton gin newly refurbished and improved, money started rolling in. He was quick to utilize any profit to purchase more slaves, which equated to more cotton.

At the height of cotton production, Louisiana was producing one-sixth of the cotton grown in the United States. But Emmanuel had gotten wind of something capable of making him even wealthier and he'd been captivated. It would involve consolidating his land and holdings with another plantation owner, but the possibilities were endless. Emmanuel had his eyes on another entrepreneur just as hungry as himself. If he'd decided to go out on that limb, it'd be with him.

Emmanuel was not one to trust others with his wealth, but there was something about Thaddeus Jackson that made him feel the two of them together would be unstoppable.

6

1857

Emmanuel Sinclair wasn't content to simply *be* wealthy—he wanted to guarantee his wealth would outlast him. Uncertain his cotton plantation would provide him with such security, he'd reconsidered his initial interest in approaching Thaddeus Jackson.

With a marriage on the horizon, Emmanuel intended to build a mansion unlike any Louisiana had ever seen. It'd undoubtedly take a couple of years of—not only his time and attention—but his savings as well. Prepared to make such a commitment, he couldn't stop in mid-stream if his finances wavered.

Emmanuel had met Thaddeus on a handful of occasions, at social events or when either man had been near the other's property. He'd struck Emmanuel as a straight shooter, and Emmanuel had learned to appreciate a man who said what he meant and meant what he said. There was little time for being coy when one was running a business.

Thaddeus had no doubt done his own homework before introducing himself to Fatima, and Emmanuel respected that. He'd never consider joining in partnership with a man who made decisions without properly investigating his options.

Thaddeus had come out of the gate running, swiftly bringing his plantation out of the red, and soon rivaling Emmanuel's production. Cotton was no doubt king in Louisiana but there was another product now promising to more than double its profit, if one was willing to risk it all. It'd involve a year to produce its first harvest, but if there was enough land to grow sufficient crops, it all but guaranteed a fortune. It'd require highly efficient machines, much more so than a simple cotton gin, but with sharp minds and combined acreage, it could work.

It was sugar cane.

IT DIDN'T TAKE a great deal of effort to convince Thaddeus that if one plantation's yield proved lucrative, then doubling its size could surely double the return. It also went without saying that two sharp minds would fare far better than one.

After much consideration, the two businessmen devised what they considered to be both a daring and somewhat conservative plan. Although sugar cane would net them a far better profit, it didn't come without risk. The high risk, high yield concept wasn't new to either of them. They were willing to roll the dice to an extent, but they weren't willing to lose it all.

Combining both of their properties would allow them to generate hundreds of acres of sugar cane yet continue to grow a smaller cotton crop at the same time, at least until the first few seasons of sugar cane had delivered the anticipated profits.

Although the business would be doubling, both men would be working together to ensure it ran smoothly. Emmanuel was willing to share the helm, provided it gave him the time he needed to oversee the construction of his new estate.

FATIMA REMAINED AS TAKEN with her new husband as she'd been the day he'd shown up at her doorstep. She'd struggled to sleep after

William had passed away because she'd been so concerned about maintaining the plantation, and then Thaddeus had arrived like an answer to a prayer.

With no male leadership in the fields or a vision for the property's future, Fatima had been certain she'd be unable to keep the business going. But her ever true friend, Prudence, had assured her God had a plan and he'd be with her through even her darkest hours. She'd been right and her faith had been confirmed when Thaddeus had entered her life.

Prudence, on the other hand, was far from convinced it'd been the Lord who'd sent the overly confident man in the tailored suit. Her initial assessment of him was proving to be spot on. It'd not been a coincidence Thaddeus Jackson had stopped by to meet her owner; he'd planned it out as systematically as he'd planned his latest business venture.

Prudence had always cared deeply for Fatima. She was a gentle soul who'd lacked the self-confidence needed to survive on her own. Prudence had been there for her when the other women had shunned her for her beauty and remained there to protect her from whatever ills her husband had up his sleeve. However, there remained a thin line between protecting her and steering clear of situations beyond her control. Prudence was a slave and even at Fatima's insistence, Thaddeus could get rid of her at any given moment. She knew it and he knew it, but Prudence kept Fatima out of his hair, and that was the only thing that'd kept her from being sold to another plantation owner.

Fatima had been so excited about her recent pregnancy and the thought of bearing an heir for her husband that she'd paid little attention to his recent allegiance with Emmanuel Sinclair. It hadn't, however, escaped Prudence's notice. The man who owned the adjacent plantation was cut from the same cloth as Thaddeus Jackson and the two of them together couldn't be an indication of anything good. She vowed to keep as much of an eye on the two as possible, while still protecting the gullible, and vulnerable, lady of the estate.

PERHAPS, somewhere in the corners of Fatima Jackson's mind, somewhere so deep she dared to visit, she was aware of her husband's deceptiveness. Maybe it was that which had concerned her far more than the nights she'd lain awake with worry when William had passed away.

Could it have been the stress of holding in her thoughts or the strain of simply denying them that caused the pain, the bleeding, more bleeding...and ultimately, her first miscarriage?

7

1858

TWO HIGHLY DETERMINED MEN, two highly intellectual minds, two driven individuals determined to succeed, and succeed Emmanuel Sinclair and Thaddeus Jackson did.

Their first sugar cane harvest confirmed the two were unstoppable. The decision to have a fallback cotton crop had proven unnecessary and they'd quickly plowed over that land and added to their cane. As the profits rolled in and the construction on Emmanuel's estate moved forward, the two men were on top of the world. But would the top be enough?

With wealth came connections to the elite of Louisiana. Hobnobbing was something both men were good at and utilized to their advantage. Whereas Thaddeus benefitted from his good looks, Emmanuel used his confidant air and track record to woo the rich and powerful. He'd left Thaddeus to tend to day-to-day operations as he'd traveled up and down the Mississippi River to meet with contacts concerning their product. It'd proved to be a lucrative endeavor and their sugar cane business had not only grown but become quite well-known. They'd become a business model, so to speak, for those aspiring to grow their capital.

❀

TACKLING the challenge of an unmanned cotton plantation, followed by merging resources with a partner to begin a sugar cane business from the ground up, had been exhilarating for Thaddeus Jackson. Unfortunately, the exhilaration had been short lived.

Thaddeus's life, as busy as it'd become, was terribly mundane. His fragile wife, Fatima, had suffered two miscarriages and had begun spending her days wallowing in her sorrows, convinced God had somehow found her undeserving of a child. Thaddeus had quickly tired of her insecurities and had little tolerance for her tears. As much as he disliked Prudence, he'd relied on her to keep Fatima occupied.

Just as Thaddeus had done his research on Fatima, Emmanuel had done his on the job experience of his future partner. He'd been most intrigued by Thaddeus's unsavory history as a privateer along the Mississippi. Emmanuel's contacts had confirmed that he'd gone far beyond the realm of his job title and made the most of his connections with the criminal element.

Emmanuel had suspected that Thaddeus had made a living bartering stolen goods but, at some point, could no longer offload them for profit. Louisiana had more free blacks than any of the other colonies and many were landowners and businessmen. However, Thaddeus would have had limited access to any connections farther up the Mississippi. His skin color alone would've caused skepticism, especially where stolen property was concerned.

Emmanuel wasn't interested in offloading many of the items being shipped up the Mississippi. He had no intention of creating more exhausting jobs for himself, like trying to find buyers for large items he'd have to store until they were sold. Nor did he need more cattle or slaves destined for someone else's plantation.

Thaddeus had prided himself in being a privateer, but Emmanuel found him to be little more than a river pirate—a fairly successful one, but a river pirate just the same. Emmanuel, however, wasn't willing to enter the dark world of criminal enterprise unless it was going to be well worth his while.

However, he had a plan, a very big, complex plan that'd only work if Thaddeus Jackson was on board.

THADDEUS WAS quick to arrive at Emmanuel's property after being summoned. Anytime he could leave his own estate, he was anxious to do so.

The two men had sat in the parlor for the first time. With the first floor almost complete, Emmanuel was chomping at the bit to begin construction on the remaining floors. He had big plans for his office and once it was complete, the two men would take their business to another level.

Since Lucretia would not arrive until the estate was finished, Emmanuel had commissioned makeshift furniture, saving the expensive pieces from New Orleans and Europe for her. The chairs in the parlor weren't chairs at all, rather overturned stumps.

It'd come as no surprise that Emmanuel had investigated his past. Thaddeus would've been disappointed had he not done so. It wasn't personal; it was business. He hadn't even been offended by the term "river pirate"; in fact, Thaddeus had been amused.

Emmanuel had also been right about his decision to abort the profession. Pirating had been under the gun for decades by military action, vigilante groups, and law enforcement of varying degrees. It was getting too risky and Thaddeus had more living left to do. He wasn't willing to gamble on the gallows.

"For someone not familiar with the profession," Thaddeus had said, "you sure did your homework."

Emmanuel *had* done his homework and the plan he'd presented proved just that. Where Thaddeus had been limited, Emmanuel had formulated a plan to expand. Texas had less than a handful of free blacks, which had eliminated it as a possibility for Thaddeus's pirating efforts. Galveston was known to be a safe haven for pirates and had direct access to the Gulf, leading back to Louisiana.

Limiting his efforts to the Mississippi River had two drawbacks. The first was it'd put Thaddeus in close proximity to his own backyard. The other was it narrowed the cargo he'd have access to. Expanding their operations to the gulf would give them contact with not only ships from Spain and the Caribbean, but Cuban vessels as well. The potential for loot would be far beyond what Thaddeus had plundered from the river. There'd be gold doubloons and jewels, the likes that the two sugar cane farmers had never seen.

A plan of this scale couldn't be carried out by the two of them alone. The profit margin would be so extensive they'd need others to cover their tracks. The powerful contacts Emmanuel had made along their shipping routes would provide a diversified group of highly respected businessmen to form the perfect collaborative.

Membership would have to be kept secret, but Emmanuel had solutions for that potential problem as well.

What had been the one thing that the elite and powerful had always coveted? An invitation to a club that others would only dream of being a member of. It'd be called the *Sinclair Oaks Hunting Club* and would be so secretive the members would only be able to attend by maneuvering through a complex maze of tunnels unknown to anyone else.

Emmanuel and Thaddeus would concentrate on designing an elaborate and foolproof method of storing the bounty until it could be sold or bartered off among the members.

The only other problem not yet addressed was coming up with the perfect liaison between the collaborative and the pirates plundering the unsuspected ships. It'd be necessary to have someone else handle that end of the business in order for Emmanuel and Thaddeus to keep their hands clean.

Fortunately, when one of the partners didn't have an answer, the other one made up for it. Thaddeus had the perfect man for the job. Samuel Thibodeaux of Kane, Louisiana.

8

LUCRETIA AUBOIS vividly remembered the day her father had told her about Emmanuel Sinclair. She'd been standing on the bank, gazing over the water, and wondering if her life would ever be anything more than relocating from one dreadful place to another. Each move meant more work to re-establish some semblance of a home and she'd hated every minute of it.

She'd had very little, if any, memory of living in Europe, but her heart told her there was more to life than what she'd experienced. Her father had just come from a trip down the Mississippi, bearing news her heart had indeed been right. There was a man, several years her elder, who was the owner of a large cotton plantation. One didn't have to be from the south to know cotton meant money and money equated a very different lifestyle.

The young girl had been instantly intrigued and yearned to learn more. Mr. Sinclair had been looking for a bride who could host parties, run his household when he was traveling, and bear him an heir. Her father had swiftly confirmed his beautiful daughter would indeed fit the bill. And so, it had begun.

Their courtship had consisted of letters delivered at the mercy of strangers. The correspondence often arrived out of chronological order and more often, not at all. The infamous Pony Express had not yet begun its short eighteen-month run before being replaced with the electric telegraph, so Lucretia's father would pass letters on during his travels and pray they were received.

It had been early one morning, as summer was nearing its end, when the culmination of the sparse courtship was finally solidified. Lucretia's tickets arrived for her long journey to New Orleans where her future husband would be waiting.

The news of her forthcoming life had spread like wildfire among the French-Acadians in Baltimore. They'd shared in her excitement; some had been envious, others downright jealous, but they'd assisted her just the same. The women had gathered together their finest fabric and sewed what was sure to be a suitable dress for meeting her future husband. It'd been folded neatly, to decrease any potential for wrinkling, and packed away for later. The trip itself would be taxing and she'd need to change into fresh clothing only as the steamboat neared New Orleans.

Lucretia had been a petite young lady with chestnut brown hair, cropped short for easy care, and eyes changing from green to gray, depending on her mood. She'd been a good-natured child, which had carried over into young adulthood, but she'd been quite decisive when it came to what she'd wanted, dreaming of a day when she'd have more control over her own life.

Exiting the steamboat in her newly sewn dress, Lucretia had vowed never to return to her old life. From that day forth, she'd be the well-respected wife of a plantation owner. She'd climb the social ladder, learn all she could about culture and the arts, and she'd support her husband so strongly he'd have to rely on her for his own success.

Many had considered her a plain young woman, but fine clothing and money could instantly remedy that. Lucretia Aubois of Baltimore would cease to exist. Lucretia would quickly become the sophisticated matriarch of the Sinclair dynasty.

9

1860-1863

By 1860, Emmanuel Sinclair had finally completed his beloved mansion and had sent for Lucretia to join him. It was a glorious time, as the estate had turned into all he'd hoped. Thaddeus had proven to be even better at running the collaborative than he'd been at running the sugar cane farms. Things were going just as the two partners had dreamed.

Fatima was the only one who had yet to find her happiness. She'd continued to miscarry, blaming herself for whatever sins she'd committed to anger God. Thaddeus spent as little time with her as possible, had limited patience with her self-pity, and often told her she was losing his children because it'd become a self-fulfilling prophecy. "Some people refuse to be happy," he'd told her over and over again.

Prudence was there to pick up the pieces from whatever damage Thaddeus had done to her heart. But Fatima remained steadfast in defending her husband and refused to allow anyone to condemn his actions. Prudence prayed Lucretia would be the friend that Fatima so desperately needed.

LUCRETIA HAD INDEED BEEN the answer to many prayers. At the young age of eighteen, she already knew what she wanted and expected from her new life and was determined to make it work.

A petite brunette, she almost resembled a child, but her personality far from reflected it. She was respectful of Emmanuel being head of the home, but she too had her own opinions and ideas for their future. It was as if getting away from her family had given her all the confidence she'd needed to grow into adulthood.

She and Fatima had become fast friends despite their obvious differences, and it was Lucretia who was able to encourage the meek woman to leave her own home and visit the vast estate. The two of them enjoyed trying on dresses, styling each other's hair, and picking out furniture for the blank slate of a home. But that was where Fatima's confidence had ended. Where Lucretia flourished in the social settings of high society, Fatima cowered in intimidation from the wealthy and cultured.

Prudence was grateful for what little time Lucretia had succeeded in building Fatima up, but knew she'd reached the peak of her comfort zone. Prudence and Lucretia often discussed Thaddeus's shortcomings but knew better than to do so with Fatima.

❦

THE ONSET of the Civil War drastically affected the prices of cotton and although Emmanuel and Thaddeus's enterprise remained virtually unscathed, they were skeptical of what the coming years had in store.

Thankfully, they'd been in a situation where they had the funds to pay any fees necessary to avoid the draft. Louisiana, although seceding from the Union early on, had portions of the state that remained dedicated to the Union. In a rare move, the US had recognized those sections and permitted them to have their own governor and congressman.

It went without saying, Emmanuel and Thaddeus chose to stay neutral rather than cut off any party who had the potential of contributing to their business. Their collaborative now stretched in every direction, which meant choosing a side would eliminate up to fifty percent of it. So as far as they were concerned, the Civil War didn't exist. War was bad for business.

As the sugar cane crop continued to thrive, along with the collaborative, Emmanuel was now spending more and more time traveling. Lucretia was fine with his absence, even in the sprawling home. With Thaddeus left behind to tend to their day-to-day operations, it wasn't long before he had his eye on more than Emmanuel's share of the sugar cane.

Lucretia was all that Fatima wasn't. She was strong and confident, a take-charge type of woman that was a rarity in both the south and the era in which they lived. There was little doubt she could've taken the reins of Emmanuel's business herself. Lucretia had a way with people—all people, from the slaves, to the upper echelon of New Orleans. She treated them all the same and everyone left her feeling better about themselves.

She'd used Emmanuel's money to make the most of her appearance, leaving her childlike persona behind. Lucretia had grown into a woman and quickly adapted to life among the elite. It was becoming more difficult for Thaddeus to ignore his growing desire for her. Emmanuel's frequent absences were almost a sign for him to act upon his feelings.

Thaddeus Jackson was accustomed to getting what he wanted. If he had to be patient, then patient he would be. It began with a few flirtatious gestures—a wink here, a laugh there, a light hug when he was leaving.

Lucretia was indeed smart, smart with business, and smart with innuendo. She'd picked up on his childish, schoolboy gestures and was determined to use them to her advantage. The lifestyle she'd married into wasn't one she'd ever be willing to part with, so Lucretia needed to learn all she could about the business should she ever have to take over. Thaddeus was merely a means to an end, but was far too arrogant to realize the player was being played.

Thaddeus wasn't trying to get Lucretia to fall in love with him. He, too, was far from willing to lose his empire. If the two were ever caught, he'd lose Fatima and Lucretia would lose Emmanuel and the whole house of cards would tumble down. No, his desires were simply carnal.

It had been a stormy night when he'd decided to make a move. Thaddeus had been working on the ledgers when the rain came, giving him an excuse to stay longer than usual. He'd made his way downstairs to find Lucretia reading in the front parlor. All the house help had gone back to their quarters and she was sipping from a dark whiskey.

"I was trying to complete my work before the storm hit," Thaddeus had said, holding up a stack of ledgers as proof of his efforts. "Didn't realize such a strong one was heading our way."

Lucretia looked up from her book, then out the window as if to verify his story. "It *is* coming down. You're welcome to have a seat. Can I get you a drink?" she'd asked, holding hers up to display what she was drinking.

"Sure," he'd answered. "Don't let me keep you up."

"I was reading," she'd said, holding up her book much like she had her drink. "Let me get one for you."

She'd returned with the drink and asked to see the ledgers. Emmanuel wouldn't have allowed her to see such things, but she'd had the advantage with Thaddeus.

"I know what you're doing," Thaddeus had said smoothly. "You're using me for information. You could simply ask."

"And you're using me for your fantasies," Lucretia had said, returning the wink, the whiskey making her lightheaded.

"And what would you know about my fantasies?" he'd asked after he'd taken a seductive sip from the dark liquid and eased his long figure over beside her.

Lucretia took too long to reply, and his full mouth was over hers before she could answer. They'd made love savagely on the floor of the parlor like animals, leaving them both breathless.

Lucretia had lain on the floor long after Thaddeus had left, tears rolling down her cheeks, as she'd stared up at the ceiling. She'd jumped up and ran to her bedroom just as the slaves made their way to the plantation for work.

She'd spent the day in bed, her eyes swollen from the tears cried throughout the long hours of the night. She was terribly angry at herself for being so weak. Lucretia wasn't as concerned about betraying Emmanuel or Fatima as she'd been about risking her future. It was an error in judgment she'd never make again.

One of the older slaves had sent for Prudence when Lucretia refused both breakfast and lunch. It hadn't taken her long to make her way up the stairs and to Lucretia's bedside. Prudence had eased her plump bottom on the bed beside her and rubbed the hair from her face. If the other women had seen her take such liberty with Lucretia, she'd surely have been scolded.

Prudence walked to the washstand and wet a rag, which she placed firmly on Lucretia's forehead. Her eyes said all that her mouth didn't... Prudence knew what had happened.

"Never speak of it, child," she'd said firmly. "Never allow your lips to form the words. 'Tis over now and will never happen again. I'll see to it myself. Never, never speak of it again."

THE HOLIDAYS HAD COME and gone quickly, but there had been much more to celebrate among the Jackson and Sinclair households. Both wives were pregnant with future heirs and Fatima's fervent prayers had been answered. She'd made it past the first few months of her pregnancy without miscarrying.

It had been a harsh February day when Lucretia felt the first pains of labor. Prudence was summoned immediately, and she'd quickly shooed the others away as she prepared Lucretia for the birth of her first child. Emmanuel had been traveling up the Mississippi to meet with brokers in New York, but he wouldn't have been the type to comfort her at a time such as this anyway. Childbirth was not yet something men took part in.

Lucretia's labor pains had progressed quickly. "I have names picked out," she'd told Prudence in between contractions. "If it's a girl, I'm going to name her Philomene. It's close to Prudence, don't you think?"

"It's lovely," she'd answered, dark thoughts entering the back of her mind. "Don't talk now, Ms. Lucretia. You need to rest in between contractions. We never know how long labor will be. Try to breathe regularly while you're not in pain, don't hold your breath."

The contractions continued to increase in severity and occurred back to back with little time in between. Lucretia was growing weak from the pain and Prudence prayed it'd soon be over. Just as she'd opened her eyes from prayer, the baby's head began crowning and Lucretia's screams could be heard throughout the entire estate.

"You're almost there, child. Just keep pushing like I taught you. Breathe, child. Don't forget to breathe..."

Lucretia's scant frame hadn't made the delivery easy, but she'd been determined to rid her body of the cause of such pain. The head made its way out and the shoulders and body abruptly followed.

It was Lucretia's turn to remain quiet while she listened for the tiny infant to cry, as air filled its small lungs, for the first time. It was the sound she'd longed to hear for nine months. She exhaled a sigh of relief and waited intently for Prudence to reveal the gender.

When Prudence remained silent, Lucretia lifted her head to see for herself.

Tears filled Prudence's eyes before escaping the rims and dripping down her dark face. She'd wrapped the infant in a blanket and swayed with it to make the cries subside.

"Prudence, what is it? Bring the baby to me. Is it a boy or girl?"

Prudence moved slowly toward Lucretia; her fears now realized. "I'm sorry, Ms. Lucretia. I'm so sorry."

"What do you mean?" Lucretia asked, panic rising in her throat.

Prudence placed the baby in Lucretia's arms, revealing the thick, dark hair and its beautiful chocolate skin. "She's a beautiful girl with mulatto skin. She's... She's... She's Thaddeus's daughter."

Lucretia literally felt her own heart stop beating. She suddenly felt faint, and her body was swimming with dizziness. The realization was too much for her mind to comprehend. The baby's cries suddenly seemed far away, as if she were merely a dream. Lucretia held her, but she felt detached, almost as though her own hands didn't belong to her. Her mind seemed to fog over, the dreamlike state returning. Suddenly her thoughts were consumed with Fatima's goodness, her vulnerability, her loyalty as a friend. And how she was the one who'd finally had a viable pregnancy. The thought made bile rise in Lucretia's throat and she handed the infant to Prudence in order to vomit beside the bed.

Emmanuel wouldn't have been as hurt as Fatima—he'd be angry and humiliated and would instantly rid his life of both Lucretia and Thaddeus. There wouldn't be any way he could maintain the combined properties, the growth of the sugar cane, and continue to do the traveling necessary to sell it. It would all fall apart, and no one would win.

The whirlwind of emotions was too much to process, there'd be time for that later. The two women locked eyes as Prudence handed the wrapped bundle back to Lucretia. The infant had quieted now, exhausted from making her entrance into the world.

Holding her close to her bosom, Lucretia allowed Philomene to suckle quietly. Once she'd fallen into a deep sleep of contentment, Lucretia held her tight, whispering a soft lullaby in her ear. Prudence turned away, allowing the young mother some privacy before she squeezed the final breath from the child's tiny body.

"*Ça y est*," Lucretia said. "It's done, Prudence. My firstborn is gone."

Prudence quickly took charge, removing the baby from Lucretia's grasp and covering her sweet face with the blanket. "There's little time, so listen carefully," Prudence said, reaching down and taking Lucretia's face in her hand to ensure she was looking at her. "Are you listening? Do you understand what I'm saying?"

"Yes...yes," Lucretia answered as the tears came.

"Stop, there will be plenty of time for tears later. *This* is what happened. The infant's face was severely deformed, I've swaddled her tightly to conceal it. The deformities made it impossible for her to breathe for more than a few seconds. The casket will be closed. I'll send for a traiteur to come offer prayers and have someone ride over to the livery to have a casket delivered. Do you understand?"

"Yes."

"Do you, Lucretia? No one must ever know. Our stories must remain the same. We have to take this to our graves."

"Yes, I understand," Lucretia answered flatly, her eyelids closing from emotional fatigue.

"You've done the right thing. Too many people would've been hurt. You didn't have a choice. Now, let it lie."

THE FUNERAL of baby Philomene Sinclair was held on a brisk February morning. Clouds covered any warmth that would've radiated from the sun, making such a sad occasion even more somber. With Emmanuel still out of town, the ceremony was held in his absence, and attended by very few. Prudence had insisted Fatima remain at home on bedrest, feeling it would shield her from any more grief, and hopefully prevent yet another miscarriage.

Despite Prudence's attempts to keep Thaddeus at home with his wife, he'd made an unexpected appearance at the funeral to express the Jackson family's condolences. For a brief moment, Lucretia wondered if he'd known that Philomene had been his. Perhaps he'd suffered the loss just as she had. If that were the case, she'd allow him the moment to celebrate their daughter's brief life along with those in attendance. But today was all that she'd grant him—from this day forward he'd be nothing more than her husband's business partner. Her focus would now be on producing an heir for the Sinclair name.

THE BRIGHT DAYS of spring promised hope and new beginnings as the birth of Fatima's first child neared. Prudence had not left Fatima's side for fear of an early labor. With the weather growing warmer, Thaddeus spent his days in the fields.

Fatima's bedrest had given her much-needed strength to prepare her body for the rigors of labor. At least she'd thought so. When the infant decided to make its entrance, it opted for a quick and hasty one. The contractions hit back to back, harder and harder until she was so ravaged with pain that she became delirious.

Her small frame was not adequately equipped to deliver such a large child. Despite Prudence's experience and expertise, there was little she could do but keep Fatima comfortable for the duration of the labor.

For two days Fatima struggled in and out of consciousness, fighting for the birth of her long-awaited child. After thirty-one hours of strenuous labor and countless prayers, Fatima succumbed to the exhaustion.

Prudence announced the death of Fatima Jackson and her unborn child at the first sign of daybreak. Thaddeus had already left for the fields.

10

1864

NOT LONG AFTER Philomene's death, rumors began to circulate about the Sinclair family curse. It was said that whatever had caused the infant's death would haunt future generations by claiming the lives of the firstborn.

Emmanuel had gotten wind of the claims and demanded they cease immediately. He'd also insisted that Lucretia never hear of such cruel foolishness. But behind closed doors, when he'd found himself alone in his office, he'd indeed worried about the scuttlebutt making its way through the grapevine.

If he'd only been home, he'd convinced himself, *none of this would've happened. It was his Creator's punishment for missing his own daughter's birth and funeral and now everyone tied to his name would suffer.*

He'd begun to look forward to his travels now, staying away longer than necessary. He'd felt guilty for being relieved when Philomene had been a daughter and not his heir. If he'd lost a son, it would have been much more difficult to accept. Emmanuel found himself leaving a day or so earlier than his itinerary required and spending a few nights in New Orleans before heading up the Mississippi.

In the beginning, Emmanuel had spent his time drinking in

taverns, boasting of his success, but that eventually grew old. After reconsidering time spent away from the estate, he planned to head straight home once off the steamboat. However, something had caught his attention—something that would alter the entire course of his life. He'd met the beautiful and mesmerizing Desiree Cazeaux.

Born a free woman of color, Madame Cazeaux was recognized as a giver, someone who helped those in need and did all she could for the sick. But those good deeds weren't what drew people to her. It was her practice of voodoo and root work along with her incredible beauty that attracted both whites and blacks. A devout Catholic, Madame Cazeaux provided people with advice and guidance.

Desiree Cazeaux had a dramatic flair for entertainment, and many believed she was simply a crafty entrepreneur. But Emmanuel fell hook, line, and sinker for her connections to the spiritual world. He attended every ceremony he could whenever he was in New Orleans and paid her handsomely for the opportunity to have sessions with her alone.

She'd encouraged him to grow his business and said she'd seen gold and jewels in his future. An *abundance* of jewels and gold, she'd emphasized repeatedly.

It was that meeting with the beautiful and well-spoken Desiree that'd sent him beating a path home to his estate. He'd been convinced that somewhere, there was a ship overflowing with booty, and he had to get Samuel Thibodeaux on top of it.

※

THE TWO PARTNERS were sitting in Emmanuel's office when Samuel knocked from behind the fireplace. He'd entered the tunnels just as the collaborative members did and made his way up the spiral staircase. Emmanuel preferred that no one, not even Lucretia, saw who entered when it concerned business outside of sugar cane. His office —and the west wing for that matter—were strictly off limits for anyone not in his inner circle. It was cleaned by Thaddeus's most trusted male slave, George. The partners threatened to take the slave's life if he ever shared any details of its contents.

"What'd you find out?" Thaddeus asked Samuel before he'd even taken a seat.

"I've got my men on it. We're best to hijack a vessel coming in from the gulf. I say we change it up and hit a Cuban container this time."

Emmanuel's face grew crimson with rage, and he slammed his balled fist on the mahogany desk. "Listen, Thibodeaux, you're clearly not listening. I have no intention of storing bales of tobacco or anyone else's slaves. I don't even want to deal with barrels of rum. You're missing the whole damn point!"

"I understood Thaddeus said you were looking for a bigger bounty. Tobacco and rum are the biggest products out there. I realize we'd be dealing with a storage issue, but the return would be phenomenal."

"And how the hell are you going to transport all of that to our tunnels?" Emmanuel asked. "That's the most absurd thing I've ever heard. We've come too far to bring that type of heat down on ourselves."

"What do you propose, Mr. Sinclair?" Samuel asked, masking his fury.

"I say we find the ships that are traveling with gold and jewels. *That's* what I propose!"

"Technically they're all traveling with gold. That's their currency."

Emmanuel sent Thaddeus a look that spoke volumes. Thaddeus stood and paced back and forth across the office. "Then what the hell have you been doing, Samuel?" he demanded. "Leave everything else and get the damn gold!"

"Hit a Spanish vessel," Emmanuel seethed. "Get the gold doubloons, garnets, and emeralds! And have them confiscate any medicines. I can't count the times I've emphasized that. In case you've failed to notice, this country's still at war. Medicine's a commodity that's in high demand from both sides. Do we need to find someone else to do your job?"

"That won't be necessary, sir," Samuel Thibodeaux insisted. "My work has spoken for itself in the past. I won't let you down."

"Very well, then," Emmanuel said firmly. "You can see your way out the same way you came in. We'll meet with the club and let them know we have the largest bounty yet in the making."

Samuel was grateful for the opportunity to leave the estate. Emmanuel Sinclair gave him the creeps. Since the death of his daughter, his mind had spiraled out of control. One moment he'd be normal, then the next he'd turn completely illogical. The less Samuel was around him, the better off he was.

After ample time had passed for Samuel to have made his way down the tunnels, Thaddeus spoke. "Emmanuel, what makes you so certain there's a big bounty of gold and gems out there? Samuel can't ensure what's in any vessel."

"It comes on good authority," Emmanuel said. "I'll leave it at that. There's been times I've had to trust your judgment and now I must insist you trust mine. The members are going to have to put their money up front on this one. It's going to pay big."

҉

AS THE RUMORS continued to circulate about the Sinclair curse, Emmanuel became convinced the only person who could reverse his family's fate was Desiree Cazeaux. He visited her weekly in New Orleans until he was able to persuade her to carve out several hours for him without interruption.

Emmanuel had spent the night at a hotel in town prior to their meeting to ensure his promptness. After what seemed like hours of poring over his concerns, Madame Cazeaux seemed to have the ideal solution. It was quite simple—all the answers lay with the mandrake plant.

"The powers and capabilities of the mandrake are immeasurable," she'd told him, leaving the room for several minutes before returning with a root carefully wrapped in a small blanket. "The root is so potent that its properties can even penetrate skin. You must be extremely careful when handling it. Beyond that, its benefits are many. It can bring wealth, power, and good fortune. If kept under a pillow at night, it can even help a woman conceive."

Emmanuel's thoughts raced. *Could such a thing exist? Why haven't I heard of it before?*

"It first grew under the gallows from the seed of a gibbeted man," Desiree continued.

"Gibbeted?"

"A man hung in the gallows. It is what the term *La Main de Gloire* was derived from."

Emmanuel wasn't accustomed to being unacquainted with a subject and he didn't like it.

"Forgive me, *La Main de Gloire*?"

"The hand of glory, have you not heard of it?"

"Not at all," he conceded. "Please, elaborate."

"The name, the hand of glory, was taken from the mandrake plant for obvious reasons. The leaves of the plant resemble hands, for one, and the mandrake is believed to shine at night much like a lamp adding light for those who are stealing."

"I'm afraid I don't understand. Was the mandrake plant also referred to as the hand of glory?"

"No," she answered, realizing Emmanuel wasn't familiar with the legend. "Allow me to begin at its origin. The hand of glory is believed to have many magical powers. Legend has it the hand had to be cut from a villain still hanging from the gallows. Any blood remaining from the hand was squeezed out and drained and the fingers were positioned." She stopped briefly and assessed Emmanuel's comfort level. He was beginning to grow pale. "Are you all right? Is this too much for you?"

He swallowed hard but answered right away. "I'm fine. Please continue."

Desiree nodded. "The hand was then wrapped in a specifically prepared cloth and placed in a solution of saltpeter, salt, and long peppers. It was left for several months to dry. Wax was made from fat of the dead man's hand and used to make a candle; his hair being utilized as a wick." She paused again to make sure Emmanuel was still following her. "If one decided to use the fingers as a candle, they were dipped in wax. Otherwise, a candle was placed in the dead man's fist or his palm. They could burn forever once alight without being consumed. The hand of glory was used by a thief to enter a house without opposition to steal whatever spoils he desired. The hand had the power to put the occupants to sleep, rendering them motionless. The light could not be extinguished by water but by blood or skimmed milk. So, in other words, the hand of glory ensured a thief's success."

Emmanuel bristled; he couldn't believe his ears. Not only was he learning of the powers of the mandrake plant, but he'd been given information to ensure his future illicit endeavors would be successful. The hand of glory, indeed.

AT THE APPOINTED TIME, with the mandrake root broken into pieces and placed strategically in his desk for wealth and success, and under Lucretia's pillow to expedite the conception of an heir, Thaddeus and Emmanuel waited for the collaborative to arrive. Samuel Thibodeaux was ready to meet with everyone concerning his plan for their most lucrative heist to date.

Thaddeus had arrived with two of his finest bottles of scotch and had already poured his and Emmanuel's second glass when the first guests arrived. Under the guise of a hunting club, the members would lodge at both the Sinclair and Jackson estates. It would be a weekend of fraternizing, and hopefully celebrating a profitable deal in the works.

Samuel was the last to arrive, along with Phillipe, one of his most trusted men. The two had obviously done their homework and were anxious to share their plan with the members. Although Samuel was bringing in an exorbitant sum of money for the members, he was treated much like a servant, never included in any socializing or hobnobbing. Emmanuel preferred to keep it strictly business, which seemed to keep Samuel in his place.

"Good evening," Thibodeaux began. "Phillipe and I have come up with a foolproof plan for what we believe to be our largest raid."

"Nothing is foolproof," Emmanuel interjected.

Samuel nodded in agreement but continued, "With so many ports being blockaded due to the war, our strategies have been somewhat limited, so bear with us. After much consideration, we believe intercepting one of the New York businessmen's shipments to the Caribbean would be our best bet. We would transfer their goods to one of the collaborative's blockade runners, hijack their captain and a few of their crew, and meet with their intended Caribbean counterparts. Their goods would then be bartered for a much more manageable bounty of smaller quantity yet greater profit. We'll hug the Mexican and Texas coast until reaching Louisiana, giving us much less of a chance of being stopped by military channels."

"What makes you so confident you can overtake the vessel coming from New York?" Thaddeus asked.

"We've had several men in that area doing surveillance for us. It appears to be much more feasible than what we've done in the past. Their manufactured goods are in great demand in the Caribbean. We'll need more upfront money than we've needed in the past, simply because we'll require more men and will be traveling farther."

Thaddeus looked around the large office and nodded in Emmanuel's direction.

"Okay, Samuel," Emmanuel began, "you may be excused while we take a vote and continue our weekend. Thaddeus and I will meet with you Monday morning."

Samuel nodded at each member before he and Phillipe took the spiral staircase down to the tunnels.

Emmanuel handed out pieces of paper and instructed the men to go to their respective alcoves to place their votes. "The fireplaces are lit, gentlemen," he added. "There are cigars for your pleasure. Enjoy yourselves."

THE VOTES from the collaborative had been unanimous, only solidifying Emmanuel's belief that his efforts would be profitable. His obsession with the mandrake plant was only deepening and he was purchasing more roots from Desiree. He had little doubt that Lucretia would soon be pregnant with a son and his money would flow mightier than the Mississippi.

Desiree had warned him about handling the root directly, but he'd sit in his office for hours running his hands across the magical rhizome he now believed would provide all his family could desire. Confident the Sinclair curse was now lifted, he was getting the best sleep of his life, but was deliriously unaware of how mad he was becoming.

Lucretia watched from a distance as her husband unraveled. She chalked it up to his guilt over missing Philomene's birth. She was also dealing with her own guilt, so she left him alone with his. It was then that she'd begun to take more responsibility in the sugar cane business, though he'd failed to notice. Her contact with Thaddeus was nothing more than professional. He needed her help and respected her business sense.

They'd both been at the mill when Samuel had arrived at Emmanuel's office, via the tunnels. Phillipe had helped to hoist their bounty up the pulley and into the headquarters before quickly making his exit. It was Samuel's turn to bask in the glory of their loot, but he had no desire to be in Emmanuel's presence. He'd been paid well for his job and didn't need any accolades.

Samuel gazed at Emmanuel skeptically. He was holding a dirty stem of some kind in his lap and had a glass of whiskey sitting on his desk. His eyes were glazed over, and a crazed smile crossed his face. "How'd it go on the high seas?"

"I think you'll be quite pleased," Samuel answered. "Want to take a look?"

Emmanuel motioned for him to place the burlap sacks on his desk. "Open one and let me take a peek."

Samuel lifted a hefty bundle up onto the desk and pulled back the material to reveal its contents.

Emmanuel audibly gasped as he took in the rainbow of gemstones and glistening gold doubloons. "Not bad," he said, standing to get a closer look. "How many of those bundles do you have?"

"Fourteen to be exact. Phillipe helped to hoist them up here, but he's gone now. The crew has been paid; the hostages taken care of."

"Good to hear," Emmanuel slurred. "Good to hear, Samuel. I do believe you've outdone yourself."

"Maybe I'm your lucky charm," Samuel added. "It'd be hard to do this without me, ya know?"

"You have one thing right, you're definitely my lucky charm," Emmanuel said as he reared back a fireplace poker and struck Samuel across the head. Aided by the element of surprise, the force of the blow knocked him to the floor, but not unconscious.

"Wha...? What the hell?" Samuel reached up to feel the side of his head and drew back a blood-drenched hand. "You ungrateful..."

Emmanuel carefully placed the mandrake root on his chair, before lifting the poker high above his head. He struck Samuel Thibodeaux several times before stopping to confirm he was dead.

"Maybe I was wrong," Emmanuel said to the bludgeoned corpse. "You *are* my lucky charm and I *can't* do this without you. At least not without *part* of you."

THE SUN WAS ALMOST SETTING by the time Lucretia got back to the house. Emmanuel was sitting in the front parlor, his breath smelling of whiskey. Her day at the mill had left her tired and dirty. She was in no mood to deal with her husband's antics.

"Where have you been?" he demanded.

"Down at the mill," she answered flatly. "Someone has to look after our business, Emmanuel. It's time for you to do your share."

"I need you to send for Thaddeus," he said, dismissing her answer. "I need him *immediately.*"

Lucretia considered a scathing response but decided against it. She'd been taught to never argue with fools or drunks. "I'll send someone," she responded before heading to the kitchen. It'd been a trying day and she was hungry.

Thaddeus was still nearby on the property when the slave reached him with the message. It was only a few minutes before he was knocking on the front door and being shown to the parlor.

"What took you so long?" Emmanuel demanded.

"You're drunk," Thaddeus said.

"You're an asshole," Emmanuel grumbled back.

"I'm not here to swap insults. What's so urgent?" Thaddeus retorted.

"Samuel was here earlier. He brought the loot."

Thaddeus perked up at the thought of what might be upstairs. "How'd it go?"

"You won't be disappointed," Emmanuel said. "However, there were a few kinks in the armor."

"Like what?"

"Let's talk upstairs."

Thaddeus helped him up before they made the trek to the third floor. They passed the alcoves where the collaborative had cast their votes and Emmanuel was unlocking his office door when he turned to Thaddeus. "We had a mild issue. I should warn you before we go in."

"What kind of *issue*?" he asked, the hair on the back of his neck bristling.

"We'll discuss it inside."

As soon as the door was opened, Thaddeus felt his heart sink. The oil lamp illuminated the ghastly scene. Blood splattered the rug, the walls, and the ceiling. "What the hell have you done?"

"Let's just say, I took care of business."

"*Business?* This isn't our *business!*"

"You weren't here!" Emmanuel yelled defensively. "He was

double-crossing us! I had to take care of it myself. He brought only a handful of doubloons and said that was the extent of their bounty. I knew he was lying. You should've seen his face. If we tolerate that bullshit once, it'll happen every time. It's not just *our* money, Thaddeus! It also belongs to the collaborative. What was I *supposed* to do?"

"Looks like a hell of a lot more than a handful of doubloons to me," Thaddeus said as he looked at the mountain of gold and jewels.

"He was conning me into paying him more. Said he left it in the tunnels, but I had to pay for it. It was in the tunnels, all right. Took me hours to hoist all of this up here."

Emmanuel continued to slur and ramble while Thaddeus struggled to make sense of it. It'd have taken two men to get those heavy bundles up to his office, even with a pulley. There was no way Emmanuel could've done it alone, but he was getting crazier by the day and Thaddeus was afraid to confront him with the truth. Maybe there was some way to get him straightened out before the collaborative saw him again. If not, they'd *both* lose everything.

"What are we going to do now?" Thaddeus asked.

"You've got to help get this body out of here. We can't take a chance on someone finding him. Granted, he stole from us, but I can't get caught with him in my house," Emmanuel reasoned.

"Look at all this blood. It'll take days to clean this place. How are we going to get him out of here? We can't carry him out the front door and we sure can't get him down that spiral staircase and through the tunnels. He's too heavy," Thaddeus insisted.

Emmanuel's eyes widened as he quickly devised a plan. "We'll let everyone go to sleep and then lower him down the dumbwaiter. Go get your wagon and we'll load him up, take him to the bayou, and feed him to the gators. With this much blood, it'll surely cause a feeding frenzy."

"You sick bastard. Damn, Emmanuel, what'd you do with his *hands*?"

HOURS LATER, when they were certain Lucretia was sleeping, Emmanuel and Thaddeus wrapped Samuel's body in a cotton tarp, folded his corpse to fit in the dumbwaiter, and lowered him down.

Quickly making their way to the kitchen, they retrieved his body as quietly as possible, went out the back door, and loaded him in the wagon. Thaddeus grabbed the reins, lashing them against the horses' backs as they wound their way toward the bayou.

When the house was no longer in sight, Thaddeus unleashed his fury on Emmanuel. "If this wasn't the *worst* idea you've ever had. Honestly, you need to stop drinking and pull yourself together. I understand you've been through the death of a child but you're out of control. For God's sakes, what did you do with Samuel's hands, *eat* them?"

"Hell no, I didn't eat them. You're sick," Emmanuel slurred. "I couldn't *believe* he'd double-cross us."

"Did he, Emmanuel? Are you certain or were you just drunk?"

"I'm too tired to argue with you. Let's throw this piece of shit in the bayou and go home."

Thaddeus was in too deep to turn back now, but he'd deal with Emmanuel in the morning when he was sober. He'd let Lucretia know what her husband had done so she'd be aware of who she was dealing with. If Emmanuel was capable of this, he could also harm *her*.

They'd gotten as close to the water as possible, but Samuel had been a husky man, tall and stout, and they'd both struggled to pull him off the wagon. Thaddeus walked down to the dock and placed both of their lanterns there so they could see where to lug him. He grabbed Samuel under his arms, giving Emmanuel the easier job of holding his feet. Emmanuel had fallen several times, making their journey to the water difficult, at best.

When they finally reached the edge of the dock, Thaddeus and Emmanuel laid the body down. At the smell of blood, several gators sensed a feast. Their approach created glistening ripples across the dark water. The gators' stealth movement made Thaddeus's spine shiver.

"Let's push him in before they get crazy," Thaddeus said, placing his foot on Samuel's torso. Emmanuel did the same to his lower body as they pushed him toward the bayou.

As soon as his body hit the brackish water, the feeding frenzy began.

"Oh my God," Thaddeus whispered. "That's horrific."

"Yes, it is," Emmanuel agreed. Suddenly, without warning, he pushed Thaddeus into the frenzy alongside Samuel Thibodeaux.

Steadying his own feet, Emmanuel wiped his hands across his bloody trousers and stepped back from the macabre bloodbath. The realization of his actions sobered him up rapidly. Riddled with remorse, he solemnly whispered into the night, "*That's* for taking liberty with my wife. *No one* takes advantage of Emmanuel Sinclair and gets away with it."

11

1864

EMMANUEL'S BUILDING anger had him reaching for the bottle of whiskey. Instead, he felt the burlap bag containing Samuel's hands. The right hand must become his personal hand of glory to ensure his future aspirations came to fruition. He grasped the bloody hand bearing a simple gold wedding band and remembered he'd meant to toss it in the bayou with the corpse. But another idea surfaced, and he'd liked it. No one had seen either Samuel or Thaddeus enter his home, but people needed to be aware that no one could cross Emmanuel Sinclair. He veered the wagon in another direction and made his way toward the Thibodeaux home.

This will make a statement no one can deny, he thought, as he tossed the left hand onto Samuel's front porch. He slapped the reins across the horses' backs and was several yards down the road before what he'd done hit him.

Panic overtook Emmanuel as he realized all that was left to conceal from the day's events. What a mess he'd made of things in his haste to prove his superiority.

Slow down and think this out, he'd told himself. *First things, first. Get away from the bayou, return the wagon, hide the contraband, have my office cleaned, get myself cleaned up and return to Lucretia.*

His thoughts shifted. *Lucretia would've never wanted a man like Thaddeus, she'd never betray me. She'd never long for another man, she's never loved anybody but me*, he continued to tell himself. *My wife is home in bed*, he thought. *There's still time for me to salvage my life. No one is privy to the details of this day. It can all be cleaned up. I can make it all go away.*

Making his way to the Jackson estate to return the wagon, Emmanuel continued wavering from one extreme state to another. One moment, his thoughts were overtaken with madness, the next he was attempting to rationalize his circumstances.

Lucretia and I can produce an heir and the Sinclair line will carry on. Thaddeus is gone. I just need to ensure that every memory of him has been erased.

As the horses raced closer to the Jackson home, Emmanuel's rage escalated. Having finished the last of his whiskey, the panic returned. He grabbed an oil lantern from the side of the wagon and entered the home.

I've got to erase his memory. I've got to erase his memory.

Stumbling through the house, he peeled off his bloody clothes on his way to the master's bedroom. He set the lantern on the floor while he ransacked Thaddeus's clothes.

Emmanuel staggered back and forth across the room in a drunken stupor—*I've got to erase his memory, got to erase his memory.* He lost his footing, knocking over the lantern.

In his haste to reach the toppled lantern, Emmanuel tripped over the mound of clothes and fell to the floor. The oil hastily ran across the hardwood planks, just ahead of the blaze, and all he could do was watch as the flames licked their way across the room, atop the oil.

Repeating, *erase his memory, erase his memory*, Emmanuel fled from the house.

***

As Emmanuel climbed in bed with his wife, a loud knocking could be heard on the plantation's front door. Lucretia turned over and placed her arm across his chest. The pounding continued as Emmanuel feigned snoring. Suddenly, Lucretia sat straight up in bed, as she realized it was too late for callers.

"Emmanuel, Emmanuel wake up," she whispered, trying to wake him. "There's someone at the door."

He rolled over, snored once more for good measure, then slowly opened his eyes. "What? It's the middle of the night."

"I don't know but they're surely persistent. Will you see what they want?"

Emmanuel tossed the covers back and got out of bed. He was still intoxicated but the run through the fields and tunnels had sobered him up considerably. His head was already pounding, an indication of how the next couple of days would play out.

"Who's there?" he grunted before opening the door.

"It's George from the Jackson estate, Master Sinclair. Prudence's husband, remember? I'm sorry to bother you, 'tis a big emergency."

Emmanuel opened the door, obviously frustrated with the intrusion. "What's so urgent? Are you aware of the hour?"

"Yes sir, Master Sinclair. Master Jackson's home is afire. We've been fighting it for a long while, but it's almost completely gone. It was far gone before anyone saw the flames."

"Oh, dear Lord," Emmanuel said, grabbing his chest in an attempt to appear overtaken with grief. "Where's Thaddeus? You all didn't let him inhale too much smoke, did you? He shouldn't be fighting a fire."

"Sir, we haven't been able to find Master Jackson. We've looked everywhere but he can't be found. The fire is still too hot to get close. He must've perished inside."

With those words, Emmanuel fell forward just in time for George to catch him before he landed on the porch. George laid him down lightly as Lucretia came outside.

"What's going on here?" she demanded, squatting down to check on her husband.

"I think he fainted, ma'am. 'Twas a terrible shock to him."

"*What* was a terrible shock? Why are you here at such an hour?"

"'Tis the Jackson estate, ma'am. It's burned to the ground and Master Jackson is nowhere to be found."

"Wha....?"

"Yes, ma'am. We didn't even know it was afire until it was too late to salvage it. Master Thaddeus must've burned up," he said, his voice breaking for the first time. "I'm not sure what to do, ma'am."

Emmanuel fluttered his eyelids and propped himself up on his elbows. "George, take me to the plantation. I have to check on Thaddeus."

"There's nothing you can do, Emmanuel," Lucretia said. "The fire has consumed the home. If he was inside, it's too late."

"Tell the others to get back to their quarters," Emmanuel told George. "I'll be down at daybreak to assess the damage."

"Yes sir," he answered. "I will pass the word."

❀

"LET ME MAKE SOME COFFEE," Lucretia said. "You won't be sobered up by daylight if you don't drink some."

"I suppose you're right," Emmanuel answered, making his way into the kitchen.

"What could've happened?" she asked. "It's hard to believe both Thaddeus and Fatima are now gone."

"Who knows? For all we know, it was Union troops who didn't want him to own slaves. For that matter, could've been Johnny Rebs who felt he should be a slave himself."

❀

EMMANUEL HAD PULLED himself together long enough to put Thaddeus's slaves at ease. They'd all been given housing and were provided for better than they could provide for themselves at that point, so there was no mass exodus.

In a kind and concerned voice, Emmanuel had explained to them there was still a possibility Thaddeus Jackson could indeed return.

Perhaps he'd been taken prisoner by either side of the war; perhaps he'd taken a trip and simply neglected to turn down a lantern in his home, causing the fire.

Emmanuel bowed his head and allowed his voice to catch. "Let's not ponder all that could've happened," he'd continued mournfully. "We'll pray for his return and well-being now. In the meantime, the best thing we can do is continue to farm this land. Mr. Jackson and I formed a partnership, and it's very important for me to keep my end of the bargain. Nothing will change here. You all continue as you have been. My home is open should any of you have concerns."

With that he'd covered his face and feigned a sob, climbed in his wagon, and headed home.

Once back in his office, he went to work breaking the bundles down into manageable sizes. He'd never shared with Thaddeus the hiding place he'd had built when the estate was in its infancy. Although he'd been one hell of a partner, Emmanuel didn't trust anyone, not even Lucretia. He'd patted himself on the back numerous times for his cleverness and doted on the realization that no one had even suspected the hidden compartment existed.

The collaborative would soon be asking questions about returns on their investments and he would have to explain the absences of both Samuel and Thaddeus. The last thing he needed was any gold or gemstones, suggestive of a heist on the high seas, near his office.

It'd taken days of strenuous labor to lower the bundles down into the tunnels before transporting them to his secret vault. Emmanuel had considered using George at one point, but quickly thought better of it. This was something he couldn't trust anyone with.

He'd allowed Lucretia to handle the business temporarily. She knew what she was doing and enjoyed the challenge. As soon as he had everything hidden and his office cleaned up, he'd get back to running things again. It wasn't as though Thaddeus was going to return.

With the treasure locked away, Emmanuel decided it was time to summon George.

Damn if I'm going to clean up all the blood and brain matter from Samuel's murder. I'm Emmanuel Sinclair after all.

George wouldn't reveal any secrets for fear of his own life, and if he shared it among the slaves, well, it'd scare them all enough to never cross him.

Emmanuel's back was throbbing from hoisting the bundles down into the tunnels, so he eased himself into the chair behind his desk. He'd forgotten about leaving the mandrake root there on the night of Samuel's murder and for the first time since the event, thought of the plant and its powers.

He rubbed his hands over it and closed his eyes. How relaxing it was to recall his sessions with Desiree. *How long had it been since he'd seen her?* He reached into the bottom drawer and pulled out the last bottle of whiskey. Removing the cork, he held the liquid up to his nose and smelled the strong aroma. It'd surely help his soreness and ease his mind and conscience. Emmanuel took several sips followed by a deep swallow. The fire slowly made its way down his esophagus and settled in his belly. It wasn't long before he felt lightheaded and carefree.

Tomorrow I'll go into New Orleans and purchase another mandrake from Desiree, he thought. *I don't think this one is doing all it's supposed to.*

🌼

THE FOLLOWING MORNING Lucretia was awakened by Emmanuel dressing in some of his finest apparel.

"What are you doing?" she asked. "It's hardly daybreak. Why are you getting dressed?"

"I'm going into New Orleans for an early appointment. I'm not sure if I'll be home tonight or tomorrow. You told me I needed to do my share and it's time for me to get back to work. No need for concern," Emmanuel assured her.

"I don't believe now is a good time for you to travel. With Thaddeus gone, I'll need help with the plantation. I'm not completely comfortable being here alone with all that's happened. What if someone burns *our* home down?"

"That's absurd, Lucretia. Who'd do such a thing?"

"I don't know. Perhaps the same person who *burned* the Jackson home."

"You'll be fine," he echoed. "As I said, I'll be back before you know it."

And with that, Emmanuel was gone, leaving Lucretia sitting on the side of her bed wondering how she'd ever make this year's harvest profitable.

If only she could get into Emmanuel's office—she was certain all she needed to learn would be there.

WHEN EMMANUEL finally reached Desiree Cazeaux's office, he was devastated to discover she wasn't there. Someone he hadn't met answered her door only to tell him she was unavailable.

"*Unavailable?* Please let her know that Emmanuel Sinclair is here," he'd said bluntly.

"She's still unavailable," the woman had answered.

"I'm confident she will *become* available if she's notified I'm here."

She'd slammed the door in his face and refused to answer his continued knocking.

Emmanuel had stood there for several minutes, staring at the closed door, his heart sinking. He'd knocked one final time for good measure before securing a hotel room in the French Quarter for the night. He'd changed into more comfortable clothing, placed a piece of his mandrake root in his pocket, and made his way to the nearest tavern.

The pub was one he'd frequented many times before and he recognized several faces. He slid onto a chair and ordered a whiskey. When the bartender poured his drink, Emmanuel placed enough currency on the bar to cover his drinks for a month.

"Keep them coming," he said flatly. "It's been a tough week."

The bartender nodded his acknowledgement and made his way to the other end of the bar to serve another customer.

Emmanuel held the glass under his nose and inhaled deeply before tossing the liquid back and swallowing hard. He sat his glass back on the bar then slid it toward the bartender's side. He waited for several seconds before slamming his palm on the bar. Everyone in the tavern turned to see the source of the commotion.

"Nothing to see, folks," Emmanuel screamed. "*What?* Are you people hard up for entertainment?"

"That'll be enough," the bartender said. "If you want to be served here, you'll have to wait your turn. I don't care how much money you've laid down. Am I clear?"

"Do you know who I am?" Emmanuel asked.

"Don't know and don't care. Everyone is *treated* the same here. Your money doesn't get you special treatment."

"This isn't the only tavern in town," Emmanuel spat. "Give me my change. I'm out of here."

The man quickly made change and thrust it in his direction. "Glad to hear it," he said. "Do yourself a favor and don't come back."

Emmanuel stood stunned for a few moments, unaccustomed to being on the opposite end of such behavior. His face burned from humiliation, but he refused to look back at the other patrons to see their smirks. He could buy and sell them all.

If they only knew, he thought. *If they only knew what's hidden at my estate, they'd all be begging me to drink with them.*

There were indeed other taverns for Emmanuel to patronize, and that he did. He'd found an isolated corner with a small table where he could drink and hold his mandrake root at the same time. The warmth of the whiskey and the high he got from the mandrake was almost too good to be true. It was like being in another place, another place where he hadn't thrown his best friend to hungry gators, where his wife hadn't shared her body with another man, and where strangers knew the Sinclair name.

A place where Desiree Cazeaux was available and had even more mandrake to sell him.

UNSURE OF HOW he'd gotten back to his hotel room the night before, Emmanuel woke with a searing hangover. He gathered his belongings, checked out of the hotel, and walked back to Desiree's residence. He saw through the windows that there was a group of people inside, most likely listening to one of her lectures. He made his way in and took a seat in the back.

He could see her, standing in front of a podium, speaking on one of the Haitian rituals practiced in Louisiana. She locked eyes with Emmanuel briefly before cupping her hand over her mouth and speaking to one of the larger men seated behind her. It was only a moment before he discreetly left his seat on the dais and walked over to Emmanuel.

"You'll need to leave, sir," he said quietly. "Madame Cazeaux doesn't want any trouble. You've become a liability to her work and she no longer wishes to meet with you."

"That simply can't be true," Emmanuel prattled. "I'm only here for a mandrake root. I'll be on my way as soon as I purchase it."

"You won't be getting any more mandrake from Desiree. You've misused its power so it will no longer benefit you. In fact, it will now be detrimental. Discard all you have before it harms those you love. You are acting erratically, Mr. Sinclair. Madame Cazeaux believes you have been handling the root with your bare hands. She warned you of its potency from the beginning. You can leave now or I'll toss you out like the trash. Pick your pleasure."

Emmanuel was speechless. In his wildest dreams, he'd never thought she'd turn on him like this. Clearly his place was in Kane, not New Orleans.

His place was where everyone knew him and turning their backs on him *wasn't* an option.

12

1864 - 1865

EMMANUEL HAD PULLED his wagon over a few miles from home and walked into the woods. It was necessary for him to dispose of the mandrake root somewhere that Lucretia couldn't ever get her hands on it. He'd become convinced Desiree Cazeaux had put a hex on its power, especially after being warned by her bodyguard that it could now be harmful to his loved ones.

I can't believe she treated me in such a way, he thought. *Desiree will be very sorry for what she's done, especially when I start selling off some of that loot. They'll all be sorry.*

🌼

LUCRETIA HAD BEEN in the fields when Emmanuel arrived home. His stomach had been in a knot for the past few days and it wasn't until he'd found his way into the lush estate that he'd felt a sense of relief. After dropping his bag on the polished floor, he'd made his way into the rotunda and over to the staircase. It was the one place that had never disappointed him.

Emmanuel stepped up a few stairs before pausing to admire the stained glass overhead. A sense of warmth had filled his insides, a sense of pride that he'd been able to provide his bride with such an amazing home.

The sound of a door slamming caught his attention.

"Emmanuel? Emmanuel, is that you?" Lucretia squealed.

"Yes. I'm here, Lucretia," he answered, quickly making his way toward the front door. "Is everything all right? I assured you I'd be home directly."

She'd been red-faced and drenched from perspiration, but it hadn't held her back from hurling herself into his arms. "I'm so glad you're home; it seems like a lifetime since you left."

Emmanuel had been thrown off guard by her greeting. It'd been many months since the two had doted on one another in such a way. "Lucretia, I'm delighted to see you as well. Is everything okay? Is the crop okay?"

She'd thrown her head back in a hearty laugh. "Yes, my darling, everything is fine. I have amazing news for you."

"Please," he'd urged. "Don't keep me in suspense."

"The doctor made a visit while you were away. It was as I'd suspected. You're going to be a father, this time to an heir. I can feel it in my soul."

Fearing that his heart might stop, Emmanuel had reached for his chest.

"What is it? *Aren't* you excited? I thought this was what you wanted?"

"Indeed, it is, Lucretia," he'd answered, stepping back from her to assure his heart was indeed beating. "I just wasn't quite expecting it. So many bad things have happened, I... I just wasn't prepared for such wondrous news."

"'Tis a new day, my love. You are going to have an heir to the Sinclair Empire."

AFTER CELEBRATING over one of his favorite meals, Emmanuel had insisted on taking to his office to finish some paperwork. Lucretia had been exhausted from her workday, so she'd been grateful for the opportunity to retire early. Kissing her husband fully on the lips, she'd walked to her room to clean up before climbing in bed.

George had cleaned his office immaculately, just as Emmanuel had expected. He was as devoted as any man he'd known. *Perhaps I should've considered partnering with George instead of Thaddeus,* he'd thought snidely. But he'd known better. George would've never considered being part of such an underhanded business.

Emmanuel sat behind his desk, unwrapped the bottles of whiskey he'd purchased in New Orleans, and placed them carefully in his desk drawers. His body was shaking from withdrawals of the mandrake root and he hoped the whiskey would supplement its high. He'd taken four long slugs from the bottle before sitting back in his chair to allow it to take effect.

After an hour of waiting for the alcohol to ease his trembling, he'd opened the whiskey again. *An heir,* he thought. *What the hell do I have to offer an heir? What example could I possibly set? My body will only continue to shake and getting more mandrake is not a possibility. That bitch will never sell me any and if she did...*

A horrible thought entered his mind. It was as if for the first time, he was realizing *if* he'd been able to get more, it'd only hurt his loved ones.

Maybe even kill another child... Or perhaps cause the return of the Sinclair curse.

Who am I fooling? I've been an idiot. Lucretia can run this business better than I can. She's shared her body with another man. I don't have proof, but a husband can sense these things. It was how her feelings for Thaddeus had changed so quickly, how she'd no longer wanted to have him or Fatima to their home, how she'd cringed when hearing his name.

He could feel the warmth from too much whiskey as it soothed his body and eased his nervousness. *The baby may be born deformed like Philomene had been. Lucretia couldn't handle such a heartache again.* She'd hid her pain very well, but Emmanuel had sensed it. He was aware of the nights she'd lain awake in their bed, tears sliding silently down her face. He had noticed the many Sundays she'd conjured up an illness to avoid going to the small church in town.

Yes, indeed, her heart had been broken.

What if Desiree has put a curse on me? What if she's determined to hurt those I love because I didn't heed her warning about not handling the mandrake root directly? What do I have to offer that would make anyone's life better? The collaborative is bound to turn on me without any profit from the last heist. It's better that Lucretia never knows where it's hidden. They won't stop asking questions about Samuel and Thaddeus, they may even open an investigation of their own. Oh, dear God, that's what they'll do. They'll call for an investigation and have me imprisoned, or even hung in the gallows. The gallows...

He dug through his desk drawer before pulling out Samuel's salted hand. "You look after this place," he'd said to the foul-smelling, rotting body part before placing it on the center of his desk.

Desiree isn't aware of you so she can't take your powers. No one can.

Emmanuel carefully placed the cork back in the whiskey bottle, unfettered the mock fireplace masking the spiral staircase and hastily grabbed a rope. It'd taken him a while to ensure the noose was tied properly, then he'd irrationally made his way to the one place he'd loved more than he'd loved Lucretia.

It was there in the rotunda, where Lucretia found her husband the following morning, his limp body hanging from a railing at the top of the staircase.

Emmanuel Sinclair would never live to see the birth of his heir or the end of the Civil War.

ON A DREARY, overcast January morning, Emmanuel was laid to rest on the property he'd loved. There were only a handful of mourners in attendance but that'd been Lucretia's preference. She'd been able to keep his cause of death a secret, but clearly there'd be talk among those in town.

Emmanuel hadn't been a man without flaws, but he'd been a hard worker and successful businessman. The Sinclair name would be carried on and Lucretia would ensure it didn't bear any tarnishing. In fact, she'd see to whatever blemishes she could erase from her husband's questionable business dealings.

Her stomach was protruding now, and she rubbed both hands across it in a loving gesture. There was no doubt in her mind it was a son in her womb. A son that'd make the Sinclair name something to be proud of once again.

The priest finished reciting the twenty-third Psalm in a slow, monotonous tone. He looked up at Lucretia and nodded, closed his Bible, and simply walked away. The slaves would arrive on the hilltop when Lucretia returned to the house and Emmanuel would be committed to the earth on the land where he'd been born and where he'd died.

Lucretia had been able to keep her tears at bay while the priest had solemnly said what few words he could conjure up on Emmanuel's behalf. But as she turned to make her way back to the house the tears resurfaced. Feeling a warm hand grasp hers, she turned to see Prudence's concerned face.

"Ms. Lucretia, do you need some company?"

"Yes, yes, Prudence, I do. But I can walk back to the house alone. You have someone summon George; I'd like to meet with both of you."

Prudence squeezed Lucretia's hand softly and waved down one of the other slaves headed back to the Jackson property.

Lucretia was met with smells of a hearty lunch, but her heart wasn't in it. Her appetite was normally good as the additional weight on her hips was beginning to show. But her heart was too heavy to tolerate a meal. Even with Emmanuel spending more and more time in his office, the place seemed awfully lonely in his absence. Lonely and disturbingly quiet.

She did, however, accept a hot tea in the parlor with instructions for Prudence and George to join her when they arrived. Lucretia wasn't one to wallow in self-pity, but she felt she deserved one day to allow the shock of losing her husband to sink in. She'd started on her second cup of tea and was considering opening a book when she heard Prudence's voice.

Their arrival was announced as they were shown to the parlor. "Would you care for tea?" she'd asked. They both declined as they took seats farthest from hers. Lucretia had considered asking them to move closer but realized they were nervous and probably more comfortable where they were.

"I'm sorry to alarm you," she'd begun, "but I realized there was no need to put off meeting with you both, even on the day of Emmanuel's funeral." She'd paused to sip from her tea, causing them both to squirm uncomfortably in their seats.

"There's no reason for alarm," Lucretia had insisted. "Prudence, you have been not only an indispensable servant, but a loyal friend. I sense the war will be over soon and the freedom of slaves is imminent. I'd like to offer you and your family a parcel of land and a job to go along with it. Of course, with that I'd be honored to grant you and George your freedom."

For a minute, Lucretia wasn't sure they'd heard her. They sat stoically silent, their eyes unblinking, their breathing stopped. "Prudence? Did you hear me?"

"Yes... Yes, Ms. Lucretia." She turned and looked at George, his eyes brimming with tears. "George, what do you say about this?"

"I...I..." He'd struggled to find words.

"I think he's saying we'd be honored to accept such a fine gift," Prudence answered.

"Very well then," Lucretia had said, a broad smile crossing her face. "I believe a hearty lunch is in order. I'll make sure they have enough prepared."

PART II

NOW

1

KANE, LOUISIANA

BEN NORWOOD'S day hadn't started off well. His coffee maker had finally kicked the bucket, leaving him without caffeine. His brother Dan had phoned the night before to inform him that his wife was going into early labor. This meant Ben would be out on the bayou alone, struggling to get as many gators as he could. Alligators meant money, which was desperately needed to supplement their taxidermy business. With hunting season only lasting thirty days, the brothers had hoped the newborn wouldn't arrive until it was over. They'd almost made it.

Ben downed a slug of orange juice from the carton and made his way outside. The sky was hinting of rain, but a smattering of bright, swollen clouds suggested the weather could go either way. The stench of his bait cooler permeated the air, and would've made the average man nauseous, but Ben was so accustomed to the smell he didn't even notice. He quickly loaded the cooler with chicken thighs for his hooks, then lathered his hands with soap and rinsed them with the garden hose. Ben threw his rain gear in the boat while doing a brief inventory of items he'd need that day.

".308 rifle, check," he said aloud as he ran his finger down the barrel of the gun. ".22 MAG pistol, bow and arrow, check. Rope, first aid kit, and ample ammo, check." After a few more seconds of mental accounting, Ben jumped in his old Dodge pickup. She sputtered, coughed, and choked like a heavy smoker, but eventually succumbed to a steady hum, signaling she was ready to proceed.

Ben wasn't a fan of riding solo, not when it came to getting gators, but he understood Dan's need to be by his wife's side. It'd be their first child and both were over the moon. While it was hard for him to imagine having a wife and child of his own, Ben was happy for Dan. Family life was good for his brother and he'd make a good father.

Tapping the steering wheel to the beat of the song on the radio, he contemplated the day ahead. Hopefully, the clouds would continue to cover portions of the sky, offering some relief from the harsh summer sun. Gators were more active in warmer temperatures and the last thing Ben needed was to run into any wrestling matches.

The drive to where he'd launch his boat into the bayou wasn't a long one. Ben made the ride so frequently he rarely noticed his surroundings. But today, he took the time to observe several deteriorating trailers clinging desperately to the long stilts meant to keep them above any floodwaters. Shaking his head, he wondered how much longer they'd hang on before eventually splitting in half and toppling over. Unfortunately, the occupants of the declining dwellings were willing to stay until it happened. Meth and heroin were both on the rise, sucking the life out of a once hard-working generation. Along with the influx of the drug trade came a cast of shady characters the once tight-knit community had known nothing about. Gone were the days of having a gun to simply hunt or protect oneself from aggressive critters. Now folks had to protect not only their property, but their lives as well.

Ben thought of his father and how ashamed he would've been to see the current state of young folks. Garrison Norwood had been a strict, no-nonsense type fella, but he'd been a good man and father. He'd taught his sons everything he'd known about the bayou and made sure they'd all worked for what little they'd owned. His wife had died before the boys had even started grade school, leaving him to raise his children by trial and error. But as far as Ben and Dan were concerned, their father had done his best.

The dirt road leading back to the bayou would've been missed by anyone not familiar with the terrain, but Ben's truck turned onto it as if it had a mind of its own. He went through the motions without much thought, and was cranking the boat, making steady progress down the bayou within minutes. Apart from the increasing drug crowd, most of the people in Kane, Louisiana were longtime residents accustomed to life in the backwoods. But even with Ben's experience in the wild, he never took for granted the hidden dangers lying in the small waterways fed by the Mississippi. At times, nature could seem so fragile, yet he was all too aware of its wrath.

Ben suddenly felt his skin bristle but wasn't sure why. In the swamp, things were often sensed, but not seen. He was probably on edge, thinking of the approaching rain and knowing his brother's baby was soon due. Either way, he needed to focus on pulling the gators he'd hooked out of the water, tagging their tails, and getting them sold.

Slowing the boat to a hum, Ben found the first tag of the day in an area covered with a thick blanket of water hyacinths. Bald cypress trees, draped heavily with Spanish moss, lined the banks. The blue ribbon wasn't visible, indicating a gator had taken the bait and would be ready to fight for his life. Ben inhaled deeply and held his breath a little longer than normal.

Get yourself together. It's not like you've never been a solo hunter. Just follow the bubbles and get the gator.

Forcing a nervous laugh, he inched the boat closer, but still couldn't locate a taut line, or any movement under the vegetation.

Damn it. Don't tell me somebody's poaching our lines. Son-of-a-bitch...

A flash of color caught Ben's eye and he squinted to focus. "What the...?" he whispered as he reached for his cell phone.

Suddenly the silence of the swamp was deafening.

2

ATLANTA, GEORGIA

TINK MABREY SHOOK the excess rainwater from her Burberry umbrella and pushed her way through the revolving doors into the law offices of Mabrey and Woodard. As summer was giving way to fall, she hoped the thunderstorms would lessen. Glancing down at her watch, she discovered she was fifteen minutes late for her morning meeting. Atlanta was well known for its gridlock traffic, but inclement weather assured motorists an even longer commute. Nothing could be done about it, so she refused to allow it to get her day off to an unpleasant start.

Tink offered a weak smile to the security guard sitting behind the oval desk before pushing the *up* arrow on the elevator.

Brushing back the tendrils of sleek, black hair escaping the pearl and silver clasp, she struggled to remember if she'd applied lipstick. As she dug through her purse for a compact, two of the firm's secretaries stepped off the elevator.

"Good morning, Catherine," Mildred Murphy said in her normal, subdued tone. "I see you got caught in the nasty rain."

Tink nodded and quickly stepped into the elevator. She'd long since tired of correcting Mildred's insistence to call her Catherine instead of Tink. As a toddler, she'd been given the nickname Tinker-bell by her father, and it had stuck. Before long everyone had called her Tink, and frankly, it *fit*.

The brief respite before the whirlwind of meetings and confer-ence calls ended as the elevator doors opened to the fourteenth floor. Candace Ramsey looked up with a phone dangling from her ear and mouthed that Tink's client was waiting in the conference room. Tink held up a finger, then made a beeline for her office to drop off her umbrella and rain jacket, apply a quick coat of lipstick, and grab the appropriate paperwork.

The phone on her desk rang and Tink debated whether to answer it. She made an effort to reach for it, then thought better of it. Turning quickly from her desk, she literally collided with Frank Potts, who softened the blow by grabbing her shoulders.

"Where's the fire?" he asked.

"Oops. Sorry, Frank. I'm late for my meeting. The rain, the traffic..."

"Here, let me take that file. Your father needs to see you and has asked Harold Barber to speak with your client. He's been working on this case as well, correct?"

"Yes, he has, but I'm already fifteen minutes late. You know how impatient Mr. Powell is," Tink replied. "And what in the world does my father want this early in the day? Can't it wait?"

"I don't assume so. He seems preoccupied and insisted you come to his office as soon as you arrived. Harold is waiting outside the conference room for the file. He's competent—you know that. Every-thing will be fine."

She let out a heavy sigh. Tink couldn't imagine what could be so dire as to interfere with consulting a client. Business always took precedence over anything else.

She passed Candace for the second time in five minutes, shrugged to signal she had no idea what was going on, then rode the elevator up six more stories. Her father's office was on one end of the top floor with his partner's on the other. Both workspaces offered panoramic views of the city. They'd been impeccably decorated by one of Atlanta's most renowned interior designers, with no expense spared, reflecting the prestige and affluence of the firm. Every time Mildred, her father's secretary, opened the double mahogany doors, Tink felt a hint of intimidation.

Augustus Mabrey indeed had a commanding presence. Known to those closest to him as August, he was a man of integrity and intellect. He was also very large and intimidating, always demanding hard work and devotion from his employees. Augustus sought out only the best attorneys and rewarded them handsomely for their efforts. He was respected and well-liked, but very few people knew him on a personal level.

An open file was fanned out evenly across his polished desk. Augustus looked up solemnly and motioned for his daughter to take a seat.

"Good morning, Tink. I assume you were caught in traffic. Looks like we'll be pummeled for most of the week."

"Yes, I was. It makes for a long ride in," she answered quietly.

Augustus looked at the file before stacking the papers and closing it. He leaned back in his leather chair and laced his long fingers together.

"What is it, Father?" Tink finally questioned. "You look so troubled. Is everything all right?"

"It seems your grandfather has passed away."

"Grandfather *Sinclair*?"

The grandfather she'd never met. That didn't seem important enough to drag her away from her meeting.

Augustus nodded. "Yes. Apparently, he passed away several months ago."

"That's odd, I suppose," she said. "I mean, I assumed someone would've contacted us. But then again, why would they after all this time?"

The two sat in silence for a few moments before Augustus spoke again. "I'm troubled, Tink. I knew it was best to bring you to Atlanta when your mother passed away. After all, the bayou was no place to raise a child. But your grandparents had a right to know their only granddaughter." He paused briefly as though lost to some other time. He'd never opened up to Tink, so Tink didn't interrupt him.

When her father looked up, she saw the glimmer of tears in his dark eyes. "Let's not go back down that road. If they'd wanted to know me, they had every opportunity."

"You've done well, Catherine, and I'm very proud of you."

She was momentarily taken aback by both his use of her given name and his compliment. It was a rarity for him to make such an acknowledgment.

"It's all behind us now," she said softly. "If he died several months ago, there's already been a funeral. I have a great deal of work to do, so I'll let you get to yours. Dinner this week?" Tink asked as she stood to leave.

"That'd be nice, Catherine, but please, sit back down for a moment."

"What's with you calling me *Catherine*? This must be serious, and I don't like it." Tink took her time sitting back down and wrapped loose pieces of hair around her index finger like an anxious youngster.

"Don't behave like a child. It's unbecoming," he said soothingly, though the words stung, nonetheless. Augustus Mabrey had never allowed her the joy of being a child, even when she'd been one. He'd never been unkind to her, but had lacked the gentle, carefree nature of a parent. Tink had never doubted her father's love, even in the loneliest moments.

As she watched her father's Adam's apple bob as he swallowed, the tenderness in his eyes changed to bitterness.

"What is it? What aren't you telling me?"

His jaw tightened as he retrieved a paper from the file he'd closed earlier and handed it to her. "It seems your grandfather has left you the family's home in Kane, Louisiana. Frankly, I'm surprised. You must be the only relative left. The plantation was repeatedly passed down to the next generation of cotton and sugar cane farmers, ensuring it remained in the family."

"A *plantation*?" Tink asked incredulously. "What would I do with a plantation? I don't even cook or clean for myself and I certainly don't know anything about cotton or sugar cane."

Augustus chuckled as he reached across to retrieve the document from her. "I've done some checking and it appears the old gray mare ain't what she used to be. In other words," he said, chuckling again, "you won't be expected to grow and pick cotton or sugar cane."

"I don't know what you find so funny, but I wish you'd share it with me."

His eyes softened as he leaned back. He seemed to relax a bit, making Tink feel less on edge.

"I can just see you having to farm and taking care of a plantation," Augustus said playfully. "That'd be quite the change of lifestyle, wouldn't it?"

"I'm sorry, but I'm still confused. Five minutes ago, I was preparing to meet with Mr. Powell and now I'm the owner of a cotton plantation in a state I haven't set foot in since my birth. How did my grandfather even find me?"

"Although your mother's family hasn't seen you since you were a week old, I feel certain they've kept tabs on you. Through the years, I'd send them photos and updates. Two years ago, I received a certified copy of your grandmother's obituary. She'd passed away six weeks prior to the mailing. Your grandfather had written there was no need for a visit or correspondence, so I never shared it with you."

"But why leave the plantation to me? I've never even met them. Isn't there someone else?"

"No, I'm afraid there isn't. That's what made their insistence *not* to have a relationship with you all the more distressing."

"So why refuse to see me? Why the determination not to have any contact?"

"I wish I could explain it, Tink, but don't take it personally. The Sinclairs migrated from France back in the mid-1700s and their life here wasn't easy. Still, they persevered and became quite successful. They were very proud of their heritage and all they'd achieved. The plantation was proof of all the family had struggled to attain.

According to Olivia, your grandparents became a little *too* proud—in many ways, they came to think they were better than others, even though their own ancestry was so mixed."

Tink sank back in her chair and slid her feet out of her still-damp heels. "So, this plantation, what's it like?"

"It dates all the way back to 1860. Your great-great-great grandfather, if I am correct, had it built for his young bride. He'd inherited his father's cotton plantation and became quite the businessman. As the cotton money flowed in, he decided to take the plunge and go into the sugar cane business. That was quite a risk back then. For lack of a better term, he went *all in*. Apparently, he was wise enough to realize he needed more land and another savvy business partner, so he joined forces with a free slave, who was experienced and brilliant when it came to business. The partnership came out of the gate running and the Sinclairs were on the top of the world."

"I don't understand," Tink said. "You said he built the home in 1860. The Civil War was still going on. I know some slaves were freed beforehand for various reasons, but did they acquire property and wealth, too?"

"Louisiana had more African-American property owners at that time than any other state. The state's history is quite interesting, a melting pot of cultures, races, religions, and beliefs."

"So, did Olivia tell you this?" Tink asked hesitantly. The mention of her mother always lent her father pause. This time, however, it seemed to humor him.

"I do believe your mother had long since tired of the family history and was convinced the story was embellished each time it was told. Her father barraged me with facts of the family lineage whenever he could. That's one of the reasons Olivia rarely took me there. She much preferred her studio apartment outside of New Orleans."

Tink hadn't heard much about her mother through the years. What she'd learned had come from her paternal grandmother. For some reason, her father preferred to keep his memories to himself.

"Tell me about her. Why would she prefer a small apartment over living on a plantation?" Tink expected the usual brush-off, but this time a broad, genuine smile crossed his handsome face.

"She was one of a kind, Tink. Beautiful—oh, *was* she beautiful, just like you. She had shiny, black hair like yours, soft as silk. It seemed to flow like satin. Her eyes were like yours too, so different from mine, a color one couldn't put into words. Some days they were a swirl of green and tan; others they seemed a deep blue mixed with hints of gray."

Augustus began to take on the faraway look he often wore when he thought about Olivia and Tink feared he'd stop talking. "Please, please, tell me more."

"Society was changing, and Olivia was never really like her parents," he continued. "She respected and appreciated her heritage, but something always kept her away. I could never put my finger on it, but Olivia had some misgivings about the place. She never shared it with me, and I never pressed her. Her folks were furious when she moved away, even taunted her about being a traitor for working in the city, as a *waitress*, of all things. After all, she was a *Sinclair*, which was deep southern royalty in Kane, Louisiana."

"Grandmother said you met Olivia while you were eating in the restaurant where she worked," Tink pressed, trying her luck.

"Yes, I was just out of law school and working for a small firm in Atlanta. I was sent to New Orleans to meet with potential interns studying at Tulane. The firm believed they'd be more apt to agree to free summer work if a younger person confronted them with tales of exciting Atlanta night life." His dark eyes lit up at the memory.

"Tell me about meeting her. Tell me everything about that night." Tink curled her feet up under her, anticipating a scolding about sitting unprofessionally, but it never came. Instead, his eyes continued to twinkle.

"We were in some tourist trap bar on Bourbon Street the students had recommended. I had a couple of beers before I agreed to try one of the more famous drinks."

Augustus laughed, a hearty laugh, one Tink had never heard.

"So, you got drunk? What happened next?" she asked, leaning forward.

"I've never been a big drinker. Sure, I've had a beer every now and then, but never anything like that." He squinted as if deep in thought. "I wish I could remember the name of the drink, but for the life of me, I can't. Anyway, it was poison. I'm convinced now it was simply a dash of every liquor behind the bar." Her father laughed again and Tink squealed with delight.

"So where was Olivia? Did she work at the bar?"

"Heavens no. She wouldn't have been caught dead in a place like that. The potential interns saw what was coming and decided they'd better get some food in me. It wouldn't have worked in their favor if I had a raging hangover the next day."

"So that's when you went to the restaurant?"

"Yes, it was," Augustus answered, clearing his throat as his voice started to crack. "I'm sure we were a sight to see coming through the door," he said. "Loud, boisterous, and inebriated. Apparently, it was something Olivia saw often because she didn't bat an eye."

Although her father's eyes were still twinkling, they were also laced with tears. Tink felt a twinge of guilt for hoping he'd continue.

"My tie was loosened, and the top two buttons were undone on my shirt. I'm sure I looked like someone who partied often." He chuckled. "Oh, the hangover I had the following morning convinced me never to behave that badly again."

"Did you know you loved her? Right then, I mean. Was it love at first sight?"

"I remember it like it was yesterday. Even in my drunkenness, I recall every second of it."

"Tell me! Please, don't make me drag it out of you." Tink had never heard so much about her mother and father's relationship and was determined to keep the conversation moving.

"I was studying the menu, which was blurry, I might add," Augustus confessed. "She walked back to our table with a pad and pen and I looked up at her. I had never seen anyone so beautiful, Tink. We locked eyes as the rest of the world seemed to melt away."

Tink settled into her seat, ecstatic to hear more about her mother, though the question of her inheritance wasn't far from her mind.

Rather than go into detail regarding her mother, Augustus Mabrey adopted his stern, no-nonsense expression. "At any rate, Catherine..."

"Another *Catherine*," Tink said sarcastically.

Augustus ignored her. "I'll send this over to Paige Simpson's office and have her handle it. You have work to attend to."

"Are you referring to the Realtor?"

"She's the only Paige Simpson I know."

"Just a bit hasty, don't you think? After all, I haven't even seen the place and only learned of it a few minutes ago. Shouldn't I at least visit before we sell it to a stranger?"

Tink caught a flash of indignation in her father's eyes, but it receded as quickly as it'd appeared, and was replaced with a hint of sympathy. "By all accounts, Tinkerbell, you, too, are a stranger."

The use of her full nickname, which she hadn't heard him say in over two decades, had her tearing up. Tink lowered her head.

"It's a headache you don't need," Augustus continued. "My advice is to sell it for what you can get."

"I just think I should visit the place before we unload it. Is that too unreasonable?"

"I can't take any time off for at least a couple of months."

"I'm twenty-nine years old. I think I can manage a short trip alone. Besides, what is it, a seven or eight-hour drive at the most?"

Augustus stood, turning his back on Tink to take in the view of the city skyline.

Tink slid her heels back on and joined him at the window. "I can't fathom why you'd be so upset about my desire to visit that part of my past. I'm aware my mother never felt a connection with the place, but I'm as much a Sinclair as I am a Mabrey." She paused, fearing an outburst.

Augustus spoke before she could summon the courage to continue. "I realize it's quite a shock to you, as it was to me. Let's allow it to sink in for a day or two before you make any decisions. Why don't I treat you to lunch? I've been craving lamb chops from Nikolai's Roof."

"Sounds delightful. Would noon work?"

"Yes, it would," he answered after referring to his daily calendar. "I look forward to spending some time with my daughter. But no talk of your inheritance. I just want to catch up on what's happening in your life."

3

Ben Norwood slowly placed his cell phone in the back pocket of his jeans, struggling to breathe. Having been prepared to find an angry alligator on his line, he was deeply shaken by what he'd discovered. Unsure of whether to move closer or back his boat away, he shifted his weight from one foot to the other and resisted the urge to vomit.

Checking his watch repeatedly made it seem an eternity since he'd placed the call to the sheriff's department. The armpits of his T-shirt were drenched, beads of sweat were rolling down his back, and he was beginning to feel lightheaded. Just as he sat down in the boat, he heard the wails of sirens.

Standing once again, Ben waved to get the deputy's attention. The hastily revved engine soon quieted as Deputy Cassius Holder slowed and floated up beside him.

"What've we got, Ben?" he asked. "Roxie said you called in a dead body."

"Damn good to see you, Cassius. Thought somebody had poached my line, then I saw this," Ben answered, pointing past the fanned-out palmetto leaves to the green ash tree. "*Merde*, man. I think his hands have been cut off."

Cassius pushed the button on his radio as if to test its ability.

Static crackled across the bayou. He reached into his cooler, pulled out two bottles of water, and tossed one to Ben. "You look overheated. Take a few swigs and splash some on your face. Can't have you suffering a heatstroke on me."

Ben opened the water and did as he was told while Cassius radioed Roxie. Cassius's words sounded more like a feeble croak than his usual, confident tone. "We're going to need an ID unit out here," the deputy muttered. "It's bad. Go ahead and send the sheriff, too."

"Ten-four," Roxie answered after a lengthy pause. "Will do, Deputy Holder."

Cassius held the small, black mic in his trembling hand. When it was obvious Roxie would say nothing more, he clipped the mic back on his belt and turned to Ben.

"What do you make of this? What time did you discover the body?"

Ben looked down at his phone. "Fourteen minutes ago," he said, his voice calmer and more even now. "I called as soon as I saw the body. Just couldn't believe it. Still can't."

"Where's your brother?" the deputy asked as he looked in every direction except at the ash tree where the body hung.

"Harriett's in labor. Dan's at the hospital. She picked a hell of a day for this—took ten years off my life and that's probably an understatement."

"Did you check it out? The body, I mean? How close did you get?"

"No closer than I am now. Wasn't sure what else I might find and I didn't want to disturb any evidence."

"Good thinking," Cassius said as he turned to look at the body. He took his sunglasses off and leaned forward in the boat to get a better look. "Don't think I know him, do you?"

"Nope, don't think so," Ben answered. "But I only got a quick glance."

Cassius pulled the boat a few feet closer and put his shades back on. "I don't want to disturb anything we could use for evidence," he said as he looked over the scene. "Yep, the hands are both cut off.

What kind of sick son-of-a-bitch would do such a thing? Can't believe the gators haven't eaten on him."

"Jesus," Ben said, sitting back down. He wasn't eager to get a better look at the corpse. The sheriff could do that—it was his job, after all. "Look, Cassius, do you still need me, man? I've got to check the rest of our lines and get back home. I'm sure Dan would appreciate my presence at the hospital."

Deputy Holder once again removed his sunglasses and looked at Ben. "You aren't leaving me out here...? I mean, we'll need a full statement."

"Figured you would," Ben said. "Sounds like the cavalry's coming."

The two men looked up to see three boats heading their way, their flashing blue lights indicating urgency. Something of this magnitude was certainly big news for Kane, Louisiana. A homicide was one thing, but torture was unheard of.

"Looks like the whole force came out," Cassius drawled.

Deputy Amos Arrowood was driving the sheriff, who was standing and holding on to the small windshield, which did little more than deflect some of the mist coming off the water. He wore a stern expression as he nodded a greeting to Ben and Cassius.

"Morning, Sheriff," Ben said. "Thought someone was poaching our lines, but I found *that* instead."

Sheriff Isaac Broussard was in his mid-fifties but looked much younger, save for his thick gray hair. Otherwise, he was as fit as any thirty-year-old. He was six-feet-four with broad shoulders and a trim waistline, and his skin remained tanned a deep bronze year round. His striking good looks were often discussed among the women in Kane, but he was a devoted family man.

"When did you find him?" the sheriff asked, shaking his head from side to side.

"Guess it's been about half an hour or so," Ben answered. "Seems a hell of a lot longer."

"I'm sure it does, son. Doesn't look familiar to me. Does he to you, Holder?"

"No, sir. Haven't gotten too close yet, but he's not a local. Could be working on one of the oil rigs."

Sheriff Broussard motioned the two other boats forward and signaled the deputies to start gathering evidence. Within minutes, they were fanned out, looking for anything that could be considered evidence.

"Ben, you can go ahead and take off," Isaac said kindly. "We've got to get this body out of here. It's gonna be a scorcher today."

"Okay, Sheriff. I'll be home later if you need anything else," Ben answered as he cranked his boat, grateful for the opportunity to exit.

"Ben," Cassius yelled from the bank, "I'll stop by your place tonight for a beer."

"Sounds good," Ben called back as he pulled away. Then, just as he was getting his mind back on tagging some gators, it hit him.

What if this wasn't the only body he'd find on the end of his lines?

4

TINK CAUGHT the elevator and rode back down to the fourteenth floor. As she stepped out, she was flagged over by her friend Candace Ramsey.

"What's going on?" Candace whispered. "You *never* miss a meeting with Mr. Powell."

"You wouldn't believe me if I told you," Tink answered with an exaggerated sigh.

"Are we still on for tonight?"

"Oh, Candace, I'm so far behind with my case load..."

"Oh no you don't!" Candace interjected. "You've canceled the last two times we planned to meet for drinks. You'll never meet Mr. Right working all the time."

"I'm awfully tired and have a lot of information to digest. Why don't you come over for a glass of wine and we'll order takeout?"

"I suppose it's better than nothing. You know I can't stand not being in on the latest scoop. Eight?"

"Make it seven-thirty. I want to turn in early."

BEN FOUND Cassius on his front porch, one hand raised and about to knock, a twelve-pack of beer tucked under his arm.

"Hope the rest of your day went better than the first half," Cassius commented as he walked past him and plopped into the leather recliner.

"Why do you always take my chair? I finally get a recliner worth a shit and you practically knock me down to sit in it."

"Well, there you have it. Guess the rest of the day didn't pan out too good either."

Ben grabbed one of the beers and sat on the sofa. "How much worse could it have gotten?" he asked. "It's not every day I come across a brutalized body."

"Did Harriett have the baby?" Cassius asked.

"Yep, thank God I arrived after the delivery. Can you believe they allow everyone in the delivery room now? I find it offensive, to be honest. The last thing I'd want other people to see would be my wife's... Well, you get my drift."

"They don't think of it like that. It's more of a celebrating life kinda thing. But I agree—it's gotten out of hand. Sort of like breast-feeding in public. Some things you just don't share."

"They had a girl, pretty little thing, has a head full of hair. She's so tiny though. Dan was holding her with his big, rough hands. Damn near gave me a heart attack. He's going to break her if he's not careful."

"I don't think you can literally *break* a baby, Ben."

"Well, if anybody could break a baby, it'd be Dan. One thing's for sure, I won't be holding her for a while. Maybe fifteen or twenty pounds from now."

"What'd they name her?" Cassius asked.

"Hell, I don't remember. Something with an 'L'. I don't know what happened to simple names like Ben and Dan."

"And Cassius."

Ben let the comment go without a reply. "At least Dan'll be back tomorrow. I couldn't handle another day like this one by myself. Did you find out who the guy was?"

"No, but they'll fingerprint him at the coroner's office."

"Fingerprints, huh? Bet that'll be difficult without any hands."

Cassius let out a loud belly laugh. "Just seeing if you were listening. You're on the ball there, aren't ya, Ben?"

"You're sick, man. This is nothing to joke around about."

"I was just messin' with ya. But seriously, my bet's on a drug deal gone bad. He probably stole somebody's stash, so they cut his hands off to make a statement. The drug crowd's nothing to play with and it's only getting worse."

"I don't know why they started bringing that crap to Kane, of all places."

"It's not just Kane, it's everywhere. There's no escaping it. It was only a matter of time before it arrived at our doorstep."

"No identification, huh?" Ben asked again.

"Nothing. Pair of Levi's, navy blue Hanes T-shirt, old Nikes. You should count your blessings the sheriff let you take off when he did. We caught hell getting him down from that ash tree. I'll never forget the smell. If you hadn't found him when you did, the decomposition would've been a lot worse."

"Spare me the details," Ben said. "Your job, not mine."

"Any gators?"

"Yep, and I'm glad I won't have to do it alone in the morning. My heart stopped every time I pulled up to a line, afraid that I'd find another body."

"Let's just hope this isn't gonna be a pattern," Cassius said. "I couldn't stomach another crime scene like that one."

TINK WAS SITTING on her Persian rug with two of her case files spread across the coffee table. No matter how hard she tried to concentrate, her mind kept drifting off to the cotton plantation in Louisiana.

What does it look like? Why'd they leave it to me? Why didn't my grandparents ever contact me? Why did my mother never feel a connection there?

An impatient and persistent knock signaled Candace's arrival. As usual, she was fifteen minutes early. Normally, her promptness frustrated Tink, but tonight she welcomed the company.

"Hey there," Tink said as she swung open the door. "I'm starving. Are you ready to order dinner?"

"Yep, I brought the wine," Candace answered, holding up the bottle. "You phone in dinner while I open this. I'm thinking Mongolian Beef."

"Really? That's a first."

"I'm unpredictable, what can I say?"

As soon as Tink placed their order, Candace shoved a wineglass in her hand and slid a barstool from under the kitchen island. "Spit it out. Something's going on and I don't like not knowing."

"Nothing like getting straight to the point," Tink said playfully.

She'd known Candace four years and the two were the best of friends. They'd started working at Mabrey and Woodard at the same time and often shared the latest workplace gossip. Candace was a great receptionist, very professional and attractive, friendly and accommodating. Everyone liked her, and she enjoyed nothing more than being in the middle of all the goings-on. Anything Tink wanted to know, she only needed to ask Candace Ramsey.

"Does it have something to do with a case?" she asked, motioning toward the disaster on the coffee table.

"No, it doesn't have anything to do with my caseload. Besides, you know I can't discuss confidential business."

"So, it's like that, huh?"

"What are you talking about?"

"You're going to make me drag it out of you."

"What's gotten into you, Candace? You're acting as if there's some type of conspiracy. Perhaps I'm the one who's out of the loop."

"No, both you and Mr. Mabrey have acted odd all day, to say nothing of him sending Harold Barber to cover your meeting with Mr. Powell."

"You don't miss a beat, do you?" Tink asked as she sank onto the sofa and motioned for Candace to join her. "I'm grateful to have someone to talk to. I've never been able to open up to my father."

Candace sat down and looked at her sympathetically. "What's wrong? You look so...troubled. I'm here whenever you need me. If it's too personal, though, I don't mean to pry."

The shock of her inheritance had weighed heavily on her as the day progressed, now leaving Tink limp from exhaustion. Her eyes filled with tears, but she refused to let them escape.

"Do you need a tissue?" Candace asked softly.

"No, I'm fine," Tink answered, clearing her throat to get rid of the lump forming there. "It just came out of the blue. I should've known it was going to be big news when Father requested I come to his office in lieu of meeting with Mr. Powell."

Tink paused to sip from her wine.

"Take your time," Candace said gently, although her tone

suggested she was salivating to hear more. Tink didn't want to frustrate her by prolonging it.

"I've told you about my mother dying in childbirth. I knew very little about her, except she and my father lived in Louisiana. After I was born, he brought me to Atlanta, believing the city would offer more opportunities for him, and be a better place to raise a child. My mother's parents were not only shocked but livid with him for moving away with me."

"I'm sure they didn't like the thought of not seeing you grow up near them."

"They chose not to see me at all," Tink said. "There's been no contact between any of us since Father left with me when I was a week old."

"Seriously? That's odd. So, you've never even met your grandparents?"

"No. At least not that I can recall."

"So, are they here in town?"

"What?" Tink asked, turning to face Candace.

"Are your grandparents in town? Is that what your dad wanted to see you about?"

"No, I'm sorry," Tink stammered. "My thoughts are so scattered right now. Actually, they're both deceased. My grandmother passed away first, followed by my grandfather."

Candace spoke just as the doorbell rang. "I'm sorry you never had the chance to meet them. It's a shame for all of you." She grabbed her purse and started toward the door.

"I paid with my credit card and put the tip on there, too," Tink said. "I'll grab the plates."

"Gregg must be delivering tonight if you left the tip."

"Why would you say that?"

"Because he's super-hot and you try to impress him whenever it's your turn to treat."

"Oh, stop it," Tink answered, waving her friend toward the door as she attempted to conceal a smile.

"Not a bad choice," Candace said, savoring the flavor of her beef dish. "Sometimes it pays to order something new. I tend to get in ruts. Want to try some?"

"No thanks, I've got more than I can eat here."

"It'll be okay, Tink. I know you're sad and it's understandable. Even though you never knew them, it's still a loss. Perhaps a loss of what *could've* been."

Tink swallowed a mouthful of her dinner. "This is going to sound cruel, but it never occurred to me to mourn their passing. Now that I think about it, I'm appalled. How unkind of me."

"You must be thinking of your mother and a part of your life you never had a chance to know."

"That's the weird part," Tink said, pushing her plate to the middle of the table. "They left me an inheritance."

"Now you're talking," Candace said. "What do I see in your future? A new car? A new loft? A new wardrobe?"

"How about a cotton plantation?"

"What...?"

6

"You can't be serious!" Candace Ramsey squealed. "A cotton plantation in Louisiana? Oh my..."

"Are you hyperventilating?" Tink asked. "Seriously? I wasn't that surprised, and I had no idea there was even a plantation in my family."

"Why are you so blah about this? What does it look like? Do you have butlers and maids?"

"For heaven's sake, Candace, I'm not rich by any stretch of the imagination. According to Father, it's in very ill repair. In fact, his suggestion was to sell it immediately and take whatever I could get."

Candace's eyes widened. "Is that what you're going to do? After all, it must be worth something. I'd give anything to have an inheritance plop in my lap."

Tink felt strange again. Something was gnawing at her and she couldn't put her finger on it. There were so many questions she feared she'd never get answers to and she wondered why she knew so little about the other half of her family.

"Tink? Are you with me? You're a million miles away."

She wasn't quite ready to share what was causing her such concern. Tink had hidden her deepest feelings throughout her childhood, and if she could harbor them as a child, she could continue to do so as an adult. Her father was a good man. He'd provided her with all the important things—a roof over her head, warmth in the winter, cool air in the sticky Georgia summers, nutritious meals, and a wonderful education. He'd loved her; Tink never doubted it. He'd loved her as much as his heart would allow.

Perhaps she was simply getting emotional about Olivia. After all, every young girl needed her mother; someone with whom they could share their most intimate thoughts. It had to have been difficult for her father as she was growing up, especially during her teen years.

"Hello? You're still gone," Candace said. "Are you all right? Do you want to be alone?"

"No, I don't," Tink replied. "I'm sorry. It's just difficult to process. I can't sell it without at least seeing it."

"Your dad didn't have any pictures?"

"None he showed me. He was very protective of the file on his desk. He closed it as soon as I sat down and offered very few details about the property. Apparently, it has quite the history, dating back to the 1860s."

"Cool! I bet it's spectacular!"

"Or it's a total teardown, but I'd still like the opportunity to see it and make my own decision about keeping it or putting it on the market."

"You're a grown woman, Tink. I, of all people, know how intimidating your dad can be, but this isn't his call."

Tink sighed and held up her wineglass. "I think this warrants another drink."

Candace carried the remnants of their dinner to the kitchen and returned with the bottle of wine. "Do you know the name of the town where it's located?"

"Cane, Louisiana. Could be spelled several different ways."

"You haven't even looked it up?" Candace asked incredulously. She pointed to Tink's laptop on the end of the sofa. "Hand it over."

Tink passed it to her, not bothering to give her the password. Candace had long since dragged it out of her. It only took a moment for the computer to power up and Candace's fingers began racing across the keyboard so quickly it made Tink's head hurt.

"How do you type so fast? Even if I was able to, I wouldn't. It grates on my nerves."

"Do you want answers or not? We can find out a lot through public records, get general info on the town, and surrounding areas," Candace said as her eyes darted across the screen.

"Okay, I'm curious, I admit it. But I'm also skeptical. Maybe Father's right. If I place it on the market, I'll never have to deal with it. At the least, it'd be a problem I don't need right now."

"Wait, here it is. Kane, Louisiana, spelled with a 'K'. Want some stats?"

"Sure, why not?"

"Let's just say it pales in comparison to the great metropolis of Atlanta. Population is less than three thousand, median annual income is twenty-four thousand. Yikes, even I make more than that." Candace paused. "I'd *never* be able to shop, not even at Nordstrom Rack. How dreadful!"

"So that's what you're taking from this?" Tink drawled. "You do realize there are less prosperous parts of the country, don't you?"

Candace ignored the questions and continued her search. "Originally settled by French and Spanish colonists, Kane's main industry is manufacturing. The good news is oil and natural gas are booming industries nearby. Kane is in close proximity to many shipping points."

"Which would explain the prosperous sugar cane and cotton industries in the 1800s," Tink commented.

"And how it's continuing to prosper," Candace continued. "Appears to be a matter of the haves and the have-nots. There's the poor, hard-working folks, and those who are large landowners. You, my dear, must qualify as the upper echelon, being as you own a plantation."

"See if you can find any property under the Sinclair surname."

Just when Tink was certain she'd scream from the rapid

keystrokes, Candace finally looked up. "It's a big one, girl. Oh my... what in the world are you going to do with *this*?"

"Hand over the laptop," she answered nonchalantly. Once she had the screen turned around, Tink let out a gasp. It was indeed an enormous estate. Even shown in a black and white photograph, it was captivating.

"This photo was taken well over a hundred years ago. I'm sure it's nothing more than a pile of rubble now," Tink said, pushing the power button and closing the laptop. She no longer wanted to discuss her inheritance.

Candace poured what remained of the wine into their glasses.

7

BEN GOT OUT OF BED, showered, and ate a hearty breakfast, hoping it'd make up for his lack of sleep the night before. He'd tossed and turned but couldn't seem to get the vision of the man hanging from the ash tree out of his mind. The shock had slowly faded to repulsion, causing him to vomit several times throughout the night.

It'd been all he could do not to plead with Cassius to stay the night on the sofa, but his pride had gotten the best of him. Perhaps he would've been able to sleep had he not been left alone with his thoughts. Ben wondered if his buddy had fared better.

Just as he placed his plate in the dishwasher, he heard a vehicle pull up, instantly putting him at ease. He knew the rumble of that particular engine.

"How's the baby?" Ben asked, as he walked out to the truck.

"Beautiful," Dan answered without hesitation. "I sure hated to leave Harriett at the hospital last night. To be honest, I wouldn't have if you hadn't found that dead guy yesterday. Figured you weren't too anxious to get back out there by yourself."

"Well, you figured right. I'm not embarrassed to say I'm damn glad to have you back. I'm sorry you had to leave Harriett though. How's she doing?"

"She's a trooper. I never knew how tough childbirth was. Don't know how women do it."

"Please don't elaborate. I prefer to remain ignorant of the details. But you have to be *careful* with the kid, Dan. Your hands are twice as big as she is. It makes me nervous, you handling her so rough and all."

"I'm not being rough with her. My God, Ben, she's my daughter."

"You just don't know your own strength."

"I'll keep that in mind," Dan muttered as he loaded up the boat.

Ben felt a sudden wave of guilt and didn't want his comments to taint the day ahead. "I know you wouldn't hurt her. I've just never been an uncle before. So, when do they get released from the hospital?"

"Later this afternoon. Harriett's mother plans on bringing them home. Not that I don't appreciate it, but it's *my* job. She's also packed enough suitcases to stay with us for a year. I'm sure we'll need the help, but damn, nobody wants their mother-in-law practically moving in."

"I hear ya," Ben agreed before steering the conversation in another direction. "I'm still jittery from yesterday. You're right—I couldn't have done this by myself. It was sick, man."

"Have they found out who he was?"

"Not that I've heard. Cassius thinks it might have something to do with drugs. It does make sense, especially since nobody knew him. I don't like strangers moving in. If you aren't from here, what in creation would draw you to Kane, Louisiana?"

"Employment, for one. Those oil rigs aren't paying too bad."

"Yeah, but the guys coming out for those jobs are sketchy, pillar-to-post type folks. They can't be trusted. Many of 'em are illegals, too. They can commit a crime and leave without a trace. It's troubling, especially with Harriett having the baby."

"Landry."

"What?"

"Her name is Landry, not *baby*."

"Yeah, I meant to ask you about her name. Where'd Harriett get

Landry from? I'll never remember it. Whatever happened to people naming babies something everyone could pronounce and spell?"

"Harriett didn't name her, I did."

"You're kidding, right? Landry's not even a girl's name, Dan. Hell, it's not even a name."

"It most certainly is," Dan answered, his defenses clearly flaring.

"Okay, tell me one person named Landry."

"My favorite football player and coach for one."

"You can't be serious," Ben said with a chuckle. "You named your daughter after Tom Landry? I'm a little offended you didn't name her Ben."

Dan turned to face his brother and glared.

This brought forth raucous laughter from both of them. "One thing about it—I won't forget her name now."

8

SEVENTY-FIVE-YEAR-OLD PALOMA LEBLANC wiped her perspiring forehead with a linen handkerchief. The gnats and mosquitoes thrived in the damp, humid air of the bayou and seemed particularly fond of her on days when the heat was searing. There was no need to allow it to frustrate her. It'd been this way for as long as she could remember and wasn't bound to change now.

After finishing the last of her hot tea, Paloma rinsed her cup and swept over the floor of her scant living space. Originally erected as slave quarters, the old cottage was balanced on bare wooden slats, constructed with clapboard siding, and topped off with a rusting metal roof. Through the years, she'd been offered more ample accommodations, but this was home and there was something about the familiarity that Paloma appreciated.

It wasn't necessary to glance down at her watch—she knew it was time for her latest appointment. Absentmindedly smoothing her hand over the worn wool blanket covering the back of her lumpy sofa, she thought of the young mother that'd been referred for her services. Her skin was as dark as a starless sky at midnight, her teeth were so white they appeared fluorescent, her eyes were large and curious, but a weakness loomed in them.

It didn't take someone with Paloma's instincts as a traiteur to surmise the woman was ill. There were symptoms even her shadowed complexion couldn't hide. Her attempts to disguise the pain running through her muscles were reflected in her eyes, the windows to the soul. A deep sadness swelled in Paloma's belly before fluttering up her windpipe.

She was contemplating another cup of tea when she heard a light tapping. Swallowing hard, she pulled the wooden door open as the hinges moaned and creaked.

The girl had lost more weight since her last visit, which Paloma guessed had been over three weeks prior. The weight loss gave her eyes the appearance of being even larger and despite her best attempts, Paloma's hand went to her mouth as she gasped. The girl pretended not to notice as she walked past the traiteur and made her way to the couch.

"Please," Paloma insisted as she pulled herself together. "Please make yourself comfortable, Zoya. I'm happy to see you again."

She nodded slightly, the only acknowledgment she offered. Her brightly patterned dress hung limply from her small frame as she gathered the excess material and nervously crumpled it in her fingers. She pulled a folded handkerchief from her bag and thrust it in Paloma's direction.

Paloma took it, feeling the weight of the coins inside. "It isn't necessary to bring me a gift, Zoya. My services do not require payment."

"It's not a payment," she insisted. "It's simply a gift. My father said to tell you he and my mama appreciate what you're doing." She closed her eyes and fought a grimace.

"The pain is worsening, isn't it, child?"

"It's nothin'. I need you to lay hands on me, pray over me..."

"Zoya, my prayers are not enough. You must see a doctor, one in town, not around here."

"No," she said quickly and defiantly, opening her eyes so wide Paloma was almost frightened. "The doctor will only give me a disease your prayers will never heal. I have heard about them; the older women talk about how they curse our kind."

"Not true, child. It is a lie; they can help you. They don't have the power to place a curse upon you."

"But you can help me. You were taught how to heal and how to say prayers that can be heard."

"I was taught nothing of the kind. My gift was passed down to me from generations of traiteurs before me. I don't heal anyone. Healing comes from above."

"Then why was I sent to you?" she asked, her voice turning weak and fragile. She narrowed her large eyes into a piercing stare. "Why waste my time? I have children who need tending."

"Prayers work hand-in-hand with medicine," Paloma answered calmly. She'd dealt with this type of behavior many times.

"You're a fake. You're not one of us, you're turning your back on your culture and its people," Zoya all but whispered as she stood. "Keep the coins. My father won't take them back."

"Please, Zoya. I can see the pain in your face. You're hurting because there's something going on with your body. I'm happy to do my part. I'll lay hands on you and say all the prayers I can for your healing. But there are still things only a doctor can do."

"Forget it," she said, pushing her way past Paloma and opening the door. "I don't need you or a doctor. I just need to rest."

Paloma reached for her and opened her mouth to speak before deciding against it. Her initial thought was to plead with Zoya to consider her young children, but the effort would've been fruitless. Deep down, Zoya knew she was ill—that was why she didn't want to see a doctor. She didn't want to hear the words, for once they were spoken, they could never be retracted.

Paloma stood at the door, watching Zoya struggle to get into the waiting pirogue. She worried the unbalanced woman would tip the small boat over, but the relative who'd brought her was able to steady it.

Paloma swallowed hard as they paddled away and wondered if

she'd ever see Zoya again. She would pray for her children—that was all she could do.

🌀

GRATEFUL FOR BETTER WEATHER, Paloma decided to check on the estate. It'd been a couple of days since she'd walked up there, so a visit was overdue. Since the ground was still muddy from the rain, she pulled on her waterproof boots and locked the door behind herself.

The water on the bayou was as smooth as glass, leaving no indication of the pirogue that had parted the waters just a few moments before. It was eerily quiet—even the crickets and bullfrogs seemed to be napping. Paloma felt the hair on the back of her neck stand just as it did every time she made her way to the house.

The estate had been quite opulent in its day, or so she'd been told, but as far back as she could remember, it'd been nothing but a decaying piece of rubble. She recalled stories from her mother and the other *staff*—as they'd referred to themselves—of more fruitful times on the plantation when money flowed like the waters from the gulf poured into the bayou. There had been extravagant parties where the ladies dressed in imported silk gowns and the men drove fancy cars purchased from out-of-state dealerships. The furniture had been new—the chandeliers had shone like diamonds hanging from the ceilings, and people from near and far knew the Sinclair name.

But Paloma also recalled other stories, told in hushed tones and wavering voices, none of the children were supposed to hear. Those had been the stories she'd been most interested in, often feigning sleep or disinterest whenever she'd heard whispered conversations.

Paloma had been born after the wealth had begun to fade, but the large house still needed to be cleaned and scrubbed, despite its deterioration. Annabelle and Corbin Sinclair had been the last of a dying breed. They'd worked hard to maintain their status among Louisiana's elite sugar cane farmers, but Corbin's failing health had taken its toll on the once-thriving estate. Without proper guidance and supervision, the business had begun to falter, and the Sinclairs' only child, Baron, only added to their mounting troubles. He'd been born with a loathsome sense of entitlement rather than the fierce work ethic that had pulsed through the Sinclairs' blood from the time they'd settled in Kane, Louisiana.

Corbin's illness had left him with little strength to discipline his growing son, and by his teenage years, Baron had been running through what was left of the family fortune like there was no tomorrow. His mother, Annabelle, doted on him as though he were a toddler, but the household staff had been convinced she feared Baron more than she loved him.

The only hope of salvaging the Sinclair name and prosperity had been a miracle. Corbin and Annabelle hoped to find it in a wife for their son. Corbin had sent for the heads of influential cane-farming families to come and meet with him, but word had already been out about their desire to marry off the bad seed of the bunch, and none had been interested. They had wanted their daughters to marry into prominent families with not only Louisiana "royal lineage" but those with an obvious sustainable future. Clearly, doubt of Baron's ability to expand the Sinclair fortune had become a topic of widespread gossip.

It had been his son's introduction to the beautiful, but socially unacceptable, Ruby Hobbs that had been the final straw for Corbin. He wouldn't allow Baron to piddle away the family fortune, and had made a conscious decision to hide a substantial amount of the Sinclair assets from Baron and bequeath it to a future Sinclair. All he had to do was hold on to his health until Baron and Ruby became parents.

Still hopeful that something would snap Baron into shape, Corbin had eventually turned the majority of the business over to his son.

Baron had quickly married Ruby. His attempts to run the family business had been laughable at best, forcing many of the devoted farm workers to find work elsewhere. The only employees remaining had been those who cared for the estate and resided on the premises.

The cottages left much to be desired, but they were home, so most of the help had stayed, despite the sporadic paychecks, dispersed whenever Baron had money from whatever scheme he was running at the time. Those surviving in such sparse conditions had been accustomed to living off the land and usually had other ways of making a few bucks.

The old antebellum home was coming into view, and Paloma heaved a sigh of regret for making the trip. The young mother had zapped her energy, making her feel the need for a midday nap. She reached into the deep pocket of her homemade apron, pulled out a ring of rusty skeleton keys, and slid the appropriate one into the lock.

Every time she entered the house, Paloma longed to feel sadness over Baron's recent death, but no matter how desperately she tried, she couldn't recall a single fond memory of the man. Ruby had been as narcissistic as her husband and neither of them had been capable of loving anyone, including each other. Their love was reserved for things, not people, which had always puzzled Paloma.

How could they not have loved Olivia? She'd been the most beautiful child Paloma had ever laid eyes on, so polite and kind-hearted.

Paloma reached for the light switch only to find the electricity had been turned off, no doubt from lack of payment. The latest news was the estate had been left to Olivia's young daughter, but no one knew what would be done with it. Until then, Paloma would continue to keep the place up as best she could.

It was the right thing to do.

9

TINK SAT NERVOUSLY on the stiff couch outside of her father's office, waiting for him to finish a business call. She could feel Mildred Murphy's stare boring into her, but refused to acknowledge it.

Mildred cleared her throat for the third time, forcing Tink to turn to her. "I know I should've given Father more notice, but I had a few minutes in between appointments and was hoping he'd be free."

"Your father is rarely available without an appointment," Mildred said firmly, reminding Tink of how she'd spoken to her as a child when she'd visited her dad's office. Well, those days were gone. Tink was now an attorney herself.

"I realize, how busy he is," Tink said flatly. "But before he's my employer, he's my father, Ms. Murphy."

Mildred's carefully drawn-on eyebrows immediately arched and her eyes widened, but before she could offer a reply, Augustus opened the double doors leading back to his office.

"Good morning, Tink. What brings you to the top floor?"

The nervousness in Tink's stomach worsened as she stood. "I was hoping you'd have a few minutes," she stammered, stunned she'd been so brash with Mildred. "I'd like to speak with you if you're available."

"Come in," Augustus said warmly, stretching his arm out to motion her inside. Tink hurriedly entered, grateful to be out of sight of Mildred's judgmental glare. Her father closed the door behind them and sat in the chair next to hers. "She's getting old, Tink."

"Excuse me?"

"Mildred. She's getting older. Don't be so hard on her."

"Oh, for heaven's sake. You must have the lobby bugged," Tink teased. "She's always intimidated me and quite frankly, I'm over it. I'm an adult, after all."

Augustus looked at her, and for a moment she thought he was going to cry, but his expression swiftly changed into a grin. "Yes, I know you're an adult."

"You're mocking me."

"Forgive me," he said. "So, what do you need to see me about?"

As though she no longer had control over them, Tink began wringing her hands. *Why was it so difficult to speak to her own father?* Her mouth suddenly felt dry and she longed for a sip of water.

"You're an adult, remember? I have a feeling I know what this is about."

"Could I have a water?"

Augustus walked to the small refrigerator under his wet bar and pulled out two waters. He handed Tink one, sat back down, and screwed the top off one for himself. "You want to discuss your inheritance, don't you?"

Tink nodded, her voice failing her. "Yes."

"If you feel as though your curiosity is in some way betraying me, please don't. I've been thinking about how I handled the situation and don't feel good about it. It was unfair of me not to share more about your mother. It's a painful subject. I've just always found it easier not to discuss her. Easier for me, that is."

There was so much Tink wanted to say, but if she didn't discuss what she'd come for, she'd lose her nerve. "I want to visit the plantation."

Augustus expelled a long breath and leaned back. "Yes, I figured as much," he said softly. "I'll get in touch with the remaining staff and have Mildred clear my calendar."

"Wait." Tink held up a hand. "This is something I need to do myself. I, I just feel the need to go alone."

Tink studied the pricey rug under her feet as her father stood and made his way to the window. It was something he often did when he was at a loss for words. He'd place his balled fist under his prominent chin and stare blankly over the city.

Tink remained silent for what seemed like hours until he turned to face her. "Do me one favor," Augustus said adamantly. "Take Candace Ramsey with you. I'll ensure she's paid and there's no time deducted from her vacation leave. And, for God's sake, fly into New Orleans and rent a car. I'll be worried enough about you driving those back roads from the airport—I sure couldn't stand to think of you driving from Atlanta."

Relief washed over her, leaving her limp and tired. "Thank you," she managed to say. "I'm sure Candace will appreciate a break."

"I'll have Mildred secure a replacement from the temp agency," he replied, taking a seat behind his desk. "I'll contact the attorney handling the estate and let him know you'll be coming. It goes without saying to contact me before you sign anything or make any permanent decisions."

"Of course," Tink agreed. "I wouldn't dream of doing either of those things without discussing them with you. It's simply a quick trip to see the property. I feel I owe it to Olivia."

"Bear in mind there was little love lost between your mother and her family and she certainly didn't have any connection to that ostentatious property."

"Doesn't that strike you as odd?"

"Don't allow it to evoke any unfounded emotions, Tink. Blood isn't necessarily thicker than water." With that, Augustus reached for a file on his desk, indicating their meeting had come to an end.

10

———

BEN WAS WASHING up with the garden hose when Deputy Cassius Holder drove up. He'd apparently just showered, his dark hair was damp and slicked back, and he had on a new shirt that still bore prominent creases from where it'd been folded at the factory.

"New shirt?" Ben asked, fighting back a grin.

"How'd you know?"

"An iron comes in handy every now and then, or as a last resort, you could throw it in the dryer for a few minutes."

"What are you talking about?"

Ben turned the hose off and looked up at his old friend. "Who are you trying to impress, Cassius?"

"Not a damn soul," he responded rebelliously, his cheeks flushing a light pink. "Just wondering if you'd like to get a beer at Syd's. She's got wings on special tonight."

"Oh, it's coming to me now. There's a new girl behind the bar."

"I wasn't aware of that, but this *is* a new shirt. Got it off Amazon. Prime's the greatest thing since sliced bread, I tell ya. Stuff gets here in two days, guaranteed. No more going into New Orleans for me. They even deliver toilet paper."

"Toilet paper? Who doesn't have time to go pick up toilet paper? Things are getting out of hand."

"Not the point. You pay a flat fee and it's delivered right to your door."

"Whatever floats your boat, Cassius. I just got home," Ben said, holding his arms out to show how dirty his clothes were. "Haven't even showered."

"I can wait. No problem."

"Need a wingman, don't you?"

"I've never understood that term, but I guess I do. How long are you gonna take?"

"Never rush your wingman," Ben answered. "There's beer in the fridge and for heaven's sake, throw your shirt in the dryer. It's embarrassing."

⁂

BEN GOT in the passenger's seat of Cassius's police cruiser, but not before offering to take his pickup. "I think it's time for you to get another vehicle. You can't possibly expect to go on a date in this thing."

"Can't say I haven't been toying with the idea," Cassius said. "But why not take advantage of the free gas while I can?" He patted the dashboard affectionately. "If we're in a crash, this is the vehicle to be in. She's reinforced in all of the appropriate places."

"I'm not anticipating a crash and you're creeping me out. Is it the car or the bartender you need a wingman for?"

Cassius ignored the comment and turned on the radio instead. "No ID on the murdered guy yet. Must be a roustabout on one of the oil rigs or something."

"How do they identify him without prints?"

"Medical examiners know all kinds of tricks, but without a missing person report, none of them help much. With no dental records or familial DNA to compare with his, we're out of luck."

"No one has missed this guy?"

"Technically, it's just been a day. If he's a drifter, chances are no one will care enough to go to the trouble of finding him."

"It doesn't make sense for someone to bring such heat down on themselves. I mean, cutting a guy's hands off isn't something you see every day."

"You've got *that* right. They're trying to send a message, but to who? It's got Sheriff Broussard on edge. He said if his hair wasn't already gray, it would be now."

"Doubt he's seen anything like that before," Ben said, shaking his head. "Mafia shit, man. I still can't believe it."

"Why are we talking about this anyway?" Cassius asked.

"You're the one who brought it up," Ben answered, turning to look out the window. He saw his hometown from a different perspective now. It was as if a dark veil had descended upon Kane and Ben silently wondered if things would ever be the same.

11

PALOMA LEFT the front door open to let in extra light while she rummaged through a closet to find an old lantern. Why hadn't she thought to put on a sweater? The rains had left behind cool weather and a shiver ran through her, making her feel ill at ease.

The sheets she'd draped over the furniture weeks earlier now resembled odd-shaped ghosts. Dust particles floated through the air like granules of sand and she could feel grit under her galoshes as she walked. There was considerable work to do on the place and whoever moved in would have their labor cut out for them.

The estate had been constructed with the highest quality materials and had good, sound bones, but neglect had caused more than its share of problems. The dirt and grime would be the least of the next owner's worries.

Once turned on, the lantern offered a soft glow, giving her the additional light needed to locate a few candles and a flashlight. Paloma's first concern regarded any perishable items remaining in the refrigerator and freezer. She lit the candles on the tarnished silver candelabra then pulled open the drapes.

Paloma would continue to maintain what she could and keep the home as clean as possible, but she'd bear in mind the residence was unoccupied and forego any unnecessary housework. She suspected whoever took over the estate would either demolish it or be in for years of renovations. Either way, a deep cleaning wasn't going to make a difference.

The furniture under the sheets not only needed refinishing but reupholstering as well. Despite their appearance, the pieces were quite valuable, and should be spared. However, their exact value would have to be determined by a well-educated collector and Paloma hadn't encountered one of those in years.

It came as no surprise to find the utilities disconnected. Even in death Baron hadn't cared about the place. Thankfully, she'd removed most of the food after his death and dispersed it among the remaining staff. Otherwise, Paloma would've had quite the mess on her hands.

Paloma filled the porcelain sink with soapy water and absent-mindedly began wiping down the warm refrigerator. Her thoughts were on the beautiful young baby that had been born almost thirty years ago. Ruby had insisted, or rather *demanded,* that Olivia pay them a visit prior to her baby's birth. The Sinclairs had been adamantly against delivering their grandchild in a hospital for more than one reason. The first was crass and simple—it cost money. Anyone who charged the Sinclairs money couldn't be trusted. The second reason was far more sinister—so much so that just thinking about it made Paloma shake so badly she dropped her rag.

She left the rag where it lay and walked over to the kitchen table where she sat and tried to calm her breathing. Paloma looked at her weathered hands, grasping them together to ease the trembling. The voices rambling through her memory were so loud and angry it was as if they were coming from the house itself.

Olivia had looked so tired that morning when Paloma had answered the door. Her rounded belly had protruded from her small frame and her ankles and feet had been swollen to the point of appearing distorted. Her eyelids had looked heavy, indicating a rest-less night, but it had been her expression that'd deeply troubled Paloma. The usual smile on Olivia's face had been gone and replaced with a mixture of frustration and fear. A nod had taken the place of her usual friendly greeting.

If nothing else, Paloma had known her place, even with Olivia, whom she adored as her own. She'd simply reciprocated the nod and added a knowing glance, as if to say she understood this was the last place Olivia wanted to be.

Paloma had led her to the parlor in the east wing where her parents had been waiting. "Where's the old man?" Mr. Sinclair had barked from his seat.

"He's working, Dad. I told you that when you called this morning."

"What kind of work is more important than attending to a woman with child? Just like his ...can't expect anything else," Baron had murmured under his breath.

"You know what kind of work he does and I'm fine at home. The hospital is four blocks away—or *was*, until you demanded I drive out here."

"Paloma!" Ruby had screeched. "What are you thinking? Get the tea, quickly please."

"I'll just have a glass of water," Olivia had turned to say. "No caffeine for me."

"I had tea and a nightcap every day of my pregnancy and you turned out just fine," Ms. Sinclair had spouted. "Is that what you waste your husband's money on? Foolish advice from incompetent doctors?"

"I'm not here to argue with you, Mother. You demanded I come out this morning despite the fact I'm due any day now and I'm exhausted. What's so pressing?"

Paloma had walked in with the silver teapot and china cups just as Baron had slammed his fist on the table beside his armchair. It had startled her so badly that she'd spilled the steaming liquid down the front of her uniform. Even to this day, Paloma could hear the expensive china teacups hitting the floor and fracturing into tiny pieces. It had happened in slow motion, the cracking and breaking seemed to last for minutes rather than the seconds it took them to scatter across the hardwood floor.

Olivia had jumped up and ran to the kitchen to get a cold, wet towel to put over Paloma's blistering chest, then eased her into a chair. Even though she'd been in pain, Paloma could recall Ruby and Baron Sinclair's outrage. It had been scathing and hateful and so magnified that it reverberated off the walls.

They'd belittled Olivia for being foolish enough to assist the incompetent help, before quickly turning their wrath on Paloma for deliberately ruining their visit with their only child.

The situation had continued to escalate, despite neither of the women offering a rebuttal. Paloma had seen the Sinclairs' mouths moving, heard their raspy voices, their anger, their disdain, but the words had been so distorted she hadn't deciphered them.

As if coming to from a fainting spell, everything had become clear again. This time it had been Olivia's turn to render her anger. "How dare you both demand that I come out to visit as though you genuinely want to see me! Why would I expect you to behave any other way than vicious and cruel? This is the last time you will see me, mark my words! My child will be born in a hospital and not in this creepy, cursed mansion that you both gloat about. If you hadn't inherited it, you'd both be living in a shack on the bayou eating crawfish you caught yourself. You haven't fooled anyone in this community and certainly not me. You may bear the Sinclair name, but it no longer means a damn thing! You both saw to that long ago!"

Olivia had snatched her purse from the sofa and turned swiftly to Paloma. "God bless you," she'd said softly, her eyes misting over. "I can't begin to imagine what these two have put your through."

Ruby had stood so quickly she'd literally fallen back onto the sofa, her expression a combination of shock and disbelief. "Baron, don't allow her to behave in such a fashion! I...I'm simply appalled!"

Baron had reached Olivia in two strides, grabbing her right arm and flinging her into the nearest chair. "You don't have any idea what it's like to be a Sinclair, you ungrateful trash! Apparently waiting tables in a low-rent tourist trap is your idea of climbing the corporate ladder."

Paloma had been conflicted as to whether to protect Olivia from her parents' fury or escape to the safety of her own small quarters to attend her wounds. Unfortunately, she hadn't been given any time to ponder it.

Olivia had screamed like a wounded animal, falling forward onto the floor, and curling into a fetal position. Her thin arms had hugged her pregnant belly, now hardened from strong contractions. The agony of Paloma's own injuries had been forgotten as she'd hurried to Olivia's side.

"Get up, Paloma!" Ruby had demanded. "This is just another attempt to get attention. Come on, Baron, I refuse to play games with an adult. I don't know why I invited her anyway. Frankly, it's getting exhausting." With that, Ruby had left the parlor, her footsteps echoing as she stomped up the stairs.

Olivia's wails had lessened temporarily but she had still been panting, and her hair was drenched with perspiration. Paloma had wiped her face with the small portion of the apron not wet from the tea spill.

"You have other duties that require your attention," Baron had seethed through clenched teeth. "Get Olivia to her car. I don't want her back here again!"

Paloma had held her breath until she'd heard the parlor door slam. She'd known the young woman enough to know this was no cry for attention. "I'm here, child," she'd whispered in Olivia's ear. "I won't let any harm come to you, but we must get to your car."

The terror in Olivia's eyes had been far more frightening than her wails. She'd tried frantically to say something, but pain had prevented her from doing so.

As Paloma had struggled to pull Olivia's arm around her shoulder, the estate's phone had rang. To be derelict in her duties would've only caused further friction.

Paloma had eased Olivia back into a chair and quickly answered.

"Hello?" she'd said, hoping she'd been able to grab it before the caller hung up.

"Paloma?"

"Please, please sir, tell me this is Olivia's husband."

"Yes, it's Augustus. What's going on? Is she at the estate? Is she okay?"

The shrieks had returned, as the veins stood out prominently on Olivia's neck and forehead. Her breathing had been erratic—at times she'd struggled to get a breath, while at others she'd been hyperventilating.

"I'm doing what I can, Mr. Augustus. She's in terrible pain but I can't get her to the car by myself..."

"Where are the Sinclairs?" he'd demanded, his voice strained and panicked. "Get their help!"

"I don't have time to explain, sir. Please, *please* call for an ambulance. Her labor has come on too quickly. She needs a doctor!"

"I'm calling now and I'm on my way. Don't leave her side, Paloma. Dear God, don't leave her side!"

12

THE PLANE LANDED SMOOTHLY in New Orleans while the captain thanked everyone for choosing their airline. Then the seatbelt lights chimed loudly as the plane pulled into the gate. Candace squealed with delight as she jumped up to retrieve their carry-on bags from the overhead compartment.

"I feel like *I'm* the heiress," she whispered to Tink as she handed over her bag. "I spent last year's vacation cleaning out my closet and painting my parents' toolshed. I'd say this is quite the improvement."

Tink remained silent as she stood among the huddled masses waiting impatiently to exit the plane. The whole idea of her owning property in Louisiana was so surreal. Even more farfetched was the fact she'd left several pending cases behind to make this journey. She was thankful to have Candace along, but didn't share her excitement. Tink's emotions were so mixed—even after struggling to sort them into several categories, making sense of them remained difficult. Perhaps she was making more of it than was necessary, but Tink never underestimated her gut, and right now her gut was in a nervous knot.

They were the last to leave the baggage carousel after waiting for all three pieces of Candace's checked luggage. "I don't even *want* to know what you have in there," Tink said, motioning toward the bulging bags. "We're only here for a few days and might not even stay that long. Judging from your in-depth research on Kane, I'm not anticipating a host of choices for fine dining or piano bars."

"Where's your optimism? How bad can it be, anyway? At the least, it's an adventure we never dreamed we'd experience."

"You're right," Tink answered, a sense of guilt and embarrassment washing over her. How could she not be excited? *Worst-case scenario, the place is a dump and I'll have to sell it. Candace is right—it's an adventure.*

"I think you'll be pleased with the rental car," Tink said, smiling broadly at her best friend for the first time since they'd boarded the plane.

"Do tell..."

"Nope, I'll just say Mr. Augustus Mabrey graciously offered the use of his Platinum American Express card."

"Wow," Candace gushed.

"Good grief, I'm building it up a bit too much. Now you're bound to be disappointed," Tink teased as she handed the card over the counter and scrawled her name across the paperwork. "We may have to leave some of our luggage behind, Candace. I didn't get a cargo van."

The two friends laughed and walked arm-in-arm to the garage to wait for their vehicle. The convertible red Mustang didn't disappoint either of them. After getting assistance with their luggage, they pulled out into the sunshine, with the top down.

As her father had predicted, it was twenty-five minutes to the Ritz-Carlton Hotel. Both girls had pulled their hair back into pony-tails and donned their sunglasses. Just as they were enjoying the sun on their faces, the hotel came into view.

"We don't have to check in right away," Candace insisted. "Let's do a little sightseeing first."

"I'd love to, but I promised Father we'd check in as soon as we arrived. I'm pushing it as it is. I don't want to upset him."

"For heaven's sake, what parent would expect their almost thirty-year-old daughter to report directly to her hotel room?"

"I'm not on restriction, Candace. I'm sure it's simply to put his mind at ease. Besides, the bellhop can bring our things to the room. We can freshen up a bit and hit the town. I've always wanted to see the French Quarter—it's so quaint and has such history."

"I was thinking more along the lines of a mixed drink on Bourbon Street, but it's your call."

Tink threw her head back and laughed heartily. "I think we'll have time to do both," she said as she eased the sports car under the elaborate entrance.

"Good afternoon, ma'am," a middle-aged man said, greeting her in a deep, professional voice. He was dressed in an ensemble reminiscent of one of the nutcrackers placed on their mantel at Christmastime. She purposely ignored Candace for fear she'd be thinking the same thing and cause her to snicker. "Will you be checking in with us today?"

"Yes, sir," Tink answered. "Catherine Mabrey. The reservation was made earlier."

He waved his gloved hand in the direction of a waiting bellhop, who was leaning against a rolling luggage cart. The young man jumped to attention and was beside the car in an instant.

"We'll just be a few minutes," Tink told the older gentleman. "We're checking in, then plan to do some sightseeing. I'm sorry to trouble you with parking my vehicle and retrieving it again so soon."

"No problem, Ms. Mabrey, but you won't need your own vehicle. It appears plans have already been made for you to have a driver. I'll ensure he's available when you come back down."

"There must be some mistake," she answered, though she suspected there wasn't.

"No, ma'am. Your law firm is providing those services for you; the limousine company has been paid in full."

"Very well," Tink said stiffly. "We'll be back down in thirty minutes."

TINK'S FACE was burning with anger as she slid the coded card into the designated slot of the elevator, allowing them access to the upper floors of the hotel. Tears stung at her eyes as they had when her father had embarrassed her in college. The other girls had been impressed by his generosity, but she'd found it overprotective and flaunting.

Neither young woman spoke until they opened the door to their room and entered to find their luggage already in place. "How do they do that?" Candace asked in disbelief. "They must have some secret, supersonic elevator that gets them here seconds before we arrive."

Tink couldn't manage a reply but did make her way over to the chocolate-covered strawberries and bottle of chilled, chardonnay. Her father knew fresh strawberries were her weakness, so she indulged in two of the largest and poured Candace and herself a full glass of wine. Foregoing the swirling, sniffing, and first sip for tasting and evaluating, Tink took an uncouth gulp from her glass.

"Don't let it ruin your trip, Tink," Candace said, although she was clearly disappointed. "I'm sure your dad thought he was doing you a favor by providing a limo. Look at the bright side—with a driver supervising us, no one will slip a roofie in our cocktails."

"So that's what you're taking from this? I'm thinking he's being overprotective, and once again, asserting his control over my life."

"Perhaps you're being a little hard on him. After all, you're all he has."

"No, I'm not," she answered defiantly, taking another excessive gulp from the overpriced wine. "He has his mother, Sully, his job..."

"You know what I mean. From what you've said, Mr. Mabrey still struggles with the loss of your mother. It must be difficult for him to see you come here alone without any guidance. The limo was probably a gesture that made him feel he was here with you somehow."

Maybe it was the wine taking effect, or her weariness from the plane ride, but Tink felt guilt-ridden. *How ungrateful of me.* Her father's feelings had been the last thing she'd considered.

"You know, you're exactly right!" She toasted to an enjoyable evening just as her cell rang. "Guess who?" she asked sarcastically before answering.

"Hi, Father, I was about to phone you. We're just settling into our suite, which is lovely by the way. I wasn't expecting a driver for the evening, but I appreciate your thoughtfulness."

"What do you mean?"

"Excuse me?"

"What are you referring to? What driver?"

"The gentleman who met us when we arrived and provided our bellhop told us transportation for the evening had been arranged by the firm. I assumed you'd taken care of it."

"I'm making an effort to stay out of your affairs, Tink, especially when it comes to this. I don't want to alarm you, but I didn't make a reservation. Let's not panic yet. I'll contact Mildred to see if either she or someone else from the firm secured the driver."

"Who would take it upon themselves to arrange a driver for me?" Tink asked bluntly.

"Don't be so defensive," Augustus answered calmly. "It's standard practice when we have associates handling business out of state."

"But this isn't related to the firm."

"I had Mildred handle the details, although it was through my personal account and not the firm's. Give me a few minutes to handle it, but don't leave the hotel. Go down and have a nice lunch. There are several restaurants to choose from. But, Tink, I'm serious—don't get in the car with anyone!"

13

SWEAT RAN down Paloma's face and she instinctively wiped it with the wet, soapy rag. Olivia's death and her daughter's birth were so profoundly etched in her mind, it was as if she were experiencing it again whenever she recalled it. She randomly swatted at the air with both hands as if to shoo away the ghosts of the past.

Her hands were still trembling as she unlocked several windows to let in some of the cool, damp air. The sweater she'd regretted leaving at her cottage was no longer needed. She took the brightest of the remaining lanterns and made her way through the mansion.

The main floor of the residence had been designed for entertaining and boasted a grand rotunda stretching up to the frescoed ceiling on the third floor. There were two extravagant parlors where guests could gather and enjoy a drink, a fancy tea cake or seafood appetizer, and often a smoke. It had an extensive kitchen capable of cooking for a decent-sized restaurant, and two large powder rooms for the women who needed to powder their noses, adjust their blustering crinolines, or loosen their corsets. Of course, the staff was all available to accommodate them although they were rarely acknowledged. As the decades had passed, these rooms had been converted to restrooms with indoor plumbing.

Paloma hesitated at the bottom of the staircase, as she always did when she was alone in the home. Even after so many years of neglect, the staircase remained as breathtaking as the day it'd been installed. At least that was what she'd been told from as far back as her memory would allow.

Paloma's eyelids felt heavy and her body weary, but she was determined to ensure a quick check of the estate since she'd made the walk up to do so. Uncertain of how long she'd stood at the base of the stairs, she reached her wrinkled fingers toward the ornate candelabras welded to the top of both volute newels. It was something she did each time she passed them, much like people who rubbed bronze statues in a town square, or the belly of a Buddha sculpture. It'd been years since she'd seen the oil-burning candles lit, but fondly remembered what a beautiful sight they'd been.

Paloma wasn't even aware of trudging up the two flights of steps or how firmly she was gripping the banister as she made her way. The knot that'd formed in her gut earlier when Zoya visited still hadn't dissolved, making her quiver. Perhaps it was in fact *she* who was ill, not the young girl who'd adamantly denied having health problems of her own.

When the house was dark, it gave off a creepy, almost haunted vibe. But Paloma quickly realized she much preferred it dim and shadowy than well-lit, which gave it a gaudy, crumbling appearance.

Paloma walked down the second-floor hallway, holding up the lantern to ensure all the bedrooms on the west wing remained closed and locked. The east wing held a large ballroom that hadn't been used in her lifetime, but remained polished and maintained as if a group of women in long gowns and men in tuxedoes might arrive at any moment. There was a large dressing room that had been built for Lucretia Sinclair, the first woman to run the estate, alongside her husband, Emmanuel. Paloma had heard many of her gowns remained in the closet, but she'd never seen them, herself.

Everything seemed in order, so she padded up to the third floor. She reached for the knob on the master bedroom and living area and was relieved to discover it locked. It was the west wing of the third floor that literally made her skin crawl. It'd been constructed under Emmanuel's strict supervision and was where he'd conducted his most important business. No one had ever been allowed inside unless he'd specifically requested their presence. Any cleaning or repairs had been done by the male slaves who had never so much as uttered a word about its contents or goings on. After Emmanuel's death, no one had found the key to the heavy cypress door that led to Emmanuel's personal office, so it had been barred shut and Paloma preferred it that way. The hushed voices sharing sinister tales of the Sinclair family had been frightening enough, but it was when the voices were silent that Paloma knew she was better off not knowing what remained on the other side.

Perhaps it was the thought of the estate changing hands and her services no longer being needed that made curiosity get the best of her. As if hiding from someone, she turned the lantern down to a faint light and inched slowly in the direction of the west wing before stopping in her tracks.

You're a foolish old woman, Paloma LeBlanc. If there's anything on that west wing worthy of secrecy, Baron and Ruby would've let the cat out of the bag by now.

Feeling a bit childish, she turned the lantern back to its full brightness and continued past the stairway, toward the west wing. The worn Persian rugs were laden with dust, along with the mahogany wainscoting and artfully carved crown molding. The whole floor desperately needed a good scrubbing and a thick coat of Murphy's Oil.

Paloma walked confidently and deliberately, lifting up prayers of safety and comfort. The hallway was wide, close to eight to ten feet, she suspected. There were several alcoves, each hosting sitting areas with bulky fireplaces adorned with ornate mantels. She paused to study each section. The hallway sprawled wider than the others in the residence, undoubtedly, to make room for heavy, upholstered armchairs and antique tables with crystal ashtrays. Each grouping was as large as the bedrooms on the second floor, roughly the equivalent to her entire residence.

How strange. Why not use his office? Why so many different sitting areas?

The mantels were each so intricate and detailed; Paloma wondered if Monroe Burke had hand-carved them. No one had ever mentioned him doing more than blacksmith work, but only someone with his immense creativity and talent could've accomplished this level of artistry. The carvings so intrigued her that she stopped and placed the lantern on the hearth to closely study one.

Paloma was unsure of the stone it was made from and wouldn't have ventured to make a guess. She wasn't a highly educated woman and certainly not a worldly one, but it was the most beautiful stone she'd ever seen. Maybe it was some type of granite or marble—it had different hues of rose and was as smooth as silk. She rubbed her fingers across it much like she had the candelabras on the staircase. The carvings were of skeleton keys in various sizes and shapes. Their different designs wound around and through the holes in the keys. Paloma reached down in the front pocket of her apron and felt the large ring of skeleton keys still used for the estate. The keys, too, were varying sizes, and original to the house. It was then she realized that anyone taking the time to compare them to these carvings would swiftly surmise they were identical.

Paloma picked up the lantern, moved to the next seating area, and again placed the lantern on the hearth to assess the mantel. Quite unlike the other one, it was made of a light wood, but certainly not cypress. She knew what that looked like. Perhaps it was poplar, oak, or hemlock. Either way, it was just as magnificent as the stone, but composed of detailed carvings of faces, both children and adults.

Paloma was so engulfed in its beauty she failed to hear someone coming up behind her. The large hand wrapped tightly around her right shoulder before she heard a sound.

14

———

"IT'S BEEN TWO SLEEPLESS NIGHTS," Dan mumbled as he and Ben made their way through the bayou. "I never dreamed missing two nights' sleep could do this to a person."

"We're getting older," Ben replied. "I thought Harriett's mother was staying over to help out."

"That's a joke. You couldn't wake that woman up with a bullhorn. All she's done is snoop through the house to find something to complain about. Apparently, our linen closet isn't even close to being organized, to say nothing of our refrigerator or kitchen cabinets."

"Well that should give her something to occupy her time," Ben said. "Mothers-in-law would have to be the worst part of being married."

"Don't get me started. Crazy Hazel just wants to sit around and hold Landry during the day when she could be helping Harriett with the house. Harriett's exhausted and can't nap during the day because she has to follow Hazel to keep her from snooping. I'm trying to get up to do the midnight feedings, but Lord knows I'm a fish outta water in this thing."

"I can't imagine," Ben said, shaking his head. "I'm just now able to take care of myself—a kid is out of the question." The sun was directly overhead and bearing down on them so brightly Ben squinted. "Have you seen my shades?" he asked, rummaging through the junk between them.

"Can't say I have, but I should have an extra pair around here somewhere."

The two men tossed everything around the boat a couple of times before coming across a pair. Ben wiped them off with his shirt tail and put them on. "Whew, that's better. I have to tell ya, Dan, Cassius is pretty close to having a kid. He's shown up the past two nights in a new shirt, expecting me to go to Syd's for whatever the special of the day is. He's got his eyes set on the new girl behind the bar."

"A cold beer at Syd's sounds like a dream right now," Dan said, a faraway look crossing his face. "You're a single guy—I don't understand what you're complaining about."

"Just saying it gets old, that's all. Sometimes a man simply wants to sit in his own recliner without interruption at the end of the day. I told you, we're getting older."

"So, who's the new girl?"

"I don't know. Syd hired her a couple of months ago. She's nice enough, I guess, but not much of a looker."

"She should pair well with Cassius then," Dan said as both brothers broke out in raucous laughter.

"Old Cassius *isn't* much to look at, is he?" Ben joked. They laughed again before settling back.

Ben felt a twinge of guilt for talking about his longtime friend. Cassius was a good man and Ben was pulling for him to win over the young woman he was pursuing. Cassius was about the same height as Ben but had a few pounds on him, and not the muscular kind. He'd gained weight in the midsection after joining the force and spending more time sitting in the patrol car than doing manual labor. That wasn't where the differences ended. Ben had a head full of tousled blond hair and Cassius had wiry, receding black hair. His complexion leaned more toward generations of mixed heritage and race, making his skin tone darker than the Norwood brothers'.

"Okay, big brother, we're coming up on the next line. Get your head back in the game," Dan said.

It'd been a decent day's work on the bayou. The burlap sacks covered six large gators, tagged, and ready to be sold for the continually decreasing market price. Only four tags were left to scout out before they headed back in.

Dan slowly eased the boat toward the bank, carefully assessing the situation. Neither brother could possibly predict what each line would hold. Some would have the bait still dangling on the pronged hook, the ribbon visible from the boat. Others might have a gator that'd somehow made it on land while attached to the line and hook, making it necessary for one of them to leave the boat in order to secure their catch. There were those hooked gators that were ready to wrestle for their lives and then the exhausted ones with no viable fight left in them. Of course, it was the latter they both hoped for.

The ribbon wasn't visible, signaling the gator had taken the bait and was pulling the line downward. But there wasn't any splashing. Both men quickly scanned the area, looking for surfacing bubbles or movement in the brush. Nothing.

"Do you see him, Ben?" Dan asked.

"I've got nothing. Maybe we've got some cannibals," Ben answered. Then the hair stood up on the back of his neck, the memory of the murdered man in the ash tree playing like a movie in his head. "Back the boat up, Dan, I don't like this. Something isn't right. Let's get outta here."

Dan kept his eyes locked on the water. "It's not another body, take it easy. We run across this all the time. Maybe he drowned himself. Either way, we can't leave a gator on the line."

After easing the boat forward another few feet, Dan removed his sunglasses and leaned forward. "I still don't see anything, but he took the bait. The line is down, but not taut. He's gotta be dead in there. You're still freaked out from the other day. I'll go check it out." Dan pulled on his thick rubber boots and grabbed the rifle. "Got my back with that .22?"

Ben wrapped his fingers around the pistol without taking his eyes off the bank. Meeting a gator on his own turf was dangerous, but without any visible signs of movement, the gator was more than likely dead or so exhausted that he was pretty damn close. "Let's leave it alone."

Dan merely grunted in response and pulled close enough to step out on solid ground. He used the barrel end of the rifle to poke around in the overgrown brush, but it yielded nothing. "Son-of-a-bitch must've gotten away. How often does that happen?"

"Like twice in our lifetimes," Ben said faintly. "So, he got away. We've got our answer. Let's hit those last four and take her in for the day."

"Ben?"

"Yeah?"

"Call Cassius." Dan stepped back toward the boat.

"Cassius?"

"Nine-one-one, Ben. Call 911."

15

THE OLDER GENTLEMAN in the nutcracker garb glanced over at the waiting chauffeur and made eye contact. As soon as the driver caught his glare, the nutcracker ran his index finger across his neck, sending the message that their plans for the evening had been cut short. As if they'd had a detailed conversation, the chauffeur eased himself into the driver's seat and was gone in an instant.

"I'm not feeling well," the shift supervisor shared with the bellhop. "I'm taking the rest of the evening off. I'll see that someone takes my place. In the meantime, ensure things flow accordingly. Don't screw up your first opportunity to be in charge—I'm retiring soon, and you'll be up for consideration."

❦

TINK AND CANDACE were looking over the menu when her cell phone rang. "It's my father again," Tink said. "Hello?"

"Listen carefully, Catherine," Augustus said firmly. "Unfortunately, we haven't found out who made those arrangements for a driver. Just as a precautionary measure, I'll need you to do as your waitress says. You'll follow her to a waiting Uber, who'll take you to another rental car, and a hotel outside of the city."

"But, Father, we had sightseeing plans this afternoon, and our bags are still in the room."

"That's been taken care of," he said calmly. "Your bags will be in the Uber driver's vehicle. Remind me to have Mildred order some decent luggage for Candace."

"Someone has removed our luggage from the room?" she asked incredulously. "And how do you know *they* can be trusted?"

"Everything has been taken care of, Ca—Tink."

"I think we're all overreacting. I mean, seriously, is someone going to kidnap me or something?"

"Now isn't the time to question my judgment. Follow the waitress and do as you're told. I'll speak with you later. Enjoy your trip, dear," he said as he disconnected the call.

"You're not going to believe this," Tink said, turning her attention back to Candace. Before she could continue, the waitress was standing over her.

"Follow me, Ms. Mabrey," she instructed quietly.

"What?" Candace asked, her eyes wide and her mouth open.

"Just grab your purse," Tink said, holding up her hand. "She's taking us to an Uber. We can't talk now."

Candace was visibly confused but followed her nonetheless.

Before the two women could grasp what was happening, they were in the backseat of a large sedan and headed outside of the city. The young man behind the wheel didn't speak until they pulled into a grocery store parking lot.

"I'm not sure what's going on here," he finally stated as he opened the car door for Tink. "But I learned a long time ago not to question my superiors."

Another man squeezed their luggage into the trunk and backseat of a small, two-door compact. He thrust a clipboard into Tink's hands and pointed to the line requiring her signature.

"What...?" Candace asked, but Tink held up her hand again.

Tink scrawled the pen across the paper, in no way similar to the signature she prided herself in. After handing her the keys, the man was gone as quickly as he'd arrived. Tink turned to the Uber driver for guidance, but he too, had disappeared.

"I don't—?"

"Just get in the car," Tink said shortly.

Candace got in the passenger side and tried to push the seat back for more leg room.

"You don't need to keep trying to force it," Tink finally said. "All of that luggage you brought is blocking the seat."

"What happened to our sexy convertible?" Candace asked as she attempted to unfold her legs. "What the hell is going on here?"

Tink noticed an envelope wedged between the two front seats. "Who knows? Apparently, Father doesn't know who ordered the car for us and he's freaking out. He's acting as though someone is stalking me, hence the getaway car." She ran her index finger under the corner of the envelope, opened it, and removed the sheets of paper inside. "This is info from our secret agent that will tell us our next move."

"So, we aren't going to Bourbon Street? I was going to surprise you with a Groupon for frozen drinks and free glasses," Candace said.

"We'll simply move our sightseeing to the end of our trip. I know you're disappointed, but Father is adamant about this." She quickly scanned over the changes in their itinerary, folded the papers, and started the car. "And just when I thought I was going to treat you to a first-class trip."

"Let me guess—we're no longer staying at five-star hotels because that'd be too obvious. Please tell me it's not Motel 6. I stayed at one with my aunt once and they hadn't cleaned the shower from the last customer. Aunt Flora made them come clean it, but I couldn't bring myself to bathe in it."

"It's not Motel 6, but it's outside of the city. Sounds like a B&B. He's also changed our reservations in Kane. Instead of the larger hotel, we'll now be staying in a motel with our own room leading directly into the parking lot. Apparently, it's safer to go straight from the sardine can gas saver directly into the room," Tink drawled.

"*Lovely.*"

"It's not a suite but boasts of a mini-fridge in the room and vending machines down the hall."

"I assumed we'd be staying at your plantation. If your grandparents were living there before they passed, it can't be too bad."

"Father talked to the attorney who's handling the will and he didn't recommend it. It seems my grandfather didn't make arrangements for the utilities to remain on, but thankfully Father took care of it." Tink looked down at her smart watch. "It's still early. Why don't we blow off this B&B altogether and drive to Kane? I have to admit I'm anxious to see it now."

"Sure, why not?" Candace answered halfheartedly.

"It'll be fun," Tink promised. "And we'll still have drinks on Bourbon Street. I promise."

16

PALOMA'S KNEES gave way and folded beneath her as she grabbed her chest.

"Take it easy now," a familiar voice said softly. "I've got ya. I'm sure sorry, Ms. Paloma, I never intended to startle you. I've been calling out for you the past five minutes."

Her cheeks grew warm from embarrassment as she tried to pull herself together. "Oh my, Sheriff, you scared the life out of me."

"So, I see." Isaac Broussard released her shoulders but stayed close. "Why don't you have a seat over here?" he suggested, leading her to the closest chair.

Paloma didn't trust herself after such a scare, so she didn't argue. "For heaven's sake," she began again, fanning her face with the hem of her apron. "I didn't hear a thing. There's never a soul in here. As you know, the rest of the staff has moved on to more prosperous employment."

"I figured they'd hit the road as soon as Mr. Sinclair passed away. No need to spin their wheels when there's no one to pay them."

"It wasn't as though he paid us regularly anyway, but I suppose something beats nothing. How'd you get in?"

"The kitchen door was unlocked, along with some windows. You should be more careful."

"I meant to lock it behind me, but there's never anyone way out here."

Isaac looked around and then back at Paloma. "Can't say as I've seen this part of the house—not that I was ever a regular guest anyway. It's quite impressive."

"This area was off limits without a special invitation. This is my first time seeing it, too, and yes, it *is* beautiful." Paloma took his hand in hers and looked up at him. "Here, have a seat. I'll be fine in a minute or two." She let go of him and indicated the armchair beside her.

Isaac folded up his tall frame and sat beside her. Paloma was always glad to see him. He was as kind as he was handsome. She patted his forearm as she took in his chiseled features. "I do declare, Sheriff, you get more handsome as the years pass. Why is it that men get better looking with age and women go downhill? I hardly find it fair."

"You're a woman after my own heart, Ms. Paloma. I came out to let you know I got a call from Blaine Biggs this morning."

"I never could understand why Esther chose that name. It sounds ridiculous. I often wondered if he was picked on as a child. It would explain why he's such an arrogant man."

"Maybe she thought it rolled off the tongue. But I agree with you, it sounds like a stage name for a B-rated actor."

"What did Blaine want with you?"

"Mr. Sinclair used him to handle the will. I'm not sure why, other than he's the cheapest attorney around."

"That'd make sense. Mr. Sinclair was a cheapskate until the end. As you can see, we're sitting in the dark," she said, waving to indicate the lack of light. "Apparently, he didn't make arrangements with Blaine Biggs to see to it the electrical company was paid."

"Biggs wanted me to know Olivia's daughter will be inheriting the estate."

Paloma's face grew warm again and she wrung her hands with

nervousness. "Oh dear, I was just remembering the day Olivia went into labor. Such a tragedy. What a beauty she was. Breaks my heart every time I think of it."

"She was a beautiful young woman and so different from those parents of hers. I'd never have pegged her for a Sinclair," Isaac agreed.

"You know, Isaac, I'm surprised to hear Baron and Ruby left the estate to their granddaughter. After her father whisked her away, they never spoke of her again. I asked about her once and thought they were going to shoot me where I stood. Olivia and her daughter were clearly off limits. As far as I know, they never had any further contact with their granddaughter."

"Apparently they felt strongly about the estate staying in the family and she's all that's left of the Sinclair line. Ironically enough, she's an attorney out of Atlanta."

Paloma nodded. "If I remember correctly, her father was an attorney. She must've followed in his footsteps. Thank the Lord he had the good sense to get her away from her grandparents. When is she coming?"

"Actually, in the next day or so. Sorry I couldn't give you more of a head's up, but Blaine just found out himself. According to her father, she's more curious about the place than anything. It sounds as though the father wants it sold, and the sooner, the better."

Paloma stood, her strength now back. "Oh my, this place is a disaster. I hope she isn't expecting it to look like it did a hundred years ago. What's the child's name?"

"Catherine Mabrey, but she's hardly a child now. I feel certain Biggs has filled them in on the condition of the place. Surely he wouldn't allow her to get her hopes up."

"We need electricity!" Paloma said as if noticing for the first time that it was disconnected. "Call that conceited attorney and tell him we need it back on as soon as possible. There's cleaning to be done, groceries to buy, and I need to put fresh linens on the beds. Did he say how many guests would be with her—Catherine, I mean?"

"No, no one else was discussed. Blaine did mention she's registered at a hotel in town. Her father has contacted the power company and they're supposedly on their way out. Paloma, this place is too much for you. Don't worry about cleaning and cooking for this young lady. I'm sure she doesn't expect it. She probably just wants to see the place, and once she realizes how run down it is, she'll be on her way back to Atlanta."

"I owe it to Olivia to do what I can for her daughter. Now shoo. Let me get to work."

Isaac stood and stretched his tall frame just as his mobile rang. "My apologies, Ms. Paloma. These can be a good thing, but more often than not, they're a thorn in my side," he said, holding up his phone. "Sheriff Broussard. What's up, Roxie?"

17

TINK AND CANDACE had picked up burgers at a fast food drive-thru and eaten in the car on the way to Kane. Both women had conceded to Augustus's change of plans and were ready to see the plantation.

"I know you're disappointed about not having more time in New Orleans, but I promise to make it up to you," Tink assured her friend.

"No worries," Candace said. "But I didn't realize it was going to be such a long drive."

"I don't think it's as far as it seems. There's nothing but open road and we're used to the constant activity in Atlanta."

"Yep, the only thing we've passed in thirty miles is a Dollar General."

"I've heard that's the place to shop," Tink teased.

"I'm not feeling it."

The two rode in silence for a few more miles before they spotted an old cinder-block gas station on the left.

"Could we stop for a potty break?" Candace asked. "We might not pass anything else for a while."

"That's probably a good idea. The GPS says we'll be in Kane in fifteen miles, but I need to stop by the attorney's office first."

They got out of the small compact and stretched their legs.

"The air smells pure and unpolluted," Tink commented. "That's a good sign. I should probably fill up while we're here."

Candace was still stretching as Tink fumbled with the gas pump. "You're not going to believe this," Tink said, looking up. "This pump is so outdated that there's not a place to pre-pay."

"Now that's something to write home about," Candace said. "I don't think we're in Kansas anymore."

"We need to go inside anyway. Besides using the restroom, we need to grab a few snacks. This is the only gas station we've seen in thirty miles, so I'm thinking we won't pass another one for a while."

The deteriorating exterior of the building seemed an indicator of what they'd find inside. However, both women were pleasantly surprised by the variety of items available.

"Afternoon, ladies," a gentleman behind the counter said. He was in his mid-to-late seventies, with a white beard and balding head, and was seated on a wooden stool playing solitaire with a deck of worn cards. "What can I do for ya?"

"I wanted to pay for my gas," Tink said. "And we need to use your facilities."

"I'll pump that for ya, child," he said. "Want me to fill 'er up?"

"Excuse me?" Tink questioned.

"Want me to top off the tank or do you want a certain dollar amount?"

"I'm sorry if I appeared rude; I've just never had anyone offer to pump my gas."

"Name's Thomas. You must not be from round heh. We don't let young women pump dey own gas—not the gentlemanly thing to do. The ladies' room is 'roun' back. Let me get you the key."

He rummaged through a few drawers before retrieving a key attached to a long, metal rod. "Have ta keep it attached to sumthin' or else I'll never get it back," he said as he handed it over.

"Thank you," Tink said, glancing over at Candace with a knowing look as if to say they'd need to go together. "Please, Mr. Thomas, just fill the tank up. It shouldn't take much, but this twenty should be enough."

"No ma'am, no need to pay now. I'd have to figure out de change. Too much trouble."

Tink nodded at him before glancing at Candace again. "We'll be right back."

The restroom was attached to the back of the building and the last occupant had left the door standing open. "Oh, dear God," Candace said as soon as they'd turned on the lights and shut the door behind them. "It's as if we've stepped back in time. How weird is this?"

"I kind of like it," Tink said. "It proves chivalry isn't dead."

"No offense," Candace countered, "but we're out of our element and it takes some getting used to. I'm surprised they even allow women to drive."

"That's not a nice thing to say. I think it's commendable men still believe in helping women."

When the two went back in the gas station, Thomas had already filled up the car. "Took eight dollars," he said in his strange dialect. "Will 'dat be all?"

"Is there a grocery store in Kane?" Tink asked. "If not, we may pick up a few snacks."

"Yup. There's a whole strip of stores right smack in de middle of town. Where ya headed?"

"I'm going to an attorney's office. I inherited my grandparents' place, but I've never seen it."

"Who'd ye folks be?"

"The Sinclairs."

What little color Thomas had instantly drained from his face.

"Did you know them?"

Seemingly taken off guard, he stammered, "Y-yup, everyone in town knows of de Sinclairs. Not well, mind ya, but knew who dey were. Didn't know dey had a granddaughter."

"I left when I was an infant and haven't been back," Tink said, aware of how awkward things had turned. "Thank you, Mr. Thomas, for pumping my gas," she added, handing him the exact change. She'd thought of giving him a ten-dollar bill, but suddenly felt a tip would be insulting. Besides, the change in his demeanor after hearing of her grandparents gave her an uneasy feeling, and she was ready to get out of there.

When they returned to the car, Candace shut her door and turned to face her friend. "How crazy was that? Did you see his expression when you mentioned your grandparents' name? I thought he was going to faint."

"That was strange. I'm just glad we're out of there. I don't know what that was about, but remind me to never get gas here again."

THE CITY of Kane was two blocks long. The strip of stores Thomas had referred to consisted of a family-owned grocery store, a bank, a pharmacy, the city hall, the police station, a small diner, a doctor's office, and a furniture store.

"The attorney's office is four miles outside of town," Tink said. "Let's go there first." She'd somehow lost her zest for visiting the plantation and wasn't ready to load up on groceries.

"Tink, don't let that old man ruin your trip. You don't know why he acted that way. Maybe he was just jealous of them. Besides, you still have me!"

"That's a relief," Tink teased. "It creeped me out, but you're right —let's enjoy ourselves. We could be cooped up in our offices right now."

"Indeed," Candace replied.

The two rode in silence for the last few miles. "That must be it," Tink said, pointing to a small, wood-framed house. "Yep, Blaine Biggs, attorney at law."

"Blaine Biggs. Is that his real name?"

"Why wouldn't it be?"

"Just a little too catchy."

"Oh, for heaven's sake. Get out and come in with me. Hopefully this won't take long."

The older home had been tastefully modified into an office. The front room served as a reception area with two armchairs and a coffee table with magazines scattered haphazardly across the top. A young woman in her early twenties sat behind a desk.

"Can I help you?"

"Yes, thank you. I'm Catherine Mabrey, here to see Mr. Biggs."

"Blaine wasn't expecting you until tomorrow—"

"*Mr.* Biggs," a voice from behind a door shouted.

The chubby redheaded girl rolled her eyes and corrected herself. "*Mr.* Biggs wasn't expecting you until tomorrow. Let me see if he's available."

Tink and Candace both stifled a laugh as she sighed heavily and knocked on the office door, then poked her head in before entering. Muffled voices indicated she was being scolded and the look on her face when she returned only confirmed as much.

"You can take a seat. *Mr.* Biggs will be out shortly." She sat behind her desk and returned to pounding on her keyboard.

The attorney made them wait an awkward fifteen minutes before making an appearance. He, too, was chubby with bright red hair. Tink assumed they were siblings.

"Ms. Mabrey?" he asked as he reached out his right hand to meet hers.

"Yes, and this is my friend, Candace. My apologies for not calling ahead."

"Come on back to my office. Fortunately, I was able to work you in. An attorney is much like being a doctor," he said brashly. "My job is seven days, sometimes sixty to seventy hours a week." He paused and heaved a deep sigh before offering them a seat in front of his desk and sliding into his own desk chair.

"I'm sure Tink would know what you mean. She's—"

Tink swiftly kicked Candace in the ankle, making her yelp. "I appreciate you working me in and my apologies again for not calling ahead. We decided to make the drive from New Orleans today. I simply wasn't thinking."

Blaine took two deep, exaggerated breaths before getting up and opening one of five file cabinets. Tink was certain they'd been placed there for effect. He rummaged through the files before pulling one out.

"Baron Sinclair, your grandfather, had me draw up his will after his wife passed away. Because of the lack of communication between you two, he listed me as the executor," he said, taking time to point out his own name on the document with his meaty index finger. "He and Mrs. Ruby Sinclair named each other as beneficiaries should the other pass away first but had yet to designate a secondary beneficiary. Mr. Sinclair put great thought into who should inherit the family estate. It was his hope you'd find your way back to Kane when you became an adult."

"I never heard from either of them," Tink said. "It was my understanding they didn't have any desire to see me. They made no effort through the years to reach me."

"I suppose communication is a two-way street," he said bluntly. "That's neither here nor there now. They're both deceased and buried. There are no plans to be made, or funerals to attend. I saw to that personally."

Tink sat across from the desk, struggling to find the appropriate words. Blaine Biggs's rudeness had flustered her.

"And it never occurred to you to contact his granddaughter when he passed away?" Candace asked, her voice shrill. "How dare you talk to Tink, um Catherine, that way. Of all the nerve..."

Tink placed her hand on Candace's arm. "Candace, there's no need to defend me. In fact, there's no offense taken. *Mr.* Biggs doesn't know anything about me. His condescending tone is simply a cover for his ignorance."

The young attorney's face grew crimson as he turned his attention to the few papers filling his file. He shuffled them numerous times before shoving them across the desk. "As you'll see, the deed to the estate and the surrounding four hundred acres is included in this packet. Mr. Sinclair sold off eight hundred acres several years ago to keep from paying property taxes on it. There's also a cashier's check for the remaining balance in the Sinclair accounts."

Tink quickly regrouped and changed her attitude. Knowing nothing about Kane, she wasn't sure how much she might need Mr. Biggs in the future. She reached over and picked up the papers and scanned over them quickly. "My apologies, Mr. Biggs. Please forgive both of us. We're drained from the trip and I'm a little defensive about my grandparents' decision not to have a relationship with me. Imagine my surprise to discover they not only had a plantation, but they'd left it to me."

Candace grimaced. "Yes, please, accept our apologies," she added.

"I understand," he said curtly. "So, will you be living there, as well? I mean...uh, are you two...?" He faltered, looking in Candace's direction.

"Oh, goodness, no," Tink said with a laugh, scooting her chair over an inch or two. "I, I can see how it could appear that way, but we're best friends. Candace was kind enough to take the trip with me. As of now, I have no plans to relocate. It's my understanding the estate needs a great deal of work."

"You're not planning to reside there? I had no idea."

"Will that pose a problem?"

"No, I'm just a little astounded. The Sinclairs took such pride in the property and it's been in the family for generations. I just assumed..."

"Unfortunately, I know very little about my heritage, Mr. Biggs. That's one of the reasons for my visit. My mother passed away during my birth and my father raised me in Atlanta where he felt there were more opportunities for both of us. As I said before, this is quite a shock, and still hasn't quite sunk in."

"I see."

"I understand you're terribly busy, and my appointment wasn't scheduled until tomorrow, but could you tell us a little about the place?"

Both the acknowledgment of his importance and the chance to

show off what he knew seemed to please him greatly. His attitude swiftly changed, a smile spreading across his face. "I've always admired the home," he began. "Even as a child, I begged my parents to ride by so I could get a glimpse of it. It's quite a looming presence."

"We saw a black and white picture online. It appears to be a massive estate. What condition is the home in now?"

"My visits have been limited, of course. I'd meet with Mr. Sinclair in one of the main floor parlors, so I can't speculate as to the rest of the home. But the house was built in 1859, so I'm certain it's taken a great deal of money and effort to keep it up. The late Baron Sinclair didn't have much interest in parting with either of those things. My apologies," he quickly added. "I didn't mean to say that out loud."

"No need to apologize," Tink said. It was clear the young attorney's arrogance was a front for his insecurities, and she felt terrible for being so unkind. "I didn't know my grandfather so it doesn't hurt my feelings. I'd be happy for you to come out and look at the estate with us. I could sure use a man's opinion on what needs repairing. I don't know anyone here and I'm sure you know the best contractors —that's assuming I can afford the necessary repairs."

"That's the strange thing," Blaine added quickly. "Mr. Sinclair, *Baron* that is, went through money like water. I don't know personally, but that's my understanding from the grapevine. His checking and savings accounts made mine look impressive, which is sad, believe me. However, there was an account he was unaware of. Had he been, I'm certain he'd have gone through it too. Corbin, your grandfather's father, was a creative landowner during the Depression. Seems he held on to most of it, selling only during good times, then reinvesting. Turns out, Corbin's intuition and farsightedness are quite the advantage to you, as sole heir."

"You don't say?" Candace scoffed, leaning forward and putting her elbows on his desk. "Do tell, Mr. Biggs."

"Candace, please," Tink said as she tried to contain her excitement. Having enough money to restore the old place was something she'd never expected, and until now, something she'd never even considered taking on. "That is strange," she responded to Blaine.

"It took quite the effort in probate, but the account was under his father's name, who had the forethought not to have any statements sent to the estate, so Baron was never aware of it. According to town gossip, Corbin and Annabelle, Baron's parents, were very conscious of their son's recklessness. The bank president, now deceased, agreed not to disclose the account to their son at the time their wills were probated. Unless you're independently wealthy, Ms. Mabrey, without their foresight, the estate would indeed end up a pile of debris. However, the stars aligned because with their will leaving all their known assets to Baron, and him leaving his to you...well, there's still money to upkeep the estate."

"Imagine that," Tink said, wrinkling her forehead in thought. "I can't believe the bank employee went out on a limb like that. It certainly put his or her job in jeopardy. I can't begin to thank you for all you've done. How'd anyone know I wouldn't be frivolous as well?"

"I'm sure it was simply their faith Olivia's offspring would do the right thing."

"I don't know what to say. So how far away is this place?"

"It's about twelve miles outside of town, but it's predominantly back roads, so it's not a quick ride. I have a set of keys here. The estate is still using the original skeleton keys if you can believe that." Tink and Candace shared uneasy glances.

"I understand the electricity was disconnected, but my father was having it put back on. I hope it's been taken care of," Tink said. "We might need to head on out there before it gets dark. We have reservations somewhere nearby for the night."

"It's my understanding that Paloma's getting everything ready for you two. She's put clean linens on the beds and even picked up groceries."

"Paloma? I haven't heard that name before."

"Paloma LeBlanc. She's an older lady who was born on the estate and has worked there since she was a child. Her family's history with the place is as long as the Sinclair's. Paloma lives in a refurbished cottage once used for slave quarters out on the bayou."

"Slave quarters? They're still there? Why?" Tink asked, swallowing hard.

"Well, I just mean that's what it was originally," Blaine said. "She loves the estate and remains very dedicated to it. Paloma's probably the only employee who's stuck around. I don't think Baron handed out paychecks on a regular basis. I'm sure you'll find her very helpful, but of course, retaining her is up to you."

Tink leaned back and exhaled deeply. "It's a lot to take in at once."

"Let's not waste time thinking about it," Candace said. "We're burning daylight—let's go see it."

"Would you like to come with us?" Tink asked, almost hoping Blaine would.

"I'd love to," he answered. "But I have some work to take care of here."

He handed her the folder, along with the ring of rusty skeleton keys. Tink was tempted to ask him if he was joking but knew he wasn't. Blaine stood to walk them out, stopping at the receptionist's desk. "I'm sure you ladies noticed the resemblance. This is my sister, Betty."

"Betty Biggs?" Candace asked incredulously, making Tink cringe. Before she could scold Candace, Blaine responded.

"Yes," he said with a childish grin. "Our mother had quite the sense of humor and a weird obsession with alliteration. You know, Peter Piper picked a peck... Well, you get what I'm saying. She assumed it would help people remember our names. We've caught hell all our lives. People refer to us by both our first and last name as if it's some form of entertainment."

"I'm terribly sorry," Candace said, stepping behind Tink as if to protect herself. "I didn't mean to poke fun..."

"Don't worry about it," Betty said playfully. "Everyone does it, especially when meeting us for the first time. Are you excited about inheriting the Sinclair place?" she asked, turning to look at Tink.

"Ms. Mabrey is a Sinclair, Betty," Blaine added.

"Yes, I'm excited," Tink answered. "I've never seen it and can't wait to get a look. Are you familiar with it?"

"Oh yes, my brother and I have always had a fascination with it. It sits so far from the road that I've never gotten a good look at it, much less privileged enough to see inside. Blaine has been in before."

"Well consider yourself cordially invited anytime."

"That's awesome," she cooed. "I'll take you up on that."

"Thanks again, Mr. Biggs," Tink said as she opened the office door.

"Blaine, please," he insisted as both he and Betty waved goodbye.

18

BEN QUICKLY JUMPED into the water, holding the skimmer tightly with his right hand. He grabbed his brother under his arm and pulled him up. Dan's face mirrored the same shock and panic that Ben had worn when he'd found the body hooked in the tree.

"Come on, man, get back in the boat. The sheriff will be here soon."

Dan waded to their boat, clearly shell-shocked.

"It's okay," Ben said softly. "I don't know what's going on around here but we're okay, little brother. Breathe." He patted Dan on the back. "I can't have you passing out on me. What'd you see? Was it a body?"

Dan nodded and swallowed hard. "Yep, right there on the ground...so much blood."

"Did a gator get it?"

"I don't think so. The hands—they were missing, like someone cut them off."

"Jesus, Lord Jesus. That's exactly the way the other guy was."

"This wasn't a guy."

"What do you mean?"

"It's a female."

"What...?"

"It's a woman."

"Are you certain? It's a woman with her hands cut off?"

"Yes, I'm sure. The hook was in her mouth...so much blood..." Dan leaned over the side of the boat and vomited.

"This can't be happening," Ben said. "I've got to contact the sheriff. I know you're not gonna want to hear this, but we better stay here and wait on him. I'd hate for the body to suddenly go missing."

Dan wiped his mouth with his shirt tail and turned to Ben. "I don't think anyone's coming back for the body. They wanted us to find her that way. Either that or they were banking on the gators eating the evidence."

Ben pulled the boat a good hundred yards from the bank and removed his cell phone from his back pocket. His palms were sweaty, making it necessary to dry them with a rag before punching in 911.

Roxie answered the phone in her usual carefree tone, another murder clearly the last thing on her mind.

"Kane Sheriff's Department, what's your emergency? Hello? Anyone there?"

"Roxie, it's Ben Norwood. I've... Dan and me... Another body," he stammered.

❦

SHERIFF BROUSSARD WAS grateful Roxie had called his cell and not used the radio. He didn't want the radio traffic going out across private scanners, nor did he need Paloma to hear news of the murder. She'd looked exhausted as it was, both physically and mentally, and he'd already startled the life out of her.

Isaac's mind whirled with so many competing thoughts. He was finally able to reel them in and concentrate on one—the coordinates of where the Norwood brothers were.

Roxie knew him well enough to remain silent while the shock of the crime sank in.

"I'm out at the Sinclair estate. Have we got anybody on the water yet? They'll have to pass by here to...to get to that location," he spoke carefully.

"Deputy Arrowood's headed that way. Holder's in town. Do you want me to radio Amos to pick you up by the bayou?"

"Yes, I'll be down at Ms. LeBlanc's place. And, Roxie, tell Cassius to hold off. After we secure the scene, I'm contacting the state police. This is over our heads."

"Ten-four, Sheriff."

Isaac appreciated Roxie's professionalism and the fact she never asked unnecessary questions. During an emergency or a crime such as this, the fewer words used the better.

He disconnected the call and turned his attention back to Paloma. "Duty calls, Ms. LeBlanc," Isaac said, reaching to help her up. "Would you mind if I catch a ride from your place? I'll pick up my car later."

"Not at all, Isaac. If it won't hold you up, I'd love to walk down with you."

"Certainly," he said. "I could use the company."

Paloma locked the house. "Is everything okay, Sheriff? Sounds as though you have something serious going on."

"Paloma, I'm growing concerned about these strangers migrating to Kane. Not that we've been completely crime-free, but with drifters you get another element of crime, and it's almost impossible to find the perpetrator."

"I wish you the best," she said kindly, reaching out to squeeze his hand. "Now run ahead of me and catch up with your deputy. It sounds pressing."

Leaving her to walk the remainder of the way alone, Isaac broke into a jog. He could hear the engine of Amos's boat just as he made it to the dock. The deputy slowed short of a complete stop as Isaac jumped on board.

"Damn if we don't have another one, Arrowood. Roxie had few details, but I'm sure the Norwoods didn't get very close. Those fellas are gonna need therapy after this one."

"Can't believe they got another one on their lines. What are the odds?"

"What are the damn odds of having two people murdered within a few days of each other? Whoever's doing this certainly enjoys the shock factor. Hell, how easy would it be to just shoot someone and dispose of them? I can't count the places where a body could be dumped or buried and never found. Besides, we don't even know any of these people."

"I heard Roxie cancel Cassius and the crime-scene team. Don't you think we need everyone on this, Sheriff?"

"Yes, I do. That's why we don't need a group of folks trampling all over the scene. Hell, Amos, you of all people know we can't handle an investigation like this. How long have you been with the department?"

"About a hundred years," he answered seriously.

Despite the situation, Isaac laughed. Amos Arrowood had, by far, the most seniority with the sheriff's department. He was sixty-four but continued to be quite an asset. He had a way with people, was respectful yet firm, and had something Isaac rarely saw anymore—common sense.

"I want an opportunity to go over the scene first," Isaac said. "Then I'll call in the state police and have them head the investigation. Now's not the time to let my pride get the best of me."

Amos sped up as the two rode in silence. The boat's revving engine made conversation difficult, but both were lost in their own thoughts anyway.

The sheriff knew he wouldn't have to worry about the brothers contaminating the scene. Not only did they know better, but both were too squeamish to get very close. Isaac was certain he'd find them in their boat.

※

Dan glanced at his watch for the fifth time in less than a minute. "What the hell's taking so long?" he demanded. "Are you sure Roxie heard you? Did you have a good signal?"

"Yes, Dan. I've told you that at least three times. It's been less than ten minutes."

"Seems a lot longer," he mumbled under his breath as he stood to get a better view down the bayou. The water was calm and as smooth as glass, like the bayou was aware of something sinister taking place. He'd turned back to face Ben when he saw movement in the vegetation.

"Ben, oh no..."

Ben stared at the rustling bushes and knew instantly what was happening. A gator had smelled the decomposing body.

"We can't let him eat that poor girl," Dan exclaimed. "I couldn't live with myself."

"What the hell are we supposed to do? This has nothing to do with us. We aren't cops."

"No, but we're human beings," Dan insisted. He reached for the rifle. "Stay behind if you want to, but if that were Landry—"

"Damn it, how'd I know you'd go there?" Ben snapped. "Let me get the boat closer." He removed his pistol from its leather holster. "Don't go storming in there, guns blazing, Dan. This is dangerous— we never confront a gator on their own turf unless it's absolutely necessary. I know this'll sound cold but she's already dead. We're just trying to protect the body for whoever claims it."

"You're right, it does sound cold," Dan retorted as he jumped from the boat onto the small piece of marshland.

"*That's* what I was talking about," Ben said as he watched Dan struggle to regain his footing. "Think before you act. Slow down, Dan. Let me get behind you, we don't even know if there's more than one."

Ben acted as backup as they moved slowly and quietly toward the rustling brush.

"If you don't hit that gator in just the right spot..." Ben whispered.

Dan turned and gave him a stern look that translated into silent, raging profanities. They held their guns steady and firm, aimed directly in front of themselves in order to react as quickly as possible. Dan held up his index finger, indicating they were dealing with one gator, which made Ben heave a silent sigh of relief.

Dan raised a clenched fist, signaling for his older brother to remain still, while he moved swiftly and deliberately in the direction of the gator. It had the young woman by the lower half of her right leg and if it got her to the water, they'd never have an opportunity to retrieve her body. With the gator's attention on his meal, Dan was able to maneuver himself into the ideal position for the kill shot.

As Ben remained motionless, the sound of the rifle reverberated throughout the bayou, making him want to collapse from relief. It was obvious from the expression on Dan's face the shot had done what they'd wanted to accomplish.

It seemed as if hours had passed, although it'd only been a matter of seconds. "Got him," Dan said. "Help me get her in the boat."

"Get her in the boat?" Ben asked. "We can't do that, Dan. The boat is full of gators and we need to leave her where she was first found. Oh Jesus..."

"I know," Dan said. "Try not to look. It's disturbing as..."

"Yes, it is," Ben said, turning his head away. "That's not the only thing, Dan."

"Let's get in the boat, Cassius and the sheriff have to be here any minute."

Ben grabbed his brother's arm and pulled forcefully. "We have to call Roxie. Cassius can't come out here. That's the girl he likes—the new bartender at Syd's."

19

BEFORE THE TWO young women left the parking lot of Blaine Biggs's office, Tink typed the address of her newly acquired plantation into her GPS.

"It's just shy of twelve miles, but according to my iPhone, we won't get there as swiftly as we would on the interstate."

"We haven't seen an interstate in quite a while," Candace said. "Aren't you a little hungry? Blaine said that woman bought food for us, but how do we know if we'll like it? You know I don't eat crawfish, blaugh." She stuck out her tongue and made a gagging noise. "They have those..."

"Little heads, I know," Tink interjected. "And the thought of pulling them off and sucking out the meat makes you want to throw up."

"I've never understood the whole concept. If you ask me, it's an awful lot of work for a miniscule piece of meat. Even crab legs, as much as I like them—"

"Are too much work, too," Tink said, completing her best friend's sentence.

"Now *lobster*, that's a *completely* different story."

Tink looked up from her cell phone and cranked the car. "I get it,

Candace. You're hungry," she said as she backed out of the parking space. "The estate is in the opposite direction, but we'd only be backtracking a few miles to go back to town."

"*Going to town*," Candace said mockingly. "It's like going back in time, reminds me of Pa taking Laura Ingalls into Walnut Grove in a horse-drawn wagon."

"Thank God we've got decent transportation," Tink said, wrinkling her forehead. The thought of being this close to the home her mother had grown up in suddenly made her anxious.

"I don't mean to be a problem, but I can't believe you aren't hungry, too," Candace rambled, oblivious to her friend's uneasiness.

"I could always eat. There was a diner and the grocery store."

"Want to hit up the diner, then grab a few things from the grocery store?"

"I'm not so sure about the diner," Tink quickly answered. The older man's reaction about her grandparents back at the gas station came to mind. "I have a feeling we'll stand out and I don't want any more attention today."

"You're thinking about that crusty old man again. Let it go, Tink."

"I don't know. I suddenly feel tired and just want to get there so I can relax. What if we just stop by the grocery store and get some things to snack on in the car and some meat and veggies?"

"Sounds like a plan to me."

Tink pulled into a parking spot, slid the key from the ignition, and stared ahead with trepidation.

"You're reading more into it," Candace said quietly. "I'll just run in and grab a few things. You need to go through the folder Blaine prepared, anyway. Besides, I'm dying to know how much that check is!"

"Oh, good grief!" Tink responded. "It'd be great if you'd go in without me. If they ask who you are, just say you're passing through. Here," Tink said, reaching for her purse. "Let me grab some cash."

"I think I can get this," Candace said, already out of the vehicle. "Be right back."

Tink spent a few minutes with her head leaned back, her eyes closed. She realized curiosity over her inheritance was getting the best of her, so she paused to calm her nerves. There'd be plenty of time to go through the intricacies of legal jargon.

20

PALOMA GOT the call from Betty Biggs announcing her guests would be arriving earlier than expected. Grateful she'd already called her cousin, Horace, to pick up some groceries for an acceptable meal, she scrambled to straighten the house. Although Paloma had been exhausted earlier, she felt rejuvenated at the thought of new breath in the lifeless estate. Paloma's thoughts remained on Isaac Broussard, but her concern hadn't hampered her anticipation of Catherine's arrival.

She continued to reflect on the secretive west wing, but quickly forced herself to change gears. That was something to address later; for now, she needed to ensure the manor would be as welcoming as possible for Olivia Sinclair's daughter.

After Horace had dropped by with the food, Paloma finished prepping the meal. She checked the roast, took it and the vegetables from the oven then covered them with foil. Paloma pulled the stained apron over her head, tossed it in the washing machine, and made her way to the bathroom. Her hands flew to her disheveled hair.

Oh, my heavens, I look awful. What in the world would two young women from the city think of me looking like this?

Paloma quickly made her way to a small closet off the hallway that held her personal hygiene items for just such emergencies. It'd be too time consuming to re-braid her long hair, so she wet her brush and smoothed the hair around her face. Never one to wear makeup, Paloma used moisturizing cream on her face and neck, adding an excess to her dry, wrinkled hands. For a moment she was tempted to put on a light shade of lipstick but decided against it.

No sense trying to be someone I'm not. They'll know immediately that I'm being disingenuous.

Clean sheets had been placed on the beds in the two largest bedrooms and she'd done her best to dust and mop with what little time she'd been given. Freshly picked flowers had even been placed on the bedside tables, although there weren't many left in the untended gardens. The electricity was back on, but it'd take hours to cool the three stories to an acceptable level.

❧

CANDACE STUFFED her face with chips and soda while Tink forced herself to nibble.

"Why aren't you eating?" Candace asked. "You've got to be hungry."

"I'm eating," Tink answered defensively. "I'm just not that hungry. It hasn't been long since we ate."

"You're nervous. Why didn't I think of that? I mean, seriously, what kind of friend am I?"

"You're a very good friend, Candace," Tink said, her voice weary. "Who else would've come on this trip with me?"

"Um, pretty much anyone you invited. What a great opportunity to be with you when you see your new estate. I wouldn't have missed it for the world!"

"Yeah, that's what I'm afraid of."

"What?"

"You've gotten our hopes up, Candace. We saw an old black and white photo of an enormous, flourishing plantation, back in all its splendor. You do realize it's not going to be like that now, don't you?

Just look around us," Tink said blandly, waving at the secluded road they were traveling down. "We don't know where we are, a thing about the culture here, or even if we'll be served something gross out of the bayou for dinner, which we must eat regardless."

Tink saw Candace making a face out of her peripheral vision. "And they'll be none of that!" she quickly added. "This woman has worked for my family for years and we'll certainly not disrespect her."

"Catherine Mabrey! How dare you think I'd be disrespectful to anyone, especially an older person."

Tink let out a long sigh, a breath she'd been holding in for miles. "I'm sorry. If I'd ever thought this would be so emotional, I would've taken my father's advice and sold it sight unseen. But we're here now, and knowing my best friend, you'll never let me turn back after we've come this far."

"Damn skippy, I won't!" Candace teased. "How much farther according to the GPS?"

Tink stepped on the brake, stopping in the middle of the road. "It should be just around that next curve. I feel nauseous."

"Do you want to get out of the car and stretch your legs?"

"No, it's now or never," Tink insisted, blasting the air conditioning as high as she could. "Besides, what am I afraid of? It's just a house. It's not like it has a life of its own or anything."

21

BEN REACHED FOR HIS HEART, certain it was failing him. It'd been bad enough to find a murdered stranger, but to discover the mutilated body of the woman his best friend was infatuated with took his reaction to another level. Ben knew little about her, but this was somehow personal. Cassius would lose his mind searching for her killer.

"Ben?"

"Yeah?"

"Still with me?" Dan asked. "We've got a situation here and I need you on your game. If one gator smelled a meal, there are bound to be others. We're more vulnerable out of the boat."

"I told you we can't move her, Dan. Isn't that the whole point of solving a murder investigation?"

"Protecting her body by getting her in the boat is the point."

"Not disturbing the crime scene so her murderer can be found is the point, dumbass. I left the safety of the boat to have your back. We killed the gator—she's still dead, and I'm not gonna be the next victim. You've been a big enough hero for the day. I'm sure Harriett and Landry would much rather you make it home than to protect some dead stranger from a hungry gator."

Apparently, his words sank in and Dan motioned his gun toward the boat. "You're right. We've done all we can."

"Listen," Ben said, pausing and leaning his head to the right. "It's faint, but I think I hear a siren. Let's get our asses out of this swamp."

JUST AS THE sheriff had suspected, the Norwood brothers were sitting safely in their boat, several hundred yards from the bank. A sudden wave of compassion washed over him as he took in their flushed faces and dirty, sweat-drenched T-shirts. Neither acknowledged him, their eyes glazed over.

Isaac nodded at both, foregoing any awkward pleasantries. "I take it he's over there," he said, pointing toward the brush.

"It's a woman, Sheriff," Ben said before breaking down. "I... It's..."

"Ben said she was the new bartender at Syd's," Dan interjected. "Cassius had a thing for her. You might not want him to hear about this over the radio."

Isaac and Amos sat stoically in the boat, taking a moment to digest the news. It'd never occurred to either of them the victim could be female. The thought of a woman being murdered and abandoned in the bayou was incomprehensible.

"Sheriff?" Dan asked awkwardly.

"Yeah, I'm with you. I wasn't prepared for... I just assumed it was a male."

"Someone needs to get her out of there," Dan stressed. "I just shot a gator that was trying to drag her to the water." The realization of all that'd occurred in such a short period of time seemed to engulf him. His chin fell toward his chest and he covered his sweaty head with his hands.

"I know you boys need to get those gators to the processing facility before they spoil from this heat, but I could sure use a few minutes of your time. Roxie's contacting the state police, but with gators already circling, we obviously can't leave the corpse there," Isaac said, motioning again in her direction. "With two bodies being found under the same circumstances, I couldn't in good conscience lead the investigation. I didn't call in our ID unit because I intended to leave that to the state police, but I wanted a look at the crime scene before they lock it down. You know how those bigger agencies tend to be. When they take over the case, the newspapers'll get information before we do."

"You got that one right," Amos said, the first words he'd spoken since arriving on the scene.

"Ben, Dan," the sheriff began, "since you're the gator hunters, we'll need you to have our backs. We'll get both boats as close to the bank as we can. The less time we're in any water, the safer we'll be. Is she a very large woman?"

"No, she's thin, and not very tall, but...she's bloated from the heat," Dan said, leaning over the boat to vomit again.

Isaac closed his eyes briefly, praying for patience. No one spoke until Dan finished puking.

"Let's make this quick," Isaac said. "We'll pull up and jump out. You two follow suit with your weapons. Point us in the direction of the body and I'll snap as many photos as I can with my phone for evidence. Amos and I will pull her back to our boat, hopefully without being eaten by any gators first."

"On three," Ben said, and he counted quickly. Both boats pulled forward and the plan was in action within seconds.

The gator Dan had shot earlier posed the biggest problem, as the brothers struggled to remove its deadweight off the victim. Isaac wasted little time snapping photos of the surrounding area, where and how the body had been placed, and the gator with the quarter-sized bullet hole on the back of its head. The sheriff also took a few seconds to photograph any nearby foliage and insects. Isaac wasn't as experienced as the investigators with larger agencies, but he wasn't without knowledge of the importance of the slightest evidence in a murder case.

With the detriment of the heat to the body, and the assurance of more gators to come, Isaac placed his phone in his back pocket and grabbed the young woman under both arms. Amos took her feet and the two quickly got her to the boat. Moving the body released the putrid smell of death, but the fear of a swift-moving gator kept them from mentioning it.

Lifting the body into the boat was more difficult than anticipated. With the additional weight, their feet sank in the muddy bottom of the swamp, causing both Isaac and Amos to stumble.

"Fellas, I need you to get in our boat and lift her up," Isaac directed firmly. "Just think of it as a gator," he continued, instantly regretting his choice of words.

The Norwoods did as they were told, each grabbing an arm and hoisting her up before gently laying her on the foredeck of the patrol boat. "We can't leave you guys with her," Ben said. "You won't be able to stand this smell for long."

Isaac and Amos had gotten back on board and both agreed there was no way of knowing how long it'd be before the state investigators arrived.

"It's not ideal, but you're right, Ben," the sheriff said as he pulled a silver blanket from one of the compartments and covered the body. "We'll take her back with us. It's best to leave her in the boat and not disturb any more evidence. Once the investigators arrive, I can show them the scene. Now get those gators processed before the whole day is a total loss."

22

Tɪɴᴋ sʟᴏᴡᴇᴅ to less than ten miles an hour as they rounded the curve leading to the estate. Her stomach was twirling with butterflies. She began second-guessing her decision to come.

What was I thinking? This was absurd. Why didn't I wait on Father to come along?

"You *can't* be serious right now," Candace said. "If someone drives up behind us, they'll rear-end us. How fast are you going, two miles an hour?"

The comment was simply a muffled noise to Tink. Though she expected the overbearing home to come into view, she was relieved to see a large mortar and rock entrance and wrought-iron gate. It was overgrown with vines but had thankfully been left open in anticipation of their arrival. The numbers matched the address she'd been given and they, too, needed a fresh coat of paint.

"Not exactly what I was expecting," Candace said. "But, hey, nothing that paint and some groundskeepers can't spruce up."

The driveway appeared to have been paved at some point but was now covered with a mixture of sand and gravel. Apparently, the concoction was cheaper than repaving. Robust river oaks lined the drive—Tink was certain they had once been breathtaking; hence the name *Sinclair Oaks*. Upon closer inspection, they appeared creepy, almost as if they were long, ghostlike arms reaching out to grab her. The thought caused her to openly shiver.

"How many times have you warned me this place was going to be a dump?" Candace demanded. "You already had the bar set low, so none of this should come as a surprise."

"I never said *dump*."

Candace released her seat belt and turned to her friend. "Don't be nervous, Tink. After all, you own this place. If you walk in the front door and get bad vibes, we can get back in the car and leave. Your dad will have it sold without you ever coming back here. Worst-case scenario, of course. But the opposite side of the coin is you find it rich in history, and something you'd like to keep, or even flip to make a profit. That'd be fun, huh?"

"I suppose I *am* being a bit childish."

"Well, at the least, there's a lady in there kind enough to have prepared dinner for us. Now quit being a spoiled brat and speed it up. I have to pee."

"Oh, for crying out loud," Tink teased.

Because of the poor condition of the driveway, they had to take it slow in the small rental car. They both squealed audibly as the estate came into view.

"Holy..." Candace whispered as both hands flew to her face. "It's enormous."

It was indeed massive, and although weathered and in need of extensive repairs, it was undoubtedly a solid structure. The term *good bones* crossed Tink's mind.

"It's like a fairy tale," Candace gushed. "I've never seen anything this big in Atlanta. It's a full-on grandiose antebellum mansion."

"Fairy tale or nightmare... Let's not get ahead of ourselves," Tink said. "I never expected this...this size of a structure."

"Structure, my ass. This is your *home*."

"Please don't use any profanity in front of this lady," Tink pleaded. "I want to make a good impression."

"You still don't get it, do you, Tink? That's not your problem. The lady inside is the one who has to impress *you*."

They remained quiet as they rode down the lengthy lane until they approached the entrance to the home. An elaborate fountain in the center of the drive leaned helplessly to the left, long since drained of any dancing water. It appeared to have given up hope of being revived and was simply waiting on a strong storm to kindly topple it over.

Before they could take in much more of the place, the front doors opened wide and an older bronzed woman with a genuine smile held out both arms. "Welcome home," she began, flashing her dazzling smile again. "I'm Paloma LeBlanc and you... Oh dear," she rambled excitedly as she dashed down the wide set of steps. She was at Tink's side in an instant, making her gasp for air.

"My apologies, child," she said, warmly now. Her soft, wrinkled hands cupped Tink's face. "You are Catherine. Oh dear, it's a miracle. It's like looking at my delightful Olivia again. Sweet Jesus, thank you for this moment."

"I'm very sorry if I've made you emotional," Tink began. "That was never my intention."

"No, no, don't apologize, child," she said quickly. She wore both a kind expression and one of deep pain. "It's me who owes *you* an apology." Paloma stepped back a few feet and discreetly wiped a lone tear from her cheek. "It is quite startling how much you resemble Ms. Olivia. I'm sure you've heard that many times from your father."

"Only a couple. It's very difficult for him to speak of her, even now."

No one spoke for a moment.

"Heavens, forgive me," Paloma said, running her hands across her hair as if to ensure it was still in place. "Who is your friend?"

"This is Candace Ramsey. She's not only my closest friend but we also work together. I don't think I would've had the nerve to make this trip without her."

"It's a pleasure to have you here, too," Paloma said, her voice excited again. "Please, both of you come in. I'm sure you're famished.

I have dinner waiting for you." She paused briefly as if to regroup. "My gracious, you have traveled quite a way, ladies. I'm sure you'd like to bring your suitcases in and freshen up before eating."

"That'd be great," Candace replied. "We could just grab our carry-on bags for now. You know how girls are—we put all of the necessities in those just in case our luggage gets lost, which happens often."

"As you can see," Paloma began, "the place needs a great deal of work. These stairs started crumbling quite some time ago, but the Sinclairs—" She caught herself mid-sentence and continued up to the front doors. "Watch your step. It's not a soft landing if you slip."

The double front doors had sheets of peeling paint, but they remained impressive. "I can't say I've ever seen such remarkable doors," Tink said.

"They were built to make a statement," Paloma answered. "Back when this estate was originally constructed, homes of this size were owned by very successful businessmen. Appearances were everything, and Mr. Emmanuel Sinclair left nothing to chance. Visitors to the estate were given the royal treatment, and believe me, they couldn't wait to tell anyone who would listen about the wealth they'd witnessed."

"I understand your family has worked here for generations."

"Indeed, they have."

"I'm sure you have many stories to share with me about my family history," Tink added.

The flash of unease that crossed Paloma's face didn't go unnoticed by Tink.

Paloma reached for the handles of both doors and opened them simultaneously to achieve the wow factor generations of Sinclairs had expected from their help. Even in its disintegrating condition, the home was clearly cared for.

Unsure of exactly how high the ceilings were or how expansive the windows, Tink found it was the staircase that instantly drew her attention. She dropped her bags to the marble floor, which hit with a thud as her eyes locked on the beautiful, yet somehow startling sight before her. The staircase was widespread and breathtaking, with meticulous detail. Tink continued to follow the stairs with her gaze, wondering how such a labyrinth had been designed.

Her feet seemed to take control and led her to the base of the staircase, where she reached for the candelabras, cupping them much like Paloma had cupped her face. The coolness of the touch seemed to awaken her from what had felt like a dream and she was suddenly embarrassed. She jerked her hands away and turned to find Paloma and Candace staring blankly at her.

"I...I, oh my," she stammered. "I don't know what came over me. It's so remarkable. I've never seen anything so..."

Paloma's eyes softened and she reached both hands out to Tink who met them with her own. "I understand, child. I get the same feeling every time I see it and I've seen it all my life. I never pass by without touching the candelabras. One day when you have time, I will tell you the story of Monroe Burke.

"I'd love to hear it," Tink said. "No time like the present..."

"Not today, dear Catherine. There is much to do, and I need to fill your bellies so you can rest. The stairs are only the first of many discoveries here. Now, you ladies grab your bags and I'll show you both to your rooms to freshen up."

Tink felt a cool breeze go through her body and a chill coursed up her spine, making her shiver despite the pungent heat in the old place.

Perhaps this hadn't been such a good idea after all.

23

THE TWO BROTHERS parted company with Amos and the sheriff and quickly made their way down the bayou. They'd lost valuable time and the law stated their lines had to be checked daily. The Louisiana Department of Wildlife and Fisheries wouldn't allow gators to suffer on the hooks any longer than necessary. Besides, it often ended in a dead gator, which didn't do anybody any good. Gator hunting was only legal from sunrise to sunset and long story short, they were burning daylight.

"No sense talking about it. The murder, I mean," Dan said, finally breaking the silence. "We'll be pushing it just to check the lines, much less pulling the gators on board."

"You know what that means, don't you?"

"Yep, another financial hit."

"Don't see any other choice," Ben said. "If we don't pay the processing plant to skin them, we'll take a big chance on ruining the meat. That'd be a double hit and one hell of a wasted day. Besides, I can't say I wouldn't welcome someone else doing part of our work today. They'll get 'em skinned, salted, and rolled up for us and we won't have to fool with the skins for three or four days. I hate to pay for something we can do ourselves, but it could be worse."

Dan glanced at his watch nervously, then turned his attention back to the bayou. "Can't you make this thing go any faster?"

"Yes, but not safely," Ben answered. "You're thinking about Harriett, aren't you?"

"Well, hell yes. I should call her and let her know I'll be late, but I don't need her worrying about some crazed killer."

"Just text her and let her know we're running a little behind. You know how women are. If you don't let them know, they instantly go to the worst-case scenario."

"And what could possibly be worse than a murdered woman with her hands cut off?"

"Thought we weren't going to talk about it," Ben replied. "Let's focus on these lines and getting home to a hot shower."

The next four hours were grueling, but luckily their lines only produced exhausted gators that gave little, if any, fight. They pulled up to the plant just in time to have their load weighed.

Ben was grateful word about the body hadn't spread like wildfire. Apparently, the grapevine hadn't gotten a hold of the murder, shielding them from unwanted questions. He and Dan used the outside hoses to spray themselves off and welcomed the cold beers another hunter offered from his cooler.

"You guys look like shit," Simon Granger commented as he walked over to the old wooden bench where they were sitting.

"Nice to see you, too, Simon," Ben said. "Long, hot day."

"I'll make sure my guys get those skins scraped, cleaned, and salted. You can pick 'em up tomorrow when you bring in your next haul. You look like two miles of bad road, figured you might want to go on home. Sunnie told me Harriett had the baby."

"Yep," Dan said. "I'm sure she'd appreciate me getting home to give her a break."

"Go on and take off. Tell her we said congratulations about the kid."

"Will do, thanks again."

BEN HAD BARELY STOPPED his truck when Dan jumped out.

"Sorry I can't stay to help clean out the boat. I've gotta get home," Dan yelled as he cranked his vehicle.

Ben stared in Dan's direction long after he was out of sight. Memories of their childhood flashed through his mind, making him envy Dan and his new family.

Then Ben turned his attention back to the bloody boat and coolers that needed washing down, and dragged over the hose and started spraying them off. Then he thought of Cassius.

He must know by now. I can't believe I haven't heard from him.

As if waiting for the thought to bloom, Cassius pulled up in the patrol car. He'd been going too fast and skidded to a stop beside Ben. He staggered out of the car with an open forty-ounce beer in his hand and slammed the door shut.

"Why didn't you call me, man? Why'd I have to hear this from the sheriff? I felt like a kid, Ben," he spat, slamming his fist on the hood of the car and taking a long gulp from the can. "It was like being called to the principal's office to be told my parents were dead. Why couldn't I have heard it from a friend, man? Why?" He staggered over to the steps and sat down.

Ben turned the hose off and wiped his hands on his jeans. "I'm sorry, Cassius, I was trying to protect you. The last thing I wanted was for you to hear about it over the phone. I thought it'd be best to hear it from Isaac. He's better with delivering news like that..." Ben tried to sound persuasive but failed miserably. He knew, as Cassius's closest buddy, it had indeed been his job to deliver the news, not the sheriff's. His excuses meant little to his grieving friend and the alcohol wasn't helping.

"Let's go inside," Ben suggested. "This boat can wait."

Cassius stumbled up the stairs and waited impatiently as Ben opened the door. "I've gotta pee," he slurred. "You better have some beer in that fridge of yours."

Ben had yet to recover from discovering the first body and today had only compounded his anxiety. The last thing he wanted to do was console a drunk man who had barely even known the murdered woman, but he was stuck with the job regardless.

When Cassius came out of the bathroom, Ben was scrubbing his hands and forearms off in the kitchen sink. "I'm going to start a pot of coffee, pal. I think it'll make you feel better than more beer. You're lucky you didn't wrap your patrol car around a tree."

Cassius ignored him, opened the refrigerator, and grabbed a beer anyway. "Geez, you stink, man. Do you smell like that every day?"

"It's called working for a living. Pull gators out of the swamp all day and see what you smell like."

"Appears you pulled more than gators out of the water today, but you didn't find her important enough to let folks know."

"Actually, I didn't even know her and other than ogling at her behind the bar, neither did you," Ben said, though he instantly regretted his words. There were times the truth simply didn't matter, and this was one of them.

Cassius turned so fast that he fell into Ben before he could swing on him. Ben grabbed him by the shoulders and shoved him into the recliner.

"Not cool, man. Sit your ass in that recliner you like so much while I take a shower. Don't you dare move from that spot or I'll call Sheriff Broussard myself," he seethed, pointing his finger in Cassius's face and wagging it. "Don't you *move*. I mean it, Cassius."

"Screw you, man. Go take a damn shower. I'll be right here when you come out, believe me."

Ben stripped off his clothes and tossed them in the washer before turning on the hot water for the shower.

If only he could wash the stench of this whole fucking day away.

He wanted to call Dan and tell him about the condition Cassius was in but refused to interrupt his time with Harriett and the baby. He just hoped Cassius didn't insist on leaving. Ben could overpower him, but couldn't hold him hostage all night, even if he was drunk. He felt bad for him, but the ugly reality was there hadn't been anything between the two except Cassius's childish crush. Ben had caught the woman checking him out but had refused to acknowledge it. She wasn't his type and he'd never dream of going after someone a friend was interested in.

If Cassius knew both her first and last name, Ben would be surprised, but he wasn't going to go there with him tonight.

Maybe drinking himself into a stupor *was* for the best.

24

"My apologies about the temperature of the house," Paloma said without turning around as she led the girls up the staircase. "I'd so hoped the air conditioning would've cooled it down more by now, but it's a big place."

Tink glared at Candace, who was fanning herself. "It's fine," Tink answered. "I understand the electricity was just recently reconnected."

"Yes, the utility company didn't show up until after two this afternoon. It's even warmer upstairs. Perhaps it won't take you long to freshen up and you can join me back downstairs until the air conditioner has worked its magic. I often wonder how we made it without such an invention for so long. I don't have it myself, but my place is down by the bayou and benefits greatly from all the shade."

"Global warming," Candace whined.

"Excuse me, dear?"

"Global warming, you know. The greenhouse effect..."

"Yes, Ms. Paloma, I'm sure it's much more tolerable with trees to block the sun," Tink piped up, again glaring at Candace.

They rested briefly on the first landing before reaching the top of the second-floor stairs and veering left. Dimly lit wall sconces led down the arched hallway, so numerous that they seemed to disappear in the distance—much like the ocean did into the horizon.

"There are many bedrooms, and you may choose from any of them, of course," Paloma said, turning to face them. "Mr. Biggs didn't give me much notice, so I only had time to place fresh linens and tidy up two of them. Most of the furniture in the house has been covered to protect it from dust, I'm sure you understand. I was unaware of who'd be taking possession of the place, but I've done my best to maintain it."

"This is an awfully large place for one person to look after," Tink observed. "Isn't there anyone else to assist you?"

"Mr. Sinclair has been gone for weeks now and his few remaining employees found work elsewhere as soon as they could. It's difficult to go without a paycheck, I'm sure you understand," she said, reaching into her apron and retrieving a ring of old skeleton keys. She carefully flipped through them until locating the appropriate one and inserted it into the lock.

The door opened wide almost as soon as the key slid in and both Tink and Candace stood skeptically in place, trying not to display their shock.

"This is your room, Ms. Catherine," Paloma began. "I chose it for you because it's closest to the stairway. I trust you will find it accommodates your needs."

"It's...it's... Well, I'm left speechless quite frankly," Tink replied. "I can't imagine anyone showing displeasure at a room such as this."

"Please, come in," Paloma insisted as she entered, and pulled back the heavy draperies, causing dust particles to float throughout the room like glitter. "All the bedrooms are equally spacious, but there's something unique about this one."

The girls remained silent, standing just outside the doorway, peering in. The canopy bed, although ridiculously overbearing, was dwarfed by the room's overall square footage. There was a window seat that ran the length of the room, which Tink estimated to be over a hundred feet. The custom draperies, which she was certain had been expensive in their day, were now worn and filled with years of dusty neglect. A fireplace, acting as the focal point of the room, was almost tall and wide enough for her to stand in.

"Please, come in," Paloma encouraged, reaching out toward Tink, who walked over to place her hand in hers. "It's a bit much to take in, child. Had I been given a chance; I would've spoken with you before you arrived."

She walked over, sat on the bed, and patted the spot beside her, suggesting Tink join her. She did. "'Tisn't what it used to be, dear, but it certainly could be again. One generation alone cannot completely taint the Sinclair name. I can sense you are different. You, my child, are an *original* Sinclair. You are from prime stock."

Tink's eyes filled with tears, forcing her to look away. Paloma stood, clearing her throat and straightening her apron. "I will show your friend to her room now, Ms. Catherine. There is a bathroom attached to each bedroom—feel free to take as much time as you need. Dinner is prepared and ready to serve at the time of your choosing."

Tink suddenly realized she'd left Candace standing at the entrance to the room. "I will walk with you, Candace," she offered. "Are all of the bedrooms locked?" she asked Paloma.

"Yes, every room stays locked," she answered. "It has always been that way and should remain so."

Tink was a bit taken aback by the sudden change in her demeanor but tried not to reveal it.

"I think I'd prefer to stay here with Tink," Candace said. "You could unlock my room after we eat. If that's okay with you," she added, sounding strangely weak and intimidated.

"Everyone needs their own space," Paloma said.

"She's fine here," Tink argued. "Candace, I'm sure you, too, feel like a fish out of water." With that, she reached for her friend's bags and walked back into her bedroom.

CANDACE SANK into one of the armchairs by the fireplace. "I'm afraid," she said, her voice just above a whisper.

Tink wondered if she'd heard her correctly. "Afraid? What in the world would've frightened you? I realize it's run down, but not nearly as much as we'd both anticipated."

"That's not it," Candace replied. "That part doesn't concern me."

"What is it then?" Tink asked as she joined her in an adjacent chair.

"I wish I could put my finger on it. I'm pretty sure it began when Pocahontas ran up on you as though you were some long-lost relative."

"Paloma. It's Paloma, Candace, and you weren't very respectful. She lives in a small place on the bayou and you act as though she regularly watches CNN."

"Because I mentioned global warming? For crying out loud, that's ridiculous!"

"I don't want her to feel as though we're trying to act like we're from the big city."

"We *are* from the big city. So, she doesn't know anything about Atlanta—

we don't know a damn thing about the bayou. And you go ballistic every time Mildred calls you Catherine and I can't count the number of times that woman, Paloma or whatever, has called you child. Child? Seriously? And you let her touch your face. That's unheard of. Your dad would've had a stroke, just sayin'."

"I...I... I was taken off guard. I didn't want to insult her, and it felt, well—it felt comfortable meeting someone who knew my mother. She said I looked just like her. Did you hear that? My father has never compared me to her except to say we were both beautiful. Every father says that to his daughter."

"The furniture has been covered to protect it from dust, I'm *sure* you understand," Candace said teasingly as she broke out into a giggle. "You are from *prime* stock, my child."

"Stop," Tink said, relieved Candace was acting more like herself.

"It's hotter than Georgia asphalt in here. Can I put on shorts after I *freshen up for dinner*?"

"Definitely. I'm going to put on a pair myself. I'm sure we'll feel better when it cools off a bit."

"I'll never be able to stay in a room by myself," Candace said, growing serious again. "This place is a castle. Do you think she'll lock us in our room tonight? Every room stays locked, *I'm sure you understand*."

"Get all of that out of your system before we go downstairs. I don't want her to overhear you mocking her. Besides, she has her own home. We'll have the place to ourselves tonight and we can snoop to our hearts' content."

"That's what I was afraid you'd say."

25

BEN SAT STRAIGHT up in bed, trying to decipher what had awakened him. Glancing at the bedside clock, he was shocked to see it was 5:30 a.m. His alarm was set to go off in fifteen minutes, yet he felt as disoriented as if it were the middle of the night.

Someone was knocking on his front door—that must have been what had awakened him—so he stepped into a pair of jeans and made his way to the den. It came as no surprise to see Cassius still passed out in the recliner from the night before. Ben could tell from the silhouetted figure outside the storm door that it was the sheriff knocking.

He could count on one hand the number of times Isaac had visited his place, and it'd never been at this time of day. Given the circumstances of the past few days, this couldn't be anything good. Ben opened the door and stepped out onto the porch. "Bad news, I take it," he said in way of a greeting.

"Mornin', Ben. Sorry to wake ya. I see Cassius spent the night," he said, pointing to the patrol car. "Have to say I'm relieved about that. He didn't take the news very well yesterday."

"No, he didn't," Ben agreed, motioning for the sheriff to walk out into the yard with him. Once he was convinced they were out of earshot, Ben felt more comfortable talking about his friend. "Showed up drunk as a skunk just as I got home. Never even got the boat cleaned out. Damn if he isn't more trouble than having a kid, I swear."

"Does he make a habit of showing up drunk?" Isaac asked.

"No, I didn't mean that. It's just ever since that woman started working at Syd's, he's had it in his head he was gonna win her over. Shows up every night expecting me to play wingman."

"I take it she didn't exactly reciprocate his feelings."

"To tell you the truth, Sheriff, I don't even know her name. She was kind of flirty, but unfortunately Cassius didn't notice it was directed at everybody but him. I'm not sure what drew him to her, but then again, we don't have a lot of women to choose from. I suppose a new woman in town would draw attention from more than just Cassius."

"I spoke to Sydney about her last night. Apparently, she wasn't too bad of a bartender, but that's where her good qualities stopped. Sydney had plans to let her go. She'd reprimanded her numerous times about flirting with customers and there were several nights that the register was missing some cash."

"Who was she and where was she from?" Ben asked. "I hate to see anyone come to Kane and stir up trouble. But nobody deserves what happened to her."

"Syd doesn't exactly require a resume from her waitresses or bartenders. The woman requested to be paid under the table, which was no surprise, and was staying in one of those extended-stay places frequented by roustabouts, men coming in off the rigs, and of course, prostitutes. The state police have taken over the investigation. I'm certain they've tossed her room by now, but they haven't confirmed an identity with me."

"Sounds like Cassius is better off without her, but he's acting as if they'd been married for years," Ben said.

"I'll talk to him later. I hate it, but he's a deputy now, and it's time for him to grow up. Sorry I woke you, but I figured you'd be up already."

"It was time for my alarm anyway. I have to get this boat cleaned up before Dan gets here."

"Listen, the investigators asked me to have you and your brother meet them at my office at nine this morning. You two discovered the body and it's bound to be connected with the other one you found by yourself."

"I figured as much, but we've got work to do, Sheriff. We had to pay Simon's guys to skin our load yesterday and that's something we've never done. It's hard enough, in the best of circumstances, to check all of our tags while the sun's up."

"I understand, son, but you know a murder investigation is going to trump any other commitment. Be there at nine and I'll try to get them out of our hair as quickly as possible."

Ben had known it would only be a matter of time before he was questioned thoroughly—he'd just hoped it wouldn't be until after gator season. No such luck. But there was no reason to take it out on Isaac.

"We'll be there, Sheriff," he said, reaching to shake his hand. "Now could you possibly help get Cassius's drunk ass out of my house?"

* * *

DAN WAS AS DISGRUNTLED as his brother to learn of their morning meeting. Apparently, the previous night had netted about as much sleep as the others and his patience and energy were wearing thin.

The state investigators were already seated in Sheriff Broussard's small office when the Norwoods arrived fifteen minutes early. Ben was grateful to be able to start immediately but regretted not having a few minutes with Isaac before they began drilling him.

Brief pleasantries were exchanged while Roxie rearranged the furniture to make room for them. Both brothers squeezed into a chair while she let herself out.

"So," the older of the two investigators began. "Ben, I understand you were the one to discover the first body, the male."

"Yes, I was."

The older fellow, whose name was Chet Westmoreland, was short and overweight with a ring of light brown hair around the middle of his head. The top of his noggin was sunburned but looked as though he took great pride in buffing and shining it. It appeared his excess weight had settled upon him without warning and he was trying to adjust to it.

Investigator Westmoreland tapped his pencil loudly on a blank legal pad. "So, you're a gator hunter, I hear," he stated in an accent Ben struggled to place.

"Yes sir, I am. But it's only thirty days out of the year," he added.

"So, do you and your brother alternate days or work separately?"

Ben was confused by the question, so Isaac spoke up. "No, it's rare to hunt solo. Dan wasn't with his brother that particular day because his wife was in labor."

Westmoreland didn't look up from his pad, but the corners of his mouth drooped into a frown.

"Exactly," Ben jumped in. "I was alone, because as Sheriff Broussard said, Dan was at the hospital with his wife, Harriett. We don't normally trap our gators alone. It's too dangerous."

"Which would explain why he was with you when you found the woman," Westmoreland said, looking up at Dan and brushing hair he didn't have away from his eyes.

"Yes," Dan agreed. "I wanted to stay home with my wife a few more days, but after Ben found that body alone, I knew he needed me."

"Do either of you find it strange that both bodies were found on your lines?" the investigator asked bluntly, looking between the brothers.

"That hasn't crossed my mind, believe it or not," Ben answered genuinely. "I guess I was more shocked this could happen here." He suddenly felt his defenses go up and turned to lock eyes with Dan. It'd never occurred to either of them that they'd be considered suspects. "Have you thought about it, Dan?"

"I didn't wonder why both were found on our lines. I wondered why they were murdered in the first place," he said snidely.

The younger of the two investigators must've decided it was his turn to play good cop. "No need to get your feathers ruffled, gentlemen. It's a routine question. No one's pointing fingers."

"I'd certainly hope not," Ben said defiantly. "Why would we kill somebody, and then call 911 on ourselves?"

"Good question," Good Cop answered calmly. He was the polar opposite of his older partner. Besides being at least thirty years younger, he seemed as laid back and green as a California surfer. Ben figured he was just out of college and not seasoned enough to suspect every person he interviewed. He was tall and lean, with shiny, almost white-blond hair, with enough length to be pushing the envelope with his agency. His name was Jon Fontenot, which, along with his accent, led Ben to believe he was from Louisiana. He'd been quick to point out that there wasn't an *h* in his name.

The five men sat quietly for a moment before Investigator Westmoreland spoke again. "Mr. Norwood, you'd be surprised at what folks do," he said in his odd accent. "Where were you on the night before your baby was born, Dan?"

"Where are you from, Mr. Westmoreland?" Ben asked directly.

"Originally Chicago," he answered, never taking his eyes off Dan.

"Well, we don't do things like they do in the big city," Ben spat. "My brother was at home with his pregnant wife the night before she gave birth."

"Were you with him?" he asked, finally turning to look at Ben. "Can you personally confirm that alibi?"

"My wife can," Dan said. "We had nothing to do with these murders. It's a coincidence they were both found on our lines."

"And how do you know that for sure?"

"We didn't even know these people."

"Just like I don't know you? Is there anybody that has a beef with you two?"

"Don't even answer this prick," Ben said.

"Does that mean you have no intention of cooperating with our investigation, Mr. Norwood?" Westmoreland asked.

"Of course, they'll cooperate in any way possible," Isaac insisted. "I've known these boys all of their lives. You're barking up the wrong tree and wasting valuable investigative time."

"You're also interfering with our workday," Ben said abruptly, pushing his chair back. "Come on, Dan. We can't lose money again today. Screw these guys."

❧

THE INVESTIGATORS LOOSENED their ties and hung their jackets on the hooks in the back seat. Westmoreland backed out of the parking spot and turned on the A/C.

"So, what was that about?" Fontenot asked. "I believe them, but you pissed them off before we could get very far."

"Ah, I believe 'em. We already have the statements they gave the sheriff. They're not our guys."

"I don't get it then. Why were you such an asshole?"

"It succeeded in pissing 'em off, right?"

"Yep...I just said you—"

"So, they'll dig deeper in this community than we ever could. Their fear has now turned into anger and defiance. Bet they get to the bottom of these murders long before we do."

26

"OH, IT SMELLS WONDERFUL," Tink said as she and Candace entered the kitchen.

"Out, out you two," Paloma said as she playfully shooed them toward the dining room with a dish towel. "You can't very well have your first meal in the kitchen like hired help."

She led them down the wide hall and into a long dining room with a table that could've easily seated twelve.

"Oh, my word," Candace said. "If we sit at each end, we'll have to shout to hear each other."

"I suppose that's simply in the movies," Paloma said kindly. "I don't think folks are that formal anymore. This is your *home*, dear," she said, placing her hand on Tink's shoulder. "Please, both of you sit where you desire. I'll bring your plates out shortly."

"Tink, you sit at the head of the table," Candace said. "This is your first meal in your new home and it's only appropriate that you take your place. I'll be right beside you, of course."

"I do believe your attitude is changing," Tink said, smiling at her friend. She was grateful to have her here. *After all, what would it have been like without her?*

Paloma walked in with steaming plates of food and placed them gently in front of each of them.

"Wow," Candace said. "This looks fantastic. And to think I was... Oh, never mind."

"You hardly needed to go to such trouble," Tink insisted. "But I'm delighted you did. Oh, my! This pork roast is to die for, Candace. Look, there's whipped potatoes with gravy too. When is the last time we've had a home-cooked meal like this?"

"Last Easter, maybe," Candace said as she dug in.

That was the last the two of them spoke until they'd wiped their plates clean.

"I can't remember ever being this stuffed," Tink said. "I may have to unbutton my shorts."

"You can't get up without dessert," Paloma said, surfacing again from the kitchen. "Hot apple pie, just out of the oven. My apologies for not serving it with ice cream, but I wasn't sure if the freezer would be back on to keep it cool." She poured them each another glass of merlot. "And I never serve a meal without iced tea, but again, without ice, I went with red wine instead."

"Just a little sample," Tink said as she savored the homemade crust and cinnamon apples. "Unbelievable. You're a tremendous cook, Paloma."

"Years of experience and watching some of the best," she answered. "But thank you just the same."

"Could we possibly eat the rest of this later? I think I need a walk or I'm going to be miserable. I'm used to eating a little here and there, mostly takeout food. Such a big meal is a treat for both of us."

"Certainly. I'll wrap this up and leave it in the icebox for you. Would you like for me to show you around the grounds?"

"That would be delightful," Tink answered.

❀

THE HEAT HAD DIMINISHED SOMEWHAT as the sun was making its way toward the western horizon. The temperature was now bearable, especially in the shade of the big oaks.

"Unfortunately for us, the city has less and less green space," Tink commented. "These trees are beautiful, and judging by their size, must be over a hundred years old."

"They've been here for as long as I can remember," Paloma said. "I remember playing under them as a child."

The three women walked leisurely through what had clearly once been well-tended gardens.

"Do you remember when someone took care of the flower gardens?" Tink asked, trying to picture what it'd been like decades before.

"Yes, my child, I do. It was something else to see. Flowers reflect love in a home," she said kindly. "At least, that's what my mother always told me. It wasn't until your grandparents took over the estate that the grounds no longer seemed important. The old folks were aghast. They considered the gardens to be merely a prelude to the home itself. I tend to agree."

They walked along for a few more minutes before Tink spoke again. "Why do you suppose they weren't concerned about the gardens?"

Paloma hesitated. "I'm not certain."

Tink could sense there were underlying reasons, as well as Paloma's reason for not disclosing them, but she didn't press the issue. "I wonder how costly it'd be to have this restored?" she asked instead.

"I would hate to hear *that* estimate," Candace said frankly. "Just think about the HOA fee at your loft! I couldn't even afford that for my rent!"

This made Tink laugh, something that felt very, very good. She hadn't laughed since she'd gotten here. "I agree with Paloma. The gardens are as important as the house itself. I've always wanted to garden—but it was never an option for me."

It was Candace's turn to laugh, which she did with abandon. "Why in the world would you want to sweat in a garden? I've never heard you even speak of such a thing."

Tink flushed, embarrassed, which instantly ceased Candace's laughter.

"I'm sorry," Candace was quick to say. "I didn't realize you were serious."

"I've always admired flower gardens, but Father refused to allow me to pick blooms from ours. That was a job for someone else," Tink said, a deep sadness emerging in her tone. For some strange reason she felt a sudden need to protect her father and quickly added, "I'm sure my education was more important at the time."

Paloma and Candace exchanged quick glances. They were getting farther from the house and the trees were forming a canopy over-head, blocking much of the sunlight.

"How cool," Candace spoke up. "You can't even see the sky."

"We're closer to the bayou," Paloma said. "You'll notice much more vegetation."

"It's so quiet," Tink commented. "You could hear a pin drop."

"Oh, but there's much life hidden just beneath the surface," Paloma said. "It's very deceiving and I must warn you to never stroll down here alone."

"Are there any alligators?" Candace asked.

"Yes, there are...many of them, and they are masters at camou-flaging themselves."

"Is it true they hibernate?"

"Yes, they hibernate between the months of November and February. They don't feed during that time, but they make their dens along the water's edge. You'll often see them sunning on the banks."

"Are they endangered?" Tink asked as she doubled her steps to catch up.

"Alligator hunting was banned by the state at one point, to allow them to replenish themselves, but they're back in force now."

Just as Tink was going to comment again about how quiet it was, they heard a loud scream, jolting both her and Candace. "What? Who...?"

"You have to learn the sounds of the bayou, child," Paloma said softly. "'Tis merely a mink somewhere nearby."

"But it sounded like a woman!" Candace insisted.

"It was a mink," Paloma reiterated. "They're like a weasel but are quite aggressive. They even attack their own kind, but you won't be close enough to one to worry about it. Stay away from the bayou when you're alone."

The women turned their heads toward the sound of a slight hum. A boat came into view just as Paloma raised her hand to wave. "Speaking of alligators," she said, walking swiftly toward the water, "you won't come across anybody who knows more about them than these two."

Tink and Candace followed behind her as she cupped her hands around her mouth and shouted a hello.

The boat slowed as it swerved toward the embankment, and its engine went silent. "Good afternoon, Ms. Paloma," a handsome gentleman said. "Or maybe evenin' by now, I guess."

"Did you have a good day on the bayou?" Paloma asked. "How's the season going?"

"Hot and sticky, but we did okay today, despite a delayed start. Excuse me, ladies. I'm Ben Norwood and this is my brother, Dan. I haven't had the pleasure of—"

"Oh my," Paloma interrupted. "How terribly rude of me. Ben, this is Catherine Mabrey. She's inherited the place from her grandparents."

A blank look crossed both men's faces, but disappeared as quickly as it'd surfaced. "Well, it's nice to make your acquaintance," Ben said. "Forgive our appearance—we've been out on the water all day."

Dan managed a lazy grin and held up his hand to wave in their direction.

"This is Candace Ramsey," Tink said, turning to her friend. "She was kind enough to make the initial trip with me. This is our first time coming down to the river—or bayou, is it Paloma?"

"Bayou," she answered, her attention remaining on the two men. "Dan, I hear you have an addition to your family."

"Yes, ma'am," he answered, a broad smile crossing his face. "A beautiful girl."

"So I've heard," she said, smiling back. "I hope she's as pretty as her mother."

"She is, thank the good Lord," Ben teased. "He's been biting at the bit to get home."

"And to get a decent night's sleep, Ms. Paloma," Dan said. "Any suggestions?"

"How long is she sleeping in between feedings?"

"About three hours, give or take."

"Try to get her to eat more at each feeding. Hopefully, she'll sleep a little longer in between. Give her a nice warm bath at bedtime and try keeping her up more during the day. She's still young yet—allow her a good month or so, she'll start sleeping through the night."

Dan looked defeated.

"These fellas are nearing the end of gator season, which lasts thirty days. That's thirty days of grueling work," Paloma said.

"Where are the gators?" Candace asked, leaning forward to see if there were any lying in the boat.

"We drop them off at the processing facility at the end of the day," Ben said, reaching to pull back the end of a wet burlap. "We do have their skins, though." He pulled one up. "It'll have to be salted, and then re-salted to dry it out, before it can be used for anything else."

"That's the coolest thing ever," Candace said excitedly. "Did you see that, Tink?"

"Yes, I did," she said, although much less enthusiastically. "It's still a little bloody, isn't it?"

The chuckle came from the men this time. "Yep, fresh off the gator," Ben teased.

"It's getting late," Paloma said. "I need to get them both back to the house. They've assured me that they won't be making any trips down here alone."

"That's good advice, ladies," Ben said. "Are you two alone in that big place?"

Tink hesitated briefly before confiming. "This is the first time I've ever seen it. We only arrived a couple of hours ago, but I agree, it's quite daunting."

Ben turned to give his brother a knowing look. He cleared his throat and turned to Paloma. "Have you heard about the two incidents involving our tags?"

She nodded slightly. "I'm being vigilant, fellows."

"We aren't aware of anything. Like I said, we just arrived..."

"It's nothing, dear," Paloma insisted. "Nice to see both of you." She waved at the boys. "Let me get these two settled in. Good luck with the little one, Dan."

Both men nodded, as Ben cranked the engine. "We pass by here twice a day, ladies. If you need anything just let us know," he said.

And then they were gone, leaving nothing but a slight wake in their path.

"THAT WAS A LITTLE ODD," Ben said. "Did you notice Ms. Paloma's reaction?"

"What do you mean? I didn't realize you even knew she was there."

"Now, what's *that* supposed to mean?"

"You're smitten, aren't you? I can't remember *ever* seeing you like that."

"I don't know what you're talking about. I was referring to—"

"She was quite a looker, I have to say."

"Who are you talking about? There were three women back there."

"Three very beautiful women. However, we can mark Ms. Paloma off the list."

"You're not right, Dan. Do I need to take care of Landry tonight so you can get some sleep? I think you're beginning to hallucinate."

"Hallucinate, my ass," Dan joked, laughing loudly and slapping his brother's back. "Both of the young women were exceptionally attractive, but you only had eyes for one. Just couldn't look away from those amazing eyes, could you?"

27

PALOMA SAID VERY little on their walk back to the house, and Tink and Candace struggled to keep up with her pace.

"The dark comes quickly once the sun begins to set," Paloma said flatly. "You'll have all day tomorrow to tour the grounds. For now, it's best to be inside."

"Will you be okay walking down to the bayou alone?" Tink asked.

"I've lived here all my life and when one is raised on the bayou, you have a keen sense of things around you," she answered. "There's no need to be concerned about me. Did Mr. Biggs give you a set of keys?"

"Yes, he did. I left them in a bag in my room."

"It's important to get in the habit of keeping them with you. This place is vast, and it'd be hard to hear if someone unexpected were inside. That's why the rooms have always remained locked—that and the fact the staff couldn't always be trusted. Although it may be difficult to see now, there are many valuable pieces here."

"I'm sure there are," Tink said, somewhat taken aback at the thought of an intruder. "Has there ever been a problem with strangers sneaking onto the property?"

"No," Paloma was quick to answer. "But one can never be too safe, especially two young ladies staying here alone. I'm sure the same is true in Atlanta—it's always best to be aware of your surroundings."

"Yes," both Candace and Tink adamantly agreed.

"I'll unlock your bedroom again so you can get your keys," Paloma answered. "I made up the bedroom next to yours for her." She pointed at Candace. "The one next door, not across the hall. I wouldn't recommend wandering around the residence tonight. There's bound to be light bulbs that need replacing."

"I have to admit I'm a little anxious to see the rest of it," Tink said.

Paloma stopped abruptly. "'Tis much you don't know about the place. Stay in the areas you're familiar with. If you need something to drink or a midnight snack, you know where the kitchen is. Your bedrooms each have a bathroom. That should be adequate until I can show you around the rest of the estate."

Tink had a sudden surge of homesickness and longed for the strength of her father. He had a way of handling awkward and intimidating situations, something her tender years had yet to teach her.

"With much due respect, Ms. Paloma, this is now my home."

"There's no need to remind me of that, Catherine. I'm well aware of it, 'tis why I'm telling you these things. I would be doing you a disservice not to make you aware of what's in your best interest. Now," she said matter-of-factly as she started for the stairs, "let's get you settled in."

Candace and Tink were walking so close together they stumbled over each other's feet. Tink was relieved to reach her bedroom. Paloma unlocked the door and moved aside for them to enter.

"Would you bring me your set of keys?" Paloma asked, her tone changing back to one of kindness. "They are separated according to wings of the estate. I'll show you which one is to the bedrooms on this wing. I doubt you use skeleton keys in the city."

Tink's mood lightened with the shift in Paloma's voice. "I've always thought one skeleton key fit everything."

"Yes, many people assume that, but it's not always the case." She waved her hand toward the hall. "This wing is made up merely of guest rooms and served as bedrooms for the children when they were old enough to be removed from the nursery upstairs."

Paloma took the ring of keys from Tink's hand and flipped through them until she found the one she was looking for. It was a long, skinny key with only two teeth.

"This is the longest key on the set so it should be easy to find. The kitchen isn't locked, obviously, nor is the dining room. Ms. Candace, I hope you find your accommodations to your liking. Again, my apologies for not having more time to spruce them up. Good night, ladies."

"Good night, Ms. Paloma," they both said.

"Be careful walking back to your place," Tink said as Paloma shut the door behind her.

CANDACE'S SNORING prevented Tink from falling into a deep sleep and kept the day's events swirling in her head. Convinced that sleep was nowhere in her future, she caved into the cravings of milk and leftover apple pie, and used her iPhone as a flashlight so as not to disturb Candace. Tink slowly pushed the covers back, used her toes to find the slippers by the bed, and eased her feet into them.

As if Paloma were there to remind her, she grabbed the set of keys from the nightstand. The house was dark and unbelievably quiet as she made her way to the stairs. Tink was halfway down when she wished she'd simply stayed in bed with her rambling thoughts.

When she reached the kitchen, she flipped on the light switch and was relieved to be able to see more than just a few feet in front of her. Feeling foolish for being uneasy, Tink grabbed a plate and glass from the cabinet and poured her milk. After lifting the foil from the pie, she used the spatula to snag the piece she'd taken a bite from earlier.

Her phone gave a loud ring as she was savoring her dessert, almost making her drop her fork. *Who could possibly be calling this late at night?*

"Hello?"

"Catherine! Thank God, I've been trying to reach you for hours. The bed and breakfast said you never checked in. I was about to book a flight. Where are you?"

"I'm sorry. I haven't had a missed call," she said, then checked her phone to make sure there hadn't been one.

"Where are you?"

"Candace and I decided to drive out to the plantation after the fiasco in New Orleans. I should've called you but got tied up with everything here. I was going to phone you first thing in the morning."

"You've got to be kidding me. I can't imagine you making a decision like that without consulting me first, especially after what happened with the car. Didn't you think I'd be concerned when I couldn't reach you?"

"I had my cell with me the entire time."

"You're in the middle of nowhere," Augustus said, his voice growing louder. "There are places in Atlanta where you lose service. For crying out loud, use your head, Catherine!"

Shaken by her father's anger, Tink was rendered speechless. She'd allowed herself to get overly excited about seeing the estate and had clearly made some hasty decisions. It was unlike her and the last thing she'd intended to do was cause her father concern.

"I'm terribly s—"

"My apologies for raising my voice but I've been sick with worry. It's not like you to be irresponsible. You're in a strange place and out of your element, Catherine. What kind of condition is that house in? Is it safe? The thought of you and Candace being there alone brings me great concern. I demand you leave as soon as the sun comes up."

"It's in better condition than we'd anticipated but will need serious renovations. We are alone tonight but Paloma is here—"

"Who?"

"Paloma LeBlanc. She knew Olivia. Her family has worked here for generations."

The phone was silent for several seconds, making Tink check to see if she'd lost service again. "Father?"

"I'm here," he answered solemnly. "You said it will need renovations. You can't possibly be considering keeping that money pit, Catherine."

"That's far too many *Catherines* for this hour. I feel a headache coming on."

"That makes two of us. I called you thirty minutes ago. Why did your phone ring now?"

"I came down to the kitchen to get a snack. I was having trouble sleeping."

"For the love of God, Tink. What has come over you, wandering all over that old house? Does it even have an alarm system? Wait, don't answer that. As of just a few hours ago, it didn't even have the electricity connected."

28

As bad as Ben felt for Cassius, he was grateful not to find him in his driveway when he got home. He was beginning to feel like Dan, desperate for a good night's rest.

Aside from the meeting at Isaac's office, the rest of their day had gone well. Each tag had netted a gator—nice-sized ones at that, and he was home at a decent hour. Ben loaded the wooden trailer with the skins Simon's men had salted the day before and the ones he and his brother had removed from their day's catch. He hooked his ATV to the hitch and drove them back to the building behind his house to be taxidermied.

His muscles ached as he heaved the heavy skins inside to dry. Dan was anxious to get home to the baby, which Ben understood, but it was the worst time of year for him to leave early. It left the cleanup and rest of the duties to Ben and he was exhausted, to say nothing of the discontented growl coming from his stomach.

It suddenly dawned on him he hadn't been to the grocery store since discovering the first body, which left nothing for dinner or the next day's lunch. Ben quickly washed everything down and took the time to spray himself off. Times like these made him appreciate the privacy of his place and the rutted, dirt road leading back to it. He could hear anyone coming long before they got to him.

After peeling off his wet clothes, he placed them in a plastic garbage bag, walked into the house naked, tossed the load in the washer, and waited on the water to heat up in the shower.

Damn, I do stink. Cassius was right. I wonder if this house stinks too.

Ben hadn't ever considered that his home could reek of the stench of the bayou, and made a mental note to purchase some air fresheners when he picked up his groceries.

The steamy shower removed the day's grime, but only served to exhaust him further. Ben eyed his bed and seriously considered climbing in for the night, but knew he'd regret it in the morning. Dressing in a T-shirt and pair of jeans made him think of Cassius showing up in his new shirts from Amazon. He'd totally wanted to impress that woman at Syd's.

Damn it, why couldn't she have just gone out of her way to speak to him? How much effort would it have taken?

The thought of hot wings from Syd's and a cold, frothy beer made his mouth water. Maybe he'd stop by and eat dinner then order a sandwich to go for lunch tomorrow. The last thing he felt like doing was grocery shopping, which meant lugging everything inside, putting it away, and preparing something for dinner.

Still halfway expecting Cassius to be in his driveway, Ben felt a twinge of guilt when he wasn't. If he'd been a decent friend, he would stop by, pick him up, and buy him beer and dinner. But Syd's place would bring back bad memories. It was early yet, only a day, and Cassius was bound to still be emotional. Besides, he had to have a monumental hangover.

During the week, the evening crowd was always the same. The weekends tended to bring out a seedier bunch from the outskirts of the parish, usually those coming in from working the week on the oil rigs. They were anxious for a stiff drink and to pick up loose women. Ben had watched the scene unfold enough times to know it wasn't the way he wanted to live. More often than not, his weekends were spent working on his property, or making repairs to his aging house.

That satisfied him just fine. If he got lonely, he'd stop by and visit Dan and Harriett, or pick up a couple of steaks and a twelve-pack and invite Cassius over.

For the first time in ages, Ben wondered if his life would always be that way. Dan had been right—he *was* taken with the beautiful young woman with the shiny black hair and mysterious eyes he'd met tonight at the Sinclair place. And he had a strange feeling in the pit of his stomach, a feeling she was in some kind of danger. Ben couldn't quite put his finger on it, but it wouldn't stop gnawing at him.

Then his mind flashed back to the gator with the bartender's leg in its jaws.

29

CANDACE PULLED the heavy draperies back, allowing the sun's bright rays to filter into the bedroom. "Wow," she said. "We're still here. I somehow thought we'd awaken to discover this had all been a dream."

Tink rolled over, still groggy, and opened her eyes. "I'm sorry, but I wasn't afforded as much rest as you," she moaned. "Has anyone ever told you how much you snore? I think you need to address that before you have any male suitors staying overnight."

"I don't snore," Candace said. "If anyone snores, it's you. This place is looking pretty dingy in the daylight, Tink. Come take a look, we're *way* up here."

Tink slid into her slippers and padded over to the window. "Yes, we are," she agreed. "Why do you suppose my grandparents didn't even paint the place? I'd imagine a coat of paint would make an unbelievable difference."

"But look at the size of this house," Candace replied. "I bet it'd have to be scraped and pressure washed before adding a coat of paint, and there's no telling how much it'd cost."

"According to Blaine Biggs, they weren't very good with their money. I suppose they no longer used it as a working plantation, which I find odd. I wonder what they did for a living."

"It sounds as though they lived off the riches of generations past. What a shame. It'd have been nice of them to leave some to you."

"Oh, but we're forgetting," Tink suddenly exclaimed. "My great-grandfather did think of other generations to come. Remember the secret account?"

"Yes! Yes, I do! Quick, where's that file? I can't believe you didn't look to see how much was left in it."

"It's in the car," Tink said. "Geez, I don't know where my mind is. I still feel like pinching myself. Oh no..."

"What?"

"Father called last night and he's not happy. Apparently, we don't have service up here. Luckily, I carried my phone with me when I went downstairs for pie last night."

"You went down for pie without me?"

"Yes, you were snoring so loudly I couldn't sleep, but that's not the point. Anyway, he'd been trying to reach me for hours but couldn't get through. I can't believe I forgot to tell him we'd decided not to stay in town."

"Do you have to tell your dad everything you do?"

"No, I don't, but after the fiasco with someone ordering a car without our knowledge, it was only natural for him to be concerned."

"It's odd but that seems like days ago," Candace said. "I'd almost forgotten. I still believe someone from the firm did it."

"Father assured me they didn't, but who knows? At any rate, we're alive and well. That's what matters."

"Indeed, it is," Candace agreed.

"It was a long day. I'll agree with that."

"Rise 'n' shine, Tink. We need to look around before that woman comes up here. It's daylight—I don't feel so nervous anymore," Candace said impatiently.

"I'll hop in the shower," Tink said. "Why don't you go take one in your room? It'll cut the time in half."

"Huh?"

"Take a shower in—"

"I heard you," Candace said. "But I haven't even seen it yet. I can't just walk over there by myself and get in the shower. Someone could be in there just waiting to kill me."

"So much for not being nervous anymore," Tink drawled. "That's ridiculous. I feel certain it's about the same floor plan as this room, so I'll grab my toiletries and take a shower next door while you shower in here."

"Okay," Candace agreed. "And it's next to this room, not across the hall."

"Candace, Paloma was simply letting us know which room had been prepared for guests. I think you have it out for her."

"Oh, come on, Tink. You have to admit she's pretty bossy to be an employee."

"I think she's just looking out for us."

"What do you suppose that guy was talking about last night? She sure did cut him off fast."

"I'm not sure, but I'll ask her about it today."

❦

CANDACE AND TINK SHOWERED, dressed in shorts and tennis shoes, and made their way downstairs to the kitchen. Paloma was already there, standing over a cast iron skillet filled with sizzling bacon while flipping hot cakes on a griddle. The house looked much more dated in the morning light, making Tink inwardly cringe.

Paloma had done her part to keep it clean, but the wallpaper and curtains had turned brown from age, and desperately needed replacing. Tink thought of her own loft back in the city and found herself comparing the two. She'd loved the renovated kitchen, which had been the deciding factor when purchasing her first home. The white marble island and glass-front cabinets had made it a place she wanted to spend time in and entertain friends.

This kitchen, as sizeable as it was, gave off a dreary, unwelcoming vibe. It had clearly been built with the help in mind and not as a space for family and friends to gather.

"Ms. Catherine, are you all right?" Paloma asked.

Tink shook her head as if to pull herself out of a daze. "Yes, ma'am. I'm sorry—I was just looking around the kitchen. You didn't need to make breakfast for us, but it sure smells delicious."

"Everyone must begin the day with a good meal," Paloma insisted. "Did you sleep well?"

"Yes," Tink answered, sneaking a glance at Candace. "My father called in the middle of the night when I was getting a slice of pie. Apparently, there isn't service upstairs. Is there a landline in the house?"

"Excuse me?"

"A phone line?" she asked again.

"Yes, well, allow me to rephrase that. It's wired for phone lines and had a working one until Ms. Ruby passed away. Mr. Sinclair saw no further need for one after that."

"They're almost obsolete now," Tink said, "except in cases where cell phones lose service because of lack of towers. I suppose the home phone needs to be reconnected."

"That should be easy enough," Paloma replied as she stacked the pancakes onto their plates and walked toward the dining room. "Breakfast is served, ladies."

They followed her to the table, but Tink had more questions. "Ms. Paloma, do you have a cell phone?"

The woman stifled a laugh while she placed the plates on the table. "No," she answered firmly. "I won't live to see the day that I would need such an instrument."

"How do you stay in contact with relatives?" Candace asked.

"You do not understand the way of life here," Paloma said. "We do not need such fancy gadgets. We are a simple people and I prefer it that way. I have no television, no phone, no electricity."

Candace gasped aloud and covered her mouth. "I'm so sorry, Ms. Paloma," she said genuinely. "I don't mean to be disrespectful. It's very hard for me to relate to that. We are from two different worlds, I suppose."

For the first time since their meeting, Paloma looked tenderly at Candace. "Child, 'tis okay to be different. The good Lord makes us all different—different colors, different hearts, different ways of life. I don't judge the life you girls are from, just as you shouldn't judge mine."

"No, ma'am," Candace said. "I certainly don't judge yours. I'm just trying to understand it, is all."

"Don't worry about me," Paloma insisted. "My uncle and cousin are nearby. I talk to my relatives on their phone. As for you and me..." She patted Candace's hand. "We can both learn from each other."

30

"THERE'S no way I could eat a big breakfast like that every morning," Tink said. "I'd be as big as this house."

"My mother always told me to eat like a king at breakfast, a prince at lunch, and a pauper for dinner," Paloma said. "That way you'll have the day to burn off any excess calories."

"I may have to steal that idea," Candace said. "I think your mother had something there."

"That was a time when people didn't spend their days in an office," Paloma quickly added. "We worked in the heat of the day."

"Oh," Candace said solemnly. "I sit at a switchboard all day so it probably wouldn't apply to me."

Paloma stifled a laugh as she removed their plates from the table. "What are your plans for the day, ladies?"

"I'd love to have a tour of the place," Tink said. "Would you have time to show us around?"

"Certainly. Let me put these plates in some soapy water and I'll be right back."

PALOMA REMOVED HER APRON, placed the dishes in the sink, and returned to the dining room.

"Where shall we begin?" Tink asked.

"Allow me to give you a brief history of the place before we start. I'm not sure how much you've learned about the estate, but I'd be happy to share what I know."

"Please do," Tink encouraged. "I've haven't heard much about it and I'd love to get its history."

Paloma nodded. "I know very little about the property prior to this mansion, except that it was owned by Claude Sinclair. He was a hardworking man who, according to his son, barely made ends meet. His only child, Emmanuel, was the one who built this home. He was a very good businessman and when he inherited the small shack he'd grown up in, Emmanuel knew he was destined for greater things. He immediately began increasing the production of cotton and purchasing more slaves. It didn't take him long to start turning a large profit. That's when he learned of a beautiful young woman in Baltimore who'd soon agree to be his bride."

"How'd he meet someone that far away?" Candace asked.

"He traveled extensively up and down the Mississippi, making contacts for his business. It was supposedly through those travels that he met his soon-to-be bride's father, who was anxious for his daughter to marry into money. With Emmanuel looking for a bride, it appeared to be a win-win situation for both."

"So, this home was built for his new bride?" Candace asked excitedly. "It's a love story, Tink. How cool."

"Yes, Emmanuel built the home to welcome his new bride," Paloma continued, "but it wasn't exactly the fairy tale he'd hoped. There were many obstacles along the way."

"Well, let's see it," Tink said, getting up from her seat at the table. "Is it structurally sound, Ms. Paloma?"

"It's an expansive place," she answered. "Some areas are better than others and some have been kept up, while others were simply closed off. It wasn't until your grandparents, Ruby and Baron, inherited the place that it was neglected to this extent. It was constructed with high-quality materials, as the old folks said, and no expense was spared. Through the years, it was cared for as best as each generation could. As you can imagine, it costs a great deal to keep an estate of this size running. Not that I'd know, mind you. My place is quite simple, and I prefer it that way."

"I understand they weren't exactly good money managers," Tink said.

"I'm not privy to that type of information nor do I care to be," Paloma said flatly.

Noted, Tink thought. *She's not ready to share any family secrets.*

Paloma walked out of the dining room toward the front of the home as the girls followed. She reached the entrance and turned to face the interior of the home. "This is my favorite part of the estate," she began. "As you'll see, Mr. Emmanuel Sinclair had each floor constructed almost in a mirror image of the other. As you enter here, you're led to the center of the home, the rotunda. I noticed you were instantly drawn to this staircase, Catherine," she said. "It, too, is my favorite. Story is that a Haitian slave by the name of Monroe Burke came up with the vision and erected it for Mr. Sinclair to impress his new bride. It worked. It not only amazed her, but everyone who visited the estate." Paloma pointed toward the roof. "The rotunda goes all the way up to the third floor. The stained glass in the ceiling came from Europe, along with many of the tiles found elsewhere in the home. As you can see, the house breaks off into two wings from the rotunda, which are referred to as the east and west wings.

"The first floor is primarily for entertaining," she continued. "There are two parlors which serve to receive and greet guests. They were initially separated by gender; the men would enjoy a smoke and alcoholic beverage, while the women discussed gossip and the latest fashions in the adjacent parlor. There were originally two spacious powder rooms, both utilized as an area where women could powder their noses and adjust their crinolines. After indoor plumbing was invented, they became bathrooms for either sex."

"I hadn't thought about plumbing," Tink said. "Of course, they didn't have a bathroom inside when the home was built. They weren't in homes until the early nineteen hundreds, correct?"

"It depended upon your social status," Paloma replied. "I believe they were first introduced into the fancier hotels before showing up in homes, but there were other means when necessary."

"The outhouse!" Candace exclaimed.

"I still have one of those," Paloma said. "But I was speaking of the chamber pot. It was placed just beneath the bed for nighttime usage and emptied in the outhouse in the morning. They were also utilized in the powder rooms when women were in their finest dresses. It kept them from going outside and risking getting them dirty."

"Let me guess who had to dump them," Candace muttered. "What a shame."

"The house was a much better place to work than the fields," Paloma added.

"I thought it was called a slop jar," Tink said.

"Common misconception," Paloma said. "The slop jar was used for, well, slop. The waste from washing one's teeth or their water from a sponge bath was poured into the slop pot, which was disposed of in another area. People back then either bathed in a tub with water heated over a fire or wiped down with soap and water at night. I've heard the history books portrayed people back then as going weeks at a time without bathing and it simply wasn't the case—at least here it wasn't. But as you saw in your rooms last night, the plumbing was upgraded as inventions progressed."

"I don't mean to pry," Tink said, "but did any of my ancestors ever offer to upgrade your cottage?"

"Yes, child," she answered kindly. "They offered many times. Even suggested I take a room in this house, but I'm quite content with my life. I want for very little."

"We're a very spoiled generation," Tink said. "But I hope you know you're always welcome to move up here. I worried about you walking back alone last night."

"'Tis a foolish waste of time to worry about me. As I told you before, I'm at home on the bayou," Paloma said, moving more quickly now toward both parlors. She opened the door then out held her hand to allow them to enter. "I've kept the doors shut to these areas simply because they are no longer in use. The sheets are protecting the furniture from dust, but truth be told, the pieces are now in ill repair. Their worth is probably immeasurable as they were shipped from overseas by Emmanuel Sinclair and have remained here since. However, no one has shown much interest in updating them. They took quite a beating with Baron and Ruby."

Candace and Tink walked into the parlor and looked around. The same heavy draperies hung over the windows while huge, greasy chandeliers were set in the high ceiling.

"Yikes," Tink said. "This is so gloomy. There's no way you could possibly keep all of this up, Ms. Paloma. The dust and dander alone must make it a hazard to your lungs. We need to get a commercial cleaning crew out here. Would you mind if we uncover the furniture? I have to admit, I'm intrigued."

"'Tis your home, child. Do as you wish."

Tink nodded to Candace and the two began lifting the sheets slowly from each piece. "Oh my," Tink said softly as she rubbed her hands down the length of the varnished wood on the sofa. "This is magnificent. I agree with you on the upholstery, but these pieces are certainly worth restoring—that is if we could find someone who's capable of restoring them properly."

"You won't find anyone in Kane who can offer such expertise. Perhaps in New Orleans," Paloma offered.

As the women unearthed each piece, Paloma spoke about the estate. "Both of the parlors are similar to one another, although you'll clearly find one larger and more masculine. We are in the east wing now, which includes the dining room you've already seen. There is a butler's pantry, which runs along the rear of the home from the dining room to the kitchen. It gives easier, and unseen, access to the employees bringing food to the table or to guests in the parlors." She paused long enough to nod in approval at a piece they were clearly taken with.

"The west wing is made up of the kitchen and laundry facilities, along with ample storage for cleaning supplies, staples for the kitchen, and so forth. It also leads to an area meant to house the help, should they decide to live on the premises."

"Appears they thought of everything," Tink said. "I can't wait to see all of it."

Paloma suddenly appeared tired and worn. "There is much to digest about this place."

"Ms. Paloma," Candace interrupted, "I've been meaning to ask you. What did the guy mean last night when he asked if you were aware of the two incidents that'd occurred?"

She looked confused, but Tink thought it was for show. "'Tis nothing," she said at last. "Just some gossip amongst the town folks. 'Tis important to separate gossip from truth when dealing with small minds."

"Should it concern us?" Tink asked.

"Not at all, dear."

"Are the Norwoods nice people?"

"Yes," Paloma answered, a smile crossing her face. "They are both fine young men. I crocheted a blanket for Dan's new little one and completely forgot to give it to him. Perhaps I'll catch them tonight when they head back in."

"Oh my," Tink said. "It'd be a shame to give a handmade blanket to him in that filthy boat. Would you like for me to take you to see the baby?"

Paloma appeared deep in thought before nodding. "It might be nice for you to make a new friend. Harriett is a sweet young lady and I can't think of anything more pleasant than laying eyes on a beautiful newborn."

"It's settled then," Tink said. "Maybe you can tell us more about the history of the house on the ride over."

From the look on her face, Paloma didn't seem to want to discuss the estate any further.

31

BEN AND DAN were packing up the boat when Sheriff Broussard drove up. "Mornin' fellas," he said as he got out of his cruiser.

"Mornin', Sheriff," Ben said as he continued to load up the day's supplies. "Don't tell me we have to meet with those assholes from the state again."

Isaac laughed and nodded. "They weren't the most pleasant, were they? But they were just doing their jobs and I can't fault 'em for that. I could see where they were going with it, as insulting as it was."

"Yeah, well tell them we're working men, and unless they have a warrant for our arrest, we won't be meeting with them again," Dan piped up.

Isaac and Ben turned to look at him. Dan was the most easygoing guy either of them knew and it wasn't like him to be defiant.

"Wow, little brother," Ben said. "You're getting ornery in your old age."

"I've got a daughter to support, Ben. I don't appreciate being badgered by a couple of bozos who think nothing of wasting our time."

"And there you have it, Sheriff," Ben said.

"I didn't come out here to interrupt your day," Isaac said. "Just wanted you to know we got identities on both the bodies. They were pillar-to-post type folks, just as we suspected. They knew each other and apparently traveled to Kane together. The state is looking for next of kin but hasn't found any yet. They both had records as long as my arm, mostly small-time stuff—scams, shoplifting, bad checks, that type of thing. They had some possession charges but none for dealing, which comes as a surprise."

"Interesting," Ben said. "But the statement is still extreme. Almost seems like some New York mob stuff."

"Definitely nothing we see in Kane," the sheriff agreed. "But, historically, cutting off hands is a punishment for thieves. They must've crossed the wrong people with their small-time cons. The drug crowd has some big sharks. You can't underestimate your opponent with that group."

"You're right there, Sheriff," Dan interjected. "At least they have identities now. As hard as it's been on us, I do hate to see anyone murdered, especially like that."

Isaac nodded and for a moment, the three men did nothing but continue to load the boat.

"Hey, Sheriff," Dan began. "What's the deal with those two young women staying at the Sinclair estate?"

"The Sinclairs had a granddaughter that they never interacted with. Their daughter, Olivia, died giving birth to her and from what I understand, Olivia's husband took the granddaughter and moved to Atlanta. She must've been the only living relative because she inherited the estate. What a mess that place is. I wonder what she'll do with it."

"Tear it down, if she knows what's best," Ben said with a chuckle.

"I was just wondering," Dan continued, "do those two girls know about the murders? I mean, how safe are they in that big place?"

"I wouldn't think they'd be in danger. This appears to be an isolated incident among a crowd not associated with Kane."

"Oh, look at you," Ben said. "Sounding like those big city cops, *an isolated incident.*"

"It's true. I believe their deaths were drug-related. I can't imagine someone hurting two young women from Atlanta. I understand the granddaughter is an attorney."

"So, they're not in any danger because she's educated?" Dan asked.

"Damn, Dan," Ben snapped. "Do you have the hots for her or what? Do I need to remind you that you're a married man?"

"No, Ben. I *know* I'm a married man. A married man with a daughter. I just got an odd feeling when we were talking to Paloma. She seemed very anxious to change the subject and not let the women know about the murders."

"So, Ms. Paloma is a murderer now?"

"What? Hell no, Ben. I just don't understand why she wouldn't give them a head's up, is all."

"My guess is she didn't want to frighten them," Isaac said. "This is their first trip to Kane and that type of information could put a bad taste in their mouth. I'm certain that if Paloma felt they were in danger, she'd tell them about the murders herself. She was very close to Olivia Sinclair. I've heard her speak of her many times."

"Have you met the granddaughter?" Dan asked.

"Not yet. I've been meaning to go by and introduce myself, but I've been tied up."

"First time in a while that I've seen my big brother so smitten," Dan said, smirking. "She's quite the looker, if you haven't heard. I must admit, I was getting a little worried about Ben. Thought he and Cassius were an item for a minute."

"That's not funny," Ben said. "We've got to get to work, Sheriff. Thanks for stopping by."

"Have you heard from Cassius?" Isaac asked, making his way back to his patrol car.

"Nope," Ben replied. "Guess he's still pissed at me for being so tough on him the other night. I can't handle him drunk. He's a lot sober, but the whole tears-in-his-beer thing is too much."

"He took the rest of the week off," Isaac said. "I've tried to talk to him but to no avail. Maybe hearing about what a con artist she was will snap him out of his grief."

"I'll go by his place after work," Ben said. "He'll come around."

"Have a good day, fellas. I'll go by and meet the Sinclair lady."

"Yeah, do that, Sheriff," Dan reiterated. "I'd sure feel better. That's a big place. Somebody could be in that house and she'd never even know it."

32

"My apologies for this car," Tink said as she helped Paloma in the front seat. "It's extremely small. I'm not sure what my father was thinking. There was barely room for Candace's luggage."

"That's enough about my luggage," Candace piped up from the back. "One can never be too prepared."

"Where to?" Tink asked, ignoring Candace's justification for over-packing.

"Take a left at the end of the driveway. It's the opposite direction of town," Paloma said, the beautiful, crocheted baby blanket folded and placed carefully on her lap. "I have to say I'm thrilled to death to see this little one. It seems like just yesterday that Ben and Dan were riding by my place with their father. He was very strict on those boys, but it's probably why they ended up as good as they did."

"Are they twins?" Candace asked.

"No, they're a year apart, I believe. Their mother passed away when they were very young, and their father died when they were in their mid-twenties. They only have each other. I was so relieved when Dan and Harriett married. She's a delightful young woman."

"Is Ben married?" Tink asked nonchalantly.

"No, he isn't. I think he still feels like he must be a father to Dan.

It's time for him to meet a nice girl. He spends all of his time working on that old fixer-upper he bought."

"Oooooh," Candace said. "So, he has construction skills. I happen to know someone in great need of a handyman."

"If you're referring to Catherine, she needs far more than a handyman!"

The observation brought laughter from Candace and Paloma.

"You ladies are hysterical," Tink said. "But seriously, he may be able to tell us how much work would be required to repair the place, or if it's repairable at all."

"Anything is repairable," Paloma said, waving to the left. "Turn here."

"Turn where?" Tink asked, slowing down and looking for a driveway.

"Right there," Paloma said, pointing again.

"I don't see anything, Ms. Paloma," Tink insisted.

"Goodness, child, it's right there."

"Good grief," Tink continued. "I'd have ridden right past that. How do they find their driveway in the dark?"

"'Tis easy. They sense it."

Tink forced herself not to look in the rearview mirror at Candace. She'd surely hear about how odd that comment was later. Instead, she concentrated on not hitting anything as she made her way to the home of Dan and Harriett Norwood.

After several curves and ruts, Tink saw the raised doublewide trailer coming into view.

Paloma wrung her hands, either from excitement or nervousness, as they pulled in front.

"Let me help you out," Tink said, jumping out of the driver's side. It was the first time Tink had realized that Paloma was an older woman. She seemed almost frail outside of her everyday environment and Tink wanted desperately to shelter her from harm. Paloma held the baby blanket tightly as they climbed the stairs and rang the bell.

A middle-aged woman answered the door and looked at them

blankly.

"Hello," Tink said with a broad smile. "Is Harriett available? Our apologies for not calling before our visit."

"I'm not sure if she's busy or not," the woman said bluntly. "I'll have to check."

"Mother?" Harriett yelled from another part of the house. "Who's here?"

"I don't know," the woman yelled back. "Someone who obviously didn't call first."

This quickly brought Harriett to the door. "Mother, you can be so rude at times." Harriett peeked her head around her mother's shoulder and squealed with delight. "Ms. Paloma! How wonderful to see you," she said, lightly pushing her mother to the side and opening the door wide. "Please, come in."

Paloma hugged her before entering. "Do tell, where's that little one I've been hearing about?"

"She's just waking up," Harriett replied. "Mother, will you get her for me?"

Her mother was none too thrilled to be brushed aside but made her way down the hall anyway. Harriett rolled her eyes and broke into a giggle. "My apologies for her rudeness. I'm sorry we haven't met," she said to Tink and Candace.

"Again, our apologies for not calling first," Tink reiterated. "I'm Catherine, but everyone calls me Tink, and this is my best friend, Candace."

"Very nice to meet both of you and it's not necessary to call first when visiting a friend. Come have a seat. Dan told me you inherited the Sinclair estate. That's a monstrous place. I mean, in a good way, of course. It's so huge."

Tink laughed before agreeing. "It *is* monstrous. And it needs a great deal of work."

The grandmother came back in, carrying a swaddled bundle.

"This is my mother, Hazel," Harriett said. "Mother, this is Ms. Paloma. Dan and Ben have known her all their life. And this is Tink, if I may," she continued, glancing at Tink for approval. "And her friend, Candace. Tink just inherited an estate here in Kane. I'm anxious to see what she does with it."

Hazel wasn't impressed and made no comment either way. "I'll get Landry's bottle," she said coolly.

Harriett handed the pink bundle to Paloma, who quickly peeled the layers away to reveal the infant inside. "Oh, she's delightful," Paloma gushed.

"Delightful? You're clearly not here for the midnight feedings," Hazel commented, returning with the bottle.

"Mother, we haven't asked you to get up once," Harriett said. "Dan has been so good to help," she whispered to Paloma.

"He's a very proud father," Paloma agreed.

"Oh! Is this beautiful afghan for Landry?" Harriett asked as she unfolded the hand-knitted blanket.

"Yes, it is. I couldn't very well show up without a gift for the little one."

"But you could've called first," Hazel spoke up.

"That's it, Mother," Harriett snapped. "It's one thing to be disrespectful to Dan and me, but it's another thing to be impolite to our friends. I've had it."

Hazel abruptly left the room and the sound of a slammed door echoed down the hall.

"I'm sorry about that," Harriett said, her cheeks turning pink. "We're all running on very little sleep and my tolerance level has reached its peak."

Paloma patted her arm. "Dan told me about it, but I assured him it'd get better soon. She's a beautiful baby—perfect in every way."

"Thank you. Would you like to feed her?" she asked, offering her the bottle.

"Yes, I would."

"Can I get you ladies anything?" Harriett asked. "I haven't been to the store, but I believe I have some juice in the fridge."

"No, we're fine," Candace spoke up. "I'm grateful Paloma brought us to meet you. I'm going to have to get back to Atlanta soon and Tink could use a friend. I mean, one her age. Ugh, I mean..."

"You aren't offending me, child," Paloma spoke up. "Catherine does need a friend. I'm sure it'll get awfully lonely here without someone her age to talk to."

"You're both acting as though I'm moving here permanently."

"I just assumed you were," Harriett said. "So, you won't be staying?"

"No, I have a job to get back to in Atlanta. This was just meant to be a quick trip to see the place. I've never been here. Well, I was born here, but my father moved us to Atlanta the week after my birth."

"I had no idea," Harriett said. "I have only been here a few years myself. I got a job teaching in Kane right out of college, then I met Dan. The rest is history, I suppose. So, are you planning on selling the estate?"

"To be honest, I'm not quite certain what my plans are. I was hoping to see it before putting it up on the market. But I must admit, I'm a little taken with it, to say nothing of the generations of my family who spent their lives there. So much history."

"That's so cool," Harriett said. "Ms. Paloma can certainly fill you in on Kane's history. Her family has been here as long as yours."

"So I've heard," Tink agreed.

Apparently, Hazel had quickly gotten over her temper tantrum and returned to the den. "You must be terribly frightened in that house if it's as large as Harriett acts like it is," she said snidely as she cut her eyes at Tink. "Especially with all that's going on in Kane these days."

"Mother, are you trying to anger me? Now's not a good time to revisit that. We're enjoying a nice visit."

"What do you mean?" Candace asked. "We've only been here a day and I'm afraid we aren't familiar with anything going on in Kane."

"It's nothing, really," Harriett answered quickly.

"Nothing? You call two gruesome murders nothing?" Hazel asked.

"Murders?" Tink asked, her voice much shriller than she'd intended.

"Yes! Ben found one of them in the bayou the day Landry was

born. Poor child, talk about putting a damper on the day of your birth!"

"Mother! She will never know about that and I don't care to be reminded, again!"

"But you said murders, with an *s*," Candace said. "As in plural, more than one."

"I'm aware of what plural means," Hazel spat. "There were two. The second was a lady. Dan and Ben found her."

"A woman?" Candace gasped. "That's insane. Is the killer still at large? I mean, this is big, and we're staying in that huge, deserted place. Ms. Paloma, we could've been killed!"

"I'd never put you in danger," Paloma replied. "Besides, don't you have murders every day in Atlanta? It's my understanding that all major cities deal with crimes such as this."

"Well...well...well yes, we do," Candace stammered. "But it's different."

"How is it different?" Paloma pressed.

"It's other people and...and we're very careful. We know where to go and where not to. Besides, this is such a small place with a small population. It's less expected to happen here. Why do you suppose they were killed?"

"We aren't sure," Paloma answered. "But they're outsiders and it's possibly related to drugs."

"Then how did your husband and his brother find them?" Candace asked.

"They were hanging from their lines," Hazel was quick to interject. "They had their hands cut off. It was terrible. Ben said it was something like the mob would do."

"Mother, that's enough and I mean it. Why would you frighten these young women? I've had all I can take of you."

"They hung people and cut their hands off?" Candace all but screamed. "You can't be serious. This is scary as hell, Tink. I'm out of here first thing in the morning."

"Language," Tink said. "I think you're overreacting, Candace. This type of thing happens when drugs are involved."

"Seriously?" Candace asked, her face reflecting shock. "We're in the middle of nowhere and no one felt it necessary to inform us of not one, but two, murders? And you're concerned about me saying *hell*?"

"Candace, are you aware of every murder that happens near us? No, we just become immune to all the news. I'm sure it's nothing to worry about."

"How many people are in this town?" Candace demanded. "How many murders have you had in the past five years? I'm serious. How many?"

"None," Harriett answered. "But we've had more outsiders coming through to work on the oil rigs. It's a job, with decent pay, requiring little skills. At least for those at entry level. They live a drifter lifestyle, going from one menial job to the next."

Candace caught Tink's glare and returned it, but thankfully remained silent.

❀

"What a nice girl," Tink gushed as they got back in the car. "Wasn't that baby beautiful?"

"Indeed, she was," Paloma answered.

"Wasn't she beautiful, Candace?" Tink pressed.

"She's too small to be beautiful. Babies have to grow into their heads, it takes a while."

"Candace! That's not very nice."

"Oh, come on. You can't say that you've *not* noticed. Their heads are always oversized. That's why they can't hold it up right away."

"Good grief, I think it's because their little neck muscles aren't strong enough."

"Whatever," Candace said. "You'll see in a few weeks when her body catches up with that head. She'll be much cuter."

"I'm anxious to get back to the house and see more," Tink said, changing the subject. "Ms. Paloma, tell us more about the second floor."

33

DAN HAD STAYED late to help Ben wash the boat down and it hadn't gone unappreciated. The clean-up time was cut in half, along with the time spent salting down the day's skins and adding additional salt to those currently drying.

"I've missed having you around at the end of the day," Ben said.

"You've missed having an extra set of hands," Dan added with a laugh.

"Same thing. You seem a little more rested."

"I'm not sure how. When I'm not up with Landry, I'm awake pondering when that ole battleaxe is gonna leave."

"Crazy Hazel still hanging around?"

"That's all she's doing, just hanging around. I'm gonna have to send her on her way. It's clear Harriett doesn't have it in her. Hazel's driving her nuts."

"I'll be glad when you guys get back to normal, if there is such a thing after having a child."

The screech of tires caused the brothers to look up. "Damn, I knew things were going too good," Ben said as Cassius got out of his car and slammed the door.

"What's up, Norwoods?"

"Just cleaning up," Dan said. "I was headed out. How've you been, Cassius?"

"Okay. The sheriff gave me a few days off. Guess he thinks I'm gonna go postal or something."

"At least you're not drunk," Ben said.

"Kiss my ass."

"Well, it's good to see some things never change," Dan said as he cleaned his hands. "You two are like an old married couple."

"Your brother's the woman," Cassius said. "You know the kind— never wants her husband to have more than one beer."

Dan laughed as he got in his truck and cranked it up. "See ya in the morning, Ben. Try not to hit your husband over the head with a frying pan."

"See ya in the morning," Ben said, not acknowledging the comment.

"Got any beer in the fridge?" Cassius asked.

"Yep, unless you drank it all when I wasn't home to defend it."

The two friends made their way up the front steps and into the house. "I'll hop in the shower before you tell me how much I stink. Grab a beer but don't drink the last one."

"Who drinks a man's last beer?" Cassius asked.

"You," Ben answered as he walked down the hall toward the shower.

BEN GRABBED a beer from the fridge and found Cassius exactly where he suspected he would, in his recliner. "Why don't you have the television on?"

"I don't know. Just didn't feel like listening to anything right now. I haven't been sleeping well."

"Do you have a baby I don't know about?" Ben regretted the words as soon as they left his mouth. Now the door was open for Cassius to host his pity party.

"Hell no, I can't even get a girlfriend. It's tough, you know?"

"What, not having a girlfriend? I'm in the same boat in case you haven't noticed."

"Did yours get murdered, too?"

"Enough of that shit," Ben snapped. "I'm sorry about that woman, but she wasn't your girlfriend, Cassius, and thank God for it. She wasn't a good person. In fact, she was stealing from Syd."

"How do you know that?"

"Well, for starters, Syd told Isaac herself. She was intending to fire her. Anyway, what did you know about her other than batting your lashes across the bar at her?"

"Damn, man. She was a nice girl."

"Okay. I'll give you that, but it's time to move on. I'm sorry about what happened to her, but you're still among the living. I can't take any more of you wallowing in self-pity."

"And there you have it folks, the reason why Ben Norwood's unattached. He's cold as ice."

"Give me a break. You don't have to come over here, ya know?"

"Oh, but look at all the fun I'd miss," Cassius said. "Damn, Ben, can't anybody kid with you anymore?"

"I'm just worn out and to be honest, finding those bodies was awful. I've been sleeping about as good as Dan has, which isn't saying much."

"Was it as bad as they said?" Cassius asked, leaning forward as if to hear better. "Tell me, Ben, how bad was it?"

"I'm not going to talk about it, Cassius."

"You brought it up. Just tell me, was she dressed? I mean, they didn't...you know?"

"No, they didn't and I'm not going to give you any gruesome details. Not that I've got any, mind you. Dan found her and all I saw was her T-shirt from Syd's bar, and her face. That's when I turned away. Nobody wants or needs to see that shit."

"Thanks for telling me that," Cassius said, leaning back. "That makes me feel better. You know, that they didn't..."

"Yeah, well, she was fully clothed," Ben said as he slugged the rest of his beer and got up for another.

"Listen, I heard a woman inherited the ole Sinclair place. That's a helluva lot of house for one person," Cassius yelled toward the kitchen.

Ben walked back in the den with two beers and tossed one to Cassius. "You don't have to scream. I'm like five feet away."

Cassius opened his beer and continued. "Wouldn't that be somethin'? I mean, to inherit a mansion like that. It's crazy."

"Dan and I met her and her friend yesterday."

"You did? You never mentioned it."

"You had other stuff on your mind. Ms. Paloma was walking them around the grounds and we stopped and spoke with them."

"What's the woman like?"

"Very nice. She's from Atlanta," Ben said before getting defensive. "And don't even think about it, Cassius."

"Think about what?"

"Give me a break. I've been meaning to check on her—it's not a good time for a single woman to move to Kane. I wish Ms. Paloma lived in that house, too. Somebody could be in there and those two girls wouldn't even be aware of it."

"You said she brought a friend, huh? Male or female?"

"Female."

"Looks like we're burning daylight, Norwood," Cassius said as he glanced at his watch.

"Well, well, look at who's already over the bartender."

"You said I was better off without her. Besides, I've always wanted to see inside that mansion."

Twenty minutes later, they were on their way to the Sinclair estate. "I'd feel better if I'd called first," Ben said. "I don't have her number and Paloma doesn't have a cell phone. Not that she'd get service down by the bayou."

"You get service while you're out on the water," Cassius retorted. "You sure as hell get through to 911."

"Thank goodness," Ben said. "And that's enough about those murders. That'd be the best way to ruin the night."

"What murders?"

"You're a funny guy," Ben said.

The two rode in silence until pulling in the drive.

Ben peered through the windshield. "This place has sure gone down. Look at the mailbox. If that's any indication of the rest of the place, it'd take a fortune to make it livable."

"It's been the envy of Kane for as long as I can remember. Have you ever been inside?" Cassius asked.

"Nope. I've been on part of the grounds—that's it. My father always had the utmost respect for Ms. Paloma, and we'd stop to say a few words whenever we saw her."

"Whoa. Look at that, won't you?" Cassius said as the house came into view. "I'd heard it was big, but this is over the top."

Ben put the old truck in park and, for the first time, was embarrassed about his vehicle. The moan and screech of the driver's door opening made him cringe. Cassius, however, didn't have a care in the world as he took the stairs two at a time and was already ringing the bell.

Damn, Ben thought. *What was I thinking bringing Cassius here?*

Just as Ben had started up the stairs, Catherine opened the door.

She's more beautiful than I remember.

She looked confused until she saw Ben. "Hello, Ben," she said. "What brings you way out here?"

"It's not very far," he answered. "I just wanted to check on you and...Candace, is it?"

"Yep," Candace piped in as she opened the door wider. "Candace is the name."

"This is Deputy Cassius Holder, one of my childhood buddies," Ben said. "Cassius, this is Catherine and Candace."

"Nice to meet you both. My buddy was worried about you ladies being here alone, but after hearing you're from Atlanta, I'm sure you're aware of stranger danger," Cassius said.

"Stranger danger?" Candace said with a giggle. "I haven't heard that since kindergarten."

"Still holds true today," he said. "This is a big place. I'm sure you're careful."

"Forgive my manners," Tink said. "Please come in and call me Tink. My father's the only one who calls me Catherine and that's when he's upset with me."

"Okay, Tink it is," Ben said as he and Cassius made their way in. "This place is well over a hundred years old. It looks like you have your work cut out for you."

"I understand it was completed in 1859, and yes indeed, I have my work cut out for me," Tink said as she led them into the first parlor. "Excuse the dust. We just uncovered some of the furniture. It's quite impressive other than desperately needing to be refinished."

Ben admired the handiwork on the antique furniture. "Nice pieces. They don't make 'em like this anymore."

"Funny you should come by," Tink said. "We were just talking about you today."

"Who is 'we'?" Ben asked.

"Ms. Paloma and me. She told us you've done a lot of repairs on your place. I was hoping you might have some suggestions for me."

"You could hardly compare my place to this. I just piddle around on the weekends."

"So, what do you ladies do back in Atlanta?" Cassius interjected.

"Tink's a lawyer; I'm a receptionist at the same law firm," Candace answered. "Real exciting stuff."

"A lawyer, huh?" Cassius asked.

Tink nodded.

"Tink, is there any wine or refreshments for our visitors?" Candace asked.

"I'm not sure. How rude of me again. I'll go check."

Candace grabbed Cassius by the hand. "Come with me. If there's any alcohol in this place, I'll find it."

Cassius released her hand as they entered the rotunda. "This is crazy. I've heard about it but haven't ever seen it for myself."

"Yes, it's a little over the top," Candace replied. "This whole place gives me the creeps. Come on, let's go to the kitchen."

Cassius wanted to stay and admire the stained-glass ceiling, but he followed Candace, who seemed anxious to get away from it. By the time he caught up with her, she was opening and closing cabinets.

"I did find a couple of bottles of red wine, but I've never heard of the brand. Who knows what it'll taste like?"

She handed Cassius the bottles and rustled through the cabinets for four glasses, which she set on the counter. "Wait, Ben said you're a deputy—as in deputy sheriff?"

"That'd be me."

"Well, well, well. Do tell me about these murders that no one seems to want us to know about."

"Who doesn't want you to know?" Cassius asked.

"That Paloma woman, for starters. Ben and his brother asked her if she was aware of what was going on and she certainly didn't want them to elaborate. Then we took her to visit Harriett, and her mother couldn't wait to scare us."

"I don't doubt that for a minute."

"Is it true about their hands being cut off?"

Cassius did nothing but squirm for a moment.

"Okay," Candace said shortly, "cut to the chase. I've been freaked out since we got here. Something just isn't right about this place. It's so huge and that woman seems to be in control of every step we make. And who in the hell still uses skeleton keys?"

"First of all, let me assure you the murders are isolated incidents. Nobody knew those people—they were drifters and probably involved in the drug trade. They both had records. Kane hasn't ever had a crime problem, at least until the drugs started coming in. Most of the drugs are down by the oil rigs anyway—not in town. I'm sure Ms. Paloma just didn't want to worry you ladies."

"Well, she hasn't even noticed that I'm here," Candace said. "It's as if Tink is some ghost of her late mother and Paloma is enamored with her."

"Sounds as if you two got off on the wrong foot," Cassius replied. "She's quite a nice lady. Just give her a chance. Her family has a long history here."

"Yeah, and if I hear that one more time I'll scream." Candace sighed. "I mean, seriously, Tink inherited this place, but Paloma even tries to control which parts of the house she goes in. I'm starting to feel like I'm in some horror movie. Anyway, I've got to get back to work. Can't say that I'll be sad to go."

"It's probably just being in this big, old house. It'd give anybody the creeps," Cassius said. "We better take this wine to them before they send out a search party."

TINK WAS TAKING notes on a legal pad, Ben sitting close to her. "So, you think it's salvageable?"

"Definitely has good bones. I don't know of another home built with such quality products," Ben replied. "Of course, you'll need to get someone out to check the foundation, but I'd say at this point, you're looking at cosmetic issues, for the most part. I have no idea when the plumbing and wiring were updated—any repairs to those could be an issue as well. Do you know what the square footage is?"

"I was looking over some of the information I got from Blaine Biggs and it's over sixteen thousand."

"Sixteen thousand!" Cassius exclaimed as he and Candace took a seat. "I'd hate to get that utility bill!"

"Yeah, me too," Tink agreed. "The electricity was cut off before we arrived and my father had it reconnected. It's just now started to cool off. I'm sure there are areas that could be shut off for the time being. There's no reason to heat and cool all of this. It'd cost a fortune."

"You'll definitely need some wood for the winter. I'd recommend utilizing as many fireplaces as possible," Ben added.

"Is that safe?" Tink asked. "I have one in my loft, but I've never used it."

"They're very safe, but you need to have them checked out first."

"Ca-ching, ca-ching," Candace piped up. "The good news is we found some wine. Would anyone care for a glass?"

"Sure," Tink said.

Candace poured. As soon as everyone took a sip, they all gagged.

"This is terrible," Candace said. "I've never met a wine I couldn't drink until now."

"I have to agree," Tink said. "I'm so sorry, gentlemen. I wasn't expecting company, or I would've had something to serve you."

"How do you two like wings?" Ben asked. "I know of a quaint little place that might just hit the spot."

34

CANDACE CRAWLED in Tink's bed, still too afraid to sleep in her own designated room. "That was kinda fun, huh?" she asked.

"Yes, it was. I like the small-town thing."

"This takes the small-town thing to a whole different level, Tink."

"I suppose so, but it feels very...comfortable."

"The jury is still out for me," Candace said. "You know I've got to get back to work. Not that I haven't appreciated your dad giving me a much-needed break, but I hate to take advantage of it. What are your plans?"

"I may stay a few more days."

"A few more days? What do you plan to accomplish in a few days? You still haven't told me how much that check was, and what are your long-term plans? Are you going to remodel this monster?"

"Monster? Candace, you haven't even given it a chance."

"I meant monster in the sense of its size, but you're right, it gives me the creeps. There. I said it."

"I understand how it could," Tink said. "But it doesn't throw off a bad vibe to me. I don't think it's the house you don't like—I think it's Paloma."

"Since you brought her up, no, I don't like her very much. There's something strange about how she wants to control what you see and don't see in the house. It's your house, for crying out loud!"

"I don't think she's trying to prevent me from seeing the house, I think she just wants me to be safe. It's an old house."

"I haven't seen any floors you might fall through," Candace said. "Sure, it needs to be updated and it hasn't been taken care of, but it's not falling in."

Tink sat up in bed and flipped on the bedside light. "Okay, what would you like to see?" she asked, grabbing the ring of skeleton keys from the nightstand. "I have the keys to the castle—let's check it out."

"Are you serious?"

"Why not? You're right; it's my house. Let's check it out."

"But it's after midnight," Candace pointed out.

"Do you have other plans?"

Candace squealed with delight and jumped out of bed, throwing on her robe and stepping into her slippers. "Let's look at the rest of the bedrooms!"

"Bedrooms it is," Tink said. "Is your phone charged? Paloma said some of the light bulbs could be blown so we'll need the light."

"Charged and ready," Candace replied.

"Then let's go."

"Do you feel like an updated version of Nancy Drew?" Candace asked.

"I've wanted to see it all, but you're right—Paloma *was* showing it to us on her own terms."

The two women opened the door leading into the hall and made a left. The long hallway before them seemed to loom, then vanish into darkness. Struggling to control the chill running up her spine, Tink stood up a bit straighter as if to exude confidence. The house was now eerily silent, unlike it'd been in her bedroom. The wall sconces offered a dim view of the doors on each side of the hall. They were much larger than an average interior door and were made of thick, rough-hewn wood. Each boasted heavy pewter locks and handles.

"Whatever happened to regular doorknobs?" Candace asked.

"I doubt they had them when this house was built. These locks look like they were made to last."

"I wonder why they kept everything locked. Don't you find it a little strange?"

"Normally I would, but Paloma explained it was to keep people out while it was vacant and to deter employees from stealing."

"And she said for you to always keep your keys with you. Have you got them?"

Tink hold up the ring of rusted keys and rattled them. "Right here. Which room would you like to see first?"

"How many bedrooms do you suppose there are?" Candace asked. "And for God's sake, what's the wattage in those bulbs?"

Tink feigned a laugh as she passed Candace's assigned room and walked across the wide hall to the one a few feet past it. "Let's check this one out," she suggested.

Tink went through the keys until she found the longest one as Paloma had instructed and slid it in the lock. The door opened with a slight nudge while Tink felt for an overhead light. When she couldn't find one, Candace used her phone to shine the flashlight.

"There's a bedside lamp over there," Tink said.

The girls had intertwined their arms and made their way to the dusty brass lamp. It was the only thing not covered with large tarps. Tink turned the switch and it lit dimly, just as the sconces in the hall.

"Again, what wattage do they use?" Candace asked. "The first thing you need to do is get some bright bulbs. That's half the problem."

"Dimness keeps you from seeing a myriad of things like wear and tear," Tink said.

"Myriad?" Candace questioned. "Seriously. Whatever happened to a *shitload* of things?"

"Candace, what's gotten into you? Your language is terrible."

"Funny, it never seemed to bother you before."

Tink didn't acknowledge that, but released Candace's arm and walked along the perimeter of the room. "It's much like the room we're sleeping in. I bet they all mirror one another, like a hotel."

"Yeah, well these tarpaulins are always spooky. What if someone were hiding underneath?"

Tink laughed. "They'd be waiting a long time for someone to come along to scare."

"Let's go all the way to the end of the hall," Candace suggested.

Tink pulled the door shut and locked it behind herself. The last thing she wanted was for Paloma to scold her if she found it unlocked.

Both used their phones to light the way this time. "I agree," Tink said. "Brighter bulbs are a must."

"You've got to be kidding," Candace said as she reached out to part the cobwebs woven across the hallway. "It's as if it's been staged to frighten us."

"I doubt someone put up fake cobwebs," Tink said sarcastically. "But seriously, how far does this hall go?"

Their rhythmed breathing was the only thing that could be heard as they walked on the thick burgundy carpeting. As they neared the end, a set of double doors, much like the single doors on the other rooms, came into view. They were illuminated by sconces on either side.

"I wonder if this is a bedroom," Tink said, fumbling once again with the keys on the ring. "Paloma said the long key was for all the bedrooms. Perhaps this is a storage closet of some kind."

"A storage closet with double doors?"

Tink thrust the key in the door to test its ability. Both doors parted and appeared to open by themselves. "Oh, my..." Tink whispered. She rubbed her hand up and down the wall in hopes of discovering an overhead light. Her heart skipped when she felt what was certainly a switch. After a moment's hesitation, Tink flipped it on. Light instantly flooded the space, displaying a bedroom that was surely three times the size of the others.

"Wha...?" Candace gasped. "Whose room do you suppose this was? Was it for the man who originally built the place?"

"No," Tink whispered. "Paloma said the master was on the third floor."

She scanned the room, noticing white sheets of varying sizes thrown across lumps of furniture. The fireplace reminded her of a horror movie she'd once seen where a group of youngsters were dared to spend the night in a haunted house. The ceilings were well over twelve feet, making the mouth of the fireplace at least eight. The hearth and mantel were a dull marble with carvings of cherubs floating peacefully on their feathered wings. Tink was moving forward to get a better look when Candace grabbed her arm.

"Tink, let's get out of here," she said, pulling her toward the door.

"What?" Tink whispered. "You're the one who wanted to look around and now we are."

"No," Candace demanded. "I'm serious," she pleaded. "Let's get out of here, *now*."

Tink turned to face her friend. "What's up with you?"

It was then she noticed it—the portrait. The portrait of *her* in a green silk gown, cut low in the front to accentuate a large emerald and diamond necklace. Her sleek, black hair had been pulled back into a chignon and her eyes were sorrowful.

"Oh my God, oh my...what is this?" she gasped as she squeezed Candace's arm and continued to back away. "Who would've done such a thing?"

A firm hand seized her arm as a deep male voice boomed, "What do you ladies think you're doing?"

35

SHERIFF BROUSSARD PULLED into his parking space at the precinct before he spotted the state vehicle parked in the lot. *Damn, if I'd noticed they were here, I'd have driven back home*, he thought. The last thing he was in the mood for was the sarcasm of Investigators Westmoreland and Fontenot.

I just hope somebody has the coffee ready.

Roxie had the men seated out front on a wooden bench, which, judging by their expressions, hadn't pleased them much at all. "Mornin' fellas," Isaac said as he took off his hat and placed it on the rack. "What brings you two to Kane?"

Investigator Westmoreland made a point of referring to his watch as though the sheriff reported to him. "A little thing called murder, Sheriff Broussard."

"Haven't solved that one yet?" Isaac asked with a straight face.

"Do you have a few minutes?" Fontenot, the good cop, asked.

"I always have time for my brothers in blue. Come on back, gentlemen."

The two followed him to his office, where Isaac gestured at the spare guest seats. "Please, make yourselves at home. Can I get you some coffee?"

"No," Westmoreland quickly answered before his partner could take him up on the offer. "We're not getting anywhere with the people at the extended-stay motel or the oil rigs."

"I'm sorry to hear that," Isaac said. "That's not a crowd who's typically tight with law enforcement, and from what I've heard about the woman, I doubt they're mourning her loss. Both victims had extensive records, and despite how petty most of their crimes were, they were indicative of a dishonest lifestyle, to say the least."

"So, the victims were to blame for their own murders, is that what you're saying, Sheriff?" Westmoreland asked as he leaned forward to eyeball Isaac.

"First of all, you can back away and get your elbows off my desk. If you think you can come into my territory and piss on it, you're sadly mistaken. I don't know how it works in your department, but we treat each other with respect here. In case you haven't noticed, we're on the same team." Isaac stood, his long frame looming over them. "I haven't even had a cup of coffee and damn if I'm going to be insulted by two bozos who think the bad guys are just gonna run up and tattle on their buddies. You can see yourselves out."

Before either of them could react, he'd walked past them. He was pouring himself a cup of brew in the breakroom when Westmoreland tapped on the doorframe.

"Sheriff? Uh, I may have, well, I didn't mean, I... Could we start this morning over again?"

"Are you asking for a do-over, Westmoreland?" Isaac asked, a grin crossing his face.

"I suppose you could say that," Westmoreland answered, clearly hating like hell to play nice.

"Does this little act you two have ever work anywhere?" the sheriff asked, enjoying every minute of this.

"We're on our way back to the motel, so we don't have much time. Could you spare us a few minutes?"

The fun was over, but Isaac had won the battle. He doubted the two men would ever approach him in that manner again. The state police often looked down on local cops. They didn't have the training or resources the state did, and most didn't have a college education. Evidently, they'd misread Isaac Broussard.

The sheriff sat behind his desk and sipped from his steaming cup. "Okay, gentlemen, let's start this conversation over. Is there anything we can do to assist in your investigation?"

Fontenot glanced over at the more seasoned investigator and nodded in his direction.

"We aren't getting any leads from the drifter crowd, as you surmised," the older gentleman said. "I don't doubt all of 'em have a rap sheet to match. There's a reason why their type is always moving."

"Yep, but unfortunately they're useful to an industry that's continually short on unskilled help. Those guys make what they can, until they burn their bridges, then it's on to the next gig. Sadly, for Kane, they tend to bring in an unsavory element, in this case drugs. Lived here all my life, and I don't recall having a drug problem until the last decade."

"No offense, Sheriff," Westmoreland began, "but that's where we're running into a problem. Why Kane? And I'm not referring to the drug issue. Undoubtedly, illegal drugs are everywhere, but why bring the mutilated bodies to Kane? They could've killed them down by that shit hole of a motel and dumped 'em anywhere. It's obvious no one down there gives a damn about what happened to 'em— they're not the snitching kind. Clearly a gruesome crime like this would draw attention, a lot of attention, especially to a small, rural town. Like your gator hunter pointed out, I'm not from Louisiana. Hell, I'm from the Windy City, but even I could figure out a place to hide a body out here. And common sense would tell anyone a body bleeding out like that would draw every gator in sight."

"I tend to agree with you," Sheriff Broussard said. "I hate to say it, Lord knows I do, but that's a point I've pondered more than once. They wanted the bodies to be found. Like you said, there's a million places to stash a body—we're on the bayou, for heaven's sake. There was the chance, maybe a big one, that the gators could've got to them, especially with blood covering the bodies. But they had to have been killed elsewhere. As much blood as there was, it wasn't enough to be the original crime scene, and there had to have been one helluva fight. I know I'd fight if I thought someone was going to cut my hands off."

"Not bad, Sheriff," Westmoreland said. "We got the autopsies back and the cause of death was blood loss. However, they were incapacitated by severe blows to the head. No doubt they were unconscious when they removed their hands."

"Yeah, I can't see anyone making it easy for the perp to cut them off."

"Even deemed unconscious, I believe we're dealing with at least two perpetrators. I can't see one person killing them and getting them out to the bayou."

"Agreed," Isaac said. "But why? My initial thought is the symbolism of removing their hands. That type of thing goes back to medieval days. Cut off the hand that steals."

"Definitely a statement, but again, why bring them here? Have you had a recent rash of burglaries? Robberies, maybe? Can you think of anyone who'd like to send out a message that Kane won't stand for such crimes?"

The sheriff wrinkled his forehead. "That'd make sense," he said, struggling to recall anything that could link such a heinous act to Kane. "But we just don't have a great deal of crime here. Don't get me wrong, we're not crime free. Hell, I don't know of anywhere that is. But people still leave their doors unlocked here. I mean most of them don't even own keys to their own houses. We get DUIs and a few barroom brawls down at Syd's, but that's to be expected when alcohol is involved. We've had some drug arrests but they're typically outsiders. I can't recall the last time we had a home break-in or a robbery."

"I take it you know most of the people in town," Jon Fontenot spoke up.

"Yep. We're spread out over a large area, but Kane has a small population—close to three-thousand. If I don't know them by name, I either know their folks, or at least that they're fairly new to our parish. Most of the drifters tend to stay closer to the rigs where they can get work. As you can see, we aren't booming with employment opportunities."

"So, no one comes to mind who'd have a motive for this?" Fontenot pressed.

"For murdering two people and cutting their hands off? Hell no. If I had any inkling someone was capable of this in Kane, I'd be on their ass like white on rice."

"So, just to revisit it briefly," the younger investigator began, "you don't have any reason to suspect the Norwood brothers?"

"Absolutely not," Isaac said firmly. "I grew up with their father and I knew them before they were a twinkle in his eyes. They're hard-working young men and honest as the day is long."

"Okay, let me go back to being from Chicago," Westmoreland interjected. "And again, no offense, Sheriff, just doing our jobs. Let me play devil's advocate for a minute."

Isaac nodded and leaned back in his chair. That was to be expected from two outsiders and he understood their need to explore every angle. At least they were sharing their thoughts with him and he wouldn't be blindsided.

"So," Westmoreland began again, "being from Chicago, I don't know a damn thing about bayous, nor do I own a boat of any kind. Let's just say, for shits and giggles, I'm a drifter. I get pissed at a fella who's robbed me of my drugs, and I want to make a statement. I decide I'll cut his hands off to let everybody know I won't stand for anybody taking what's mine. Hell, let's say he stole from me when we were drinking at your local watering hole, Syd's. So, I happen to kill him when he leaves. Where do I find a boat and how do I know the damn gators won't get me? How would I know where someone's gator bait and lines might be?" He paused briefly, his eyes taking on a faraway look. "Then, I wait another day or so and a woman, who happens to shack with the fella who initially stole from me, steals from me, too. So, I do the same thing. Only find another line that happens to belong to the same set of brothers. Does that strike you as feasible?"

Isaac didn't answer, his thoughts also faraway.

"Let me tell ya, Sheriff, I don't get the feeling it was your boys either, but it doesn't pass the smell test. Something keeps bringing us back to Kane and for the life of me, I just can't put my finger on it."

36

BY THE TIME Paloma made it to the house, Candace and Tink were sitting at the kitchen table with mugs of coffee in front of them.

"I see you've met my cousin Horace," she began.

"Yep," Candace said stoically. "He scared the shit out of us."

Tink didn't bother to scold her for the language because she felt the same way.

"I understand he saw lights on at the end of the house and was concerned."

"He saw the lights on in my house, so he decided to come in?" Tink demanded.

"Catherine, I have people watching out for you. This is all new. I had my reasons for wanting to show you the place first and this is one of them."

"And how were you going to tell me that someone painted a portrait of me without my permission? I agree with Candace—this place is creepy and I'm going home."

"The portrait isn't of *you*, Catherine," Paloma said softly.

"Apparently you haven't seen the portrait," Tink said, her voice cracking and the tears starting to flow. "Please don't..."

"The portrait is of Olivia. That was her bedroom. Horace, could you get her a tissue?" she asked before sitting beside Tink. "Now you see why I was so taken with you when you arrived. You're a spitting image of your mother. Have you never seen a picture?"

"Yes...yes, but I've only seen profile views where I didn't see her face very well." Tink buried her face in the handkerchief Horace handed her. "That's just...well, it's crazy," Tink said in between sobs. "Why didn't Father ever tell me that I was a dead ringer for her?"

"That might not be the best way to phrase it," Candace said under her breath.

"Your parents made a beautiful couple," Paloma said. "It's only fitting you are so lovely."

"I look like her twin," Tink muttered flatly.

"Not exactly," Paloma replied. "I'm sure the resemblance was uncanny enough for you to assume the portrait was of you, but if you examine it further, you'll discover many differences."

Tink blew her nose on the handkerchief, wiped her eyes, and looked up at Paloma. "I can't believe Father didn't talk more about her. I know so little about my own mother."

Paloma nodded at Horace. "I think I've got it from here," she said, placing her hand on top of Tink's. "Thanks for checking on them. I remember so much about Olivia. She was as beautiful inside as she was out. Her kind spirit would fill a room. I can tell you all that you desire, but I want to do so at the appropriate time. You've had so much to absorb already. I don't want to put too much on you at once."

Tink leaned over and wrapped her arms around Paloma's neck before sinking her head onto her bosom. The tears continued until they became racking sobs. "Thank... Thank you... I can't thank you enough."

"It's been a long night," Paloma whispered. "Go to bed and get a good night's sleep. Tomorrow will be much easier."

IT WAS after two in the morning when the women crawled back in bed. They'd made their way to Tink's bedroom like they were sleep-walking.

"Do you see what I'm talking about now?" Candace asked. "It's just too much. Let's get out of here first thing in the morning."

"I can understand how you could feel that way," Tink answered. "But please see my side. You and Paloma didn't hit it off at first, but I believe she has my best interest at heart. Candace, my mother wouldn't want me to leave so soon. There was a reason why she never fit in here. I have to find out why."

"Listen to yourself," Candace said. "She didn't fit in here—that's all you need to know."

"Try to understand," Tink pleaded. "Go back to work and I'll stay for a few more weeks, maybe even have some improvements done to the place. But I beg you, don't say anything to Father that would bring him concern. He's on the verge of coming to drag me home as it is."

"I don't like it, but I do trust you, Tink. If this is something you must do, then do it. I won't say anything negative to your dad."

"That's why you're my bestie," Tink said with a broad smile. "What will I do without you, Candace? It'll be so lonely."

"For starters, don't go wandering around in the middle of the night. Lock yourself in this room and stay put."

37

TINK HELPED Candace lug the last of her luggage down to the car just as Paloma walked up to the house.

"Good morning, ladies," she said warmly. "I was afraid I might miss saying goodbye, Ms. Candace."

"I can't believe I'm already leaving," Candace said.

"Yes, Ms. Catherine will be quite lonesome without you."

"Please make sure she visits Harriett and you, too," Candace said. "I'll miss her, but I'll keep her updated on the latest gossip at work."

Paloma reached into the pocket of her apron and pulled out a hand-stitched handkerchief. "This is for you," she said, thrusting it toward Candace. "It was made by my ancestors before me. One can never have too many handkerchiefs, I suppose. A woman should always have one nearby. 'Tis for your sad tears and happy ones as well. May you shed more tears of joy than of sadness."

Candace was clearly touched by Paloma's display of kindness. "It's beautiful, Ms. Paloma. I will keep it in my purse always," she said, leaning over to hug her. "Wow, what will you two do without me?"

"Oh, I think we'll make it," Tink said as she and Paloma broke into laughter. "We better get on the road or you'll miss your plane."

"I'm going to take care of some cleaning," Paloma said. "I suppose

I should remove the covers from more of the furniture since you'll be staying awhile."

"That'd be nice," Tink said as she cranked the car. "I can't wait to see what's underneath."

🐚

"I NEED TO RETURN THIS CAR," Tink said after they'd gotten a few miles from the house. "I'm thinking of buying a crappy used car. What do you think?"

"You're thinking of staying that long?"

"Did you not hear me say 'crappy'? I'm talking about a thousand bucks—that's what I'd spend on a rental for a few weeks."

"I don't know, Tink. What if you break down out in the middle of nowhere? Did you forget about the murderer who's on the loose?"

"Well, maybe two grand then," Tink considered. "Would you mind if I stopped at one of those mom-and-pop used-car places on the way? I'd need someone to drive the rental to the airport and something tells me Paloma doesn't have a license."

"Ha! That's a hoot! I'd love to see you negotiate for a clunker. Wouldn't miss it for anything. Your dad would freak out if he could see you."

"But he isn't seeing me and he's not going to hear about it, *is* he?"

"Nope, but I was just thinking of something. Did your grandparents not have a vehicle? If they did, it'd be left to you since everything else was."

"You're right," Tink answered. "That's odd. I'll ask Paloma about it when I get back."

The friends rode silently for over twenty minutes before they saw a used-car lot on the side of the road. "Did you see that?" Tink asked. She quickly made a U-turn and headed back toward the rows of older cars. "This is so exciting!"

"Seriously? I know a lot of people who'd beg to differ with you, myself included," Candace said. "And again, I'll say, your father would have a stroke if he knew what you were doing. Not only are you doing business with a shyster, but you're about to pay for an unreliable piece of—"

"Okay, point taken, but I'm not going to purchase a new car. Father did teach me that's the quickest way to lose money."

They got out of the compact only to be met by the quintessential used-car salesman. "Good morning, beautiful ladies," he said. "What can I do for you today?"

"I'm looking for a reliable used car," Tink replied.

"Like, there is such a thing," Candace muttered.

"Do we have a skeptic in our midst?" the man asked, his left eyebrow raised.

"Been here, done this," Candace said.

"Well you haven't purchased a fine pre-owned vehicle from Lucky Al's Autos, have you?"

"Catchy name," Candace mumbled.

"We aim to please. Name's Al," he said, extending his hand to Tink.

"I never would've guessed," Candace interrupted.

Tink turned to give her the stink eye before turning back to greet Lucky Al. "I'm Tink, nice to meet you."

"As you can see, we have a vast array to choose from," he said as he waved across his limited inventory. "I can point out the best features of each or you could peruse them yourself."

"I love a salesman with an extensive vocabulary," Candace said with a straight face.

Neither of them acknowledged her comment. "I don't want to spend much," Tink continued. "But I don't want anything that's going to break down on me either. What do you recommend?"

"I have a nice 1999 Ford Escort SE in stock," he said.

"You do realize what year it is, don't you?" Candace asked.

"Just ignore her," Tink said. "Do you think it'd be reliable on these back roads?"

"Oh yes," he said. "Come on over. It's the burgundy one in the corner. It's only had one owner and..."

"Does anyone ever buy into that story?" Candace asked. "Let me guess—it was a little old lady who just left it in her garage and never drove it, just polished it every day."

"Candace, really," Tink said. "I don't want you to miss your flight."

"As I was saying," Lucky Al continued, undeterred. "It only has 95,000 miles on it."

"That's because it's already turned over eight times," Candace said.

"It has alloy wheels, a CD player, and rear window defrost. I don't have to tell you how important *that* is," Al said sternly. "Power steering and air-conditioning are some other fine features as well."

"Do they even manufacture cars without those two things anymore?" Candace chimed in.

"Gets thirty-one miles to the gallon and if that don't sell you on it, nuthin' will."

Tink allowed him to open the door before she slid in behind the wheel. "Not very roomy, but I suppose that's not the point. Smells like Granny was a smoker," she said.

"She smoked in it while it was in the garage," Candace added.

"How much?" Tink asked.

"Are you freaking kidding me?" Candace asked. "You *cannot* be serious."

"Two grand," Lucky Al answered.

"She'll give you eight hundred cash," Candace said, stepping up and confronting Al. "Take it or leave it. Otherwise I'll call her father right now and let him know what she's up to. He'll fly down here from Atlanta and have this place shut down in less than an hour for fraudulent odometers."

"You have a deal," Al answered, as he handed Tink the keys. "I'll meet you at my trailer with the paperwork."

With that he took off in a brisk walk in case she changed her mind.

"I can't believe you talked him down twelve hundred dollars! You've missed your calling, Candace," Tink gushed. "It's sort of cute, in its own little way."

"We'll be lucky if it makes it to the airport, but you weren't going to be satisfied until you took part in this low-class escapade. Wanna stop by the pawn shop and sell your jewelry while we're at it?"

"Funny. Real funny. I'm simply saying it makes sense to purchase something rather than renting a car. I can always sell it back to Lucky Al when I fly home."

"Yeah, good luck with that!"

38

"MABREY AND WOODARD, Mildred Murphy speaking, how may I help you?"

The familiar voice gave Tink mixed feelings. Her initial thought was one of homesickness, but that was quickly followed by resentment. Mildred had a way of making her feel like an adolescent.

"Mabrey and—"

"Mildred, it's me," Tink interrupted. "Is Father available to take my call?"

"I'll check, Catherine," she answered.

She knows how much I dislike her calling me that, Tink thought. *When will she retire? I swear she'll work until the day she dies just to anger me.*

The thought was so childish it made Tink giggle. She missed Candace already and had just dropped her off at the airport. Her friend would've understood her hostility toward Mildred.

"Tink?" her father asked. "It's great to hear from you."

It was so good to hear his voice—it was so smooth and confident that it caused a lump to form in her throat. "Father, I'm so glad you were able to take my call. I've missed you."

The comment seemed to throw him off a bit. It wasn't often they shared such sentiments. "And I as well," he countered. "I was beginning to wonder if you'd dropped off the face of the earth."

"Well, I'm pretty close," Tink said with a laugh. "It is Louisiana after all."

"I understand Candace is headed back to work. Do you have any idea when you'll be back?" Augustus asked casually.

"That's what I was calling about," Tink said, stepping into uncharted territory. "I was wondering if I could take a few more weeks."

"A few more weeks?" he asked, his voice growing concerned. "Tink, it was my understanding this was to be a short trip made simply to look at the place. What's going on down there?"

"I literally just got here and there's more that I'd like to do."

"Perhaps you could fill me in," Augustus said, a hint of coolness in his tone. "I haven't even heard the condition of the home."

"It's not as bad as I'd initially anticipated," Tink offered, noting the change in his voice. "Of course, it needs a great deal of restoration, but it's an amazing place, with great bones."

"Restoration? It sounds as though you could be entertaining the idea of remodeling that albatross. I certainly hope that's not the case."

Tink paused long enough to confirm his suspicions. "Father, you know I'm not experienced in that type of thing. But surprisingly there's money left to do so. I can't deny I'd love to see it back to its former glory."

"First of all, what do you know about its former glory?" he asked smugly.

The bluntness of the question, and the tone in which it was presented, hurt her tremendously. But she knew her father and if she allowed his intimidation tactics to work now, she might as well catch the next plane back to Atlanta.

"I don't know anything about its original state, Father, but I can see its potential. I'd like to take the opportunity to learn about my heritage while I'm here. It sounds as though the Sinclairs were incredibly determined people."

"They were boastful and cruel," Augustus stated flatly. "That I *know* to be fact. If you want to delve into the history of a greedy family, I suppose you have the right to do so."

Tink had never heard her father speak so unkindly about anyone and realized there was much she didn't know. "Maybe you'd like to share with me," she suggested. "Why don't you start with how I look exactly like Olivia?"

"She was your mother, Catherine. I've allowed you to refer to her as Olivia through the years because you never knew her, but it's terribly disrespectful."

"And here we go with *Catherine* again. That's always the first clue you'd rather steer away from the subject at hand. But it's long overdue, Father, and I want answers. You've shared so little with me—I find it hard to believe you're surprised by my curiosity. I deserve to know more about her and the Sinclairs, and if you refuse to tell me, I'll find out on my own."

"You sound like a spoiled child."

"Would you like to hear about the house?" Tink asked, deciding to change the direction of the conversation altogether.

"Is it going to fall in on you? That's all I need to know," her father said, a hint of humor in his speech.

Tink went from the verge of tears to excitement in an instant. He wanted to hear about something in her life and she couldn't tell him fast enough. "Well, it's touch and go," she teased. "I know you've been here, many years ago, of course, but isn't it ridiculously large?"

"Indeed. I paid the arrears on that electrical bill, but the next one's yours. Might want to have somebody blow some insulation in those walls."

"Yikes, I don't even want to know what that bill will be."

"You said something about there being money to restore it. I find that hard to believe after knowing Olivia's parents. How much are you talking?"

"Over four million," Tink replied.

"Four million *dollars*?" Augustus asked incredulously. "I have to admit I'm shocked. Why didn't they keep the house up?"

"They weren't aware of the money," Tink answered. "According to the attorney, Olivia's—I mean Mother's—father was quite reckless with money. His father hid the account from him."

"Account? As in the four million was in an account at a bank? You've got to be kidding me."

"Apparently so."

"Is it still there?" he asked, his voice rising with concern.

"No. Believe it or not, I have a cashier's check."

"Where are you?"

"What?"

"Where are you right now?"

"I just dropped Candace off at the airport."

"What did you do with the cashier's check?"

"It's in my purse."

"Jesus Christ, Tink," Augustus said. "Don't drive back to Kane with that check and don't leave New Orleans until I figure something out. I knew I should've taken off and gone with you. This is the most absurd situation I've ever heard of. Besides the fact the money has been sitting in a bank making minimal interest, it's a miracle it's still there at all."

"I believe I've handled things fairly well so far," Tink said defensively. The last thing she wanted or needed now was for her father to fly out to Kane.

"And you're certain you'd like to restore some of the estate?" Augustus asked.

"I'm not ruling it out. Don't worry, Father, I'm not leaving Atlanta, but I'm not sure what I want to do with the property. Besides, you've always told me real estate was the safest investment."

"I wasn't referring to the bayou," he noted dryly. "But here we are. Let me think. That money needs to be invested and the sooner the better."

"But it needs to be accessible," Tink said. "I don't want to put it in a CD where I'm penalized when I take some out."

"We're not talking about a CD," Augustus said. "You're so naïve, Tink."

Normally the comment would've stung, but he hadn't called her Catherine, which softened the blow.

"We're talking four *million* dollars."

"I'm aware of that," Tink said. "I'm on the highway now. Do I pull over at the next exit?"

"Yes, go into town and have lunch, preferably at one of the finer hotels. I'd feel much better knowing you're at a safe place. New Orleans has more than its share of seedy places. I'll contact some investors I know in that area to discuss the best way to capitalize on your money."

"All right. I'll take the next exit and go back into the city. I take it you want me to wait on your call."

"Exactly. And whatever you do, don't let anyone get their eye on that cashier's check."

39

BEN AND DAN NORWOOD gave each other a high five followed by a hearty bear hug. It felt damn good for the gator season to be over. The older they got, the longer the season seemed to last, but the end of the hunting season was indeed a time of celebration. They'd used all the tags they'd been allotted, sold the meat at market prices, and had forty skins drying that'd net them one helluva profit. Now it was time to get back to the daily routine of running their taxidermy business.

"Let me buy you and Harriett dinner in the big city," Ben offered. "This has been the most difficult season yet and we deserve an indulgence."

"Sounds good to me, but I sent Hazel back from whence she came, so we don't have a sitter. Not that she'd be a trustworthy one, might I add," Dan said.

"What about Paloma?" Ben asked. "I bet she'd be delighted to keep Landry. You know how she loves babies."

"Hmmm," Dan considered. "That could be a possibility. But there'd have to be a catch."

"A catch? Want me to spring for the babysitter fee?"

"Hardly," Dan said with a laugh. "You'd be the odd man out on a date."

"The old third wheel adage." Ben pondered. "So, you want me to babysit *and* pay for the dinner I don't get to enjoy? Not very considerate of you, but I guess I'd do it for Harriett."

"You honestly think I'd let you babysit? Now *that's* a stretch. I was talking about you getting a date. I know it's a foreign concept, but you're a big boy now, and I'm tired of you tagging along like a puppy."

"Oh, no you didn't," Ben said, feigning shock. "A *puppy*? Come on, you can do better than that. Want me to bring Cassius?"

"I'm not even going to dignify that with a response. You know what I'm hinting at; if not, you're beyond help."

"Maybe I just want to hear you say it," Ben teased.

"You're such a child, no wonder people think I'm the oldest."

"They think you're the oldest because you're an oversized Goliath."

"Just give her a call," Dan concluded. "Harriett and I will reach out to Paloma."

AS BOTH MEN were finishing up the final cleaning on the boat, Sheriff Broussard pulled up. "Evenin' gentlemen," he said as he removed his hat and offered his hand to both.

"What's up, Sheriff?" Ben asked. "I hope you aren't the bearer of bad news."

"Not any *new* bad news," he quickly added. "Just more of the same. Do you fellas have a few minutes to talk?"

Ben looked at his brother who nodded in agreement. "I guess so, Sheriff," Dan said. "It's the end of the season, so hopefully this will be the last time I'll get home late for a while."

"Come on in," Ben said as he dried off his hands. "Can't promise the place is tidied up, but I haven't been home much lately."

Ben grabbed three beers out of the fridge and offered his recliner to Isaac. "I hope you aren't here to tell us we have to meet with those two clowns from the state again."

"No, they don't consider either of you suspects, but they had to play the game."

"And what did it accomplish?" Dan asked. "It was a waste of everybody's time."

"Well, when you find two dead bodies, you have to expect to be questioned at some point," Isaac said. "They were at my office when I got there this morning and weren't very happy about not having a suspect."

"I don't doubt it," Ben said.

"They're not bad guys—just a little arrogant is all. I don't have any doubts they want these murders solved as much as I do."

"They've got to have *something*," Dan said. "Don't they have *any* suspects?"

"No, not really. But they did bring up a valid question," Isaac said, pausing to twist the cap off his beer. "What does Kane have to do with the murders?"

"How could Kane have anything to do with it?" Ben asked. "I assumed it was just a dumping ground for two no-good cons who came looking for work at the rigs."

"That's what everyone assumed," Isaac agreed. "But, let's think from their vantage point. If it was someone in that group of drifters who killed them, why would they come all the way to Kane to dump their bodies? And ultimately, how would they get them out onto the bayou? They'd have to have a boat. And think about how both bodies were found on your lines. Kind of a coincidence, don't you think?"

"Don't tell me you think we're behind all of this," Dan said.

"Oh, good Lord," Isaac grunted. "You boys know better than that."

"Then who would kill two strangers and dump them where Dan and I would discover them?" Ben asked.

"I've known you both since the day you were born, and I'd never believe either of you are capable of such a thing. However, I do wonder who'd have a motive to make it appear as if you did."

"Everybody we know lives in Kane," Dan said. "And I can't imagine any of them doing something so horrific. And they'd certainly have no reason to frame us."

Isaac took a swig from his beer and furrowed his brow. "Let's think about this, fellas. Are either of you aware of anyone with a closet drug problem? Anyone who might be buying drugs from those motels?"

"Hell no," Ben said. "There's no way we'd have anything to do with drugs. That's absurd."

"Whoever this is has to have access to a boat and have some knowledge of the bayou. Agent Westmoreland was right when he said there's no way a novice could know where your lines would be. It'd make more sense for the murderer to just dump the bodies in the water. They clearly wanted them to be found."

"And be found on *our* lines," Ben said.

"But think about it, Ben," Dan spoke up. "Why kill two people we don't know and place them on our lines? We've never had a problem with anybody, not even a stranger."

"Maybe someone's doing it to throw off their motive," Ben suggested. "That'd be the only thing that makes any sense. Have you looked into the people who've moved to Kane recently, Sheriff?"

"It'd be virtually impossible to do that," Isaac answered. "I could run the records of anyone who's rented a residence or purchased one recently, but there's no accounting for all the visitors coming and going, to say nothing of those purchasing illegal drugs. It'd put a terrible strain on us just to account for those listed on rental agreements. We're a small department."

"Maybe it's just coincidence they found two lines in our territory," Dan said. "There's hundreds of men working those rigs and let's face it, Louisiana's full of bayous. If you know one, you know them all."

"So, we're at square one," Isaac said, dropping his head to look at his laced fingers. "Sadly, we don't know if this is the end of it. I keep going back to the hands being cut off. As crazy as it sounds, it brings me some sense of relief. What does that type of act suggest to you?"

"My initial thought is it'd be payback for a thief and would certainly send a message to anyone else even considering stealing," Dan said.

"My thoughts exactly," the sheriff agreed. "So hopefully it's the end of it."

40

Tink sat down for lunch at the Roosevelt Hotel while she waited on her father to give her further instructions. Her phone rang just as her chilled tomato soup with pickled shrimp and cucumber arrived. She thanked the waiter and reached for her cell. "Hello, Father?"

"Hi, Tink. I was able to reach Justine Waterstone at Morgan Stanley. She can see you in thirty minutes, but no later. She's squeezing you in."

"What do you want me to do?" she asked. "Am I to trust her judgment and sign the check over to her?"

"You aren't signing the check over to her," Augustus said. "She'll invest it in what she feels is best."

"My only concern is if I'll have access to the funds when I need them. If I decide to make some renovations, I'll need a steady flow of cash."

"It typically takes three to four days to make a draw from a particular investment but it's not a problem. I'll have her transfer some of the money to your account with Bank of America, which should get you started. However, you don't need to jump into a project like that headfirst. Neither of us have any knowledge of building, much less restoration. You'll need a well-respected contractor."

"I know, Father. I'm not even certain I'll do it. I just want the option available should I decide to."

"Very well, call me after you meet with her. And Tink..."

"Yes?"

"Stay in touch. It causes me tremendous concern when I can't reach you."

"I will, Father, and I'll see you soon, I promise."

TINK WAS RELIEVED to leave the office of Ms. Waterstone and head back to Kane. She'd parked four blocks from the office to ensure the investor hadn't seen the rusty old car. She'd surely think Tink was crazy.

Halfway back to Kane, the air conditioning had pooped out and she'd considered stopping by Lucky Al's but decided it'd be a fruitless effort. He had the money, she had the car—the deal was over.

She made a mental note to herself to inquire about her grandfather's vehicles. Surely, he had an automobile. She passed the ramshackle gas station that'd belonged to the strange old man and instinctually looked down at her gas gauge.

Great, it's almost empty. Like I expected Lucky Al to fill it up. Tink checked her rearview mirror before making a U-turn to fill up her gas tank. It was the last place on earth she wanted to purchase fuel, but it beat running out along the desolate roadway.

Tink pulled up to a pump and dug through her purse for a twenty. She planned on a quick in and out, making conversation unnecessary. She opened the door, expecting to see Thomas, but was shocked to find a woman behind the register.

"Good afternoon," the lady said kindly.

Tink struggled to mask the flash of astonishment crossing her face but it didn't go unnoticed.

"Expecting a grumpy old man, were you?" the woman teased.

"I'm sorry. I've only been here once and wasn't sure what to expect."

"Allow me to introduce myself," she began with a strong southern twang. "I'm Opal Bailey-Blanchard. Thomas is my husband."

"It's nice to meet you," Tink said. "Is that a Georgian accent I detect?"

Opal covered her mouth as she laughed. "Close. I'm from Tennessee. Where are you from?"

"I'm from Atlanta," Tink answered. "I'm just here visiting."

"You're certainly a beautiful young lady," Opal said. "I'm originally from Chattanooga, but that was many, many years ago. I never could drop the accent—not that'd I want a Cajun one, mind you."

The comment made Tink smile. She instantly liked the woman with shoulder-length brown hair and an inviting smile, though she had no idea why she would have married Thomas.

"It's nice to meet a neighbor of sorts," Tink said genuinely. "I haven't been here long but I'm certainly out of my element."

"Oh dear, if anyone can relate, it's me. I met Thomas through a cousin who'd moved here to purchase a shrimp boat. He highly oversold the place, so I moved down the summer after I graduated from college. Thomas was young and handsome, and very persuasive. I stayed to keep the books for my cousin's business and before I knew it, Thomas had proposed."

"What a nice love story," Tink said, wondering just how persuasive and good-looking Thomas could've been in his youth.

"It wasn't all a bed of roses," Opal continued. "I insisted on hyphenating my name when we married, which went over like a lead balloon around these parts." She paused to playfully roll her eyes and reminisce. "People thought I was a women's lib fanatic from the big city and never took too kindly to me after that. But, hey, I'm still here so there must be something good about the place."

"Well, it's been nice to meet you, Ms. Opal Bailey-Blanchard," Tink said with a smile. "And I can't imagine anyone not taking to you. Hopefully, I'll see you again before I head back."

"Same to you, dear," Opal said as she put the twenty-dollar bill in the cash register. "Would you like for me to pump that gas for you?"

"No ma'am," Tink answered. "I'm used to doing that myself."

As Tink rounded the curve near the estate, she was reminded of when she and Candace had arrived. Her stomach had been in such a knot she'd almost denied herself the privilege of seeing the place.

Turning into the drive, she couldn't help but wince at the entrance. It had initially appeared creepy to her, but now simply looked dilapidated. The thought of it being the first part of the estate visitors would see made her cringe. Perhaps she'd use it as an excuse to phone Ben Norwood. It'd be her first project and quite possibly a deal breaker.

Even with her window rolled down, she could feel sweat running down her face. The sun was directly overhead, illuminating all the shortcomings of the property. No doubt it had tremendous potential, but it'd be months, maybe even years, before everything could be done. Provided, of course, there were no major issues. Tink had seen enough renovation shows on television to know the biggest problems were hidden underneath the first couple of layers.

When the house came into view, Tink released a sigh of relief. She was looking forward to getting out of the hot car. And even though she'd miss Candace, she was looking forward to rummaging through the house alone.

The front door was standing open so Tink assumed Paloma was busy cleaning inside. She grabbed her purse from the passenger's side but didn't bother getting her key ring. Wiping the sweat from her brow, she pulled her black hair back and put it in a ponytail.

"Hello?" she called as she entered the home. "Paloma? I'm back and don't want to startle you." Tink closed the door and locked it before making her way toward the kitchen.

Before she could get there, she saw it, and her mind went blank. She tried to scream but nothing came out. Tink felt her hands reach for her throat as if to coax it into shrieking. Still nothing. Her breathing was erratic, and she feared losing consciousness. She planted a hand on the wall to steady herself until she could regulate her breathing.

Get your cell phone, her mind urged.

Tink dug through her purse, running her fingers over every object until feeling the thin cell phone. After pulling it from her bag, she punched in 911 and waited for a connection. When she didn't hear it ringing, she moved closer to the kitchen in hopes of getting service. After about eight seconds, it rang.

"Kane 911, Roxie speaking, what's your emergency?"

"I...I need someone to come out. My home's been vandalized. There are threats. I'm petrified..."

"What's your address, ma'am?"

Tink struggled to remember the address, even the street name, but came up with nothing. "I can't remember," she stammered. "It's the... It's the Sinclair estate. Please, send someone quick. I'm not sure if they're still in the house."

"Are you in a situation where you can exit the home, ma'am?" Roxie asked.

"I'm not sure," Tink answered, breaking into tears and shaking uncontrollably. "I locked the front door behind me and I'm halfway in the estate. I'm afraid to move one way or the other. Can you *please* just get someone here for me?"

"Can you hear anyone?" Roxie asked softly. "Do you hear any movement in the home?"

Tink tried desperately to be quiet but her breathing was so frantic that it was difficult to hear above it. "I don't know. I'm panicking and I'm seriously afraid I'll pass out. Help me."

"They're on their way, ma'am. Stay on the phone with me. You'll be fine."

Tink dropped her cell and ran for the front door, unaware if anyone was running after her. She unlocked the front door and ran out into the sunshine. With her purse inside, she didn't have her car keys, so she turned and fled behind the house and toward the bayou. She wondered if she was losing her mind or if she heard the crunching of gravel under tires.

She hid behind a large oak to catch her breath. It was indeed a car pulling up the drive and it had come to a stop. Someone got out and

Tink heard a car door slam. Peeking from behind the large tree, she recognized Cassius.

"Cassius! Cassius!" Tink screamed. "I'm here. Wait for me."

Cassius put his hand on his weapon as a precaution. "Tink? Are you okay?"

She ran to him and fell into his arms. "Oh my God, someone was in the house, they left the door open and…"

Cassius awkwardly put his arms around her and patted her uneasily. "It's okay, I'm here. Did you see anyone?"

"No, the door was open when—"

"Catherine! Catherine!" Paloma was screaming as she ran toward them. Her face was bright red and she was gasping.

"I'm okay, Paloma," Tink answered, running to meet her. "Help me, Cassius. She's going to have a heart attack!"

Cassius and Tink had Paloma by her arms and were practically carrying her to the police cruiser. Cassius cranked it and turned on the air as high as it would go. "Here," he said, thrusting a bottled water toward Paloma. "I've already had a couple of sips from it, but it's cold."

Paloma sipped slowly and leaned toward the cool air flowing from the vents.

"Someone's been in the house," Tink said. "You shouldn't have run in this heat, Paloma."

"I'm okay, child," Paloma said as she sipped from the water again. "I was just so frightened. Is anything missing?"

"I only got a few feet inside and…"

They were interrupted by someone screaming out for Paloma. Cassius walked to meet the newcomer.

"I need to see Paloma," Tink heard him tell the officer. "It's urgent."

"Ms. Paloma," Cassius said in a soft voice, "Horace is here. Do you feel up to speaking with him?"

She nodded and started to get out of the car. "No, ma'am, not yet," Cassius cautioned. "Stay near the cool air and continue taking small sips from the water. I'll bring him over here."

"Paloma," Horace began as he, too, gasped for air having run from the bayou. "It's urgent, very urgent. Zoya's father has brought her in the pirogue and she's barely alive."

"Sweet Jesus," Paloma whispered. She paused briefly to instruct Cassius to help Horace get Zoya to his cruiser to transport her to the hospital.

"I'll radio for an ambulance, Ms. Paloma," Cassius said. "I don't have medical training and—"

"There isn't time for that, Cassius. Do as I say."

The two men ran toward the bayou, leaving the two women alone.

"Who is Zoya?" Tink asked, feeling as if her whole world was falling apart.

"She's a very ill young woman who is frightened of doctors," Paloma answered.

"Why come to you?"

"I'm a traiteur, child," Paloma answered. "I'm not a witch doctor so don't go letting your mind run away with you. I simply lift prayers up on others' behalf. But my prayers, like your own, work hand-in-hand with those God has blessed with medical training. Many people here believe doctors mean us harm."

A dark, older man was running beside Cassius and Horace, screaming in a language Tink had never heard. She stood back from the vehicle as they put a bundle of bright, patterned material in the backseat of the car. Apparently, there was a young woman inside, too small and frail to see.

Horace stepped away from the chaos and closed the car door. The father had exchanged the front seat with Paloma, who had gotten in the back with the ill woman.

"I'll radio the sheriff," Cassius said. "He'll be here right away. Horace, don't leave her side, and Tink, don't go back in that house until the sheriff has arrived."

Tink stood dumbfounded, unsure of what to do or say.

41

HORACE AND TINK were sitting on the front steps when Sheriff Broussard and Ben Norwood pulled up. Tink was too hot and too nervous to stand to greet them, but Horace was beside the car before they got out.

"Afternoon, Sheriff," he said. "It's been a tough day and the sun hasn't even set. I'm afraid the worst has yet to happen."

"What makes you say that?" Isaac asked. "What's happening, Horace?"

"One of the young women who's been seeking prayers from Paloma has been rushed to the hospital by one of your deputies. Paloma and the woman's father are with him. And to top it off, Ms. Catherine here got the wits scared out of her."

"What happened, Tink?" Ben asked, rushing up the stairs and offering his hand to pull her up. The sheriff and Horace joined them on the porch.

"I'd just gotten here, and the front door was ajar. I assumed Paloma was here cleaning, so I went on in. I had just made it a few feet toward the kitchen when I saw it... It..." Tink was struggling not to break down but was failing miserably. Ben reached for her hand and held it firmly.

"It's okay, Tink," he assured her. "We're here now and nobody can hurt you. Is someone hurt inside?"

"No, no one's inside. There's a dummy—a mannequin, I mean. It's covered in blood...or something that *looks* like blood...and has on a long, black wig. The hands aren't attached and..."

"Sheriff, why don't you go check it out?" Ben asked. "I don't have a gun with me and someone could still be inside. If not, we need to get that shit out of there so she can get in the air conditioning. It's too hot for her out here and she's so upset."

"Ben, can I speak to you a second?" Isaac asked, nodding away from the stairs. "Horace, would you sit with Catherine while we figure out what's going on here?"

"Yes, certainly, Sheriff," Horace answered as he reached for Tink's hand and walked her toward the row of rocking chairs.

🦪

As soon as they were out of earshot, Isaac spoke quietly to Ben. "I don't like this. I don't like it at all. If it's a mannequin with the hands removed, it's clearly related to the murders or, at the least, a warning Catherine could be next. I'll go inside to make sure all is clear, but I doubt they're still here. This has just taken a twist I never suspected."

"She doesn't know anybody here. Why *warn* her at all? Warn her about *what*, for that matter? They didn't bother to warn the other two."

"Well, we don't know that, Ben."

"Know what?" Ben asked, his mind whirling.

"We don't know that they weren't warned. And frankly, we don't know anything about this girl either. If you ask me, she's the newest person in town and—"

"And what, Sheriff? She may be cutting people's hands off and lugging them through the bayou? And then to top it off, she's placing a staged mannequin in her own house to scare herself?"

"Ben..."

"Just go check out the house, Sheriff. This whole thing is unsettling as hell," Ben seethed as he walked back to join Horace and Tink.

42

AFTER GETTING an update from Zoya's father on the girl's condition, Paloma made her way to the waiting room to find Cassius. By the time she located him, she was frantic all over again.

"Have you spoken with the sheriff?" she asked as she slid onto a chair beside him.

"Not yet," he answered. "I'm sure he's taking care of everything. He called when he was almost there, and Ben was with him. How's the girl?"

"She's anemic, her iron was extremely low. She'll be fine but I'm certain they'll keep her overnight for observation."

"Listen, Ms. Paloma, I know this sounds callous, but I'm sure the sheriff's expecting me back at work. Are you going to stay here with them?"

"That won't be necessary. I'm sure her father will stay. I'll need to speak with him and the nurses because of the language barrier and... Well, he's very skeptical of hospitals and doctors."

"I sure wish they'd get past all those fears," Cassius said. "I mean, she could be dead right now."

"It's their culture," Paloma replied warmly. "I'm certain it's difficult for others to understand, but somewhere in their lineage their ancestors had reason to feel the way they do."

"But things are different now," Cassius insisted.

"Yes, some things are, but some aren't. Perhaps time will begin to change their outlook. Situations such as this," Paloma said as she waved her hand across the waiting room, "will do wonders to encourage them to seek medical help."

"So, are you going to catch a ride back to Kane with me?"

"If you could wait just a few minutes for me to explain everything to the proper people. Cassius, I was running to the estate in such a hurry that I forgot my keys and everything. I don't have any money on me, and I hate to leave Zoya's father without anything to eat all night. Could you possibly loan me a few dollars? I can pay you back as soon as we get back to Kane."

"Certainly," Cassius said, digging in his wallet and pulling out two ten-dollar bills. "Don't worry about paying me back. Everyone needs to do something good every now and then."

"I agree, Cassius. Looks like you're turning into a man after all," Paloma said as she leaned to kiss him on the cheek. "I'll be back as soon as I can."

43

HORACE HAD ROCKED SILENTLY on the porch beside Tink. Although she knew nothing about him other than he was Paloma's cousin, he provided a sense of strength. He had the same comforting persona as Paloma, which had been the only thing keeping her from getting in the old car and heading straight to the airport.

Horace was clearly a patient man, but Tink could sense his need to talk about what had happened. She turned to face him and forced a smile. "What's this about, Mr. Horace?" she asked.

"I don't know, Ms. Catherine, but the sheriff will get to the bottom of it. He's a good man, a good sheriff, and he won't let anything happen to you."

"Could I just be Catherine?"

"What do you mean?"

"You don't need to call me Ms. Catherine. I'm just Catherine. Ms. Paloma does that too."

"You just did it."

"Excuse me?"

"You called my cousin, Ms. Paloma, and me, Mr. Horace. We are simple people. There's no Sinclair blood in our veins."

"So that's what this is about," Tink replied. "You're calling me that out of respect because my family owned this house. It doesn't make me any more important than you. We're all people."

"That's big city talk," Horace said, reaching over to pat her arm. "That's not bayou talk."

"Clearly bayou talk needs to change," Tink said. "I appreciate your respect, but the way I see it, we're somehow family and I like that. I have plenty of friends, but not near enough family."

That seemed to please Horace, whose eyes glistened as he looked out over the land.

The screen door slammed behind Isaac and Ben as they came out on the porch, wearing expressions of concern. They leaned on the railing in front of Tink and Horace.

"That was some sick stunt someone pulled," the sheriff began. "It's just a mannequin and the blood isn't real. It has a sweet smell to it, so they must have made it—looks pretty damn real though. I'm sure it scared you."

"Yes, it did," Tink agreed. "Who'd do something like that and why?"

"That's the fifty-thousand-dollar question," Ben said. "Who do you know here in Kane?"

"Absolutely no one," Tink said. "I mean, I know Paloma and Horace. But I only met them when I arrived. I left Kane when I was a week old and haven't returned until I got the news about inheriting the estate. My father told me next to nothing about my mother's side of the family, so I don't even recognize the people in the portraits inside what is now my house."

"I wish I had some answers," the sheriff said. "But I'm at a loss. What do you think, Horace? Have you seen any strangers around here or on your property?"

"No, sir," Horace quickly answered. "You know we keep our eyes out for folks who don't have any business around here."

"Do you own property nearby?" Tink asked, having assumed he lived down by the bayou near Paloma.

"Yes," he answered. "Our family inherited property from the

Sinclairs a few years after this house was built. It's been passed down through the family just as this has."

"Is it very far?" she pressed.

"No, it's right next to you, a few acres away. We have an old home house, but Paloma has always had a love for the bayou. She chose to stay in those quarters when she was young, and I could never convince her to live with us."

"How's Jericho?" Isaac asked.

"Doing okay. Could be better, but at ninety years old you're not going to be as spry as you once were," Horace answered.

"I can understand that," Isaac agreed. "I have days when I feel ninety, myself."

That brought a chuckle from Horace.

"Who's Jericho?" Tink asked.

"My father and Paloma's uncle," Horace told her. "You'll meet him soon enough. He doesn't leave home much anymore—too old and set in his ways."

"First the murders, now this," Ben interrupted. "And it all started around the time Tink showed up. What's the connection?"

"I swear," Tink began defensively, "there's absolutely no connection between me and any murders."

"I'm not suggesting you had anything to do with it," Ben quickly assured her. "But you have to admit it's odd that it coincided with your inheritance and arrival in Kane. Normally I'd never connect those two things with the murders, but now we're dealing with this." He waved toward the house in disgust.

"Speaking of that," Tink said, pointing to the screen door, "would you and the sheriff mind taking it out of here? I'm not going to allow anyone to scare me away. It's hot as Hades out here and I have work to do inside. I have a house to restore."

Ben, Horace, and Isaac looked at her as though she had two heads.

"You can't be serious," Isaac said. "That mannequin may have been placed there to frighten you, but they could've just as well killed you. It's not a game."

"How dare you even suggest I consider this a game?" Tink fumed. "The last thing I expected to come home to was a scene staged to scare the life out of me."

"I'm sure the sheriff didn't mean any offense by that," Ben said.

"How do you know what he meant, Ben?" Tink asked angrily. "All I know is that I arrived home to find that...that bloody thing in the house and when the sheriff arrived, I was suddenly blamed for his unsolved crimes. In fact, I'll get the damn thing out myself," she said defiantly. "I believe we're finished here."

"Ms. Sinclair—" Isaac began.

"It's Ms. Mabrey," Tink corrected, instantly ashamed of her abhorrent behavior.

"Ms. Mabrey, please allow me to apologize. It seems we've gotten off on the wrong foot and it's no one's fault but my own. I take this display in your house as seriously as I'm taking these murders, I *assure* you. There's no reason for me to suspect you're involved in any way, but I do have cause for concern about your well-being. Things, bad things, are happening here, and I don't have an explanation for them. That's not a good position for me to be in."

Tink hung her head. "Forgive me, Sheriff. It's so unlike me to lash out at anyone. I suppose it's because I've been determined to take care of this...well, this house situation without anyone's help. Clearly, I'm failing miserably. I should've just put it on the market without even coming out here like my father said."

"You don't mean that," Isaac said. "I'll have one of our deputies keep an eye out around here, but please be careful."

"I will," she assured him.

Cassius pulled up with Paloma before they continued. Paloma looked tired and much older than she had when she'd left for the hospital earlier.

"What happened?" Cassius asked. "I didn't expect you both to still be here."

Paloma made her way to Tink and gave her a light squeeze. "How are you, dear? I'm terribly sorry this has happened. I'll stay up here with you tonight."

"I'll be glad to stay," Ben said. "I think you ladies need a man here, especially at night. With gator season over, I don't have anything pressing. I can work my own schedule and be here should you need me. What do you think, Tink?"

"The house is certainly big enough," she said, looking to Paloma for guidance.

"I'm not against having a man here," Paloma said. "But my first concern is why something like this happened in the first place. Isaac, I'm sure you'll be looking into what's going on."

"Yes, I will," the sheriff promised. "But unfortunately, I'll have to share this with the two investigators from the state. They're in charge of the investigation and this incident has to be tied to the murders, same MO."

"Not those two goof-offs," Ben moaned. "I understand why you need to let them in on it, Isaac, but I don't like dealing with them, especially the older fella."

"They have access to a great deal of resources, Ben," Isaac said. "I'm not their biggest fan either, but there are times when we simply have to suck it up."

"Thank you for your time, Isaac," Paloma said. "I'm sure you have more work to get to before getting home to your family."

"You're the only person who ever concerns themselves with my life outside of the department," he said warmly. "That's what makes you special, Ms. Paloma. Are you going to catch a ride, Ben?"

"Guess I better. I have to pick up my truck, ladies, but I'll be back later so keep the light on."

"Can we give you a lift, Horace?" Isaac asked. "I don't see your truck here."

"That'd be appreciated, Sheriff. I should be getting back to Papa, I'm sure he's wondering if I've left for good by now. I walked down to visit Paloma when Zoya's father came up in the pirogue. It's been quite a day since then."

"Indeed," Paloma agreed. "She's going to be fine but could still use our prayers."

44

HORACE'S HEART was heavy as he rode in the backseat of the sheriff's cruiser. His father was now an old man, his heart weak, and he'd be troubled to learn of what was happening in Kane. Horace hadn't told him about the murders, neither had known the couple, and without a television or newspaper to bring it to Jericho's attention, he was certainly no worse for the wear. But it was closer to home now and involved the Sinclair home. Horace could no longer justify keeping such news from his father.

It was a short ride home; one Horace could've easily walked within minutes. But his concern for Jericho was so deep that getting to him even a few seconds earlier would ease his mind. Ben got out of the front and opened the back door of the vehicle for him. The two men shook hands and Horace waved at them both as the sheriff drove away.

He quickly opened the door and called for his father. Jericho had been standing on the back porch throwing bird seed out for the red birds that'd eat the seed in the early morning hours.

"I'm out here," he shouted in a raspy voice.

"Sorry," Horace began. "Didn't mean to be gone so long. Are you hungry?"

"I'm not an invalid," Jericho said. "I had a sandwich about an hour ago. What happened to you? Is Paloma alright?"

"Yes, I ran into a couple of problems," Horace began. "A young woman who's been seeing Paloma was near death when her father brought her to Paloma's quarters."

"That's not good," Jericho commented. "Was Paloma able to help her?"

"She prayed for her, Papa, but there are times when doctors are needed. God gives them the ability to heal," Horace added as if his father would have a better chance of understanding if he gave God the ultimate credit.

"I see," was all Jericho commented. "You mentioned a couple of problems. Were there more?"

"Unfortunately there were," Horace answered, pausing before he continued with what would surely upset his father.

"Spit it out," Jericho said bluntly. "I'm ninety years old, I don't have time to waste."

"Here," Horace suggested. "Have a seat. It's troubling."

"Troubling you say?"

"There was trouble at the Sinclair place."

Jericho placed the seed in his hand back into the sack and turned to his son, the youngest of his thirteen children. "What kind of trouble?"

"It's a long tale, Papa."

"I don't have a bus to catch."

"Let's go inside and sit at the table. It's not something one would discuss standing up."

Jericho's eyes reflected deep concern making Horace wonder what he could possibly think had happened. As far as his father knew, the last of the Sinclairs had passed away when Baron died.

The two men walked solemnly into the house where Horace ran water in the kettle and put in on the stove. He rambled through the cabinets for an acceptable snack to place on the table at a time such as this but failed to locate one.

"Enough stalling, cut to the chase."

His father was right, he was indeed delaying the news. "There have been two murders in Kane in the past week. Both were drifters from down by the rigs, no one here knew them. The Norwood brothers found them on their lines, it's gator season, you know?"

"*I* know when gator season is. It's been the same for years, don't patronize me."

"All right. The victims were mutilated. No one's sure why. Did you know the Sinclairs had an heir?"

"I know Olivia had a daughter, but I wasn't sure if Baron would leave the estate to her. He, well... you knew Baron. He was unpredictable. But, get back to the murders. Why were they mutilated and more importantly, why didn't you share it with me?"

"It wasn't important," Horace said. "Why worry you over a couple of murders that had nothing to do with us?"

"Kane is our home, son. I may be old but I'm not insensitive. Hopefully Isaac will get to the bottom of it, but in the meantime, stay away from those gypsies. They're up to no good. I never thought I'd live to see such foolishness."

"Yeah, it's not good."

"Horace, I know you as well as I know myself. I love all my children, but God blessed me double with you. You're the only one who's loved this place as much as I have."

Horace nodded in agreement but what he wanted to say was that it wasn't the bayou he loved; it was his father. It was his father who'd taken the time to teach him all he knew about the land; the land passed down by a brave woman named Prudence.

"So, tell me about Olivia's daughter," Jericho pressed. "Is she as lovely as her mother? Kind too?"

"Yes, and yes, but this isn't easy on her. She's from Atlanta, and Kane is a foreign place to her, and..."

"What aren't you telling me? There's something troubling you."

"Yes, it is, Papa. This young lady is kind and strong, although she doesn't yet realize her strength."

"Then what's the problem? We all learn of our strength when we're required to use it."

"Someone is trying to either frame or intimidate her."

"*Frame* her? Frame her for *what*?"

"These murders in town," Horace said quietly.

"Speak up, son," Jericho insisted. "Perhaps it is time you found your strength as well."

His father was right, and Horace knew it. He wasn't afraid of his father; Horace just didn't like sharing news that would upset him. He'd worked hard all his life, and if nothing else, Jericho deserved peace in his later years.

"It's the oddest thing," Horace began, "but whoever murdered the couple cut their hands off."

When his father didn't immediately respond, Horace looked up at him and was shocked by his expression. Jericho's eyes were opened wide with shock and his mouth was agape. His breathing had quickened.

"Are you alright, Papa?"

"Sweet, sweet Jesus," Jericho gasped. "I've prayed ten thousand prayers that I'd never live to see the Sinclairs' sins come back to haunt them," he whispered. "Some secrets should stay buried where they belong."

"Wha... what are you talking about? Papa? Please tell me what you're talking about?"

His father seemed almost trancelike and it was frightening Horace. He shouldn't have shared any of this with him, he was too old, it was wrong.

"Horace, listen to me, son," Jericho said, as his eyes seemed to clear and come into focus. "Go into my room and get the wooden box out of the cedar chest at the end of the bed. Don't waste time, go."

Horace walked quickly into his father's room and opened the chest. He found the wooden box under a quilt and returned to the kitchen.

"Now get the key from the drawer next to the refrigerator," Jericho said firmly. His gnarled hands struggled with the key, but he refused to allow Horace to open it for him.

"My days on this earth are numbered, son. God blessed me with more children, grandchildren and great grandchildren than I've deserved. I've been honored to father thirteen college graduates now scattered across this country, with fancy careers and thriving families. I'm especially fortunate you chose to farm this land after finishing your master's in agriculture. You've brought me joy *and* you are a *fine* cane farmer. Son, I have no regrets when the good Lord calls me home. You shouldn't either, do you hear me?"

Horace nodded, not trusting his voice to speak. He struggled to keep the tears pooled in his eyes from overflowing down his dark cheeks.

"Although you're a Leblanc, you're just as much a part of the Sinclair family, don't forget that. Although their sins have been many, there was much to be proud of in their lineage. They were kind and hard-working people, minus a couple of bad seeds, which every family is destined to have. Understand, son?"

Horace nodded affirmatively.

"I don't doubt they loved us, the Leblanc's, as deeply as they loved their own, in the best way they knew how. Olivia was different, she was strong, she wasn't going to stand for wrong. You make sure her daughter knows that, understand?"

Again, Horace nodded.

"There were only two tangible things, other than land, that have been passed down through generations of Sinclairs, two *important* items, that is. I'm not referring to furniture, or paintings, or frivolous non-sense – no, sir." He said as he pulled a linen handkerchief from the box slowly unwrapping it to reveal a beautiful, old pocket watch.

"Traditionally the Sinclair men handed this down to their male heirs. When it was Mr. Corbin's time; he came to me instead of Mr. Baron." Jericho paused to catch his breath.

"You see, Mr. Baron was one of the bad seeds; Mr. Corbin was deeply hurt by all Baron's shenanigans. So, he chose me." Jericho paused again. Horace wasn't sure if his father was reminiscing or becoming too emotional to speak.

"Corbin made me swear to secretly keep these in the LeBlanc Family."

Handing the watch to Horace, Jericho explained, "This belonged to Claude Sinclair, the man who originally purchased this land. Now, he was a man of character, a man who worked hard for what he had. Claude worked alongside his slaves to make a better life for everyone. This gold watch here was passed on to his son, Emmanuel. Sadly, it was the only thing about his father, they say, Emmanuel was proud of."

"What was the other item?" Horace asked, as Jericho laid back in his chair.

Sputtering a cough, Jericho added, "The other item is this small key, attached to the link here on the watch. Just look at the artistry of this tiny skeleton key."

Horace took the key from Jericho to closely examine its skillful design. They set in silence for a while, as Jericho gathered his thoughts.

"Mr. Corbin told me he had no idea what the key unlocks; but it sure is a pretty thing. It must have unlocked something really special. Now, I never mentioned to Mr. Corbin it might unlock something Mr. Emmanuel had in his office. Remember son, like I said, some secrets are best left unlocked."

Horace continued to listen carefully to his father's story. He had so many questions. It was hard to stay silent and not interrupt.

"See, the LeBlanc men didn't have a fancy watch dating back to Claude's day." Jericho continued. "But they sure had secrets, secrets our menfolk were superstitious about sharing. We all knew Mr. Emmanuel's office had been barricaded shut by Mrs. Lucretia – even Mr. Gabriel, Corbin's father and Emmanuel's son, had never been allowed in. Mr. Gabriel warned Mr. Corbin to keep it locked up too. So, Mr. Baron wasn't allowed in either."

"What kept Mr. Baron from going in anyway?" Horace asked.

Jericho responded with a low chuckle before continuing. "Superstition is a powerful thing down here on the bayou, as you know, son. It can get the best of both black and white men alike, even if they aren't quite believers. *And*, as far as I know, that Mr. Baron, he never wasted one dime of *his money* nor *his energy* fixing anything, much less taking down a barred door. That office was sealed after Emmanuel's untimely death and has not been re-entered since, nor should it be. Secrets are best left buried or locked away, understand?"

Horace nodded, the tears now escaping the rims of his eyes.

"Find your strength, son," Jericho said. "It's been there all along. You've always believed *I* was your strength, but that's not true. Listen to me," he insisted, his breathing quickening again. "You are to take possession of these two things now, and they are to remain in our family unless..."

His breathing was becoming erratic and Horace was frantic. "I'm taking you to the hospital, better yet, I'm calling an ambulance."

Jericho reached across the table and grabbed his son's hand firmly, much harder than Horace believed he was capable of. "You'll do nothing of the sort," his father commanded. "If God calls me home, He'll do it from here. You are to keep this in our family unless Olivia's daughter bears a child, her first born, and it lives beyond the first year. If that happens, you pass the watch on to her. The Sinclair curse will be gone, and the blood line will continue in good graces, understand?"

"Yes, Papa, but I have so many questions. Please..."

"The answers to your questions are all here, but for now, go and summon Paloma. My days are numbered..."

His eyes pled with Horace who grabbed his truck keys and sped to the plantation. His cousin and Catherine were still rocking on the front porch when he arrived. He skidded to a stop and screamed for Paloma to come with him. She pulled Catherine by the hand and the two jumped in the passenger side.

"What is it, Horace?" Paloma demanded.

"It's Papa, he's not well, he wants you by his side."

It seemed like only seconds before they were at the small, wooden house that'd been home to many generations. Jericho was lying on the couch when they ran inside. Tink stood at the open door, unsure if it was appropriate for her to enter.

"Uncle Jericho," Paloma gasped as she leaned over him. "I'm here, I'm here to offer prayer just as you passed on to me," she wept.

"No, child, there is no time for prayer now. God hears our heart anyway. Is that the girl? *Olivia's* girl?"

Paloma turned to find Tink in the doorway and motioned for her to join them. "Yes, 'tis Olivia's child."

Tink knelt beside Paloma and looked tenderly at the older man. "Horace was right," Jericho said, his voice faltering. "You *are* beautiful, just as your mother was. I pray God gives you her strength," he said, a tear escaping his eye. "Horace?"

"I'm here, Papa. We're all here."

Jericho seemed faraway, his eyes clouding over, his breathing decreasing. His final words were scripture, "The fathers shall not be put to death for their children, neither shall the children be put to death for their fathers; every man shall be put to death for his own sin."

45

ISAAC DROPPED Ben off at his house and headed to his office to phone Westmoreland. Ben went inside to grab some toiletries and a change of clothes. There was no doubt in his mind that someone intended to hurt Tink. It was just a matter of finding out who they were and why they wished her harm—and hopefully, before anyone else was hurt.

He was about to phone Dan when his cell rang. It was Isaac. "Didn't get enough of me earlier?" Ben asked playfully.

"Got some bad news," the sheriff prefaced the conversation. "Horace just called to inform me Jericho has passed away."

"Passed away?" Ben repeated. "How can that be?" It was hard for him to wrap his head around. After all, he and Isaac had just dropped Horace off at home. "Please tell me Horace was there when he died."

"Yes, he was, thank the good Lord," Isaac answered. "I don't have the details but according to Horace, he passed peacefully."

"I sure wasn't expecting this," Ben said. "Where's Paloma?"

"She's there with him, along with Catherine. Apparently, Horace drove back to the house to get Paloma and they took Catherine with them. Thank God for that. She sure didn't need to be left there alone."

"Where are they now?"

"Still at Jericho's," Isaac continued. "I'm sure it'll be a while before the mortuary arrives to take his body."

"I came in to grab a few things. I was planning on staying at the estate tonight. It's not safe for Catherine there alone and I certainly don't like the thought of Paloma down by the bayou by herself either."

"Neither do I," the sheriff agreed. "I'm grateful you're there for them."

"Would you do me a favor?" Ben asked. "I'd appreciate it if you'd phone Horace and let him know I'll come by and pick up Catherine. I'm sure she feels uncomfortable."

"I'll call him now. And Ben, don't take anything for granted. We don't know who we're dealing with and what they're capable of."

❀

BEN THREW his bag in the truck and cranked it up. "Damn," he muttered as he glanced at the gas gauge. It was unlike him to let the fuel get so low. He'd need to stop by Thomas's station and fill up.

Ben utilized his time to call his brother and fill him in on the latest developments, which would surely derail their plans for a night on the town.

"This is getting a little crazy, Ben," Dan insisted. "Mega crazy. I'm not so certain you should get this involved."

"Involved?" Ben asked. "I didn't choose to get involved. The killer involved both of us when they placed murdered bodies on our lines."

"I understand where you're coming from," Dan said quickly. "And I hate like hell to say this, but frankly, we don't know anything about Catherine. She seems like a very nice lady, but let's stand back and look at the situation objectively."

"Objectively, as in she could dismember two bodies and hang them on our lines? That's absurd, Dan."

"Isaac has a point, Ben, and you know it. Nothing like this has ever happened in Kane and the only new equation is Catherine."

"I'm disappointed in you," Ben said harshly. "If she's the cause of anything, she certainly isn't aware of it, or to blame, for that matter. I'll be staying at the Sinclair place with her and Paloma should you need me."

"Ben, please, let me—"

But Ben hung up before his brother could finish, furious even if he understood his motive. They were protective of each other and had been taught to be wary of newcomers. But Catherine—Tink—was unlike anyone he'd ever met and there was no way she could be involved in anything so sinister. She was beautiful, and classy, and well-educated, but most of all, she was vulnerable. That was what drew him to her. Ben wanted to shelter her from all that was bad with the world.

His mind had been racing with so many thoughts that he'd driven right past Thomas's station.

Get it together. How can I protect anyone else when I'm not even aware of my own surroundings?

After making a quick U-turn, Ben pulled up beside a gas pump and turned off his truck. There was a twenty and a ten in his wallet. He expected Thomas to be sitting at the cash register playing solitaire, but found the building empty. Which wasn't alarming since Thomas would often be working in the back or stocking the shelves. Locals knew to leave their money on the counter, then pump their gas or take their purchases.

Ben placed his thirty dollars on the counter and headed back to pump his fuel when he heard a frantic commotion in the back.

Opal was rushing toward him, her face flushed with panic. "Ben, oh my God…"

"Ms. Opal, what's the matter? Are you all right?"

She opened her mouth to speak just as Audrey West and her three small children came in. "Good afternoon, Ms. Bailey-Blanchard," Audrey said. "I promised the kids they could pick out a treat today. They've done all their chores, so I agreed to let them look over the candy aisle."

"Yes, how nice," Opal agreed, somehow pulling herself together. "How nice…"

Ben looked confused, but Opal shook her head quickly and discreetly. "Is this your money, Ben?" she asked.

"Yes, ma'am," he answered, concerned

"Very well, then. Let me get you a receipt."

"That won't be necessary," Ben said. He'd never gotten a receipt in all the years he'd done business with Thomas, but figured Opal ran a tighter ship.

The old cash register spiraled out a short strip of paper which she ripped off before scrawling a note across the back. "Have a nice day. I'm sure mine will get better. Look, I already have these precious children to visit with while they choose their treats."

Ben shoved the receipt in his front pocket and filled his truck up with gas. As he was opening the door to get in, Opal called him from just outside the store. "Don't forget to make sure that receipt was correct, Ben."

He nodded and pulled it from his pocket. The note on the back read: *Come back at closing time. 6:00.*

That's weird, he thought, but his mind rapidly went back to Tink and how uncomfortable she must be at Horace's home. Ben cranked the truck and headed to get her.

❀

THE ATMOSPHERE at Horace's home was much like Ben had expected. A sense of gratitude for ninety years of life was mixed with the deep-seated grief of losing someone who'd been the family's pillar of strength.

Paloma was standing over the stove, cooking. The smell made Ben's mouth water and he wondered when he'd last eaten.

Horace jumped up and met him as he stepped through the door. "My dad's gone," he began as the tears came again. It was an emotion Ben was all too familiar with and he struggled to find the words that'd somehow make a difference.

"Isaac called me," Ben said, almost in a whisper. "I'm sorry, Horace. I truly am. Your father was a good man."

The two men embraced briefly before Horace made his way back to the table and wiped his face with a paper towel.

"Ben," Paloma said warmly, "I'm so glad you came." The lines on her forehead seemed to be much more defined than they had earlier in the day, as if somehow, she'd aged within the past few hours. "Have a seat. I'll have something ready here in a few minutes. How about a cup of coffee?"

"I've already eaten," he lied, "but I'd love a cup of coffee. I'm sorry to hear about Jericho."

"They'll never be another one like him," she said as she poured him a cup of steaming brew from an old tin kettle.

Ben glanced across the table at Tink. The rims of her eyes were pink from tears shed throughout the day, her makeup long since worn off. No doubt the heat had also played a part in that. Ben found her to be even more beautiful without any. She had an exotic yet wholesome look, just the same.

"You've had one hell of a day," he commented as their eyes locked.

Tink shook her head and looked down at her cup. "I hadn't met him. Jericho, that is. Not until today. I met him in time for him to die. And before he died, he said something strange. I think it was about the estate. Something about sins of the father... It's nuts, but when he said it, it seemed like he was talking about what's happening right now."

"You mean the murders?"

"All of it, I guess. I know it sounds crazy."

It did and it didn't. Ben didn't know what else to say, so he decided to drop the subject. Instead, he said, "I thought after I paid my respects, I'd offer you a ride home. I won't leave you there alone."

Tink nodded. "That'd be nice."

Ben's cell phone rang. "Excuse me," he said. "It's the sheriff, I'll step outside."

He excused himself, took the call, then knocked lightly on the door before coming back inside. "Horace, Paloma, I'm sorry but I need to take Tink back to the estate. The two investigators from the state are there to take some photographs and gather forensic evidence. Again, my condolences about Jericho."

Paloma turned from the stove and hugged him tightly. "You two be careful and for heaven's sake, child, watch over Catherine."

Tink hugged them both before joining Ben outside by his truck. "Thank you for coming to get me," she said. "I mean…"

Ben reached for her hand. "I understand what you mean. I'm sorry I left you in the first place. You'd already been through enough and then this."

❀

BOTH INVESTIGATORS WERE WALKING around the grounds but headed back to the house when they saw Ben pull up.

Chet Westmoreland's face was beaded with perspiration and his shirt looked like he'd just gotten out of a swimming pool. "I'm sweatin' like a whore in church," he seethed in Ben's direction. "I swear Louisiana has its own sun!"

Jon Fontenot looked as though he'd just stepped out of a photo shoot for surfer's weekly. It didn't go unnoticed that he was instantly taken by Catherine. He held his hand out and stepped toward her. "Good afternoon, ma'am. I'm Investigator Fontenot, but feel free to call me Jon. It doesn't have an *h*."

"Does that make a difference in how it's pronounced?" Ben asked, unable to contain himself. "The missing *h*, I mean. This is Catherine and she's had a hard day, Investigator Fontenot."

"Yes, I'm Catherine Mabrey," she interrupted, reaching out her hand to meet his. Ben refused to look at her. "I had quite a scare today."

"The sheriff filled us in on your inheritance, Ms. Mabrey," Westmoreland said. "Mind if we look inside? Hope it has air conditioning."

"Indeed, it does," Tink answered, clearly entertained by his bluntness. "Please, come inside."

Westmoreland waited impatiently behind her as she unlocked the door. As soon as the cool air met him, he heaved a sigh of relief. "There *is* a God," he mumbled. "Where's this mannequin, Ms. Mabrey?"

"It's...right through here."

"Damn, would you look at that, Fontenot? That's one hell of a stairwell."

"Language," Ben said. "We're in mixed company."

"Broussard said Ms. Mabrey was from Atlanta. I'm fairly certain she's heard profanity before."

"It's this way," Ben said, leading them toward the kitchen.

"I'd prefer Ms. Mabrey show us," Westmoreland grunted.

"As I told Jon 'without an *h*', she's had a difficult day."

Ben's comment went unacknowledged while Westmoreland directed the conversation to Tink. "If you'd be so kind as to walk us through the day, up to the point you discovered the mannequin, that'd be extremely helpful."

"Okay," Tink relented. "I discovered the door open when I got back from taking my friend to the airport."

"Open or ajar?"

"Ummm...well... I could make out it was open, but not completely. It was as if someone hadn't shut it completely behind themselves, kind of like when you push a door, but it doesn't completely close."

"Is that how you secure your place in Atlanta? Kind of push the door shut, but not completely."

"Of course not," Tink responded, unfazed. "I assumed Paloma was cleaning inside. I locked the door behind me when I left, so it didn't concern me it was open, or not completely closed—however you choose to categorize it. Paloma had arrived to clean and met us in the drive as we were leaving."

"Have you heard about the recent murders?"

"Yes."

"I'd categorize a locked door, now ajar, as a concern," Westmoreland pressed.

"This is bullshit," Ben said, stepping in between them. "Does she need a lawyer?"

"I *am* a lawyer," Tink said calmly. "I don't have a problem answering any of this gentleman's questions. He has a job to do, Ben, and if I can somehow expedite it, we're all safer for it."

Westmoreland ignored Ben altogether. "So, you came in, assuming your cleaning lady was busy at work. Did you see or hear anyone or anything?"

"No, nothing. I was calling out to Paloma so as not to startle her. It's a big house."

"You got that right."

Fontenot must have sensed Ben was ready to blow, for he stepped in. "So, you entered the house, called out for her, and didn't hear any movement of any kind, like a person running to get away?"

"No, I didn't hear a thing. I still wasn't alarmed," Tink said. "I see now how foolish I was."

"When you came through the door, did it appear to have been forced open?"

"Again, no. A broken doorframe would've sent up a red flag," Tink persisted, remaining calm and consistent.

"So, it didn't appear anyone broke through the door, but you remember locking it?"

"Nobody broke through the fucking door!" Ben shouted. "For fuck's sake, get to the point already."

"Gentlemen," Tink continued firmly, "the door was ajar. I walked in, calling out for Paloma. I continued toward the kitchen, where I assumed I'd find Paloma working. Before I made it to the kitchen, I discovered this mannequin, noticed the black wig, the missing hands, and the blood splattered everywhere—blood I assumed was real. I immediately grabbed my cell phone from my purse and dialed 911, before running out, and heading toward the back of the house. I heard what I thought was gravel crunching under tires, so I hid behind a large oak tree. The vehicle stopped in front of the house and a car door slammed. I peeked from behind the tree and saw a police car, then recognized Cassius, a deputy I'd met the day before. I ran toward him and lost it."

"Thank you, Ms. Mabrey," Fontenot said sincerely. "Investigator Westmoreland, I believe we can let this young lady go for now, do you agree?"

"Yeah, that'd be fine. We've got an ID unit en route to take some photographs and dust for prints. I'm sure you'd be more comfortable not being here, if you have somewhere else to go."

"When do you want her back?" Ben asked.

"It'll take us a few hours," Fontenot stated. "We could always lock the door when we leave."

"We'll be back in two or three hours," Ben said flatly.

"Thank you, gentlemen," Tink said as she followed Ben to the truck.

"Are you hungry?" Ben asked as he fought the urge to go into an angry rant about what assholes the two investigators were. "We could eat at the diner in town. I'm starving."

"I could certainly eat," Tink agreed. "The food Paloma was preparing smelled delicious, but I couldn't bring myself to eat in that setting. How sad."

"I couldn't believe it when Isaac called. What a day."

"Indeed."

"I'm sorry about those two," Ben said as he pointed toward the house. "They have a way of making you feel guilty about something you had nothing to do with."

"No worries, I'm used to that. I see all kinds in my business. They're just trying to see what type of reaction they can get. Believe it or not, detectives are amazingly intuitive."

"I don't like either of them, intuitive or not."

"You don't know what intuitive means, do you?" Tink teased.

"It means insightful," Ben said, grinning back at her. "Not all gator hunters are idiots."

"I wasn't insinuating that."

"Enough with the big words. I happen to know several myself, but find it unnecessary to use them."

"Big words, huh? Like what?" Tink asked, amused.

"Mayonnaise and warehouse," Ben said seriously before breaking out into laughter.

"I appreciate you saving me today, more than once," Tink said. "Now that I think about it, I'm starving too. I had lunch earlier but rushed through it because my father wanted me to meet with an investor in New Orleans. Has this been the longest day ever or what?"

"Definitely the longest day in history," Ben answered.

"I haven't been to the diner. Tell me about it."

"Not much to tell," he continued. "Little family-owned place, nothing special, but it serves its purpose. I could eat a cow right now."

They rode the next few miles, making small talk about Kane, intentionally excluding anything about the crimes or Jericho's death.

"And here we are," Ben said, pulling his truck into a spot in front. "Guess we've missed the lunch crowd and the dinner crowd hasn't arrived yet."

He held the door open for her and waved to the man behind the counter. "Afternoon, Reggie," he said. "Have you met Catherine Mabrey?"

"Can't say I've had the pleasure," he responded, wiping his hands on a dish towel before offering his right hand. "Name's Reggie, as Ben said. I've owned this money pit for the past fifteen years. Visiting Ben or new in town?"

"Well... I'm not quite sure how to answer that. I inherited the Sinclair estate, but I'm not planning on staying here full-time. I live in Atlanta."

"So, you know what I mean when I say money pit," Reggie said with a smile. He was a handsome fella in an odd sort of way, tall and broad shouldered. Tink imagined he'd once been the athletic type, but had fallen weak over the years to fried food and sweets. His hairline was receding a bit, but he had a warm smile and welcoming personality. She liked him.

Ben swiveled a bar stool in her direction, so Tink slid onto it as Reggie handed her a menu. The restaurant was small, with a long bar covered in speckled Formica and topped with sugar canisters, salt and pepper shakers, and straw dispensers. There were about ten to twelve tables scattered sporadically throughout. Tink imagined customers shuffled them about at will to make room for larger groups. It boasted outdated seventies décor which Tink assumed had been left by previous owners. She sensed Reggie's deep pride in the diner, which shone from constant cleaning. The smell of seasoned food lingered from the earlier lunch crowd.

"What do you recommend?" Tink asked.

"I still have some gumbo in the pot, but I make a mean cheeseburger, at least to hear Ben tell it. Of course, he sets his bar pretty low," Reggie said, discreetly adding a wink.

"Best burger in town," Ben said. "Of course, you haven't eaten anything from my grill."

"A burger it is," Tink agreed.

The three of them chatted as Reggie tossed spices and a few splashes of Worcestershire sauce onto a mound of ground beef before forming it into thick patties.

"I'm starving," Tink commented, "but I'm not quite *that* hungry."

"Just wait until you taste it," Reggie assured her. "If you can't eat it all, I'll package it to go."

"Okay, I give up," Tink conceded, pushing her plate toward Reggie. "I agree with Ben—it was amazing, but I'm stuffed."

"Want me to pack the other half up?" Reggie asked.

"No, thanks," Tink said, rubbing her flat belly. "I may never eat again."

"I've heard that before," Reggie said. "Good luck with that house. You've got quite a road ahead of ya."

"Thanks," she said. "I'm hoping Ben will consider helping out. I don't have any idea what I'm doing."

"Ben can do anything. Have you shown her your place?" Reggie asked him.

"No, I don't want to run her off," Ben joked. "Don't build me up too much."

"I'd love to see your place," Tink said.

Ben slid the check across the bar and reached into his pocket for some cash. "Oh shit," he mumbled quietly as he noticed the receipt Opal Bailey-Blanchard had written on. He threw a twenty on the counter and told Reggie he'd see him soon.

Tink walked briskly behind him as he hurried to the truck, and by the time he'd cranked it and they'd fastened their seatbelts, she was perplexed. "What's up with you? We've only been gone an hour and a half at the most. I'm certain the investigators are still at the house."

"It's the craziest thing," he began. "I stopped by Thomas's place to get gas when I was headed back to your place. His wife was working and—"

"I met her today," Tink interrupted. "I have to admit I was a little shocked. She's not exactly who I expected to be married to such a strange guy."

"Thomas isn't strange," Ben said defensively. "He's never been anywhere but Kane and he's quite loyal to it."

"So, what was so crazy about your stop to get gas?"

"No one was there when I went in to pay for my gas, so I put my cash on the counter. That's something we often do when Thomas is busy in the back, so I didn't think anything of it. But just as I was leaving, Opal came rushing toward me in a panic. She started to tell me something, but another customer came in with her children. She insisted I take a receipt, which I've never done, so I put it in my front pocket. While I was pumping my gas, Opal made a point of making sure that I check it and make sure it was correct."

"That's odd," Tink said.

Ben handed her the printed receipt. "Look at what she wrote on the back."

She turned it over and stared back at Ben. "It's ten minutes after six now. How far away are we?"

"Just a few miles," Ben answered as he sped up.

"Surely Opal would've called the police if she were in danger. Why would she want to talk to you when no one else is around?"

"I can't figure that one out. She seemed out of sorts when she came from the back of the building, almost as if someone were after her."

"Then why not tell you, or at least insist you stay until after the other customers left?"

"I don't know, but I should've stuck around. I was so concerned about what had happened at the estate that I was anxious to get back there."

"Are you close to Opal? Would she share her problems with you?"

"I've known her most of my life, but I wouldn't consider us close friends. Thomas and I have been pals for years. He knew my folks."

"But she would've trusted you if she was frightened by something?"

"Certainly."

"How much further?" Tink questioned as her concern grew.

"A couple of miles," Ben answered, pressing harder on the accelerator.

The gas station quickly came into view. Opal's white Volvo was the only car in the parking lot.

"She's here," Ben said. "Thank God. I feel terrible about leaving her when she was obviously distressed."

"I'm sure everything's fine," Tink assured him. The two got out of his truck and walked into the station.

"Ms. Opal?" Ben called. "It's Ben Norwood. I don't want to startle you. Ms. Opal?" Nothing appeared to be disturbed as Ben did a quick scan of the business. "She's got to be here, her car's out there."

"You said she came from the back earlier. Perhaps she's working back there," Tink suggested.

Ben didn't respond but headed toward the back. When he reached the curtain separating the public section of the store from the back-storage area, he called for her once again. "I don't want to scare you, Ms. Opal. It's Ben Norwood."

The area was eerily quiet and none of the lights were on, making it difficult to see.

"Maybe she was having car trouble and had someone pick her up," Tink said.

"Tink," Ben said gravely, "she wouldn't have left the store unlocked."

"You're right," she whispered back. "Let's go. Something's not right."

He called out for Opal one more time before pulling the string to illuminate the bare light bulb overhead. "Tink, run! Go crank the truck and lock the doors. I'll be right there," Ben shouted. "Go!"

46

Tɪɴᴋ ᴡᴀꜱ ꜱᴏ ᴛᴀᴋᴇɴ ᴀʙᴀᴄᴋ by Ben's stern demands that she didn't question what had given him such a scare. The panic in his voice had reflected the gravity of the situation. She jumped in the driver's side of his truck, relieved to find the keys still in the ignition. The engine started just fine. Just as she was leaning over to lock both doors, he came running out and opened the driver's door.

"Move over, Tink, hurry," he insisted.

After sliding over to allow him to get behind the wheel, Tink fastened her seat belt and heaved a sigh of relief. "What happened back there?" she asked. Ben gunned the accelerator, slinging her against the passenger door and leaving dirt and gravel billowing like a cloud of smoke behind them.

"Sorry about that," he murmured as he adjusted his rearview mirror.

"Slow down," Tink said. "You almost ran off the road. Where are we going?"

"Back to your place. Who would've figured I'd be grateful those two investigators are there?"

"Watch out for that tr—"

"Oh my God," Ben said, slamming on the brakes and making a U-turn. "That was Thomas. I can't let him go in the store."

"Why? Ben, tell me what's going on?"

"Call the sheriff's department and have Isaac meet us at Thomas's gas station."

"Do I dial 911?"

"Yes!" he screamed as he focused on catching up with Thomas, who was pulling an old fishing boat behind his pickup.

"Sheriff's office, Roxie speaking, what's your emergency?"

"I'm not sure," Tink stammered. "I'm with Ben Norwood and he said to have the sheriff met us at Thomas Blanchard's gas station."

"Who am I speaking with?"

"This is Catherine Mabrey, something's happened there."

"What's the emergency?" Roxie insisted. "The sheriff will want to know what's going on, ma'am. Can you put Ben on the line?"

Tink shoved the cell phone in Ben's direction. "She needs to know the details of the emergency and because I'm not privy to those, you'll have to fill her in."

"Roxie," Ben spit into the phone. "Get Isaac out there now and try to reach the investigators out at the Sinclairs'. They'll need to meet us there, too."

"Ben, just tell me what the hell's going on. I can't send the sheriff or even those two assholes into a situation they're not prepared for."

"Shit, I'm driving a hundred miles an hour to stop Thomas before he reaches the scene and I didn't want to scare Catherine, but you're obviously not going to take no for an answer. Opal's dead. Murdered. I just found the body. Her hands are cut off." With that Ben tossed the phone to Tink and passed Thomas's truck and boat before skidding to a stop in the gravel parking lot.

Thomas got out of his vehicle, his face flushed with anger. "What the hell's goin' on here, boy?" he demanded. "You damn near made me jackknife my trailer. You betta' have a damn good excu—"

"Thomas," Ben began as he started to tremble uncontrollably. "You *can't* go in there—"

"What's dis about?" Thomas insisted, turning to Tink for answers this time. "Has Ben done lost his mind?"

"Please," Tink pleaded. "There's been an accident. The sheriff's on his way."

"What kind o' accident?" he asked, searching the area for clues before resting his eyes on Opal's Volvo. "Opal? Oh, Jesus, not Opal! Is she in de car?" Thomas rushed to the vehicle.

Tink looked to Ben, but he'd succumbed to the shock of it all and was leaning over his own truck, racked with sobs. She reached for the older gentleman and took his arm to steady him. "She's not in the car, sir. The sheriff should be here any minute."

As soon as the words left her lips, the flash of red and blue lights crested the hill from both directions. The state investigators were in an unmarked, brown vehicle with blue lights blinking from the dash while a bar of lights flickered from the top of the sheriff's cruiser. Tink stood motionless while the scene unfolded in slow, methodical detail. Her head swam while the world spiraled around her, around and around and around...

The young investigator, Jon without the *h*, was kneeling beside her, his face uncomfortably close to hers, as she opened her eyes. "Ma'am? Ma'am? Are you all right? Can you hear me?"

He appeared blurry at first, then Tink realized what'd happened. She'd fainted. Embarrassed and anxious, she struggled to sit up.

"Not yet," Fontenot insisted. "You hit the gravel pretty hard. Let's make sure you aren't injured."

Ben knelt beside her. The tears had stopped and were replaced with concern. "Tink? I'm here, I'm so sorry. Are you hurting anywhere?"

"We need to make sure her head isn't bleeding," the investigator instructed. "Can you lift it slightly to see?"

"I don't want to move her neck," Ben said.

"Oh, for heaven's sake," Tink interrupted. "I'm right here and can hear everything you're both saying. I simply fainted. I'm fine. Now if you'll help me up, you can attend to more pressing matters."

Ben and Fontenot rose to their feet, then each grabbed an elbow and pulled her up. Thomas, the sheriff, and Westmoreland were standing by the sheriff's car as if a fainting spell was something they'd never witnessed.

Just wait until they get inside, Tink thought, wiping the dirt from her clothes.

"Ben," Isaac began, "what's going on here?"

Ben nodded in Thomas's direction as if to telepathically alert the sheriff they shouldn't speak of it in his presence, but the effort went unnoticed. "I came by earlier," Ben started. "Opal was acting strange... As if—"

Cassius skidded up in his patrol car, jumped out and grabbed Ben by both arms. "What's happened? Is it Opal?"

"She's dead," Ben said in a flat, defeated voice."

Thomas gasped. "Where... Where's my wife?"

Isaac reached for the radio attached to his belt and pushed the mic button. "Roxie, send an ambulance out to Thomas's store, ASAP."

"Ten-four, Sheriff," was her response.

Cassius broke away from the group and ran toward the building, pushing his way through the door.

"Shit!" Isaac yelled. "Don't touch anything, Cassius! Westmoreland, you and Fontenot grab that boy. He has no business here. It's too close to home. Put him in the back of my car if you have to."

Cassius's wails could be heard from inside. Tink watched Ben and the younger investigator run after him. A few minutes later, he was dragged back outside, blood covering the knees of his uniform, hard sobs racking his body.

Ben and Jon without an *h* looked rough, too, like they'd slipped in blood.

"What a shit show," Westmoreland bellowed, pointing at Ben, Cassius, and Fontenot. "You're *all* idiots! There's no calculating the damage you've done to the evidence. Son-of-a-bitch..." He held both hands up. "I'm getting too old for this bullshit! Investigations are hard enough without having them contaminated by your own people!" Still sputtering, he wiped his face with a wrinkled handkerchief and pulled his cell phone from the car's console.

Tink was certain he'd have a stroke before the person he was calling could answer.

"It's Westmoreland," he spat. "You've had enough time to get everything you need from the house. We've got another crime scene, if you can believe that shit. At least what's left of it. I'll text you the address. Get here yesterday."

The ambulance arrived and while the paramedics tightened the blood pressure cuff around Thomas Blanchard's biceps, Isaac made his way over to Westmoreland and the three men covered in Opal Bailey-Blanchard's blood.

Tink observed from the sidelines.

"I can't believe we have another one," she heard the sheriff say. "Apparently the drifter's murders weren't an isolated, drug crime."

"No shit," Westmoreland muttered.

"That's enough," Isaac said sternly. "You need to put a lid on it. I've listened to you spewing profanities for as long as I intend to. This is my town and I handed the investigation over to another department because I believed it was in the best interest of the victims. You're acting as though this crime spree is a personal attack on you, Westmoreland. I'd expected more professionalism."

"More professionalism?" Westmoreland asked. "It was one of *your* men who not only trampled over the crime, but also wallowed in the victim's blood!"

Cassius made a quick move toward the investigator, but Ben grabbed him before he could make contact. Tink jumped but didn't make a sound.

"My deputy was raised by the victim after both of his parents were killed in a boating accident. Before he's a deputy, he's a human being. My apologies if he allowed his emotions to get the best of him!"

Before Westmoreland could respond, one of the paramedics called for Isaac. "Sheriff, we need to transport Mr. Blanchard. His blood pressure's off the charts and he's fighting us."

The group followed the sheriff over to assess Thomas's condition.

Tink's stomach dropped. *Not now.*

"Two-twenty over one-fifty," the EMT stated. "Stroke level, Sheriff."

Sweating profusely, his face blood-red, Thomas continued to resist any efforts by the paramedics. "You can't make me go to da hospital!" he shouted. "You know dey can't, Sheriff. Last I checked, it was against de law."

"Thomas," Isaac said gently. "The last thing we need is to lose you too. Please, let them take you to the hospital. I'll meet you there."

"I need to be here with...with... I haven't seen her."

"You've got to go to the hospital. There's nothing you can do here," Isaac pressed. He turned to Cassius, motioning for him to urge Thomas to go, but Cassius failed to respond. "Damn it, Cassius," the sheriff began, "you need to ride in the ambulance with Thomas. He needs you."

With that, Isaac turned on his heels and walked over to meet with Westmoreland.

47

IT WAS WELL after midnight before Ben and Tink were allowed to leave the scene of the latest murder. They were both mentally and physically exhausted as Ben pulled into the drive of the estate. The lights were on inside, making Tink's stomach churn with that uneasy feeling she was becoming accustomed to. Before she could ponder who might be inside, the front door opened, and Paloma and Horace walked out onto the porch.

Tink heaved a sigh of relief. "As we say in the south, you're both a sight for sore eyes."

"Come inside," Paloma insisted. "The evenings are getting so cool. We heard what happened and neither of us could believe it."

"Nor could we," Tink said. "Ben and I are the last people who needed to discover another body. It put us right in the crosshairs of the investigation. Why didn't anyone bother to tell me Cassius was raised by that strange man?"

"Thomas just isn't very fond of strangers, especially when they're Sinclairs," Paloma said. "He and Baron had words more times than I care to count. Unfortunately, he considers you the enemy simply by association. But Thomas did step up to the plate when Cassius's folks were killed. He and Ms. Opal raised him as though he were their own."

"Cassius isn't having it too easy these days," Ben said. "Poor guy."

Paloma directed them toward the kitchen where she had coffee on the stove.

"Thank you," Tink said, "but I'm exhausted, and coffee would just keep me awake. Can we discuss this in the morning?"

"You aren't safe here," Paloma insisted. "Something sinister is going on and we need to get to the bottom of it before you and Ben are either framed for murder or murdered yourselves. Come with me to Horace's for the night. I need to be there for him after losing Jericho."

"How selfish of me," Tink said. "Forgive me, Horace, I'm sure you want to be at home right now. I'll be fine, Paloma. Ben has agreed to stay with me. Let's all get a good night's rest and we'll talk in the morning."

Paloma shot her a concerned glance. "Ms. Catherine, I'm not..."

"I'll be fine, we'll be fine," Tink said, gesturing toward Ben.

"Horace and I set up one of the old rollaway beds in your room. I figured you'd insist on staying here. Horace has a house and cell phone. Call us if you need us."

BEN STOOD in awe at the expansive bedroom when they'd finally gotten upstairs. "I knew this place was big, but wow, just wow."

"You're not going to believe this, but I haven't even seen it all," Tink commented. "This has been so crazy, this whole ordeal."

"Let's try to get some sleep," Ben said. "If it's even possible at this point. Tomorrow may prove to be an even longer day, and we need to be prepared. For whatever reason, someone is framing us for murder."

48

Glancing at the clock, Tink was surprised to discover she'd gotten nine hours of uninterrupted sleep. Her body and mind felt rejuvenated. Ben wasn't in the rollaway bed, so she assumed he'd already awakened and gone downstairs.

Tink took a long, hot shower and spent a few extra minutes on her makeup before blowing her hair dry and getting dressed.

Unsure of what the day would hold, she opted for a pair of jeans before pulling on a sweatshirt over her T-shirt. After putting her hair in a ponytail, she stepped into a pair of flats and made her bed.

The sun shone brightly through the stained glass above the rotunda, giving off gemstones of light much like a kaleidoscope. Tink glanced up and paused to take in its odd mixture of beauty and ominous foreboding. She was somehow able to control the shiver before it traveled completely up her spine.

You won't run me away, she thought. *Not this house, nor its past, nor its secrets.*

Tink could hear bits of conversation coming from the kitchen, so she followed the voices and the smell of coffee. "I thought I'd find you here," she said when she saw Ben and the sheriff seated at the table.

Ben jumped as if he'd been caught taking liberties with her home.

"I'm sorry. You were sleeping so well, I hated to wake you. Can I get you a cup of coffee?"

"Good morning, Sheriff," Tink said. "No thanks, I'll get it. Sit back down, Ben. What have I missed? I'm almost afraid to ask."

"Good morning, Ms. Mabrey," Isaac began. "My apologies for not letting you know I was here. Ben let me in and insisted we let you sleep."

"Please, call me Tink, all my friends do. It's an odd name to those who haven't always known me, but you'll get used to it."

"Tink it is," he answered. "Do you have a few minutes?"

"Are you kidding me?" she asked. "What's going on here, Sheriff? Is Kane usually this exciting?"

Ben and Isaac shared a forced smile for her benefit. "Can't say that it is," Isaac answered. "I don't know what to make of it. It's always been a small, uneventful place...until now."

"I suppose you're both thinking it was uneventful until *I* arrived. I can assure you; I'd never even heard of Kane until my father told me of my inheritance. This place," Tink said, waving her hand around halfheartedly, "was where my mother grew up. I never knew her. She died giving birth to me. My father scooped me up and took me to Atlanta where he limited the bits and pieces of her that he divvied out to me."

"So, you were unaware of the estate?" Isaac asked incredulously.

"Totally unaware. I knew I had grandparents, but never had contact with them. My father explained it was their choice, so I left it alone. The letter didn't arrive about my grandfather's death until weeks after he was buried."

Isaac shot a glance in Ben's direction. "So that would explain why you weren't at his funeral. Many of us wondered what had happened to you, but Baron and Ruby weren't the type of people you'd approach with personal questions."

"Baron, my grandfather, wrote to my father after my grandmother's death, and long after her funeral. It was apparent they had no interest in a relationship, which didn't seem to bother my father. In fact, he seemed relieved. Now, I can understand why. I have so many questions..."

"I'm sure you do," Isaac said kindly. "I wish I had more answers for you. This whole mess, the murders—it doesn't add up. It's as though someone took pieces from different puzzles and threw them in one box. The pieces don't match. There's no common denominator."

"Except for me," Tink added.

"Technically, I found the bodies before you arrived," Ben said. "Which doesn't add up either. I mean, why would the bodies be placed on our lines? We certainly don't have any connection with the Sinclairs. My mother died when Dan and I were young boys and my father's been dead for several years now. We don't have any money to speak of and had never even met the Sinclairs, at least not formally. I had seen them a few times, but they didn't know me. I'm close to Paloma and Horace, but everyone in Kane knows them. They're good people, kind people."

"Explain that to me," Tink said as she took a sip from the strong, black coffee.

"Explain what exactly?" Ben asked.

"The link between Paloma and the Sinclairs. I understand her family has worked for them for generations, but to be frank, why? They're complete opposites."

"Maybe I can help you understand the dynamic here," Isaac suggested. "It's not like Atlanta, or any other place, for that matter. People have a connection to their land in Kane. It goes one of two ways. They either feel a deep loyalty to their heritage, or they want to get as far from it as possible—there's no in between. I'm sure if you go back far enough, you'll see that Paloma's family was once slaves on this land."

"Indeed, they were," Paloma said, startling them all.

"Ms. Paloma," Isaac croaked, jumping to his feet. "No disrespect intended."

"Of course not, Sheriff," she said kindly. "Please, take your seat. My apologies for not being here earlier to start the coffee. I was cooking breakfast for Horace. He thinks he's fooling me with his strength, but he's heartbroken."

"I should go visit him," Ben said.

"A little later," Paloma suggested. "Perhaps some time alone is best for now."

She took off her sweater and hung it on the back of a chair before pouring herself a cup of coffee. "Any idea who was responsible for that foolishness here yesterday, Isaac?"

"None at all," he answered.

"Does your father know about any of this?" Paloma asked Tink. Her eyes were dark and sorrowful, making Tink's throat burn from emotion.

"No, and I intend on keeping it that way. He'd be down here before I could blink, and this place would be on the market."

"That might not be such a bad thing," Ben said.

"Paloma," Tink began, "what did your uncle mean when he spoke of a father's sins?"

"It was scripture, child. They were rambling words from a delirious man."

"No," Tink insisted. "They were strong, determined words from a man's deathbed. You know what he was talking about, Paloma. Please, now is the time to share it with us."

49

After two hours with the sheriff and another one with state investigators, the house was finally empty, leaving Tink and Ben alone.

"I know they're expecting me to tuck my tail and go back to Atlanta," Tink said, determination resonating from her voice. "But I won't do it. If anything, it's making me more resolved than ever to stick around and find out why they want me gone."

"I'm not sure if they want you gone or if there's something else they want," Ben said. "But I agree—you can't allow them to run you away. There's a reason why you're here and a reason why you didn't just sell the place to begin with."

"I need to know *why* my mother wasn't particularly fond of the place," Tink continued. "There are some strange undercurrents at play, and I can't leave until I understand them."

"I hear ya," Ben said, holding up his hand to solicit a high five. "What's your plan?"

"I want to tackle the grounds, starting with the entrance. It's the first impression people get of the place and it's not a pleasant one."

"You're right," Ben agreed. "What do you say we take a walk around? I think getting out of here might do us some good."

"I agree," Tink said. "Do I need a jacket?"

"I think your sweatshirt will be enough, but you'll probably shed it before we're done."

Tink locked the front door behind them, pausing long enough to ensure it had indeed been locked. "You're my witness," she told Ben. "If someone is in there when we get back, I didn't leave it ajar."

The comment made them both laugh, lightening the mood.

I won't tuck my tail, Tink assured herself.

"Let's start in the back," Ben said. "That's the area I'm more familiar with. I'm sure you're most concerned about the front but you said you haven't seen it all yet, and I have to admit, I'm a little curious myself."

The shade from the large trees made it difficult for grass to grow, but it was still green and full of foliage. Remnants of old gardens left hints of a once thriving botanical showplace, something Tink dreamed of having on the estate again. In the city, having this much personally owned land was unheard of.

They wound their way through the property before Ben stopped and turned to face the house. "Take a look at her from back here," he said. "She's enormous. This has been my only view of the place through the years. Dan and I pass by here often on our boats, but only stop when we see Paloma out at her place."

"It leaves me speechless." Tink said. "How in creation could I ever restore this? Even if I could, I'd never be able to maintain it."

"Have you ever heard the old Chinese proverb, *the journey of a thousand miles begins with one step*? Just take it one day at a time. Besides, consider it a labor of love like I do my place. Otherwise, it's simply work without an end in sight."

"That's one way to look at it," Tink said. She stood in the same spot for several minutes, gazing over the estate from one end to the other. "Hey, Ben, what's that over there?" she asked, pointing toward a large structure situated to the west of the house.

"Wow, that's the biggest one I've ever seen," he answered as he headed in its direction. "Would you look at *that*? I can't believe I've never noticed it from the water."

"Okay..." Tink urged. "Do you suppose you could fill me in on this thingamajig?"

Ben didn't speak until they'd made their way almost to the house. "This, my dear, is a cistern," he began, still in awe. "They've been used for over a hundred years as a source of water for homes and gardens." He rubbed his hand over the wood and looked toward the top of it. "I guarantee you this was waterlogged cypress. Takes damn near a year to dry even after it's been milled and planed."

Tink was struggling to understand his fascination with the contraption. "Is it like those plastic barrels people use to catch rainwater?" she asked. "I know a couple who has one to water their plants when we're in a drought. They insist on being praised for their efforts to improve the environment."

"It's a little different here in Louisiana," Ben said. "I'm sure Atlanta has an impressive infrastructure for their water system."

"Ha, that's laughable," Tink said. "It's a crumbling mess. My water bill is four times higher than the same household in a neighboring city."

Ben was clearly tuning her out, his focus on the enormous wooden barrel. "The stave height alone has to be over fifteen feet," he said, his eyes glazing over.

"You sound like a man who's buying his first muscle car," Tink said flippantly. "But I'll appease you. What's a stave?"

"See this slat of wood?" he asked, again rubbing his hand down one of the individual slats, held to the others by a few evenly spaced bands of metal. "That's a stave. Sorta like the pieces of wood that make up a whiskey barrel. This is the largest, and probably the oldest, cistern I've ever seen. Bet it was built when they constructed this place. Had to be made of cypress or it'd have never held up this well."

"It's pretty big," Tink agreed. "Did they have that many plants to water?"

"This area has a high water table," Ben said, never taking his eyes off the cistern. "Well water is unsuitable for drinking and cooking and is too brackish to bathe in. There wasn't any city water back then, so I'm certain this cistern provided not only the water for household needs but for their vegetable gardens too. Would you look at *that*? Through the years, someone added a roof to her. Looks like a thirty-degree pitch if I were to guess."

"That's *exactly* what I was thinking," Tink agreed dryly.

Again, Ben ignored the comment and continued. "The original Sinclair who had this built undoubtedly had a great deal of money. These were typically installed on a gravel foundation or a concrete slab. This one was constructed on a stout rock and mortar base. No doubt it's a thirty- to forty-thousand-gallon tank. Impressive."

"All right then," Tink interrupted as she grabbed his hand. "I get the point."

"My apologies," Ben said, slowly coming out of the trance. "It's just—"

"*Impressive*, I know. Let's walk up front. I want to show you the first phase of renovation." They were halfway up the drive when her cell rang. "Give me a minute," she said. "It's my father."

Ben hastened his pace and walked ahead toward the crumbling entrance.

"Hi, Father, I was just about to call you."

"Why do I find that a little too convenient?" he asked playfully.

"I'm sorry, I've been busy. I have a local man here looking at the entrance. It's in deplorable shape."

"I suppose that means you're staying for a while."

"Just a little longer, if that's all right with you."

"Again, a simple phone call goes a long way," he said sternly. "I'm trying awfully hard to give you your space, but I'm finding it difficult, especially without any correspondence on your part. I will say this, and you can take it for what it's worth. The first thing I'd do would have a professional conduct an extensive home inspection, followed by an appraisal. Then you'll know what you're up against."

"Great advice," Tink said. The thought of her father even half-heartedly supporting her efforts thrilled her. But as quickly as her enthusiasm surfaced, the thought of the murders returned. If her father ever got word that anyone had been killed, he'd surely come for her himself. "I'll get right on it," she added.

"There's also the small dilemma about your job," he continued. "I'm sure it's somewhere down on your list of priorities right now, but your clients beg to differ. In fact, I have no doubt Harold Barber would like nothing more than to wrap his hands around your throat. His caseload was pushing the limit without adding yours to it."

"Poor Mr. Barber," Tink said, ashamed she'd put so little thought into what her absence was doing to others. "I'm terribly sorry, Father, how selfish of me. Could I possibly do some work from here? There's clearly no Wi-Fi at the estate, but I can go into town and use the library."

"I was hoping you would've considered that before now, but I'm happy you've had this time for yourself. I'll have Harold FedEx your cases to you overnight. It goes without saying you should contact him as soon as they arrive. You won't be doing any of the construction work yourself, so there's no reason why you can't spend some time on your workload."

"Thank you so much," Tink said sincerely.

"That gives you today to contact an appraiser and a home inspector," Augustus reiterated. "I'm serious, Tink. And don't make the mistake most women do and employ the first contractor you meet."

"I'll shop around, I promise, and Father, I miss you."

"Miss you, too, Tink. Now stay in touch," he added before disconnecting.

🐚

Tink found Ben standing at the entrance, deep in thought. "Is there any hope?" she asked.

"You want my honest opinion?" Ben asked.

"Nothing but your honest opinion."

"I'd tear all of this down," he said, referring to the rock wall and wrought-iron gate. "And I'd start with that mailbox."

Tink laughed at his honesty but fully agreed. "But wouldn't it leave a big void?" she asked.

"Not at all," Ben assured her. "It's all hanging on by a thread—

might as well push it over. Once it's removed, they can put some sod down, and you'll never know this catastrophe was ever here. I call it my *less is more* design."

"My, aren't you clever?" Tink teased.

Ben bent down to massage his right knee before scouting out the sky. "Looks like we're gonna get a storm this afternoon."

Before Tink could question him, his cell phone rang. "Good morning, Horace," Ben said. He listened intently, nodded, then listened some more. "Okay, please let me know if I can do anything, and I mean anything." Another pause. "I thought so. My knee never lies to me. We'll head back to the house, now. Again, we're both here if you and Paloma need us."

"Looks like a storm's headed our way," Ben said, turning to face Tink.

"The sky is blue," Tink rebutted.

"My knee never lies to me."

"Magic knee?"

"Yep, became magical after a bad sprain in high school. My knee turned one way and the rest of me the other. Still scored though, so all was not lost."

"Football or basketball?"

"Football. Didn't help that several of the opposing team members piled on top of it after the fact."

"I get the point," Tink said, feeling squeamish. "I've never understood the fascination with sports, especially brutal ones like football and boxing."

"Whoa. Don't say that out loud," Ben suggested. "Not around here anyway."

"What did Horace want? Was he calling to tell you there's a storm on the way?"

"He was calling to let us know the funeral will be Saturday at the family cemetery. The heads-up on the storm was an afterthought."

"Family cemetery?"

"Yes, they have one on their portion of land and the Sinclairs have one on theirs. You weren't aware of that?"

"Certainly not. Is that legal? I mean burying people on your actual property?"

"Is there a difference between owning property and owning *actual* property?"

"Funny. You know what I mean, Ben. I would think there'd be regulations about that sort of thing."

"I'm pretty sure your family is grandfathered in by now, no pun intended."

"It's a little unsettling," Tink admitted.

The two walked in silence until the estate came into view. "Look up, Ben," Tink said. "I can't believe it. The sky is getting dark."

"Stick with me, kid. The knee never lies. I come in handy every now and then."

"I'd laugh but there's not much to laugh about these days."

"The fact we haven't heard from either the sheriff or the two clowns from the state is a good sign."

Tink pulled the old key from her pocket and unlocked the door.

"You can't be serious," Ben said. "This place still uses skeleton keys?"

"Yes, it does. Creepy, huh?"

"Cool. Let me see those."

Tink pushed the door open before handing him her keys. "How about a cold beer? We could sit in the parlor."

"Sure." Ben turned to enter the parlor while Tink went to the kitchen. When she returned with two bottles of beer, he was studying the rusty keys. "I thought the whole point of skeleton keys was that one opened every door. A master key of sorts."

"My thoughts exactly," Tink agreed. "However, it's not necessarily the case. Certain keys open all the bedrooms, others different areas of the house. I've never heard of having a key to bedrooms in one's own house."

"You weren't acquainted with the Sinclairs," Ben added.

"What have you heard about them?"

"They were more of a legend, an urban legend, I should say. People made up all types of stories about them because they were different from the rest of us. Money changes the dynamic. Add to it a creepy old mansion in ill repair and you have the recipe for a perfect ghost story."

"People feared the house?"

"You know how people are. I assume they're the same everywhere, but everyone relishes the thought of a haunted house. Not that there's any truth to it, but it makes for a good story just the same. You have to admit this makes the perfect backdrop. But to answer your question, I can only speak from my own experience. Your grandfather was an extremely arrogant man. It was almost as though he thrived on people not liking him. He wasn't very approachable, which only added to the mystique. I'm sure that's how he preferred it."

"Tell me more about Thomas Blanchard. I remember the first time—well, the *only* time—I met him. Candace and I stopped there for gas and he was quite accommodating. That is until he found out I'd inherited this place."

"Yeah, he wasn't very fond of Baron Sinclair. As you've seen, there aren't many places to do business in Kane and Thomas has about the only gas station around. Even though Baron lived in this big place, he blew through his money—at least that's what I've heard. He'd put things on a tab with Thomas then take months to pay him. Thomas would inevitably cut him off at some point, then the games would begin. On and on it went until Baron died, leaving quite a bit on his tab as word has it."

"Oh no," Tink said. "That makes sense now. I feel terrible. I should go settle the tab as soon as possible."

"I think I'd give it a while," Ben said. "He still has to bury his wife."

"Yikes. Not that I'd forgotten or anything, but let's start there. Why would someone murder Thomas's wife? I've been trying to find a connection between two out-of-towners, Opal Blanchard, and me."

"Opal Bailey-Blanchard."

"Huh?"

"She insisted on the hyphenated name. Not sure why, but it was important to her. Many people didn't like her for it, thought it was some type of feminist BS, but she wouldn't back down. I respected her for that. At any rate, she was one of a kind. Never understood what she saw in Thomas, but she loved him."

"I was wondering the same thing," Tink said. "They seem as different as night and day."

"I can see how you'd think that," Ben said. "On the outside looking in, they were quite different, but they had a lot more in common than you'd think. Ms. Opal was a lady, a refined lady from the big city, much like yourself. She was well-read and traveled, and quite attractive. Thomas hadn't ever left the city limits of Kane when he met her, or so the story goes, and refused to leave it even after they married. But they both cared about people and about Kane. I bet old Thomas has given away more gas than he's sold. Ms. Opal never minded though. They live in an old house not far from the station—nothing like she came from, I'm sure, but she made it a home."

"Did they ever have children? Aside from raising Cassius, I mean."

"Yes, one daughter, Esther. She got pregnant right out of high school and married the high school quarterback. A few years later, he was killed on one of the oil rigs, leaving her with two kids to raise. Pretty sad."

"Oh no. Does she still live in Kane?"

"Yes, I believe Ms. Esther lives with her parents now. I haven't even thought about her during all of this."

"It doesn't sound as if anyone would have a reason to kill Ms. Opal," Tink continued.

"If I had to pick a suspect, it'd be Baron Sinclair. No offense, of course. But that isn't possible."

"Why try to scare me away with that mannequin? I don't have a horse in this race, I just got here."

"I don't know," Ben answered. "I've thought about every angle, and frankly, there isn't one."

"One what?"

"An angle. No common thread between the three incidents, the first murders, then Ms. Opal's, and the staged scene here. Maybe there's no connection at all and someone's simply trying to make it appear as though there is."

"That's an interesting take," Tink said. "But what about you and your brother? You're both in the mix, too. Did you forget you found all three bodies?"

"Hell, no, I haven't forgotten," Ben said, his voice void of animosity despite the comment.

"Getting back to the keys," Tink said, "and the reasoning for locking the bedrooms. Paloma said she kept everything locked to keep people from stealing. That'd make sense since the Sinclairs had employees who cleaned the place. I'm certain there's bound to be some valuable pieces here. And money, even if Baron wasn't very wise with his."

"That's true. Every family has a black sheep, I suppose."

"Paloma acted weird about me looking around without her, almost as though there was something to hide. Candace and I were sneaking around one night, after Paloma had gone back to her place. One of the bedrooms, my mother's when she lived here, had a portrait of her above the mantel. She looked *exactly* like me. It freaked me out. Paloma said that was one of the reasons why she wanted to show me around personally, which could be true, but I find it odd. She was either being protective or hiding something—I'm not sure which."

"I can ease your mind on that one. Paloma's a good woman. She's been around here since her birth and I bet she knows a lot of family secrets. You can trust her. She'd never hurt anyone."

"How do you know her so well?"

"Paloma has always loved children, although she never married or had any of her own. With my mother passing away, my father often relied on her advice and babysitting services. We loved staying with her. It was quite interesting to learn of her culture and her skills as a traiteur."

"What is that exactly? Is it like a shaman?"

"That's a common misconception," Ben answered as he sat back further in his chair and placed the keys on the table beside him.

"People often use the term *witch doctor* too. Traiteurs use prayer for healing and supposedly act as a conduit to a higher spiritual power. In Paloma's case, that higher power is God. She's a devout Catholic and uses faith healing by prayer and the laying on of hands, coupled with medicinal remedies. She's a firm believer in modern medicine and often refers her clients to hospitals and local doctors. Unfortunately, her clientele comes from deep in the bayou and none of them trust anyone in the medical field. They believe going to a modern doctor will only make them sicker. It's very sad. Take the young mother that Horace brought to the estate yesterday. She could've very well died had she not come to Paloma when she did. The very fact she was unconscious saved her life. Otherwise, she'd never have agreed to go to the hospital. We can only hope she'll share her experience with others."

"Forgive me, but I don't completely understand. Why would they need her to pray for them? Why not pray for themselves?"

"Traiteurs' prayers are supposedly heard before those of others. Don't ask me exactly how it works, but it's quite an honor to be chosen. It's handed down from one generation to the next by a member of the opposite sex. Jericho chose Paloma to receive the calling for her generation."

"I remember her trying to pray for him as he lay dying," Tink said. "He refused her prayers, insisting there wasn't time."

"Jericho was a fine man."

"Why didn't Paloma ever marry?"

"I suppose she was too busy taking care of everyone around her. My father said she was a born matriarch. Even as a child, she was a caretaker."

"Just one more question," Tink pressed. "Why would Paloma and her family continue to work for the Sinclairs? It sounds as though my grandfather wasn't a very nice man."

"You should ask Paloma about her family sometime. They are very loyal people. They were initially slaves owned by the Sinclair family before Paloma's great, great grandmother was granted her freedom by Lucretia Sinclair, the woman this home was built for. I'm not certain of the details because I was so young when she told Dan and me about it, but Lucretia also granted her a parcel of land. That land was passed down through the generations and is the house Jericho lived in."

"That's amazing," Tink said.

The two sat in the parlor and drank their beers until Tink decided it was time to eat. "I'll go see what I can scrounge up for lunch," she said.

Tink was rambling through the refrigerator when she heard someone knocking on the front door.

"I'll get it," Ben said. "You stay back here."

50

Tink could hear conversation coming from the foyer and Ben sounded comfortable, putting her at ease. She closed the refrigerator and eased into the hall. Just as she was straining to hear voices, Ben and Horace rounded the corner.

"Hello, Ms. Catherine," Horace said. "I'm sorry to visit without calling first."

"You don't need to call," Tink assured him. "I'm happy to see you."

Paloma was behind him with a large picnic basket smelling of fried chicken.

"What's that I smell?" Tink asked, a broad smile crossing her face. "How'd you know we were hungry?"

"It's lunchtime and there's not much in way of a meal in that kitchen. Mind if we eat with you?"

"I've been waiting for you to join me," Tink said. "Kitchen or dining room?"

"Kitchen," Paloma said as she eased past her and placed the basket on the counter. "Would you grab the plates?" she asked Tink. "Hope everyone likes iced tea."

The four of them indulged in more than their share of fried chicken, potato salad, and fresh biscuits.

"I've never eaten this well in my life," Tink confessed. "I'll never fit in my business suits if I keep this up."

Paloma took her time wiping her mouth and placing the napkin back in her lap. "Horace has something to talk to us about," she said. "He believes it's important."

"What's going on?" Ben asked.

"I'm not sure," Horace confessed quietly. "It's just that..."

"It's okay, Horace," Paloma said. "You're among friends."

"I felt guilty for not telling my father about what's been going on," he began. "I intentionally kept the murders from him because there was no need to worry him." Horace cleared his throat and looked to Paloma for encouragement. She nodded at him. "I believe what's going on around here has something to do with the Sinclairs."

"The incident with the mannequin would certainly confirm that," Tink said. "But Ben and I have been talking and there's not a common thread among the murders or the staged scene, at least that we can find. What makes you so sure it's all related to the Sinclairs?"

"It never occurred to me that the first two murders could've had anything to do with your family," Horace said. "The fact that they were outsiders and, well, lived that type lifestyle made it appear their murders were related to criminal activity. My father loved Kane and I'm grateful he never learned of the recent drug problems here. I found no reason to tell him about it. I mean, why upset him at his age? I felt he was better off not knowing. We weren't acquainted with the victims so I was certain what he didn't know couldn't hurt him."

"That makes sense, Horace," Ben said kindly. "We all made the same assumptions. Appeared to be a drug deal gone bad, especially with the hands removed."

"The hands, that was the part that frightened him," Horace said.

"What about the hands?" Tink urged.

Horace was twisting his napkin like a nervous child.

"It's okay," Paloma said, slowly removing the material from his fingers. "Start from the beginning. We're not in a rush."

Horace cleared his throat and forced a cough into his cupped palm. "It was after you came home to that—that bloody doll with the black wig. I knew it was put there to frighten you and I couldn't understand why someone would do that. My father would've been very upset if he'd found out about it from anyone else, so I knew I had to tell him. Your family, the Sinclairs, are like our family. Our two families have lived on this land for generations. We lived a different life from this," he said, motioning in a wide circle meant to encompass the estate, "but we are loyal to your family just the same."

Tink squirmed uncomfortably. The thought of her family treating these kind people as their help was unsettling, to put it mildly. "I'm sorry if the Sinclairs made you feel you were any less important than they were. I would never..."

Paloma held her hand up to stop Tink. "Times were different back then. 'Tis nothing to apologize for, child. Now isn't the time to revisit old wounds. There were many good times here. Let Horace finish."

Tink nodded in his direction and diverted her eyes to the kitchen table. She swallowed hard in hopes of easing the burning sensation in her throat.

"It was after you discovered the mannequin in the house that I realized I had to share it with my father. I could no longer keep things from him—word was bound to get out." He forced another cough into his hand and continued. "I explained the first two murders to him, and he was saddened such a thing could happen in Kane. But it was when I told him about their hands being cut off that he got terribly upset. He was so upset that I pleaded with him to let me take him to the hospital. His exact words were, 'I prayed ten thousand prayers that I'd never live to see the Sinclairs' sins come back to haunt them.'"

Tink and Ben both gasped. "What did he mean by that?" Tink asked, just above a whisper.

"I'm not sure. He muttered something about secrets traveling down through generations of menfolk. Secrets so terrifying they were never meant to reach the ears of others, secrets so treacherous they should be buried deeper than the dead. I pleaded with him to tell me more, but his breathing was growing labored. He wanted me to get

Paloma and..." Horace's voice cracked, and he cleared his throat. "He wanted me to bring Paloma to him so I drove here as quickly as I could. But he did assure me of one thing."

"What was that?" Tink asked, leaning forward to encourage him to continue. "What did he assure you of, Horace?"

"I told him I had so many questions and he assured me the answers to all of my questions were there. He was referring to his home. My father said, 'The answers to all of your questions are here.'"

With that, Horace leaned back in his chair, clearly exhausted.

"I don't understand," Tink said, also suddenly exhausted. "How could any of this be tied to my family? Why would the murders of two strangers and Opal Blanchard be traced back to them? I'm the only living Sinclair on the planet and I certainly didn't do any of this. Dead people can't murder anyone."

"We know that," Ben said. "Perhaps something from the past resembled these crimes, right, Paloma?"

Paloma shook her head slowly, her eyes misting over. "I... I wish I knew. But one thing is certain, if Jericho said the answers are there, then they are."

"If your family has been on this land as long as mine, Paloma, you have to know something," Tink said flatly.

"There were generations before us," Paloma said, taking no offense to the insinuation she knew more than she was sharing. "We were, as they say now, on two opposite sides of the track. Their life was very different from ours, not better or worse, simply different. We longed for little, so material things didn't mean much to our family. On the other hand, material things equate to wealth and with that comes power. We knew our place."

"That makes me very uncomfortable," Tink said.

"It was a different time, far from what the world is like now. But don't feel sorry for us," Paloma said playfully. "Not all of our family chose to stay here in Kane. We have doctors and lawyers and Indian chiefs among us. Horace has a brother who practices law in Boston and a sister who's a nurse practitioner in Seattle. We," she continued, pointing to Horace then herself, "are here because it is the life we chose. Don't carry the weight of the past, Ms. Catherine. 'Tis not your cross to bear."

"Please, please," Tink pleaded, "don't call me Ms. Catherine. I don't think I can take it anymore."

"Tink," Ben urged, "don't be disrespectful. It's out of respect that Ms. Paloma calls you that."

"I'm not an elderly person and I'm not more important than she is," Tink said bluntly. "I don't feel comfortable."

"Very well, then," Paloma conceded. "I shall call you Catherine. My apologies for making you uncomfortable but old habits die hard. Let's move forward, dear."

It was then that the tears came. Tink could no longer keep them or her raw feelings inside. Large drops rolled down her cheeks, followed by racking sobs. Ben slid his chair closer to her and held her as she heaved and heaved, until she was too exhausted to shed another tear. Tink raised her head from Ben's embrace and wiped her face with a napkin. As she looked up, Horace and Paloma's eyes were cast downward.

"I'm so sorry," she said, standing and walking to the sink to wet a cloth. The cool rag brought instant relief. "I don't know what's wrong with me, but apparently I've needed that meltdown since I got here. It's been too much to deal with at once."

Paloma busied herself with stacking the dirty dishes in her basket. "I'm sorry, child. We shouldn't have burdened you with this foolishness."

"No," Tink said, rushing over to grab Paloma's arm. "Please don't go. I'm going to be okay. At least we know there are answers somewhere. Without the answers, there's no way to stop this."

51

PALOMA, Horace, Ben, and Tink sat at the kitchen table, deep in conversation. One thing was certain—they needed to find the answers to many lingering questions.

"My mother, Clementine, was a midwife," Paloma said. "I never had any interest in inheriting her calling, although I do love children. My uncle passed his gift down to me, which was a blessing in many ways. I do recall whispers, but knew it was in my best interest to let them remain just that—whispers."

"What kind of whispers?" Tink asked.

"There was always talk," Paloma answered. "As much as you don't like to hear it, our family has always worked for your family in some capacity or another. My great-great grandmother, Prudence, was the first of our ancestors here. She was originally a slave for a neighboring plantation that eventually went into the sugar cane business with Emmanuel Sinclair."

"That's interesting," Tink said. "Does that family still live on their estate?"

"The estate is no longer there. I can only speculate as to what became of it. At some point, Prudence was moved over here. She was Lucretia Sinclair's midwife. The two women were very close and just before the Civil War ended, Lucretia granted Prudence her freedom and a parcel of land. That is the land and original home where Horace now resides. The history gets a little fuzzy through the next generations, but there *was* talk among our family through the years. You must understand we were trusted with many family secrets the Sinclairs didn't want revealed and it was in our best interest to ensure they were kept."

"Now isn't the time to keep quiet," Tink pleaded. "Please, share what you know."

"I worked for Baron and Ruby the years they owned the estate. I also worked as a traiteur from my place on the bayou. I'm certain both my mother, Clementine, and her brother, Jericho, tried to shelter Horace and me from the Sinclairs. They kept their secrets close to the chest, and most likely believed we were better off not knowing them. Baron was the black sheep of the family. He was reckless and uncaring, and well, lazy. It was as simple as that. Many of us believed he'd go through what was left of the family money and the estate would eventually land in the hands of another owner."

"Do you know why my mother didn't like this place?" Tink asked, fearful of what she'd learn.

"Her grandparents, Corbin and Annabelle, were very fine people. They had a daughter, Penelope, who only lived five weeks. Baron, Olivia's father, was born next and they both doted over him like there'd never been a lovelier child in all the world. It soon became evident he had no intention of carrying on the family legacy. His wild antics were what put poor Mr. Corbin in the ground and Ms. Annabelle soon followed."

"What did he do to them?" Tink asked.

"He never physically harmed them. He just filled their days with disappointment and heartache. Baron scoffed at the thought of running a sugar cane business while walking around with his hand out to his father. The final straw was when Baron brought Ruby home to meet his parents. Mr. Corbin knew then, according to my mother, the Sinclair name would forever be tarnished. He and Ms. Annabelle had hoped Baron would soon change his ways, and mature as he got older. But when he married Ruby, they gave up all hope."

"So, my mother didn't like it here because of her parents?"

"Sweet Corbin lived long enough to see your mother born and he was overheard praying many nights that she'd change the hearts of Baron and Ruby. Unfortunately, Olivia couldn't. They never treated her kindly, Ms.—um—Catherine. They never knew what a jewel they had."

"Is that why she moved to New Orleans?" Tink persisted.

"Yes, I'm sure she was much happier away from them, as sad as it sounds. But we have other matters we need to discuss now."

"Yes," Ben said. "They'll be plenty of time for you and Paloma to talk about your mother. I'm sorry to press forward, but what family secret could be bad enough to tie the Sinclairs to these murders?"

Paloma looked at Horace and shook her head. "We both wish we knew. For the life of us, we can't recall anything that in any way links the two. As I said before, we are the youngest in our family, and they tried desperately to shield us. It was never as if our family met and discussed such things anyway. There were some conversations that were very hush-hush."

"But I'm the only one left," Tink said. "I don't know any secrets and I sure haven't killed anyone. Horace, you said your father told you all the answers were at his place. We should start there."

"Why don't you let Horace and me comb over his place while you and Ben start here?" Paloma suggested. "There might be something here my uncle wasn't aware of."

Tink sat silent for a moment before turning to Paloma. "Is there a reason why you didn't want me looking around without you?"

Paloma smiled kindly. "You were so fragile when you arrived, even with your strong-willed friend. I thought this place would be too overwhelming for you all at once. I preferred showing it to you in pieces. I believed it would be easier for you. I felt horrible the night you walked in Olivia's bedroom without warning you of the large portrait. I was trying to protect you, Catherine, not intimidate you."

Tink reached for the older woman's hand and gently squeezed.

"I'm glad my mother knew you. I have a feeling you protected her, too."

"Okay, enough of the sappy talk," Ben interrupted playfully. "Let's be productive, folks. What do you say I pick up dinner from Reggie's later and we meet back here about six?"

A loud boom evoked a scream from Tink, who jumped up from the table and cowered toward Ben.

"'Tis simply the storm rolling in," Paloma said softly. "We get more than our share here on the bayou. Be grateful for those that aren't harsh squalls, or God forbid, strong hurricanes."

Tink rubbed her hands up and down her arms. "I remember you mentioning it, Ben, but I'd forgotten." She turned to Paloma and asked, "Can I help you with that basket?"

"Oh, no, I'm fine. Horace drove us over."

"Let us walk you out," Tink suggested as she followed the pair to the front door. "Call us if you find anything."

"We certainly will," Paloma promised. "But, Catherine..." She stopped in the foyer to make direct eye contact. "Whatever you do, don't enter the west wing on the third floor. It was Emmanuel's office and it's been locked since his death. Apparently, his wife insisted on it. No one has a key anyway, but it's been sealed since 1865."

"That's odd, isn't it?" Tink asked.

"It may be odd, but do as I say, stay out of the west wing. There's nothing good about that place."

52

OPAL BAILEY-BLANCHARD'S body had been transported the day before to the closest medical facility capable of doing an extensive autopsy. Westmoreland was convinced a thorough post-mortem would be their only chance of salvaging any evidence that hadn't been contaminated by the overzealous imbeciles who'd trampled over the crime scene. The investigator was still fuming over their recklessness and reminded Sheriff Broussard of it every time it re-entered his mind.

To Westmoreland's dismay, Fontenot had turned out to be an asset. The young investigator had undoubtedly been attentive when he'd taken the forensic classes at the academy. He'd scoured over the scene of the latest murder with a fine-tooth comb, leaving no stone unturned. As far as how much would be admissible in court, should the time come, no one could know for sure, but Westmoreland was willing to risk the time Fontenot had invested.

The surrounding parishes had sent all the deputies they could spare to set up roadblocks on the roads leading in and out of Kane. Every car was stopped, and every driver questioned at length about anything unusual they might have seen or heard. It had proven to be a waste of time and manpower, but in a case such as this, it was a necessary gamble.

Westmoreland and Fontenot were heading the state's investigation, and both were getting antsy. Not only were they racing against time to catch a killer before they struck again, but their reputations were at stake. At his age, Westmoreland was taking his failure personally. He was nearing retirement and something like this would tarnish his well-earned standing among the more seasoned cops.

"This is bullshit," he seethed to Fontenot. "I find it hard to believe we can't find anybody in this little pissant town who knows something. They're lying out their asses."

"I'd tend to agree with you, but they don't appear to be hiding anything. They aren't acting like they're afraid of retribution, should they talk."

"So, think about that. What does it tell you?"

"That they clearly *don't* know anything," Fontenot answered flatly.

"If the people here don't know anything, it's because they don't know the perpetrator."

"Which would mean it's an outsider," Fontenot continued, squinting. "If it's an outsider, they'd stand out like a sore thumb."

Westmoreland motioned for Fontenot to get in his car. He was tired of the looks they were getting from the locals and didn't need the slew of out-of-area deputies listening to their potential theories.

"Let's think about this," Westmoreland began. "We have the new girl who just rolled into town to inherit a huge estate."

"The huge part I'll agree with," Fontenot said. "But unless she's sitting on a shitload of cash, she'd come out better to strike a match to it."

"Hey, the fat lady hasn't sung. You say that flippantly, but it just might turn out to be the case. So, she rolls into town, takes over the crumbling empire, and woos the alligator hunter, who, might I add, has personally found all three bodies. Coincidence?"

"It would be one hell of a coincidence, but on the flip side, what murderer would be foolish enough to put himself in that situation?"

"Don't ever question the mindset of a criminal," Westmoreland insisted. "Most serial killers are narcissistic and thrive on being the center of a circus like this."

"But Ben Norwood? I just don't see it," Fontenot said. "I don't doubt he's infatuated with the big city girl—she *is* a beauty, about the only one I've seen since we've gotten here."

"Don't tell me you're infatuated, too. A pretty face can be very misleading."

"No, I'm not infatuated," Fontenot said defensively. "I'm not saying it *couldn't* be her, but Norwood has been here his entire life and has no criminal record. The sheriff thinks a lot of him and..."

"Okay, he's got no record, and he's won the hearts of the locals, but he's never seen a beauty like the Sinclair woman, and she's an attorney to boot. She's leading him off to slaughter, I'm telling you."

"But did you see how distraught she was? That mannequin really scared her."

"Did you also see how well she handled our investigation? Norwood was all over the place, raging and cursing, and carrying on, but she kept her cool," Westmoreland added.

"I chalked her attitude up to her being an attorney. Atlanta's a huge metropolitan area so she's out of her element. I bet if we took her out on the bayou in a skimmer, she'd pee on herself."

"That's a thought," Westmoreland said. "Perhaps a field trip is in order. Maybe if we take little Ms. Prim and Proper out in the wild, she won't see it coming. In the meantime, I want to get warrants for her and Norwood's cell phone history. I bet you lunch we get a hit on something."

53

PALOMA AND HORACE had just climbed in the truck when the rain started falling in sheets. Tink shut and locked the front door and went into the parlor with Ben. "I can't believe it's so dark out," Tink said. "It's just mid-afternoon."

Ben pushed the curtain back and looked out. "Yep. It's gonna be a good one," he said. "Do you know where the fuse box is in case the electricity goes off?"

"I have no idea," Tink said. "I don't even know where the fuse box is in my loft back in Atlanta. Women like me aren't aware of those type of things."

"You better get aware," he said bluntly. "Especially in a house this size. I'd recommend getting that landline reconnected too. Cell service is spotty at best around here and you don't need to be without a phone should you have an emergency."

"I certainly agree with you there," Tink said. "That should be the first thing on my list."

"Do you know who to call?" Ben asked as he searched his phone contacts. "Here, call this number."

After being transferred several times, Tink had an appointment for the technician to come out the following day. "I haven't even seen any telephones," she said, the thought suddenly hitting her. "I'll need to purchase some before they come out. I know Father will be relieved to know he can reach me when I'm upstairs."

"You have to start thinking," Ben said. "Safety first, especially being a single woman alone in such a big place."

"You don't need to frighten me," Tink said.

"I'm just being honest. It's something you should always consider. I can spend a few hours with you today, but I'll have to go home and get some work done before coming back to spend the night. I haven't spoken to Dan today, but our gator hides need to be salted again, and some need to be laid out in the sun. It's a long process and we can't afford to lose any of them."

"What do you and Dan do exactly?" Tink asked.

"We're taxidermists," Ben answered. "It's big business here."

"What exactly does that mean?" Tink asked. "You mount deer heads and things like that, right?" She fought the urge to shiver.

"Yes, deer heads among other things," he said. "But if you didn't grow up around hunting, which I suspect you didn't, I'm not sure you'd take to it very well."

"You're probably right," she agreed. "I know you have other commitments, so let me get as much out of you as I can while you're here."

"You're just using me for my awesome personality and flawless good looks."

"Would you have a problem with that?"

"Not at all," Ben answered with a grin. "What part of the house should we start in first?"

"I'm not sure," Tink said, suddenly nervous.

"Okay, let's go up to the second floor. Bedrooms, right?"

"Yes, to the left of the stairwell. The west wing, as Paloma calls it."

"What's on the east wing then?" Ben asked as he stood to make his way to the rotunda.

"I think it's the ballroom."

"You have a ballroom?" Ben asked incredulously. "Forgive me, I'm trying to act as though I travel in such circles, but that's crazy."

"I'm not very optimistic. Judging from the entrance, I'm not thinking a great deal of upkeep has been done on it."

"Ye of little faith," Ben said, grabbing her by the hand. "Let's check it out."

Tink struggled to find as many light switches as possible. The storm had darkened the sky, making overhead lights and lamps necessary. The distant lightning generated sporadic bursts of light as the claps of thunder grew louder. The rumbling seemed to rattle the very foundation of the old place.

"Judging from that thunder, it's highly likely you could lose power," Ben said. "Do you know where the flashlights could be?"

"No. Like I said, I haven't had an opportunity to ramble around. Let's look in the storage area."

They retraced their steps to the kitchen and into the butler's pantry. "I'll never learn where all the switches are," Tink said as she felt around near the door. "There it is."

She flipped on the light. Ben rummaged through the cabinets until he felt he'd found enough batteries, two flashlights, a lantern, and a few candles.

"Doubtful we'll need all this, but better safe than sorry," he said.

"I can't find my way around with the lights *on*," Tink said playfully as they made their way back to the staircase.

"This could give you a good workout every day," Ben commented as they trekked up the stairs.

Tink slowed to marvel at the polished railing. "This is magnificent, isn't it?"

"Definitely the highlight of the home," Ben agreed. "Let it be your inspiration while you're renovating. I don't doubt this was a showplace in its day and certainly could be again—with a great deal of money, that is."

"Yep, I've heard that more than once," Tink said, slowly making her way to the second floor. "My father suggested I get a home inspector and I tend to agree. If we're dealing with some serious structural damage, it may not pay off to restore it."

"I haven't taken a real good look at her, but nothing indicates there's any foundational issues. It appears to have been built well. But a place this size requires constant maintenance. I'm sure just the few weeks since your grandfather passed away, it's suffered from being unoccupied."

"How is that exactly?" Tink asked. "How can a place go down with no one living in it?"

"Just think of how many times you open and close the outside doors daily and let in fresh air. Then you also have the heat and air running at an acceptable level, which helps."

They'd reached the top of the stairs and made a right. "I don't have any idea where I'm going," Tink said as she searched the wall for a hall light.

"These hallways are wide enough to be rooms," Ben said.

"This hall is even wider than the other wing. I'm sure they wanted to make a statement to guests coming to their balls, and it certainly would have."

The patterned carpet displayed dark, jeweled tones and, judging by its appearance, was original to the house. Over the years, filthy stains had set in along with several areas tattered so badly the hardwoods shown from underneath.

"Bet this carpet cost a pretty penny when it was put in," Ben said, squatting to run his fingers over it. "I would've loved to see it back then. When it was new, I mean."

"What a shame," Tink mumbled as she kneeled to inspect it. "There's no way this could be salvaged. I can't imagine my grandparents living here without replacing the carpet. Look at the places where it's completely worn through."

"I suppose it's all about priorities," Ben said. "But I understand what you're saying. The good news is there are some amazing hardwood floors underneath. If I were you, I'd just have these carpets taken up."

"Easier said than done," Tink said. "Let's find the ballroom."

The thunder and lightning were moving in, sounding like waves crashing against the shore. The lightning flashes were now long bolts zigzagging across the sky.

"I feel like I'm in a horror movie," Tink admitted. "I don't know what the hell I'm doing here. If you'd told me I'd be in this situation a month ago, I would've sworn you were crazy." She headed toward the ballroom with determination.

Ben followed behind until Tink opened the large double doors to reveal what was surely a gem in its prime. The two gasped as they took it all in. The parqueted floors still shone from over a century of repeated polishing, while crystal chandeliers gave off a dim, romantic glow. Chairs lined the walls, interrupted every few feet by small tables, perhaps to offer a place for the partygoers to place their drinks and fancy finger foods as they socialized.

Tink held her arms out wide and spun around, dancing to inaudible music as she dreamed of what it must've been like to be one of the lucky ones who'd received an invitation to the ball. "Wouldn't you have loved to be here when this place was alive?" she asked Ben. "Just imagine what it was like. I bet the women were beautiful, their dresses flowing as they walked up that staircase, their hair piled high, and wearing their best jewelry. I wish I could've seen it then."

Before Ben could reply, another bolt of lightning lit up the room followed by a crack of thunder that sent Tink darting into his arms.

"It's okay," he assured her. "The storm will blow over soon." As soon as the words had left his lips, lightning again struck, and the house went dark.

The ballroom suddenly felt full of people, and the warmth of their bodies was suffocating.

54

PALOMA FILLED the kettle with water and placed it on the stove. It was the only thing she could think to do that might bring solace. The old house seemed so empty without her uncle. Perhaps sitting together at the kitchen table with a warm cup of coffee would offer Horace some comfort.

They sat together in silence until the steam caused the pot to squeal. The warm liquid did seem to relax him. Paloma hoped the search for clues would take his mind off his loss.

"What secrets do you know, Paloma?" Horace asked. "I'm sure you've heard some."

"We were the youngest generation," she answered. "By the time we came along, there weren't so many secrets to be kept. And let's face it, Baron and Ruby didn't exactly hide their dirty laundry."

The last comment made Horace chuckle. "You're right about that," he agreed. "What ultimately caused the empire to crumble?"

"Corbin was a good man," Paloma began, sitting back in the old cane chair with her coffee. "He worked hard to keep it up, but he wasn't well. Baron's behavior didn't help. It was clear early on, according to Jericho, that Baron would never put in an honest day's work."

"You and Baron were about the same age, weren't you?" Horace asked.

"Yes, we were, although it didn't seem like it. He was wild as a buck, that boy. We never had anything to do with each other as children, your Auntie Clementine made *sure* of that," Paloma said. It was her turn to chuckle. "Mama always saw right through him. To hear her tell it, as soon as she delivered him, it was painfully clear he'd never amount to anything."

"Why didn't they have any more children? Was Baron too much work for them?"

"Too much work for *them*?" Paloma asked before bursting into laughter. "He was too much work for *Mama*. Corbin was struggling to keep the business above water and poor Ms. Annabelle was frightened of Baron. By the time he brought Ruby home, they were ready to throw in the towel."

"How'd Baron and Ruby meet?"

"Through mutual friends. Ruby had gone to high school a few towns over and when she set her eyes on the estate, she saw dollar signs."

"And a gullible man, apparently," Horace added.

"Ruby was a looker back in her prime and knew how to use it to her advantage. But Corbin and Annabelle saw through her façade and even anticipated the train wreck around the bend."

"So that's how she ended up a Sinclair?"

"It wasn't very difficult for her. But getting back to your first question—Annabelle had a daughter before Baron was born. Penelope was her name. She was only a few weeks old when she died."

"What happened to her?" Horace asked.

"Many children died young back then. If they lived to the age of three or four, they were considered out of the woods."

"Very sad," Horace said. "I wonder why the two of us never married or had kids of our own?"

"It must not have been in the cards. Just wasn't meant to be."

The two cousins nursed the coffee until it grew cool. "Here,"

Paloma said, standing and taking his cup. "Let me refill these, and I'll tell you about the curse."

"Sounds interesting."

"It was one of those things they whispered about. I'm sure you know what I mean."

"Indeed, I do," Horace agreed, accepting the refilled mug she handed him. "Papa knew to check around the corner before he started talking about that family. He'd always find me hiding, trying to hear something I had no business hearing."

Paloma nodded. She also recalled times where the voices were so foreboding that she struggled to get as far from what they were saying as possible. She shivered and pulled her wool cardigan tighter around her midsection.

"Are you okay, Paloma?"

"Yes, I am, just recollecting things I'd rather forget."

"Papa told me over and over that some secrets are best left buried. Do you think we should leave the Sinclairs' past alone?"

"Under any other circumstance, I would be the first to agree with Uncle Jericho," Paloma replied. "But we don't have a choice now. Innocent people are dying and if we can find out why, the good Lord would want us to do so."

Horace seemed to ponder this before shaking his head. "So, you never told me about the curse."

"I never got it firsthand," Paloma said, settling in the chair again. "But I've heard talk that's come from generations before us. You know our great, great grandmother Prudence was the first of our family to live on this land. She and our great, great grandfather George. Prudence was a midwife to the black family who lived adjacent to this property before moving to the Sinclair land."

"A black family? Did *they* own slaves?"

"Indeed, they did," Paloma replied. "That's where it gets a little hazy though. Apparently, they merged businesses with the Sinclairs and were quite prosperous. I'm not sure what happened to them, but their slaves were transferred over to this estate."

"That's interesting," Horace mused. "What happened to their home?"

"Not sure, but at any rate, Prudence and George moved here and she birthed the Sinclair children. At least during her lifetime. She passed that gift on to her daughters, but thankfully it bypassed me. I was frightened of that much responsibility and your papa was kind enough to see the traiteur characteristics in me."

"Okay, so let's get back to the curse. What *was* it?"

"For some reason, the Sinclairs believed there was a curse on their firstborn. And, true enough, the firstborn of each generation died, either shortly after birth, or within the first few weeks of their life."

"Stop there," Horace said, holding his hand up. "Remember what Papa said, the scripture he recited? The one Catherine was referring to?"

"Yes," Paloma answered, before walking over to the table beside Uncle Jericho's chair to retrieve his worn Bible. She opened it and located the scripture in question. "It comes from Deuteronomy 24:16," she said. "And look," Paloma began, turning the Bible so Horace could see the scripture, "Jericho highlighted it. It reads: 'The fathers shall not be put to death for their children, neither shall the children be put to death for their fathers; every man shall be put to death for his own sin.'"

"What do you suppose that means?" he asked.

"It sounds as though something occurred that led them all to believe the family was being punished, or cursed, rather. Perhaps a sin so big their family would have to pay for it forever."

"Pay for it by losing their firstborn child?" Horace asked, just above a whisper.

"But Uncle Jericho never believed it. That must be why he highlighted this particular scripture. He knew God wouldn't put a child to death for the sins of his father."

"But apparently each generation did lose their firstborn," Horace said.

"Indeed, they did. But many children died young during that time."

"So, it could've simply been a coincidence?"

"Exactly. I'm certain there was a reasonable explanation for their deaths, but the Sinclairs must have been convinced otherwise."

"But Olivia lived and so did her child," Horace added.

"Yes, but my mother was always tight lipped about Baron and Ruby. There was some sort of uneasiness among the three of them that was left unspoken. She loved Olivia and so did I, but her parents were terribly hateful to her. To say there was no love there would be an understatement."

"Why was that?" Horace asked. "I remember her being such a sweet girl, to say nothing of her beauty."

"Perhaps Ruby was jealous of her, but Baron made it painfully clear he wanted a son to leave his estate and business to."

"What was left of the business at that time?"

"Very little," Paloma replied. "It killed Baron's father. Jericho continued to work our land and sell off the cane each year, but as Corbin became too ill to keep the mill going, Baron did nothing to salvage their business. He thought the money was unlimited, but soon found that wasn't the case. When the money started to run low, Ruby was livid, but by then her looks had begun to fade and her options of finding another wealthy man to take her in were long gone."

"Where did he spend the money?" Horace asked. "Certainly not on the house."

"Who knows?" Paloma said. "Baron liked to be a big shot. Corbin knew he'd go through the money like water, but whispers suggested Corbin had set some aside that Baron wasn't aware of. I don't know if there was any truth to it."

"Is it true Baron and Ruby never reached out to Catherine?"

"I'm certain it is," Paloma said, nodding. "I was there the day Olivia went into labor with her. They were treating her deplorably, bullying her as they often did. It sickened me, but there was little I could do. They were certain she was faking her labor. I knew different. Olivia was so unlike them. She'd never have feigned such a thing. Her pains were so intense she was barely coherent by the time her husband arrived to take her to the hospital. I desperately wanted to ride with him, to ease her suffering somehow, but that wasn't to be."

"Did they make it to the hospital before she passed away?" Horace asked.

"An ambulance caught up with them on the road and they transported her the last few miles. She didn't deliver Catherine until after they'd reached the hospital, but from what I understand, Olivia wasn't conscious when she was born." Paloma's eyes filled with tears. "Such a waste."

"Who would want to harm her daughter now?"

Paloma shook her head, lost in the memories of the horrible day. "Someone who is terribly twisted."

"So, you never found out why Auntie Clementine was so uncomfortable around Baron and Ruby?"

"No, she'd completely shut down whenever I questioned her."

"Do you think it was because of how they treated their daughter?"

"No," Paloma was quick to say. "It was something far more disturbing than that."

"That has to be the key to what's happening now," Horace surmised.

"I think it's something from much further in the past," Paloma said. "Clearly, there are some secrets we need to unlock. Otherwise, Jericho wouldn't have mentioned them."

55

FONTENOT SIGHED, straightening up in the seat as a pair of headlights hit the windshield. Then the vehicle came into view—not their guy. He sighed and dropped his head into his hand, aware that he was biding time and his partner was awaiting his opinion. Truth was, though, he wasn't very confident in their ability to get a communications warrant on Ben or Catherine's phone call logs. "A judge would never agree to it. We have zilch in terms of probable cause."

"So, we have a confidential informant who suddenly gives us probable cause," Westmoreland said.

"You can't be serious," Fontenot huffed, agitated. "We don't have a CI and if we did, they'd have to sign an affidavit swearing to their information. I know you aren't suggesting we falsify that shit."

"No, I'm not suggesting we falsify a damn thing," Westmoreland spat. "The fact Norwood was at every scene is circumstantial evidence."

"It's evidence he found the bodies, not evidence he murdered and dismembered them." Fontenot sighed heavily and slumped back in the passenger seat. The two sat in silence for several minutes before Fontenot spoke again. "We could always ask them to agree to release their cell phone logs," he said. "If they truly want to be cleared, they'd be happy to do so."

"What's to say they don't have a burner?" Westmoreland asked. "Of course, they'd agree to give us their legit phones."

"Give me a damn break," Fontenot said as he rolled his eyes and cracked the window. "Do you seriously think those two are using burner phones? That's the craziest shit you've ever said."

"Look, we've got to come up with something real soon or it'll be our necks on the chopping block."

"What about the victims' cell phones?" Fontenot asked. "When do they expect to retrieve the information from them?"

"I put in a call to the communications specialist and he's moving it to top priority. However, they were cheap burner phones, purchased with cash, and severely damaged from the filthy bayou water. I'm sure the chips are damaged too badly to give us anything. Opal didn't receive a phone call on her cell the day of her death and the landline at the gas station doesn't have caller ID."

"Great, just our luck. Anything on any of the fingerprints?"

"There were a few on the male's wallet and hopefully a partial on the girl's necklace, but I'm not holding my breath," Westmoreland replied.

"Anything in their motel rooms?" Fontenot asked.

"Yeah, prints everywhere, all belonging to the crowd they hung with, but their rooms weren't where their murders occurred."

"I just don't see a connection between Norwood, the girl, and that other crowd. Doesn't add up. Besides, if the girl knew Norwood prior to coming here, it'd get out," Fontenot pointed out.

"Okay, so what does that leave us?" Westmoreland asked, looking at his young partner.

"Hell, I don't know. If I did, I wouldn't be sitting in this car—I'd be making an arrest."

"What about the old man, Thomas Blanchard? Pretty convenient he had to be whisked away to the hospital, huh? Got him out of being questioned at the scene," Westmoreland said.

"I'd tend to agree with you, but you can't fake blood pressure that high," Fontenot argued.

"My damn blood pressure runs that high all the time."

"I'm not married, but I do find it odd he'd leave his wife in charge of a gas station while he went fishing."

Westmoreland let out a deep laugh. "I know that's right. If I made my wife work at a place like that, I'd come home to divorce papers. But apparently, he has a standing date with a buddy every other Monday to go fishing. Sheriff verified it."

"So, what's Blanchard's story?" Fontenot asked.

"Same as the rest of these yahoos," Westmoreland answered. "Born and bred here, hasn't ever left the city limits. The wife moved here out of college and they started the business."

"Look around," Fontenot suggested. "Not a lot of businesses here. Bet there isn't another gas station for miles. Maybe he was selling more than petrol, which could possibly link him to the couple from down by the rigs. The wife's murder could've been payback for some bad business. Any other business partners or family?"

"Blanchard owns the business outright," Westmoreland said. "The sheriff said they have a daughter, a couple of grandchildren, and of course that knucklehead of a deputy."

"I say we start with their marriage and finances," Fontenot began. "Maybe the wife didn't know of any illegal dealings and wouldn't have gone along with it."

"It's definitely a lead we have to pursue. Somehow I already see the feathers ruffling when we start that line of questioning."

"Speaking of feathers ruffling," Fontenot said, pointing to the sheriff pulling up in his vehicle. "Let the games begin."

The torrential rains kept the state investigators from getting out of their vehicle, so Westmoreland cracked his window to speak to Isaac. "Got anything, Sheriff?"

"Nothing but a bunch of lazy deputies to babysit," he yelled over the sounds of the storm. "Can you guys meet me back at the precinct?"

"Sure, why not?" Westmoreland answered. "Got nothin' else to do."

❦

ISAAC STRUGGLED NOT to allow the investigator's lackadaisical comment to get under his skin. It was something said out of frustration from their lack of progress, but it irritated him just the same. Although Kane was a small department, and rarely dealt with serious issues, Isaac ran a tight and professional ship. He was unaccustomed to dealing with big egos and condescending cops, and it didn't sit well with him.

The flooding rains slowed the drive to his office, making the drive take almost twice the usual time. Isaac was appreciative of the extra few minutes to allow his exasperation to recede. Having a chip on his shoulder would only impede the investigation. He pulled into his parking space and grabbed the bright yellow rain slicker from the passenger seat. It was already drenched and would only succeed in getting him wetter, but he held it over his head as he ran into the building.

Westmoreland and Fontenot had done the same. None of the men owned an umbrella. They were considered a messy waste of time and cops never had extra time. Isaac tossed them both a hand towel as he made his way behind his desk.

"What's the latest on Mr. Blanchard?" Fontenot asked.

"He's still in the hospital. It took quite a while to get his blood pressure down, as I'm sure you'd expect. They're going to keep him one more night as a precautionary measure. Any news on when they'll release Ms. Opal's body to the funeral home?" Isaac inquired.

"It'll be sometime today," Westmoreland spoke up. "They assured me the autopsy would be completed by early afternoon. Hopefully, we'll get some DNA."

"Then we'd need someone to match it to," Isaac added. "We haven't gotten any matches on the DNA retrieved from the other two bodies."

"It's time consuming," Fontenot added. "But a call could come in at any minute confirming a match. It's a waiting game."

"Let's just hope we don't find another victim in the meantime," Isaac said.

"Tell us more about Blanchard," Westmoreland interrupted. "Everyone around here can't be the perfect citizen. How was his marriage? Are you certain it was a stable one?"

Isaac took a slow, deep breath before answering, trying to maintain his objectivity. "I suppose we never know what goes on behind closed doors, but they're still together after all these years. That has to say something. Other than being quite different, the two seemed to be as happy as any married couple can be."

"Any financial troubles?" Westmoreland pressed.

"Not that I'm aware of. They live modestly but have a nice home. The business has been around for as long as I can remember. They do a fair amount of traffic, being as they're one of two gas stations in the city limits."

"Who's their competition?" Fontenot asked.

"Another small station just behind the town square. It's owned by the McCain brothers, who do mechanic work. They also have an account with the city, so we fill our patrol cars up there. I wouldn't call the two competitors. Thomas's place is on the outskirts of town, so he caters more to the people in that area."

"I find it odd that Thomas leaves his wife in charge of a gas station while he fishes," Fontenot threw in.

"As I said, if anyone needs car repairs, oil changes, that type of thing, they go to the McCain's. Everyone pumps their own gas nowadays, so it wasn't as if Ms. Opal had to get her hands dirty. She just had to ring up any snack items or gas purchases."

"And Mr. Blanchard has had this standing fishing date for quite some time?" Fontenot asked.

"For as long as I can remember," Isaac confirmed. "He and Simon Granger fish every other Monday, rain or shine. I suspect we'll have a guesstimated time of death from the coroner."

"Yes," Westmoreland said. "But as you know, our best bet for getting the most accurate time would be to talk to the last person who saw her alive."

"I'm looking into that," Isaac said. "It sure would be convenient if Thomas had installed security cameras, but he's never needed them...until now."

"Hindsight has a way of biting you in the ass," Westmoreland said. "Any chance of him dealing drugs out of his business?"

"I'd be very surprised," Isaac began before catching himself. "Look, fellas, I've known Thomas all of my life so I'm sure it appears I'm taking up for him, but he's a good man. If you can't find him at the gas station, he's either fishing with Simon or he's at home. I don't believe he's ever left Kane in his life. Didn't even go with Ms. Opal to Tennessee when her parents passed away."

"Doesn't sound like the kind of guy who'd want to bring any illegal business to his town," Fontenot concluded.

"Exactly," Isaac agreed. "I just hope he doesn't have a heart attack when he sees Ms. Opal in her casket."

"Speaking of her funeral," Westmoreland said, "I guarantee you the killer will be there. It's the perfect opportunity to see the grief they've caused."

56

BEN TENDERLY PEELED Tink's arms from around his waist, though she didn't want to let go, and switched on a flashlight. He shone it around the circumference of the room, confirming they were indeed alone.

"The lights will be back on soon," he said. "Would you feel more comfortable downstairs?"

"No," she insisted. "I want the truth if I have to search this whole house in the dark." Tink reached for the flashlight but Ben resisted.

"No, I've got it," he said. "I'll hold it for you."

"Don't treat me like a child."

"I didn't mean—"

"I'm sorry," Tink said, reaching again for the light. This time Ben surrendered it. "Let's start with the tables and chairs. Turn them over and see if anything is taped on the bottom."

"We aren't doing a shakedown in a prison," Ben said. "I don't think they would've been intentionally hiding things to be found generations later."

"Maybe you're right, but let's not take any chances."

Ben fumbled around until he had the lantern up and going, giving them two sources of light. "That's much better," he said. "I'll start on this end. You check that set of doors on the other end."

Tink made her way across the expansive room, shining the light across the floor as she walked. The flashes of light from the storm added a movie-scene vibe she was growing accustomed to. She tried both crystal doorknobs, but neither were unlocked, so she fumbled through her set of keys. The smallest key on the ring slid easily into the lock. Expecting a small closet of some kind, she was surprised to see an elegant dressing room and closet filled with magnificent gowns of every color. Some were covered with protective, cotton covers—others clearly visible and unobscured. Tink pulled one from the many racks and held it up as she viewed herself in the mirror.

Absolutely stunning, she thought. *How many can there possibly be?*

After placing the silk gown back on the rack, she stuck her head through the double doors. "You have to see this. It's unbelievable."

Ben quickly made his way to the dressing room. "Wow, this is something. How old do you suppose these dresses are?"

"Gowns," Tink corrected. "Beautiful, expensive gowns. If I were going to hide any secrets, any documented ones, I'd certainly store them in my closet or near my personal items."

"What type of documented secrets are you referring to?" Ben asked.

"I was using the word rather flippantly," Tink said. "I didn't mean a certified document or anything of that sort, although we can't rule it out. I was thinking more of diary entries or personal letters."

"Let's close the doors," Ben said. "This lantern should provide enough light for us to look around."

Tink did as he asked and turned the flashlight off in case the power didn't return anytime soon. "How many do you suppose there are?"

"I have no idea, but it's a lot. I don't know anything about dresses, I mean *gowns*."

Tink pulled a couple from their rack and handed them to Ben. "Hold those up for me. Look, they all appear to be the same size. I know historically, women were much smaller back in the 1800s, but what are the odds they were all the same size? I bet the bulk of these belonged to one woman and my bet is on Lucretia Sinclair. The estate was built for her by her husband. Think about it—that was when this place was in its heyday. I bet there was nothing within hundreds of miles to even compare to its grandeur."

"That's true," Ben agreed. "This house wasn't just built for the two of them—it was built as a showpiece."

"Indeed," Tink added. "The tattered pieces of furniture that remain were surely fine, expensive pieces ordered from big cities and even other countries. The draperies and soiled carpets and rugs were nothing but the finest back then. And what would've been more important than an elegant ballroom to showoff than a beautiful wife dressed in the most expensive silk gowns that money could buy?"

"Women," Ben said, shaking his head. "Still the same today as they were hundreds of years ago. Some things never change."

"Women?" Tink asked smugly. "I'm referring to the men who prided themselves on showing off their trophy wives."

"Let's just be honest. It was both. This kind of money becomes a game of who can top the next guy."

"I'll agree with that. But, if we're going to find anything, I guarantee you we'll find it in here. Let's start with the dresses. Go over each of them with a fine-tooth comb. Run your fingers over the inseam and look through the layers of crinoline," Tink said. "I'll hand you one and I'll take one; when we're finished, I'll place them out in the ballroom to keep them separated. Are you okay with that?"

"Sure, whatever you say," Ben replied. "But I have to call Dan in a couple of hours, then head home to get some work done."

"Okay, Lucretia," Tink said softly, "give us some help here. We need answers."

As the words left her mouth, the power flipped back on in the house, providing Ben and Tink with much-needed light.

57

PALOMA HAD DELEGATED the attic of the small home to Horace, seeing as he was physically in better shape and could handle retrieving the boxes much easier than she could. He didn't mind that Paloma would be going through his father's chifforobe—better her than him. The loss was still too raw for him to handle.

Horace made his way up the attic stairs, unsure of what he was looking for or what he'd find. It'd been years since he had visited the space, and he wondered when someone last had. That alone gave him pause. The steps were still in decent shape, providing a stable footing for his dense frame. Through the years, the muggy humidity had caused the heavy wooden door to warp, but it opened without much effort. A host of cobwebs had joined forces and produced a makeshift barricade.

Horace placed his hands out before him and parted the combination of insect and rodent habitats to make his way to the long string dangling from the ceiling. To his relief, the light bulb was still in working order and didn't blow when he pulled on the lanyard.

Once the attic was illuminated, Horace was thankful to find himself alone. A sea of large dust particles forced him to pull a handkerchief from his back pocket and cover his mouth. An array of cardboard boxes were scattered about, along with a couple of old trunks, and a wide assortment of household items that had seen better days.

Horace opened a rusty toolbox and pulled out a flathead screwdriver. Paloma believed the darkest family secrets were further in the past, so he decided to start with the trunks. He couldn't recall ever seeing them, so he presumed they'd been stored in the attic before his time. A dry-rotted leather strap held the lock in place, and since he had no plans for the antiquated containers in the future, Horace made the executive decision to tear the leather. It'd be much easier than prying the locks open.

It took little effort to rip the aged leather and just like that, Horace was able to open the trunk. He half expected a cloud of dust to greet him but instead, everything had been packed away neatly, and protected from dirt. Uncertain of what he'd find inside, Horace was mildly disappointed to find nothing more than paperwork of plots and surveys of land. He lifted the top stack of papers out of the trunk and carried them closer to the exposed light bulb.

Horace could make very little of the legal verbiage. It referred to something called the arpent, long-lot division, and made comparisons of the square arpent mile. According to the document, 180 x 180 French feet were equivalent to 192 x 192 American feet, and one square mile was equivalent to 750 arpents. He rubbed his eyes again before studying what appeared to be a survey of their land. Certain the deed to the property had been filed with the City of Kane, Horace figured the documents were still important and should be saved. He flipped through them slowly, but decided trying to make anything of the legalese would be a waste of valuable time.

After straightening the papers neatly, he placed them at the top of the stairs leading down from the attic. He dug through the rest of the trunk only to discover the remaining papers were much the same as the survey of their own land. He did find a larger survey plan that was a cadastral map of the Sinclair property. It appeared to have been drawn at the height of their sugar cane production. He unfolded and spread the large paper across the floor before deciding the lighting was just too poor to make much out of it. He placed it on top of the other papers to take with him when he finished in the attic.

PALOMA BEGAN with removing Jericho's clothes from the chifforobe and laying them across his bed. She'd take the time to fold them and box them up later. It was important to see if there were any Horace wanted to keep first. Otherwise, she'd ask Ben or Dan to take them to a homeless shelter outside of Kane. That would've been what Jericho wanted.

Although his clothes bore years of use, they were all hung neatly in the old walnut wardrobe that had been used for decades. Paloma's eyes filled with tears as she recalled him wearing the different items through the years. Possessions hadn't been important to him, but he'd taken care of his belongings and prided himself in looking presentable when he wasn't working in the fields.

With that part of her task complete, Paloma removed his shoes. Before lining them along the wall, she took the time to feel inside each one to ensure he hadn't hidden anything inside. Her face stung from shame as she placed the last shoe on the floor. It seemed wrong to go through her uncle's belongings like this, an invasion of his well-deserved privacy. But she was doing what needed to be done. Jericho wouldn't have told Horace the answers were here if he hadn't expected him to search for them.

Once the clothes and shoes were removed, it was hard to make out the remaining items without a flashlight. Paloma walked to the bottom of the attic stairs and called for Horace.

"I'll be down in a second," he called, before making his way down the steps.

Paloma had moved to the kitchen, looking through the cabinets. "Have you seen any flashlights?" she asked without turning around.

"There should be one in the drawer of Papa's nightstand," Horace answered, shuffling behind her. "You should find some extra batteries in the cabinet to your right."

Paloma shifted and opened the cabinet beside the one she'd been rummaging through. "Yep," she answered. "Here's a brand-new pack of double As." She turned around and looked at the paperwork stacked high on the kitchen table. "What's all that?"

"I think it's the plot of our property," Horace answered. "I'm sure the deed's on file at City Hall, but we should keep these." He pointed to the large stack. "There's also a big aerial drawing of the land before the big house was built. That goes way back, huh?"

"Indeed, it does," Paloma answered. "I'd like to look over it this afternoon. It'd be interesting to see the changes over the years."

"I'm heading back up to see what else I can find in the attic. Are you making much progress?"

"Not so far," Paloma answered, deciding not to share she'd been removing his father's clothing from the closet. "Hopefully the flashlight will help."

"Let me know if you don't find it in the nightstand," Horace said.

Paloma located the flashlight and shined the light along the inside of the chifforobe. Her uncle had been a minimalist, so his clothes had made up most of the items inside. However, she was relieved to find a stack of notepads and papers in the far-left corner of the wardrobe. Paloma slid the pile out and carried it into the den where she placed them on the coffee table. The storm had finally subsided, allowing the sun to peek through the dark clouds. She opened the draperies, instantly brightening up the space. Breaking the stack down into several equal parts made the task seem more manageable. After briefly scanning over the tops of each pile, Paloma realized they'd been stacked in chronological order. Apparently, they were notes taken through the years by the women of the family and appeared to be personal journals.

Paloma knew it'd be best to start furthest back in her lineage, but the excitement of reading her own mother's thoughts got the best of her, so she flipped through several bound books before spotting the familiar handwriting. Paloma hugged the thick manuscript to her chest and walked to her uncle's chair to indulge herself in her mother's memories.

It wasn't until her tears ran past her jawline and down her neck that she realized she'd been crying. Paloma brushed them aside with the back of her hand and cleared her throat. She'd always found her mother's handwriting to be a beautiful combination of swirls and loops, much like calligraphy.

She'd hoped to discover more of a diary rather than insignificant notes relating to household duties, and what she found left her feeling less than enthused. She'd have read it word for word simply to learn more of her mother's day-to-day life, but time was critical. She glanced over the menial, repetitive tasks Clementine had completed each day but paused for the more intimate comments about her dealings with the Sinclair family.

Paloma pored over her mother's thoughts and concerns about Annabelle's suppressed fears of her son, Baron. As he grew older, his poor mother seemed more frightened of him than ever. In reading through the accounts, time started to seem inconsequential, which was why Paloma was shocked to see how much time had passed. She was about to put the journal to the side and start preparing a late dinner when something caught her eye.

SINCLAIR CURSE.

Paloma rolled her head to ease her aching neck and closed her eyes for a few seconds to rest her weary eyesight before easing back in the chair to read in earnest.

Ruby is growing more concerned about the Sinclair curse with each day. I can no longer try to reason with her as she becomes almost combative. Her second missed menstrual cycle all but confirms her pregnancy, yet she refuses to disclose the fact to her husband. Baron is growing more distant as he finds her irrational and needy. I continue to complete my daily tasks in a timely manner and avoid unnecessary contact with Ruby. Ms. Annabelle and Mr. Corbin are none the wiser of an impending grandchild and all but welcome Ruby's days spent wallowing in her bed. As a nursemaid and midwife, it remains my priority to see she is tended to where her health is concerned. Some priorities are more difficult than others and Ruby makes this one of those times.

Paloma put the journal to the side and filled the kettle on the stove. A cup of coffee would help to energize her. *Why would Ruby be so worried about the curse, yet treat her daughter so poorly when she survived?* It didn't make sense.

She called Horace from the bottom of the stairs to see if he wanted a cup of coffee.

"I'm fine." Horace assured her. When the kettle cried out, Paloma poured herself a large mug and sat back down to read again.

Today was perhaps the oddest of all the days I've spent in the employ of the Sinclairs. Ruby grabbed me fiercely by the arm and pulled me into her darkened closet, insisting I hear her out. I assumed she was losing her mind, but Ruby claimed she was completely sane.

Certain that her firstborn will fall prey to the curse, Ruby is convinced her child's only hope is to be given away. She has all but threatened me should I confide her pregnancy to anyone, and thus far I have honored her wishes. However, it is becoming more and more difficult. My head is telling me to go to Corbin and Annabelle, but my heart is telling me to go along with Ruby. Not that I believe in such foolishness as a curse placed upon a family, but because a child has no future in a place such as this. Ruby and Baron do not have the ability to provide for themselves and a child would be at risk. 'Tis as simple as that.

Paloma placed the journal on the coffee table and walked over to the window to look outside.

I don't understand. What am I reading?

Unsure of how long she'd stood there, Paloma returned to her coffee, only to find it had turned cold. Coffee no longer seemed appetizing. Paloma was unsure of what she was about to discover, but her stomach tightened, an indication it wasn't going to be good.

58

TINK AND BEN were exhausted as they ran their fingers over the last group of dresses. "This is an extreme waste of money," Ben said as he pointed to the growing pile of taffeta and chiffon, silk and charmeuse. "There's no way she could've worn all of these in her lifetime."

"Oh, you'd be surprised," Tink countered. "A woman of such wealth wouldn't have been caught dead wearing the same gown twice. It would've been a fashion faux pas of biblical proportions."

"You're talking about stuff I don't understand," Ben said. "That was the last dress and we've still got nothing. Apparently, she didn't hide any steamy secrets in her crinolines."

"Not so fast," Tink refuted. "We may have cleared out the gowns but there's still the shoes and boxes of hats, to say nothing of the evening bags. Ye of little faith."

"Good grief," Ben said as he glanced at his watch. "I hate to do it, but I've got to cut this fun short. I promised Dan to help out and I can't let him down."

"I understand," Tink replied. "I'll continue going through this while you salt your gators."

"I think not," Ben insisted. "Have you suddenly forgotten all that's happened? I'd *never* leave you here alone."

"You're right," Tink said, standing and stretching her back. "I should go with you."

"It's not that far," Ben assured her. "Let me call Dan and we'll head over."

Tink nodded while Ben walked into the ballroom to call his brother.

"Ben?" Dan questioned as though his brother was being held hostage. "What the hell's going on?"

"Everything's fine, Dan. I was just calling to let you know I'd meet you at the house to help with our hides."

"Harriett and I have been worried as hell about you! For all we knew, you were as dead as Ms. Opal. The least you could've done was call."

Ben dropped his head. He did feel bad for not staying in close contact with his brother. "Look, can we talk when I get home? So much is going on."

"No shit," Dan spat, clearly agitated. "I'm bringing Harriett with me. I don't feel comfortable leaving her and the baby alone. How long until you get there?"

"I'm leaving the Sinclair house in about five minutes. I'm bringing Tink with me, too. No woman should be left alone in Kane right now."

"I can't say I'm exactly comfortable with that," Dan said.

"Comfortable with what?" Ben questioned.

"With you bringing Tink to the house. It's no coincidence all this started when she arrived."

"Dan, it started before," Ben insisted, attempting to keep Tink from overhearing.

"Well, be that as it may, trouble seems to follow her, and I don't want my family involved."

"Wow," Ben said, more to himself than to Dan. "That's pretty cold. So, you're suggesting I leave her alone?"

"Hell no," Dan conceded. "We'll see you in a few minutes."

Ben remained in the ballroom for several minutes. He and Dan hadn't ever dealt with anything like this before. Their most difficult times had been the illnesses and loss of their parents. Placing the phone in his back pocket, he walked back into the dressing room. Tink was stacking the hat boxes in groups of four to go through later.

"Everything all right?" she asked.

"Yeah, why do you ask?"

"You look, well, pale."

"Dan's not happy with me," he said. "The gator meat isn't the moneymaker of the season. Sadly, it's the hides. If we lose those, we're in trouble."

Tink stood and brushed off the knees of her jeans before swiping across her behind. "I can't believe how much dust is in here. I could use some fresh air."

"Fresh air you shall have," Ben assured her. "It's always refreshing after a good rain."

"I'll be relieved to get out of this place," Tink muttered. "Between the storm and this dressing room, I was feeling as if the walls were closing in on me."

After going through the new regimen of double checking the locked door behind them, the two got on the road to Ben's place.

"Don't expect much," Ben said. "I don't have a grand estate."

"I'm sure it's lovely."

"I wouldn't exactly call it lovely. I got it for practically nothing, but it was what I could afford at the time. I've been restoring it ever since."

"Sounds like my *grand* estate," Tink teased. "If I end up keeping it, which isn't looking very promising, I'll be restoring it for the rest of my life."

"Ah, the joy of being a homeowner."

"So, tell me about your home," Tink said.

"It's not far from the bayou and where Dan and I put our boat in the water. My closest neighbor is over two miles away. That's what initially drew me to the place. I liked the thought of having several acres, not only because it was more isolated, but it gave us a place to house our business. We'd been renting a building and I was getting tired of throwing that cash away every month. You haven't told me about your life in Atlanta," Ben said, turning to look at Tink. "I know you're an attorney—that's about it."

"Picture a place that's the complete opposite of Kane and that's Atlanta," Tink replied. "Atlanta's a busy city, there's constant construction on the roads, making detours a continuous cycle. Did I mention the traffic?"

"What's traffic?" Ben teased. "Tell me about your place."

"It pales in comparison to Sinclair Oaks. I have a small loft but—"

"Loft? As in a barn?"

Tink laughed a little too long for Ben's taste, but he didn't mention it. "No, investors have been transforming old mills and other deserted factories into industrial-type apartment spaces. Some are rentals but others, like mine, are purchased outright, making me the proud owner of a loft. You'd probably faint if you knew how much I spent on a condo with exposed duct work and crumbling brick walls."

"Is your apartment, or loft rather, in the middle of the city?"

"Yep," Tink replied. "It's off Peachtree Street which is the main artery running through the city. The big selling point for me was that the Fox Theatre is within walking distance."

"Our entertainment is limited here, I'm sure you've noticed," Ben said blandly.

"It's been entertaining since I got here," Tink noted. "I thought I was getting away from it all."

The remainder of the ride was spent discussing clogged expressways and the continual construction of swelling skyscrapers. Enough was said about Atlanta to convince Ben it wasn't the kind of place he'd want to live.

The ruts in the dirt road brought the conversation back to his place. "Almost there," Ben assured her. "Like I said, don't expect—"

"Stop," Tink said, reaching over to place her hand on his arm. "I'm sure I'll love it."

"We'll see in a second," Ben said as he turned into his driveway.

"Oh," Tink whispered as she held back a gasp. "It's so...homey. I love it."

"Right," Ben drawled. "You don't have to go overboard."

"No, I'm serious, Ben. I love the front porch. It's so warm and inviting. Are those rockers on the porch?"

"Those were my parents'," Ben commented. "I had to re-cane and stain them again, but it was well worth it. It's one of the few memories I have of my mom. She loved to sit on the rocker and watch Dan and me play in the yard."

Tink swallowed. "That's nice," she said. "I would love to have a memory like that."

"I'm sorry," Ben said as he turned off the ignition and faced her. "I'm sure your mother would have been a great mom. But you had your dad. You haven't spoken much about him."

Tink opened her mouth to speak just as Dan and his family pulled up. She smiled broadly as she waved at Harriett. "I can't wait to see Landry."

"Me too," Ben said. "That's a distraction we both need."

59

Paloma leaned against the kitchen counter in an attempt to steady herself. The words she'd read were weighing heavy on her and the tepid coffee had made her nauseous. Afraid that she might faint, Paloma edged her way slowly toward the sink and ran water over a dish cloth. Her hands shook as she wrung out the excess water and wiped it across her face.

"Paloma? Are you all right?"

"Horace! You startled me," she answered, her knees feeling weak.

"Here, let me help you," Horace said, guiding her to the table. "You're shaking, Paloma. Has something upset you?"

"No, no, I'm fine. It's just getting late and we should've eaten long ago."

"I'll make us a sandwich," Horace offered. "We had a heavy lunch and a sandwich should suffice. How does a BLT sound?"

"That'll be fine," Paloma answered, realizing how much the past few days had taken out of her.

Horace pulled a package of bacon from the refrigerator and placed the heavy, cast-iron skillet on the stove.

"Would you mind if I take a shower?" Paloma asked.

"Not at all," Horace answered. "I'll have the sandwiches ready when you're done."

A few minutes later, secured in the bathroom, Paloma turned the water on as hot as she could stand, something she didn't have the luxury of doing in her own quarters. It seemed a foolish indulgence, but one Paloma relished just the same. Her dark skin turned a hot pink as the steamy water pelted her. She lathered the bath cloth with soap, then scrubbed her body until it felt raw. Surprised that her uncle Jericho had a large bottle of shampoo, Paloma massaged the sweet-smelling liquid deep into her scalp. She'd exhausted the hot water by the time she turned the shower off.

The warmth of the water made Paloma weary and she struggled to keep her eyes open. She grabbed a towel and quickly dried off her long hair before braiding it and twisting it into a bun. She pulled a thick cotton gown over her head and let it cascade over her lengthy frame. With every intention of going back to the kitchen for a sandwich, Paloma found herself sidetracked by the sight of her uncle's featherbed and couldn't help herself. The second the soft mattress wrapped around her thin form, Paloma was fast asleep.

HORACE WAITED for her long after he'd heard the water stop before going in to check on her. Paloma was sleeping so soundly he didn't dare wake her. She not only needed the sleep, but had earned it as well. He ate his sandwich alone at the kitchen table, then washed the dishes and left them in the drying rack to put away later.

The thought of a good night's rest didn't sound too bad to Horace either. It'd been a long day and he ached from the raw emotion of losing his father. The search of the attic had been a temporary fix to take his mind off the loss, but as the sun began its descent, the quietness of the house was a stern reminder that Jericho had gone to be with the Lord. Horace would've enjoyed a shower, but the only bathroom was off the master bedroom and he'd never disrupt his cousin's rest.

He filled a large ceramic bowl with hot, soapy water and a

matching pitcher with warm water and placed them on the wash-stand in his bedroom. It'd been the only form of bathing his ancestors had before they'd been able to put aside enough money for indoor plumbing. But none of them had ever gone to bed without a proper washing either way.

He'd barely dried off before collapsing in his bed. The hard rains had returned, but Horace never heard the accompanying thunder.

❀

PALOMA'S deep sleep was marred by disturbing dreams. She finally awakened around midnight, her gown soaked with perspiration. She changed into another, the second of the two she owned. The images of her dreams continued to run through her head until Paloma conceded her busy mind wasn't going to allow for sleep.

Rather than waste electricity, she lit the old oil lantern and carried it into the den. The soft light was less likely to wake Horace. She sat and reached for the journal, which was still open to the last page she'd read.

Paloma scanned over days and weeks of menial tasks completed at the estate with no mention of Ruby's pregnancy.

What's going on? Ruby would have to be showing by now. Has she lost the baby?

She went back through the daily entries again to make sure she hadn't missed anything. She hadn't. Paloma scanned over two more weeks of her mother's duties before Ruby's name finally came up.

Ruby's morning sickness is perhaps the worst I've encountered. It's all I can do to keep chicken broth and water down her. If Ruby becomes dehydrated, she'll be forced to admit herself into the hospital. I stress to her daily the importance of keeping food and drink down. To date, Ruby has lost twelve pounds. Baron has moved into another room and is spending more and more time in town. I dare consider the possibility he is courting another woman. Ruby's temper keeps Annabelle and Corbin in their portion of the house.

Ruby is consumed with giving her baby away and spends most of her day spinning wild tales of how her firstborn will live a long, prosperous life, but only if I assist her in this grand scheme.

It is times such as this when I long to turn to my family. But I've learned we are to be the guardian of secrets, 'tis part of our namesake. When we have a load too heavy to bear, we do two things: take it to the Lord in prayer and write down our feelings on paper. I pray that I am capable of doing the right thing both in God's eyes and in the eyes of my ancestors.

Paloma ran her wrinkled fingers across her mother's writing. There were several places where the ink was smeared, and Paloma was certain it was where Clementine's tears had fallen.

Another three weeks passed without an entry about Ruby and her pregnancy. Paloma's eyes grew heavy and she feared she might overlook something important. But there it was—the longest entry to date about the conniving mother-to-be.

The good Lord has answered my fervent prayers for Ruby. She is now past the awful weeks of morning sickness and is eating with the appetite of a man coming in from the fields. 'Tis only a matter of time before her secret is discovered by Ms. Annabelle and Ruby knows it.

Ruby has been phoning a woman in New Orleans, Pat Walsh. She is a nun who runs a shelter for unwed mothers. Ruby has convinced Ms. Walsh that her boyfriend left town after learning of the pregnancy and told the kind nun her family would disown her should they find out she is with child and unmarried.

Ms. Walsh assured Ruby everything would be kept confidential and her baby would be adopted by a loving and caring family. That was all Ruby needed to persuade herself to get to New Orleans.

I see more trouble in Ms. Ruby's plan than she does. One cannot simply disappear for several months, then return as if they'd never been away. Ruby has concocted a cousin who lives in Michigan and is supposedly suffering from late-stage cancer. She told me what type, but I struggle to recall it. Perhaps the form of cancer is a fabrication as well.

Ruby insists on having loud, animated phone calls with this nonexistent cousin where she promises her she'll find a way to assist her in the final months of her life. Those phone calls are difficult for me to stomach as I worry her deceit will come back to haunt her.

Mr. Baron has now come back to the fold and spends several nights a week in their marital bed. If he's noticed any change in his wife's body, he does not mention it. His drinking has increased two-fold, so I am left to surmise his jaunts into town didn't pan out for him.

It's on those days, when he sleeps in their bed, that I can concentrate on maintaining the household. It allows my mind freedom from the growing deception no one else seems privy to.

Mama has noticed I am carrying a burden and I feel her gaze linger upon me when I return home at night. She is old now, worn and tired, and doesn't need to be concerned with me. She has taught me well.

The worry over Ruby and the baby awoke me last night from my slumber. Mama heard me in the kitchen, and she came to my side. Her eyes, a mixture of kindness and strength, stared deep into my soul. I will never forget her words to me... "Child, I know you are troubled, but the Lord sees your suffering and his Grace is sufficient. Our family has survived on very little, but our name is more valuable than silver or gold. 'Tis not for us to judge. Tuck the secrets away, and leave them there. The world will be better for it."

CLEMENTINE HAD SHARED the same lessons with her children, nieces, and nephews. She'd preached the importance of family, hard work, loyalty, and in the end, ensuring the family name was one to be proud of.

Paloma blew the oil lamp out and sat in the dark, listening to the sounds of nature outside the small clapboard house. She was thinking of how, never once, had any of the LeBlancs envied the Sinclairs. The big house, the beautiful possessions, all seemed like a curse rather than a blessing. Even during peaceful, prosperous times, there was always foreboding just beneath the surface.

60

"LOOK," Tink squealed. "Landry has grown so much already!"

Harriett laughed as she offered the sleepy infant to Tink, who took her skeptically.

"Don't be nervous," Harriett encouraged her. "She won't break."

"If Dan hasn't broken her, it can't be done," Ben said as he pulled the pink blanket from around the baby's face to get a better look. "Thank goodness she took after her mother."

"Listen to this comedian," Dan said. "Don't quit your day job."

Ben turned to give his brother a playful hug. "Let's get to work," he said. "We're behind. Harriett, will you show Tink around? The door's unlocked."

"Unlocked?" Tink asked incredulously. "You've got to be kidding. You haven't been home since yesterday."

"It's what we do in Kane," Ben answered. "Somebody may need something."

Tink was stunned and watched in silence as Ben and Dan walked back to their shop. "I don't even know what to say," Tink said, turning to Harriett. "That's beyond my comprehension."

"It's just the way of life here," Harriett replied. "Let me take Landry and I'll show you around. Not much to see around here, but

Ben's place is pretty cool. He's worked hard on it. I wish you could've seen it when he first bought it. I have to admit, I was skeptical, but it's coming around."

She led Tink up the steps and onto the front porch. Narrow and running the length of the house, it was far from the expansive porch of the estate, but the caned rockers offered a beautiful view.

"This is so cozy," Tink said.

"It's a great place to relax. Ben spends a lot of time out here." Harriett shifted Landry to her other arm and turned the knob. "Yep, it's open. Come on in."

"You're so at ease with her," Tink said. "Have you had experience with young children before you had her?"

"A little. I have nieces and nephews, but when you have a baby of your own, you're forced to get comfortable quick."

Tink laughed nervously. "Maybe there's hope for me yet."

Harriett flipped on the lights and Tink walked into the den. There was a beautiful stone fireplace and a worn, comfortable sofa and armchair.

"That's his pride and joy," Harriett said, pointing to a brown leather recliner. "Ben ordered it online and practically waited on the front porch for days until it arrived. Cassius plops down in it every time he visits and pisses Ben off to no end."

"It's so homey," Tink agreed, taking her time to walk around the room.

"He gutted the whole inside," Harriett continued. "New fireplace, new hardwood floors, new kitchen and bathrooms."

"That's a lot of work," Tink said. She wound her way through the small home, taking in all the details Ben had worked so hard to make special. "Are these his parents?" she asked as she picked up a framed photo of a smiling couple.

"Yes, that's them," Harriett replied. "Ben even made that frame."

"You can't be serious," Tink said. "He's very talented."

"He can do anything," Harriett said. "He just needs somebody to share his life with. Ben's been so busy working that he hasn't taken the time to meet someone. I'm glad you're here."

Tink turned and smiled at her. "I'm glad I met you."

"Same here. I don't have many friends and it gets lonely. Do you think you'll move to Kane?"

"I don't see how I could right now. I have a job back in Atlanta and I'll need to get back to it soon. But I can't leave with all that's going on," Tink said, slumping her shoulders.

"Let's sit down," Harriett suggested. "Can I pass Landry to you? I'll see what Ben has to drink in the refrigerator."

Tink sank into the couch and took the infant from her mother. She felt much more comfortable holding her when she was sitting. Wisps of light hair stood on the baby's perfectly shaped head and her tiny fingers wrapped gently around Tink's pinkie. "Hey there, little one," Tink said softly. "You're beautiful."

"Beer or orange juice?" Harriett called out from the kitchen. "Pick your pleasure."

"I'll take a beer, no glass, please," Tink said.

Harriett handed her a beer and sat in the armchair. "So, tell me everything," she began. "Dan only gives me bits and pieces, but I know it's much worse than he's letting on. He's been a bear to live with, especially after finding that woman on their line. It's crazy."

"Yes, it is," Tink answered. "I'm sure the townspeople think I brought all of these horrible things to Kane."

"Why in the world would they think that?"

"I think it's somehow tied to me—or the Sinclairs, rather."

"Why would you say that?" Harriett asked. "The man and woman found on the guys' lines had nothing to do with the Sinclairs or anyone around here. That drug crowd is nothing but trouble. They work for a couple of paychecks and move on to the next place. If you ask me, most of them are probably on the run."

"What about Opal Bailey-Blanchard?" Tink asked. "There's no way she had anything to do with that crowd."

"I can't believe she was murdered," Harriett murmured. A faraway look crossed her face. "Maybe it was a robbery. I wouldn't put it past that crowd down by the rigs. Drugs can make people desperate, or so I've heard."

"That would be my first thought too, but the hands... That's the calling card that links all three murders."

"Wha...? Please don't tell me they cut poor Opal's hands off too. That's the sickest thing I've ever heard."

Tink didn't know how to respond. She'd assumed everyone in town was privy to the details by now. Unfortunately, she'd opened her mouth and told Harriett the disturbing news.

"Forgive me," Harriett said. "I know I sound as though I think I'm better than everyone else, but that's not the case."

"Not at all," Tink reassured her. "I understand where you're coming from. No one wants their town invaded by the criminal element. And to have such a hardworking woman... I'm sorry."

"No, don't be," Harriett said. "Tell me more. I need to know all of it. I'd find out eventually anyway."

"Did you know about someone breaking into the estate?"

"No!" Harriett exclaimed, leaning forward. "Were you there when it happened?"

Tink looked down at Landry, who was fast asleep in her arms, her innocence such a contrast to the evil happening around her. Tink closed her eyes and took a long, deep breath before telling Harriett all she knew about the incidents involving the murders.

"I can't wrap my head around it," Harriett whispered. "It just doesn't make any sense. What's the motive?"

"That's what we're trying to find out," Tink answered. "And we need answers soon before anyone else is killed."

"Let me help," Harriett said firmly.

"I appreciate the offer," Tink said, "but you have Landry, and this could get dangerous."

"This requires a woman's intuition," Harriett pressed. "If there are secrets hidden in that old place, it'll take a woman to find them."

"I tend to agree with you," Tink said. "But if someone broke in once, they have reason to return."

"Ben and Dan both have a slew of guns and rifles. If we aren't safe with them, we can't be protected by anyone. Let's go talk to them. If Dan agrees, you and I can get clothes and toiletries from our house, and they should be finished when we get back. What do you say?"

"I say we're burning daylight," Tink said.

❦

AFTER MUCH RESISTANCE, Dan finally conceded and agreed to follow Ben and Tink to the estate. It only took a few minutes to get the family settled in their bedroom and Harriett was ready to help Tink go through the dressing room, though Tink was now convinced there was nothing of significance to be found. Harriett insisted they go through the hats and hat boxes next. She had a feeling, as she continued to say.

The two women were astonished at the many hats, all in pristine condition, they pulled from the boxes.

"This is amazing," Tink cooed. "I've never seen anything like it."

"They're so elaborate," Harriett said. "Can you imagine what they cost back then? Even now? I bet whoever wore these was the belle of the ball."

"Lucretia."

"Who?"

"Lucretia Sinclair," Tink answered. "She was the woman this home was built for, the matriarch so to speak." Her vision went fuzzy as she thought of her own bloodline, something she'd never done before.

"Are you okay?" Harriett asked.

"Yes," Tink answered. "Let's see what we can find."

The women kneaded their hands through the ruffled hats and boxes until their fingers ached.

"Wait," Harriett said excitedly. "I think I've got something." She loosened the lining from the old hat box and two letters floated out.

Tink reached for them as if they would somehow evaporate. "There are four here," she confirmed. "I'll put them to the side. Let's go through every box again and then check the ones we haven't been through. Looks like we've hit pay dirt."

As soon as the words left her mouth, the sound of deep organ music reverberated throughout the house. "What the hell?" Tink whispered as her eyes darted around the small space.

"I think it's the doorbell," Harriett answered. "Are you expecting anyone?"

"Tink? Tink?" Ben yelled as he ran in the room. "I think there's someone at the door."

"Oh my," Tink said, remembering her father's promise to overnight her cases. "It may be a delivery for me."

Dan was immediately beside Ben, anxious.

"I'm certain that's what it is," Tink assured them, suddenly feeling foolish. "We're all overreacting." She stood and stretched before making her way to the staircase. The two brothers flanked her on both sides as if the mob were waiting to snatch her as she opened the door.

Tink took the steps two at a time and walked swiftly to the front door. After looking through the peephole and verifying it was a legitimate deliveryman, she relaxed. "It's some paperwork from my job," she assured them before opening the door.

A young man asked for Catherine Mabrey and when she confirmed her identity, he thrust a clipboard toward her and said he'd be back. Tink scrawled her signature across the bottom of the document while he retrieved her cases. Ben and Dan's jaws dropped as the courier loaded eight large boxes on a hand truck and returned to the front door. Tink handed him the clipboard; he verified the signature, and the transaction was complete. She turned around to two astounded faces with their mouths agape.

"What is that?" Ben asked, pointing to the pile of boxes that were as tall as himself.

"It's some of my more pressing cases," she answered. "My father's getting rather upset with me."

"Some of your cases?" Dan questioned. "You've got to be kidding me. I haven't even read an adult book since I got out of high school. You'll never finish all of that."

Tink's attempt to suppress a laugh failed. "It's much less daunting than it appears. I've become quite the speed-reader through the years. It won't affect what we're doing here."

Both men stood, shaking their heads. "Gentlemen!" Tink said firmly, clapping her hands several times. "Let's get back to work. Where are you two looking for clues?"

They continued to look at her in disbelief, but Ben managed to answer. "We're up in the master bedroom, as if they all wouldn't qualify for that title. Figured any dirt on the family would be kept there."

"Good Idea," Tink said. "Harriett is worth her weight in gold. Appears some letters were stashed in the lining of a hat box. Go figure. Let me get back to her and Landry."

Tink once again took the steps two at a time and found Harriett feeding Landry, who was dozing off to sleep as she suckled her bottle. When Harriett spotted Tink, a broad grin crossed her face. "I found several more letters. She was quite clever to hide them inside the linings of those hat boxes."

"I can't wait," Tink said as she glanced over the beautiful handwriting on each envelope. Each one was dated and addressed to Philomene. The dates would be helpful in creating a chronological trail.

"I feel certain these were written by a woman, judging by the penmanship," Harriett said. "It's quite lovely. That and the fact they were found in women's hat boxes gives it away. Who is Philomene?"

"I have no idea," Tink answered. "I suppose we'll find out soon. Let me get these in order and we'll start with the first one written."

Harriett placed Landry on her shoulder to burp her, then rocked her back and forth in her arms until she'd fallen into a deep slumber. She wrapped the soft blanket around her and placed her on a cushion she'd removed from one of the vanity chairs. By then, Tink had organized the letters—seven of them, to be exact.

"Here," Tink said. "You read one, then I'll read one, aloud of course."

"No, it's your family. I'm honored to get to be a part of this discovery. You read them. I'll listen. Hurry, I can't stand the wait any longer," Harriett urged.

Tink slowly opened the pale pink envelope. "It's almost like linen," she commented. "Okay, it begins…"

My precious Philomene,

Today was both the day of your birth and your death. I've never known such joy and yet suffered such grief. Devastating grief that will never leave my body; I won't allow it to abandon me. The absence of grief would be to have forgotten you and that shall never happen. Your breath was so sweet, like a wild rose blooming in a field all alone. Oh, what a lovely one you were. The most beautiful child to ever grace this earth, an angel, so perfect, so exquisite; but you arrived in a world not yet ready for you.

I cannot express the depth of my sorrow. I am so sorry, my darling. So very sorry, I dare not ask your forgiveness. As difficult as it was for me, I know it was best.

Prudence, my dear Prudence, I am forever in her debt, forever in the debt of my friend, my confidant.

The angels have summoned you, sweet Philomene, you have no doubt been given your wings by now. Fly, my beautiful angel, fly.

Love,

Mommy

Both women were silent for a moment, the tears in their eyes threatening to escape.

"Dear Lord," Harriett whispered. "That's the saddest thing I've ever heard. Who was the mother?"

"Judging by the date on the envelope, it had to be Lucretia Sinclair. The date was 1863, so Philomene had to have been Lucretia and Emmanuel's first child. I wonder what happened to her. Lucretia said *her breath was as sweet as a wild rose* so she must not have been stillborn. I wonder how long she lived."

"Born in a world that wasn't ready for her…what did that mean?"

"Perhaps she had medical problems the doctors weren't able to help."

"That's true," Harriett agreed. "That was over a century ago. Who was Prudence?"

"I've heard that name," Tink said as she struggled to recall when. "I believe she was an ancestor of Paloma's, but don't hold me to that. Some of these names are hard to remember."

"Hurry. Open the next one," Harriett urged.

Tink carefully opened the next envelope. "This one is dated two days later," she said, prefacing the letter.

There are times when one believes they cannot bear any further sorrow, but today my sweet Philomene, your mommy endured even more. Prudence handled everything as she always has, a steadfast and unwavering friend, a woman the world refuses to accept in the manner it should. Perhaps when I am returned to the dust and the years pass, things will be different in this place.

But, today was about you, my beautiful daughter. Your tiny coffin was a reminder of what could have been, what should have been. Emmanuel was away, far up the Mississippi brokering a deal to ensure the Sinclair name will carry on for generations to come. I had no ill will concerning his absence, 'twas for the best. There were just a few of us in attendance, as your coffin sat beside the small grave, waiting to be lowered into the cold, unforgiving earth. There was a fitting prayer and tears shed. Thaddeus... he came, although he had been told to let me grieve your death alone. His eyes remained downcast, as did mine and no words were exchanged. I wonder if his grief was as deep as mine.

He left Fatima at home, no doubt shielding her from such anguish, as she is with child now.

You were wrapped in our finest linens from head to toe and your tiny coffin remained securely sealed. Your flawless, little body seen only by Prudence and me. I will always love you, Philomene.

"Okay that was strange," Harriett said as soon as Tink began folding the letter and placing it back in the envelope. "Is there something weird going on? Do you get an odd vibe?"

Tink wrinkled her forehead in thought. Harriett was right—something was off.

"I don't know," Tink answered slowly. "It's very odd, indeed. Who is Thaddeus? Prudence is undoubtedly a slave who works for Lucretia. They are quite loyal to each other and it seems as though she's being discriminated against—a racial divide, perhaps. But let's think for a minute. It sounds similar to the words in Lucretia's first letter. *A world that is not ready for you yet.*"

"What are you saying?" Harriett asked. "Was the baby biracial? Oh my. What would've happened to her? Lucretia would've been killed."

Something clicked. "Or, she felt she had to kill her own baby," Tink whispered. "Oh my God, that can't be true. *No way.* We're getting way ahead of ourselves. Let's read the next letter." Her hands shook as she opened the pink envelope. This letter was dated a week later.

Sweet Philomene, my heart aches as badly today as it did on the day you drew your last breath. I am beginning to wonder if life will ever be as it once was. My body has not healed from your birth, yet I don't have an infant to hold to stave away my physical pain. I have remained in the bed since your funeral. 'Tis a fitting place for me as the outside world continues to go on, something I am not yet ready to do.

It is cold out and I worry that Prudence should've wrapped your body with more linens. Are you cold in that grave, Philomene? Do you need more linens?

"I FEEL SICK," Harriett said, as she reached over to stroke Landry's face. "This is *quite* disturbing, Tink. You don't suppose she's thinking of—"

"Don't say it. Maybe we should take a break. This is getting far more upsetting than I'd anticipated," Tink said, looking over at the sleeping infant. "It might be better if Ben and Dan did this."

"No, no..."

"Are you sure?" Tink asked, questioning her own judgment about continuing.

"Yes, let's finish them while Landry's asleep. Then we'll take a break."

"Okay," Tink said uneasily. "This is the fourth one and the last of the pink envelopes."

"The pink ones were all found in a hat box together. The cream envelopes were in another one."

Tink swallowed, studying the letter. "This one is dated two weeks after the last one."

Today, my Philomene, Prudence came to visit. Fatima has kept her busy at the Jackson estate with her fifth pregnancy. She is in her seventh month which is the furthest she's yet to get in a pregnancy. Fatima will finally give birth this time, Prudence will see to it. She has made Fatima stay in bed and made sure no one bothered her with trivial household issues.

Not that Fatima could handle them anyway. She is not like us, tiny Philomene, she is weak and coddled. Fatima has no desire to lead. She wants to be a child herself, and she wants Thaddeus to take care of her. Her husband resents her docile personality. In the beginning, men see a woman for her beauty, but it isn't long before they desire more.

Thaddeus has brought much to the partnership, just as my husband expected he would. He and Emmanuel have learned from one another, but I intend to learn all I can from both. I will not lie in bed and wait for my food to be brought to me; I will provide the meal.

Only weak, dull women allow others to take care of them, understand Philomene? It is a tough lesson to learn, but one you must understand. Only the strong survive, Philomene, only the strong.

Tink looked over at Harriett as she folded the letter. She'd grown pale and Tink longed to put all the letters away and sit in the parlor with the guys and drink. Butterflies were dancing in her stomach and she wanted nothing more than to step out of Lucretia Sinclair's life. Perhaps the best way to get through the letters was the Band-Aid approach. Read through them quickly and get it over with. She reached for the first of the cream envelopes.

"This is dated April 1863."

Sweet Philomene, your mommy hasn't talked to you in a while. I have been busy getting stronger and wiser. 'Tis been two long months since your death, two months that your body has laid in that grave, two months since you've earned your wings. You now have another angel with whom to share flight. Fatima gave birth today to a daughter almost as lovely as you. But Fatima once again displayed her weakness.

Prudence had worked with her, taught her how difficult childbirth would be, but even with months of rest, she couldn't fight hard enough. Fatima was frail and weak and she lost the battle. When she could no longer fight, both Fatima and her infant drew their last breaths.

She was my friend, and I have suffered another loss. I tried hard to make her stronger, little one, but she wouldn't listen. She wouldn't listen.

"Just two more, thank God," Tink said as tears streamed down her face.

"Want me to read them?" Harriett asked.

"Yes," Tink said quietly. "But this is something I have to do. This one's dated 1864."

My correspondence with you is further apart now, my dear Philomene. Your mommy is stronger now, although life is far from easy. Emmanuel is losing his way, I struggle to believe it, but he is going mad. His visits to New Orleans only add to his madness, but he refuses to listen to me. I know something isn't right with the so-called collaborative he and Thaddeus have formed. Listen clearly, little one, just because men have money it doesn't mean it came to them honestly. I do not respect these men although I have not laid eyes on any of them. Emmanuel thinks I am foolish, and I will continue to let him believe it. 'Tis not a bad thing to never show your hand, remember that, Philomene.

Emmanuel is insistent his office is off limits and I respect that, but many nights I can hear a group of men in there, yet they haven't come through the front or back door. 'Tis not honest.

I have seen a man here from town. His name is Samuel Thibodeaux and I hide my suspicions about him. Emmanuel speaks out in his dreams about him, something about the biggest one to come. I lie awake trying to decipher his words, but I cannot make sense of them. Madness is hard to witness; I struggle to understand.

Before I could hide these words away, more has happened, have you seen it? Can you look down and see, little one? Emmanuel was crazed today, coming and going many times, his hands shaking, his clothes dirty. I pretended not to notice, was easiest that way, remember that, Philomene, 'tis okay to play a fool as long as you aren't one.

Emmanuel hurried into our bed, his breathing strong and fast. He feigned slumber although I knew he was awake. I know his breathing when he sleeps, a wife knows these things.

George came to the front door, loud, frightened and out of breath. He brought news that Thaddeus had burned up in his home. He is gone now, too, little one. Thaddeus will be returned to the dust leaving the sugar cane all to the Sinclair line. It will take someone strong, Philomene. It will take someone strong to keep the Sinclair name going, to keep the name respected.

"I'm exhausted," Tink said. "Are you?"

"Yes," Harriett said. "Read the last one. I'm ready to get out of this room and away from those words."

"I am too," Tink answered. "This one is dated February 1865."

Little one, are you watching? Are you willing me the strength I need? Do you see the heir growing in my womb? The madness, it was getting worse with every passing day. Fearing I might hear the truth, I refuse to ask Emmanuel about all that has transpired. Samuel Thibodeaux's wife has fallen prey to the madness just as Emmanuel has. She beats on our doors and windows screaming crazed nonsense about her husband's hand that bears his wedding ring. George is now handling her fits of rage and no longer allows her on our land. I welcome his assistance as I am busy ensuring the crop is planted, harvested, and milled.

Emmanuel is no longer fit to handle business. He stays locked away in that office, his self-imposed prison. Perhaps it eases his conscience to exile himself from the life he once knew.

I never knew it would end like this, little one, I never knew. I will tell you and only you and you mustn't share it with anyone, not even Fatima's baby. In his madness, Emmanuel's office could no longer offer him the punishment he felt he deserved. I am still unsure of his sins, even now, but their weight was far too much for him to bear alone. This morning I found him hanging from the top of his beloved staircase, the jewels from the stained glass reflecting beautiful prisms of light above him like the star of Bethlehem. But he wasn't the Savior sent to save the world. He was a weak and sin-filled man.

It was up to me to save the legacy of our family. Did you see how difficult it was for me to sever the rope? Emmanuel was much heavier than I'd anticipated, his weight pulled against the tightened noose. I didn't watch as his lifeless body fell. It seemed an eternity before I heard him hit the marble floor. Did you see me toss the bottles of liquor from the top of the staircase? It was necessary you see, sweet Philomene, to cover his final sin. This world would not understand him taking his own life and it would mar our name for decades. Thank goodness the only eternal sin is disbelief in our Lord and Savior, Jesus Christ.

I must go now, little one, it will be up to you to watch over me. This will be my last letter. I have work to do. I have a legacy to build. I have an heir in my belly.

61

SOMETIME DURING THE NIGHT, Paloma had slipped back in bed and drifted off to sleep. When she awoke, the sun was shining brightly through the curtains and the sounds and smells of breakfast were coming from the kitchen. Paloma washed her face, brushed her teeth, and dressed quickly.

"Good morning, sleepy head," Horace teased. "How'd you sleep?"

"Very well, thank you. Jericho's featherbed feels like a cloud."

"That's good to hear," Horace answered, not mentioning he'd been awake himself when his cousin roused from her sleep during the night. "Did you discover anything yesterday?"

"Indeed, I did," Paloma answered, reaching for the warm plate of food he handed her. "But we don't need to share it with anyone until I've finished reading the journal entries. I don't want to reach unwarranted conclusions."

Horace sat at the table as Paloma shared all she'd read with him.

"Do you know what this means?" he asked. "There could be another living Sinclair somewhere! They could be the killer."

"Let's not get ahead of ourselves," Paloma said, although her thoughts were the same. "We aren't even certain the baby was even born. Ruby could've miscarried for all we know. Or the baby could've died after birth and no one discussed it."

"We definitely would've heard about another Sinclair baby being born, Paloma. You know that."

"Yes, you're right," she answered softly. "But, as I said, I don't know the whole story yet. I'm learning a lot about my mother. She was a good, strong woman."

"So are you," Horace added.

"Enough of that," Paloma said. "What did you find?"

"Nothing of any importance. Mostly legal papers, deeds, things of that sort."

"Hmm," Paloma said, reaching over for a few of the papers. "I'm sure these are copies and the others are documented with the city, but we don't need to toss them out. It's nice to know the land was given to our family legally."

"Yes, it appears to have been handled in a professional manner," Horace commented. He walked over to the aerial drawing and unfolded it. "This is an interesting sketch of the land. Apparently this was drawn at the height of the Sinclairs' empire. I noticed several structures that are no longer here, probably torn down when they stopped producing their crop. Who knows, over a century some things are bound to deteriorate."

Paloma took one last bite of toast and removed her plate from the table. She and Horace looked over the map carefully, discovering buildings still located on the property, and relishing the thought of a time when the land had been thriving and valuable.

"Mr. Corbin operated the last of the business," Horace said. "He was capable of expanding it, but his health got in the way. At least that's what Papa thought."

"Mr. Corbin was a good man," Paloma said. "His heart was broken when Baron turned out the way he did. I'm sure he never dreamed his son would be the end of the Sinclair name."

"But he wasn't," Horace said. "Catherine is a Sinclair and appears to be a fine person. Yet she knows nothing of her own family, which I find peculiar."

"I believe not knowing them was best for her. What a blessing Baron and Ruby didn't reach out to Catherine and bully her as they did Olivia."

"I've never understood that either," Horace said. "After Auntie Clementine got older and could no longer handle the house, you took over the duties at the estate. How in God's sweet name could you tolerate them?"

"It wasn't easy," Paloma said. "But, when Mama began to tire, it was time for me to step up."

"But why?" Horace asked.

Paloma frowned. "Because that's the kind of people we are," she answered firmly. "We work hard and see to it that everyone is taken care of."

"Forgive me," Horace said. "I'm sorry to doubt you, but why do we hold an allegiance to that family? Is it because they gave us a concession of land in 1865 just a few months shy of the thirteenth amendment being ratified? Do we still owe them our best years?"

Horace was expecting a harsh scolding, but instead, Paloma reached over and tenderly took his hand in hers. "No, my dear cousin, we don't owe them anything. We are two very different families with two very different views on life. We have different priorities and needs. But, in the end, the Sinclairs are family. Not because they freed Prudence just months before the Emancipation Proclamation was issued, but because they needed us. Through the generations, God has had his hand on us, leading us toward them, to guide them and keep their secrets...to protect them. God has given our family longevity. I know it is terribly painful to lose your father, just as it is for me to lose my uncle, but Jericho lived a long and happy life. He worked in the fields he loved so whole-heartedly, and he lived to see all his children to adulthood. Jericho also lived long enough to pass on to me his knowledge and his blessing of being a traiteur."

"I never even considered the idea of being needed by a wealthy family," Horace said. "I've always felt inferior to them."

"Because your home isn't large? Because your clothes aren't flashy?" Paloma asked earnestly. "Believe it or not, I'm certain there were many times the Sinclairs would've changed places with us. We always had enough food, and we ate it on a wobbly table surrounded by the whole lot of LeBlancs." She paused to laugh at the fond memory. "And we had books, books, and *more* books. We've lived a thousand lives through those books, Horace. Did you know most of them came from Lucretia Sinclair herself? When the 15th Amendment was ratified, black males were given the right to vote, but there was a clause built in to ensure they wouldn't be able to."

"What are you talking about?"

"They had to know how to read," Paloma said. "And *very few* freed slaves were literate. It was quite a convenient clause, but Lucretia wouldn't be party to such a travesty. She ensured that all freed slaves working for the Sinclair family had access to as many books as they could read. She even provided a teacher every evening in the front parlor of the Sinclair estate. The family continued to offer books to any blacks who wanted them, allowing them the opportunity to learn everything from how to survey, to bake, to the likes of world history."

"I'm younger than you, Paloma, but I don't recall Mr. Baron pushing any literature on me."

"Baron was the beginning of the end," Paloma agreed. "But for now, we have much work ahead and time is of the essence. Let's look over this map and I'll return to the journals."

The two noted several points of interest before Paloma placed her index finger on a small square notation. "Look at this, Horace. It's an enclosure of some kind, between our two properties, close to the bayou. It has the initials CS."

Horace leaned closer to the sketched map, focusing on the portion Paloma was referring to. "CS would be Claude Sinclair. He was Emmanuel Sinclair's father."

"Interesting," Paloma said. "I didn't know that; you're one up on me."

"Papa told me about him. Look, it's the same illustration as this, to the rear and right of the Sinclair estate." Horace pointed to another section of the map.

"That's the old root cellar," Paloma said, referring to the image near the Sinclair house. "It's rarely used anymore but was a necessity many years ago."

"I'd like to check that one out," Horace said. "I don't know why, but maybe there's something there that might help us."

"I agree," Paloma said. "Maybe a late afternoon field trip will allow my eyes to rest. But, for now, I'll return to the journals. Don't give up on the possibility of the attic holding important clues."

"I'll take care of the dishes first," Horace said. "Go back to your reading."

Paloma opened the curtains and turned on the lamp beside Jericho's chair. It took a few minutes to get settled in and find where she'd left off in the journals. The following week's worth of notes had the Sinclair household in a dysfunctional state. Baron and Ruby were arguing over the smallest things, Annabelle and Corbin were desperately seeking asylum in their portion of the estate. The fractured home life appeared to be by design, as all of them were delighted to see Ruby pack up and take the bus to some small, indiscriminate town in Michigan.

She slowed to read the details of the day Ruby departed.

As Ruby pulled away in the truck with Jericho, it seemed the house itself heaved a sigh of relief. I, too, exhaled deeply when they disappeared in the distance. 'Tis sad to feel pleasure when someone departs. My conscience will deal with me heavily as I lay my head down tonight. But for now, I will have the ability to maintain this place without the interruption of Ruby's childlike behavior.

My heart and mind continue to be at war with one another over her pregnancy, but in the end, my heart has won out. Any situation would be more beneficial to an infant than this place. I pray without ceasing for the welfare and health of this child and for the guardian angel, Pat Walsh, who has the compassion and desire to help others.

Paloma scanned the journal for two hours before reaching for the one that followed. Clementine notated every detail of her day, from her duties at Sinclair Oaks to the state of the family. It appeared

Baron was quite delighted to be free from his wife in the beginning. His days were filled with alcohol and boorish behavior. Corbin and Annabelle tried everything to reason with him but failed miserably in the end. The one issue Corbin stood firmly on was his son bringing other women into the home. Corbin's threats ranged from calling the police to disinheriting him, the latter being what ultimately stopped Baron from arriving with unwanted guests.

Corbin continued to suffer from various ailments which required all of Annabelle's mental and physical strength. She remained at a loss as to what to do with her son, who had long ago dismissed her reprimands. Baron towered over his petite mother, using his brutish appearance to intimidate her. In turn, Annabelle found solace in doting over Corbin like a mother hen. The parents cared deeply for one another, but their son was a dark, unpredictable cloud. Corbin and Annabelle never dreamed they'd long for Ruby's return, but she was the only one capable of restoring any semblance of balance back to the home.

Ruby's calls were intermittent at best, but she assured everyone she'd be back as soon as she could. The death of her fabricated cousin was imminent, but she was a stubborn woman who was fiercely fighting the grim reaper.

Paloma noted there were phone calls weekly to Clementine, more to ensure she was maintaining the secrecy of Ruby's plan than to reveal any updates.

The final months of the pregnancy seemed to weigh the heaviest on Clementine, who struggled terribly with her conscience. She prayed relentlessly and fought the urge to vomit every time she ate.

Cate, Clementine's mother, began to fear she was ill. *Our mind is capable of inflicting a great deal of damage to our body*, Clementine had penned.

The convoluted tale ended anticlimactically. Ruby strode in one afternoon, luggage in tow, as though she'd simply gone to purchase groceries. Baron was the first to comment on the additional twenty pounds she was carrying, mostly in her backside.

Corbin and Annabelle had been in the front parlor when Ruby

had arrived, and had sat dumbfounded as she had flippantly detailed the long, painful death her cousin had endured. She'd shared with them her relief to be home, and her intention to relax in a steaming bath. If they should see Clementine, Ruby had instructed, have her deliver a cup of hot tea, to be followed by a glass of Corbin's best scotch. And with that, Ruby had pointed to her luggage and wiggled her index finger toward her bedroom before exiting the parlor as quickly as she'd come.

She'd literally collided with Clementine in the hallway, leaving the older woman as astonished as Corbin and Annabelle had been. Ruby had flashed a knowing and threatening glare before demanding a hot tea be delivered upstairs as soon as possible.

Paloma scoured the pages of the journal like a starving animal finally being thrown table scraps. Her heart ached as she read of Ruby's contemptuous behavior to Clementine.

In the weeks following Ruby's return, the dysfunctional dynamic had resumed, and was embraced, oddly enough, by the four adults residing there.

The only entry from Clementine concerning the birth of Ruby's child was as follows:

I have waited patiently for Ruby to share any information of the happenings in New Orleans. She is clearly taunting me, waiting on me to inquire. She is carrying a heavy load; of that I am certain.

Just as I was beginning to believe none of this even happened, Ruby pulled me into the butler's pantry, her hand spread over my mouth to ensure my silence. She pleaded with me never to share the details of her secret, and I willingly conceded.

In the delirium of birth, Ruby is convinced she heard the midwife confirm the delivery of a healthy baby boy. That detail alone concluded her recollections of the birth and the following few days. As soon as Ruby was well enough to travel, she was offered minimal funds, equivalent to travel expenses home.

She caught a taxi to the bus station in New Orleans where she waited on Jericho to pick her up and return her to the estate. Ruby assured me my brother is unaware of the events that transpired, and I vowed to never place the details on his heart.

Ruby's main concerns are reinforcing my silence and getting pregnant as soon as possible. She believes she will birth a healthy boy, an heir to the Sinclair name. Ruby asks me repeatedly how soon she will be able to once again conceive. I can only surmise, as soon as her body has had time to heal.

She has not verbally threatened me, but her eyes certainly place fear in my heart. Ruby is a dangerous woman, one who doesn't want to lose what she has.

PALOMA LEANED BACK in the chair and closed her eyes, her thoughts swirling with the realization there could be another Sinclair among the living. She hadn't even heard Horace coming down from the attic.

"Paloma? Are you asleep?" Horace asked.

"You startled the life out of me," she answered, sitting upright. "No, I wasn't sleeping, I was allowing this to sink in." Paloma lifted the journal from her lap. "It was as we suspected. Ruby did indeed have a baby, a son, or so she believes. He was put up for adoption. That's the only information I've read so far. I'm sure the records are sealed, and even if they weren't, she would've certainly used a fictitious name."

"Wouldn't it be just like *that*—"

"Don't," Paloma interrupted. "There's no need for name-calling, Horace. We're above that."

"I think we need to contact the sheriff. This could be a big break, Paloma."

"And what do we have? An old journal suggesting Ruby bore a son? We don't have any names, any adoptive relatives, nothing. If anything, we'd have years of chasing our tails on a prospective heir who, for all we know, could be dead by now. We need more before we start alarming folks. What else did you find in the attic?"

"Still nothing that sends up red flags. It's almost lunchtime. What do you say we take a break and go check out that root cellar?" Horace inquired.

"Root cellars aren't very exciting, but I'd welcome a walk," she said. "Bring along a lantern and I'll grab a broom. They're dusty places, although I doubt there's much left of it by now."

The two cousins wound their way through the property, enjoying the sites notated on the old map. The sounds of the bayou united to create a beautiful symphony, erasing any remnants of the violent storm the day before.

"I feel like I've been inside for weeks," Paloma said. "The air is so fresh after a good storm."

"Indeed, it is. We're getting closer to the water." Horace paused to review the map. "It should be close."

Paloma reached over to hold one side of the unfolded paper until Horace could locate the root cellar. "Some of these points of reference won't be applicable. The land has evolved, yet eroded at the same time."

Horace studied the map. "It should be about a hundred yards west. I don't understand—it just looks like a mound of dirt over there. What exactly are we looking for, Paloma? I assumed there'd be trap doors in the ground."

"Not always, most were storage areas constructed above ground. They were later covered with dirt and brush, not only to stabilize the structure, but to maintain a consistent temperature. Root cellars were utilized to store vegetables, jarred preserves, and salted meats. Their ability to retain a constant temperature kept food from freezing in the winter and spoiling in the summer. 'Twas a fabulous idea back before refrigerators. The one you've seen at the estate is located just off the back of the house, like a detached basement of sorts. The ones located away from the house also stored things such as ammunition. A century ago, homeowners feared digging under the house might later affect the foundation."

"Interesting," Horace said as he reached for the broom Paloma had insisted on bringing. He used the handle to pull away the vines that had wrapped themselves around the doors like thick ropes. "It's been decades since this thing's been opened."

"I bet it was left vacant as soon as the home was built. Emmanuel doesn't sound like the type who'd store anything all the way down here by the bayou," Paloma commented. "His father was probably the last to utilize it."

"There's one hell of a lock on her," Horace said, continuing to struggle with the brush. "These doors are almost rotten, Paloma. I could go back to the house and get something to try to cut through this lock or I could just kick open the doors. What do you think?"

"Technically, it's on our property," Paloma said uneasily. "And it's not as though we are damaging anything that isn't already ruined, but..."

"But what?" Horace asked, turning to face her. He was out of breath from clearing the underbrush and anxious to see what was inside. "We're not breaking into someone's house. The whole idea of this is to get answers. I say I kick the doors open and we see what's inside. It's probably nothing anyway."

"You're right, it's probably empty, but I have an uneasy feeling. I need to check on Catherine and see if she slept well. Let's go to the estate and you can bring Ben back out here with you. This is men's work."

62

It was midday before everyone was out of bed. Tink had started the coffee just as the unnerving melody of the doorbell reverberated throughout the estate.

Tink joined Harriett, who was feeding Landry a bottle at the kitchen table. The boys were digging through the storage room, according to Harriett, though they popped right up when the bell rang, insisting to be the ones who answered it.

Once they were alone, Harriett pointed to a chair. "Come sit down, Tink, we have to talk. We can't act as if we didn't read those letters."

"I know," Tink agreed, slumping into the nearest chair. "I hardly slept a wink. Then this morning I slept so hard that I felt like I'd been drugged."

"Me, too," Harriett said. "But we were exhausted. That was a great deal of information to take in and the thunderstorm didn't help."

"It was creepy to say the least. But I don't see how any of what we read could be tied to what's happening here."

"But we can't discount it either," Harriett asserted.

"Discount what?" Dan asked as he entered the kitchen, followed by Ben, Horace, and Paloma.

"Oh, nothing, we were just talking," Harriett replied. "Look at who's here, Landry."

"Look at that precious little one," Paloma gushed. "Here, let me take her. I'll finish feeding her."

Harriett did not need to be told twice.

"What brings you two over here?" Ben asked. "Were you able to find anything that could help us?"

"I'm still a little uncertain of *what* I've found," Paloma answered. "Horace found an old survey of the property and located the original root cellar. It must have been built by Emmanuel Sinclair's father. Horace knows his name—it fails me now."

"Claude," Horace piped in.

"Yes, poor Mr. Claude never got any accolades for this land, did he?" Paloma asked. "It has always been about Emmanuel Sinclair, the amazing businessman who put Kane, Louisiana on the map."

Tink and Harriett exchanged a coded glance.

"Yeah, Ben, I found the old root cellar out by the bayou," Horace began. "It's covered in vines and debris, but I'd sure like to see what's inside. Paloma stopped me just shy of breaking in the doors. Has a serious lock on it but we don't have any use for it, so it'd be easiest just to break through the doors."

"You won't find anything in that old hole but a few jars of fruit preserves," Paloma said. "But men have an odd sense of adventure I'll never understand. I told Horace to get you to go along, Ben. There's no telling what kind of creatures he may come up on. It's a waste of time if you ask me."

"Let's check it out, Horace," Ben said. "Dan's here with the women, so they'll be fine."

Paloma turned to Dan and smiled warmly. "You go along, too, dear," she said. "You'd be miserable here wondering what they're up to."

"No ma'am, Ms. Paloma," Dan insisted. "I couldn't leave ya'll alone. I wouldn't feel right."

"Leave your shotgun propped by the door," Paloma said. "If they can get through me and that rifle, there wouldn't have been anything you could have done anyway. Now shoo, all three of you. Just like when they were little boys." She stifled a laugh. "Always getting into something. Men never grow out of that; I'm telling you ladies now. Big kids are all they are."

The women shared a laugh as Paloma encouraged the boys out the door. She took the shotgun from Dan, propped it up against the kitchen doorframe, and returned to the table. "Now hand that little one back to me. I see she's finished her bottle. Bet she's sleeping better now that she's eating more."

"Yes, she is." Harriett beamed. "That was good advice to increase her formula."

"What was that look about earlier?" Paloma asked, glancing between Tink and Harriett.

"What—?" Tink began, her eyes growing wide.

"No sense playing dumb," Harriett said. "Ms. Paloma never misses anything."

This brought a chuckle from the older woman. "The sooner you come to terms with it, the better off you'll be," Paloma said. "You two found something, didn't you?"

Harriett turned to Tink and nodded. "Tell her everything, Tink. Maybe she can make sense of it."

Over the next half hour, Tink nervously shared it all, from her and Ben going through the gowns, to Harriett discovering the letters in the lining of the hat boxes. She also shared the disturbing content of the notes written to a deceased baby who she and Harriett suspected had been killed by her own mother.

Paloma had remained silent throughout the whole summation of what'd been found in the dressing room, but it was clear her mind was sorting through the information.

"What do you make of it, Paloma?" Tink asked.

"There's probably more details in what you two read than initially believed. We will need to read between the lines, as they say," Paloma said, her eyes glazing over. "First, there is the issue of the infant. We know very little of this Thaddeus fellow other than he was a free black man who owned a cotton plantation adjoining this one. I remember hearing talk that Prudence and George, the oldest of our known ancestors, were slaves at the Jackson estate prior to moving onto Sinclair property. If Fatima died in childbirth and Thaddeus died in a house fire, it would make sense for them to be moved here. And certainly, Lucretia bearing the child of a black man, a *married* black man and her husband's business partner at that, would have had significant consequences." Paloma paused, closing her eyes as if in prayer. "Lord Jesus, that poor child, drawing her last breath at the hands of her mother," she whispered. "Could you get the letters for me? We'll need to go through them line by line."

"Yes," Tink answered. "I'll get them." She tucked her cell phone in the back pocket of her jeans before leaving the kitchen.

"Do you want me to come with you?" Harriett asked. "Are you scared to go alone?"

"No, I'm fine, I'll just be a minute. I have to take care of some of my work later or my father will kill me."

Tink's heart quickened as she made her way up the staircase. It was different now that she knew Emmanuel Sinclair had hanged himself from the one object he was most proud of.

This beautiful rotunda, with all the colors of the rainbow filtering down like diamonds, was the last thing he saw before his death. The thought made Tink hasten her step and wish she'd taken Harriett up on coming along. *I'm being foolish. I need to be at peace with this place. There had to be many good times here.*

Tink flipped the light on in the ballroom, not lingering this time to take in its splendor. She was anxious to grab the letters and get back downstairs, back with Harriett and Paloma, and back where the large shotgun was propped against the wall. She and Harriett had decided earlier to return the letters to their original hiding place because it seemed only fitting. It had also squashed their childish fears of Lucretia returning to haunt them for invading years of her privacy.

Those irrational fears now returned and Tink felt her heartbeat hasten as she opened the dressing room door. She wasted no time in pulling down the appropriate hat boxes and sliding her fingers along the loosened silk linings.

Tink counted all seven letters carefully and paused long enough to gently tuck the century and a half-old envelopes into the pocket of her blazer. She turned off the light as she pulled the door closed behind her. But before she could make her way out of the ballroom, the chandeliers overhead went off, leaving her completely in the dark.

"What have you been doing in there?" a husky female voice demanded. "What did you find?"

"Who is that?" Tink asked, placing one hand on the wall and stretching out the other. "This is my house. Why are you asking me such a thing? Why are you here?"

"We're the ones asking the questions," the voice answered. "What are you doing up here?"

Tink's thoughts instantly went to Paloma, Harriett, and the baby. "How'd you get in here?" she demanded, trying to sound unafraid. "Where's Paloma? You'd better not have hurt them!"

"You should be concerned about yourself," the strange voice cautioned her.

The initial shock faded into a combination of fear and determination. Tink knew the direction of the door leading into the hall, so she held both arms out and broke into a run. A bright beam of light from behind helped illuminate the way, but also established that Tink's visitor had the benefit of a flashlight. Loud, heavy footsteps confirmed there was more than one uninvited guest in the ballroom, and both were gaining on her.

Just as she reached the doorknob, Catherine "Tink" Mabrey's world turned black. She never felt the crushing blow of the aluminum maglite or the two intruders picking up her crumpled body and tossing her down the stairway.

※

It didn't take the three men long to locate the old root cellar.

"I can't believe you haven't noticed this before," Ben said as Horace pointed out the rotting double doors.

"I didn't even know it existed," Horace replied. "Just looks like a mound of dirt to me. I knew about the cellar under the Sinclair house, but this one's way before my time."

"Ours too," Dan spoke up. "So, these root cellars were used for canned goods?"

"That's my understanding," Horace answered. "With the cellar underground, it maintained a constant temperature. Not too cold, not too hot. Paloma said it was a way of storing vegetables and salted meats."

"Wonder what century-old vegetables taste like?" Ben teased as he pulled at some of the vines covering the doors.

Horace handed Dan an ax and kept one for himself. "Let's cut as much of this brush back as we can, then we'll just chop our way through what's left of those doors. It shouldn't be too difficult."

Horace had been right—both men were accustomed to hard work and within minutes, there wasn't much left of the doors but kindling.

"I'm thankful we're doing this in the daylight," Ben noted. "It looks like a setting for a bad horror movie."

"That's why we brought the lanterns," Horace said. "I'm sure this is a waste of time, but it's kept my mind off the loss of my father."

Ben and Dan both lowered their eyes and fumbled for words of solace.

"It's still recent and raw," Dan said quietly. "All I can say is it gets better with time."

"So they say," Horace agreed as he turned the lantern on. "Let's go in and see what we've got. My bet's on four dirt walls."

"I'll put twenty on that same bet," Ben said. "But it got us out of that house for a few minutes."

Horace and Ben waited on Dan to go in first, which was usually the case whenever they did something for the first time. It went without saying that Dan was the largest, making him a good point man.

"These stairs could use some work," Dan said, holding the lantern down to show them what they were dealing with. "I didn't expect this many steps. Figured on three or four at the most."

The collapsing stairs led down into a cavernous, square room about twelve by twelve feet. Wooden shelves lined the walls, but they, too, hadn't withstood the test of time.

"This is what I expected," Horace said as he held up his lantern and walked the circumference of the small cellar. "Feels a little strange to be the only people in here after all this time. I was expecting something on the shelves."

"It's served its purpose, I suppose. I'd hate to have to dig this out, imagine what a job it was," Ben said as he wiggled the disheveled shelves. "I'm surprised these hung on as long as they did, especially underground."

"They should've used cypress," Dan said. "These couldn't have been very sturdy, even when they were new," he added as he wiggled another set of wooden shelves. Just as he pulled his hands back, the set of shelves tumbled down like a set of dominoes.

The men stood speechless for a moment before Ben spoke. "Good thing you didn't have plans for the place, Horace. Per usual, Dan is like a bull in a china shop, but even I didn't expect him to disintegrate a set of shelves with one touch." Ben chuckled as he walked back toward the steps. "Nothing to see here folks." He stood at the bottom of the steps and turned to find Horace and Dan still standing at the foot of the pile of lumber. "It's not going to rebuild itself if that's what you two are waiting for," he said. "We've left the women alone long enough; we need to head back."

Horace and Dan remained in the same position until Ben walked over to join them. "What's going on?"

"This set of doors looks like it did the day they were constructed," Dan began. "That's what cypress can do."

"Why would you make doors of this quality down here and not at the entrance?" Horace asked. "That doesn't make sense."

"It'd make sense if you wanted everyone to believe this was merely a root cellar used to store salted meat and canned preserves," Dan replied. "First of all, you'd have to know there was a root cellar here in the first place, and if you did, why break in for someone else's stored food? And, to play the devil's advocate, if you needed food, you'd just break in and take it. Would you think to move shelves around to see if there was a hidden door?"

"No," Horace said. "You wouldn't. So, the question is, what's behind that door?"

"That's what we're here for, buddy," Dan said. "Ben, go grab those axes we used outside."

"You aren't going to break through those nice doors, are you?" Horace asked.

"Nope, not unless we absolutely have to. With enough muscle, we should be able to pry them open."

Ben hurried up the steps and immediately returned with the tools while Horace moved over to give Dan room to navigate. Dan did his best not to damage the doors any more than necessary while still wedging the ax in and pulling with all his might. He strained and grunted until it finally gave way.

Dan grabbed his shirttail and bent awkwardly to wipe his perspiring face. "I'm beginning to think you guys just use me for my strength."

"Here he goes," Ben said, "getting all arrogant again."

"It's the truth," Dan rebutted. "What the hell would you guys do without me? You wouldn't have even had the nerve to come down here."

Horace ignored them and concentrated on the open door. "Are we going to take a look inside or head back to check on the women?"

"We're here now," Dan said. "Let's take a quick look and find out what's behind those hidden doors. What do ya say, Ben?"

"Let's make it fast," Ben said. "One thing I'm sure of—if we go back and tell the women we found a hidden set of doors but didn't go inside, they'll be furious."

"Grab the other lantern," Horace instructed Ben. "Let's see what we've got here."

"I've got it," Ben said after retrieving the lamp. "Let's not get our hopes up."

They followed Dan, once again, as they squeezed themselves through the pried-open set of doors. They made it a few feet before Dan stopped and surveyed what was before them. "Look at that, would ya?" he commented, pointing to the complex underground passageway. "It would've taken an army of Hebrew slaves to construct something this elaborate."

"Or an army of *black* slaves," Horace corrected dryly.

"Horace," Dan began. "I'm so—"

"No need to apologize," Horace interrupted. "It wasn't your doing."

Dan nodded shortly and considered attempting another apology, but thought it'd be even more insulting, so he continued down the tunnel. "This brickwork is impressive. Ben, check out these support walls. That's something else."

"Dan, have you ever seen capping beams this large?" Ben asked as he gazed up above. "This place was made to last. What in the world would they need this for?"

"Who knows? I wonder how far it goes, and more importantly, where it ends. Horace, I can't believe you haven't heard about this."

"My family kept many of the Sinclair secrets, but I've never heard anyone even allude to something like this."

"Listen to those big words," Ben teased. "The only way I know what *allude* means is how you use it in conversation. Do you and Paloma study the dictionary or what?"

"Damn, Ben," Dan scolded. "Can we insult our friend any more in one day? I'm sorry, Horace."

"It was a compliment," Ben said defensively. "I find it impressive, and yet unbelievable that *we* can have such an intelligent friend."

"We read a lot," Horace said, continuing down the tunnel. "My father didn't allow us to have a television. Instead he handed us a book. You two should try it some time."

"That's a joke," Dan said. "Clearly you two don't have an infant. I barely have time to shower."

The men continued moving forward until Ben spoke. "We've walked at least five hundred yards. We were headed north but have slowly turned eastward. Where do you think we are—if we were above ground, I mean?"

"I'd have to say we're close to the Sinclair mansion," Horace answered.

"That'd make sense," Dan said. "But why build an expensive and time-consuming tunnel from the bayou to the estate?"

"Again, we have nothing but questions," Ben said. "And we have no idea what we're walking into. I don't like this at all."

"I have to agree," Dan said. "We've discovered the tunnel so let's cover it up with brush and come back with the sheriff."

"I think we're close to the house," Horace said. "I think we should keep going. If someone was setting us up, they'd have caught us off guard by now. This tunnel must end up somewhere in the estate. Maybe it's how they transported any goods brought by water up to the home."

"It seems a little strange to go to so much trouble to build an elaborate tunnel system to transport household commodities. Seems like it'd be easier to bring your horse and buggy down to meet the boat."

"Unless it was contraband," Horace said. "It'd be pretty clever to disguise a tunnel as a root cellar. It was originally built for legitimate reasons and even notated on the official plat of the property."

"I wonder what they would've been smuggling back then," Ben mused.

"It could have been any number of things," Horace replied. "Louisiana has more than its share of waterways and ports."

"But the family was already rich," Dan spoke up. "They had hundreds of acres, to say nothing of the cotton and sugar cane crops."

"One thing I've learned," Horace said, "is that the rich can never be rich enough."

"We can't narrow it down to one particular generation," Ben said. "I mean, think about it. There were years of pirating and years of prohibition. Then years of slavery and years of war. It could've been built for any number of reasons."

"That's not important right now," Dan said. "Let's get to the end of this thing and check on the women. I don't like leaving them this long. It's not a good idea."

"You're right," Ben said, now anxious to get back himself.

The men hastened their steps until they came to a long spiral staircase. The tunnel went a few feet farther, but they weren't willing to see how much.

"We've got to be at the house," Horace said as he started up the metal stairs.

"Don't want me to go first?" Dan asked.

"I'm ready to see where we are," Horace said. "Besides, these steps are narrow. You both follow behind."

The brothers did as he asked until finally Dan spoke. "This has to be the third or fourth flight of stairs, Horace. Do you see an end in sight?"

They were all sweating and out of breath now.

"We're almost to the top. There's a small landing. I think we can all stand on it."

Horace stood on the metal area while he waited on Dan and Ben to join him.

"Looks like one hell of a thick door," Dan said, wiping his forehead with the back of his hand. "This has turned into a lot more work than I anticipated."

"We should've thought to bring the axes along," Ben agreed. "How are we going to get through that?"

Horace reached out and pushed down on the bar-type lever. "There you have it," Horace said with a chuckle. "Who would've figured?"

"I'll be damned," Dan said as he patted Horace on the back. "I was ready to turn back around. I'm sweating like a hog."

"Something's moving, it sounds like some type of pulley system," Horace warned as he stepped back. "I hope we aren't walking into a trap."

Ben leaned against the door, listening, before he opened it farther. He slowly bent forward to peek in before stepping into the room. "And I thought the secret tunnel was a surprise," he said. "I just came in through a fireplace."

Dan and Horace were immediately behind him and the three stood dumbfounded inside Emmanuel Sinclair's dust-laden office.

"Listen, do you hear that?" Ben asked. "Shh..."

A panicked voice was screaming several rooms away, shrill but incomprehensible.

"I think it's Harriett," Dan yelled, making his way toward the door that led to the rest of the estate. He turned the doorknob and pushed. "Help! It's like it's barricaded. Help me push!"

The men pushed with their shoulders before looking for something in the office to break through the door.

"I have heard they closed this office off, blocking the entrance," Horace said. "It's going to take more than our strength to break it down."

"Shh... Listen," Dan ordered.

They all leaned against the door and listened intently.

"Call 911. She's dying," Harriett screamed.

"I'll run back and get the axes," Ben yelled.

"You dumbass," Dan spat. "By the time we run back through the tunnel, we could just run back to the estate without the effort of breaking through this. We don't have time to spare. Let's all push the door with our shoulders, on three."

The men's collective efforts made progress. They heard a loud crack and the door gave way, but it took two more attempts before breaking completely through the boarded-off room.

They quickly pushed through the boards; Dan was the first to break into a run. Horace and Ben followed.

"Help, Paloma, help," Harriett was screaming.

Dan followed the sound of his wife's voice but couldn't see her until he made it to the staircase. Harriett was down a flight and a half of steps, holding Tink in her arms, yelling at the top of her lungs.

"Harriett!" Dan screamed. "I'm coming!"

He reached her just as Paloma had made her way up the steps

with Landry. The baby was crying at all the ruckus, making the situation even more chaotic.

"I was trying to get to her," Paloma said to Dan. "Oh, dear Lord in heaven. What's happened?"

Ben and Horace had made their way to them. "What the hell happened? Is she alive?" Ben asked as he bent down next to Tink. There was blood everywhere and Tink was unconscious. "Oh my God, somebody do something!"

Dan grabbed his cell phone and dialed. "Get an ambulance to the Sinclair estate ASAP," he shouted. "Something has happened to Tink—um, what's her real name, Ben?"

"Catherine Mabrey," Paloma interjected. "Have them hurry. She's critical."

He nodded absently. "Yes, it's Dan, now get an ambulance out here. She's unconscious. There's a lot of blood. I don't know what happened, and it doesn't matter, she's dying. What part of *that* don't you understand?"

He quieted, then shook his head. "I...I don't know," Dan mumbled, and put Roxie on speaker. "Ben, do you see a gunshot wound? What happened?"

"She came upstairs to get the letters we found," Harriett said, her voice shaking. "Paloma and I were in the kitchen and it was taking Tink longer than it should have. I decided to check on her and found her right here on the stairs, bloody and unconscious. Maybe she was rushing and fell. I knew I should've come with her."

"Are there any injuries? Anything not caused by a fall?" the woman on the other end, Roxie, pressed.

"Her head is bleeding," Ben said. "But I can't find the cause. I think she must've fallen."

"How's her breathing? Is it fast or slow? Can you detect a pulse?"

"She's breathing," Ben said loudly. "But it's very fast and I can't find a pulse. Wait, there it is. It's very weak and she's clammy."

"Don't move her," Roxie instructed. "And don't lift her head."

Paloma pointed upward on the staircase, tears rolling down her cheeks. "She came out of both shoes. Those slip-on shoes are an accident waiting to happen. I should've known better, child." She reached for Harriett.

"It appears to be a fall down the stairs," Dan confirmed. "How much longer on that ambulance?"

"It's on its way, Dan," Roxie said. "It's on its way."

63

BEN RODE in the ambulance with Tink while the others rode with Sheriff Broussard.

"Rapid heartbeat, shallow breathing, bleeding from the back of the head, swollen abdomen," the young man said, speaking slowly and deliberately into the mouthpiece attached to his collar. He spouted off several numbers related to Tink's vitals to a voice on the other end of the radio.

"Preparing trauma bay four," the methodical voice responded. "Trauma staff is preparing for arrival. ETA?"

"We're ten to fifteen minutes out. No traffic—the sheriff is escorting us."

"Ten-four. Keep us updated on any change in the vitals."

"Ten-four."

The world seemed to fog over as Ben struggled to stay calm. Tink's dark hair hid most of the blood from sight, but her shirt and shoulders were saturated. Ben rubbed her face softly until the EMT instructed him to sit back.

"Swelling in the abdomen and lower legs," he spoke into the small black radio. "BP is slowly going down, heartbeat becoming more rapid."

"Ten-four. Age?"

The EMT looked up at Ben, who suddenly felt more helpless than ever. "I don't know," Ben answered. "Wait, the sheriff gave the driver her purse. Her license has to be in there."

"Hey, Eric, do you have her purse up there?"

"Yeah, do you need it?"

"Hand it back if you can."

A large black purse was thrust back from the front of the ambulance. Ben reached for it and offered it to the man across from him.

"I'm a little busy here, dude," he told Ben. "Think you could handle that for me?"

Ben sat, looking awkwardly at the designer bag. He'd never had the occasion to invade a woman's privacy and didn't feel comfortable doing it now.

"Sir? Can you speed it up a little? The hospital's waiting on an answer."

"Yes, sorry," Ben stammered. He pulled Tink's license from her wallet and calculated the dates. "She's twenty-nine."

"She's twenty-nine. Breathing continues to be shallow."

"Trauma bay and staff are standing by. We've cleared her for an immediate CT scan."

"Ten-four," he reiterated into the mic. "What the hell are you doing up there, Eric? Can you speed it up?"

"I'm going as fast as I can. The sheriff's in front with his lights and sirens on. We're five minutes out."

Ben felt the world swirling around him like an out-of-body experience.

"Don't pass out on me," the EMT said. "I can't help you. I've got my hands full. You need to pull yourself together. I'm sure this woman needs you. Better pull out any insurance cards while you've got her purse. The hospital will be asking for them. Do you have any emergency contacts? Why am I asking you? You didn't even know her age."

He was steadily monitoring his patient while giving Ben tasks to keep his mind occupied. The two paramedics dealt with this often. Although they saw injured and sick people daily, others didn't.

Her dad, Ben thought. *I don't even know how to reach him.*

"Ryan, we're pulling up now," Eric yelled from the front. "Got a big crew out here, so be prepared."

As soon as the ambulance had slowed to a stop, the whirlwind of medical personnel swarmed in. A sea of people in surgical scrubs pulled the gurney from the ambulance and rolled Tink into the hospital before Ben could realize what had happened.

Ben was sitting alone in the back of the ambulance, his heart racing, when Dan shouted at him. "Ben? You okay? Come on, let's go in the hospital."

"Dan, I'm so glad to see you. This is crazy."

"Are you in shock? I called out to you like five times."

"I'm okay," Ben answered, getting out of the ambulance and handing the purse to Dan. "Where's everyone else?"

"They're inside by now. I've never been so nervous in my life. The sheriff was speeding, and we didn't have the car seat for Landry..."

"Let's go in and find them," Ben said. "I don't think she's going to make it, Dan. It's bad. We need to get in touch with her father."

The two brothers sprinted down the hall and spotted Isaac talking to one of the nurses. When he saw them, he pointed in the direction of the others. Harriett and the baby, Paloma, and Horace were all huddled together in a small waiting room. Paloma was trying to console Harriett, although she needed consoling herself. Horace jumped up from his seat when they came in.

"How could this happen?" he asked quietly. "We were trying to protect her from someone hurting her and she falls down the stairs. I can't understand it. I never should've taken you two to that root cellar."

"I'm sure there'll be enough blame to go around before all is said and done," Dan said. "No need to start claiming any now. I hate to do it, but I need to call my mother-in-law to come pick up Landry. I know I'll never get Harriett to agree to leave with her. Is Paloma going to be all right? Maybe we should have a doctor look at her."

"She'd never agree to that," Horace said. "Paloma thinks she needs to help everyone else. Go make that call, Dan. The baby doesn't need to be around any germs and I'm sure a hospital has more than its share of them."

Just as Dan stepped out, Isaac came in. "They're doing all they can," he said. "It's crazy in there right now, but I'm certain it's organized chaos. She has the best trauma surgeon at the hospital."

"We need to get in touch with her father," Ben said. "I don't have any idea how to do that. I don't even know the name of the law firm she works for. Wait," he said suddenly, "she got some paperwork from her office delivered to the house. We could get someone to go look at the return address."

"We locked the house up," Horace said.

"I'll call Blaine Biggs," the sheriff said. "He contacted her father about the will, so he'll have his information."

"Might want to do that right away," Ben said.

"You're right," Isaac said, resigned. "I'll step down the hall and make the calls. Find me if anything changes."

BEN AND HORACE sat with the women, taking turns assuring them the fall wasn't their fault. It wasn't long before a doctor and nurse located them in the waiting room.

"Hello, I'm Dr. Hightower. Are you the family of Catherine Mabrey?" the tall, lean doctor asked.

"We're friends," Paloma answered. "She's from Atlanta and doesn't have any family here. How's she doing?"

"She has a tremendous amount of internal bleeding and is going to need a blood transfusion," he said. "That's all we can determine until we get her into surgery. Her blood type is rare, O negative, which acts as a universal donor. However, it's in short supply, and high demand. We're running extremely low now due to a recent car accident. That's the downside to having that blood type. O negative can only receive O negative blood. Our blood bank is currently checking with recent donors."

A lady dressed in a pantsuit quickly entered the small area and motioned for the doctor. "Have you seen the sheriff?" she asked.

"No, I haven't, Donna," Dr. Hightower answered.

"He's down the hall making a call," Ben interjected.

"He's here in the hospital?" Donna asked.

"Yes, want me to get him?" Ben asked.

"Yes, hurry! He's one of our O negative donors."

PALOMA SAT DUMBFOUNDED FOR A MOMENT, slowly comprehending what should've been obvious all along. The eyes, Isaac's beautiful eyes—why hadn't she thought of it before? They were so much like Olivia's and Catherine's. For the first time in many years, Paloma was reminded of the story of Isaac's birth. It'd been quite the news in Kane and had made the first page of the local paper.

Isaac's mother, Paula, was a reclusive writer who'd found her inspiration in the dark basement of their lavish home. Her husband, Preston, was the opposite. He was friendly and gregarious and loved the outdoors. He worked in the oil industry, traveling often to Dallas and Houston. Paula, however, was more comfortable to be home, either writing or tending her beautiful gardens. It wasn't that she was unfriendly, just more introverted than her sociable spouse. The two made a beautiful couple. When they were seen out together, everyone commented on it, making it only fitting they'd have such a handsome son.

No one in Kane had known Paula was pregnant, but it hadn't seemed odd as she was such a private person. Preston had been driving her to the hospital when the baby was born. He'd had to pull over on the roadside and deliver their son himself, before turning around and taking his family back home. Preston had been hailed a hero and his wife quite the trooper for enduring the pains of childbirth in the less-than-luxurious surroundings of an Oldsmobile F85.

"That wasn't a pleasant phone call to make," Isaac began, making Paloma jump. "Didn't mean to startle you, Paloma."

"I take it you reached the dad," Ben said.

"Yes, and he was beside himself, to put it mildly. He's catching the first flight out of Atlanta. Poor guy, I feel for him. Any more news?"

"They were looking for you," Paloma said immediately.

"Donna found me. That's what took me so long. I donated blood and had to drink juice and eat a cookie before she'd let me leave."

"Oh, thank God," Paloma sighed.

Harriett's cell phone rang. "Mother's here," she said nervously, glancing at the screen. "Lord, I hope she can take good care of Landry."

"She must have done good with you," Isaac said with a grin.

"Yes, I did!" Hazel snapped loudly as she burst into the waiting room. "If you didn't think I could handle it, you shouldn't have had *him* call me." She pointed at Dan. "I bought the formula *he* said she takes on the way, along with diapers and other essential supplies."

"His name is Dan, and her name is Landry," Harriett said tersely.

"I'm well aware of everyone's name," Hazel continued. "And I'll take excellent care of Landry while you play private investigator."

"Everyone is tired, dear, and we're worried about Catherine," Paloma said quietly. "I'm sure everything will work out fine."

"I don't know what they've told you about me, but I ain't hard of hearing," Hazel replied with a sneer. "I'm parked in a crippled person spot and I can't afford the fine so…"

"Handicapped parking, Mother," Harriett corrected.

"Tomato, tomahto," Hazel retorted. "Dan, are you going to carry the baby to the car? And, yes, I picked up a car seat. And to think you were wondering if I was up to this."

Paloma nudged Harriett.

"Mother, thank you for everything. I never doubted you; it's just hard being a new mother."

"Yes, I know. I've been one. Thanks for elbowin' my daughter to remind her to thank me," Hazel said to Paloma. "One of these days ya'll will realize I don't miss a trick."

64

A NURSE RETURNED a couple of hours later to inform them Catherine was in surgery. Her CT scan had detected significant internal bleeding and the source would need to be found and repaired.

There was little doubt Isaac's blood donation had saved her life and the hospital's cell saver machine would be crucial in keeping her alive. It would collect any of Tink's own blood lost during the surgery, process it, and return it to her. The nurse promised to come back as soon as she had any updates, and encouraged each of them to pray for Catherine, as the next few hours would be critical.

Paloma struggled to conceal her thoughts, her deep concern about what was inevitably the truth about Isaac Broussard Sinclair. *Does the sheriff know who he really is? Did his parents even know? Could he be behind what's happening in Kane? No, I refuse to believe it.*

"Paloma? You're a million miles away," Horace said.

"I'm sorry," she said, trying to bring her thoughts back to the present.

"Wait a minute!" Harriett interrupted. "How'd you guys find me? I mean, how'd you come from the *top* of the stairs? It just dawned on me."

"It's a crazy story," Ben said.

"We've got nothing but time, apparently," Harriett said. "Humor us."

"You tell 'em, Horace. This was all your discovery," Ben said. "I'd hate to take the credit."

"But you guys were headed to that old root cellar," Harriett said, frowning.

"Yes, we were," Dan said. "And it would've gone unnoticed for another hundred years if Horace hadn't spotted it on that survey."

"Cut to the chase," Harriett said. "Horace, tell us how you got to the top of the stairs without coming through the house."

"Well, we started by cutting all that brush away from the cellar doors and..."

"That's it!" Harriett exclaimed. "*Without coming through the house!*"

"Excuse me?" Horace asked. "I haven't even told you about the tunnel."

"It was in the letters we found," Harriett began. "There were letters Lucretia wrote to her dead baby, Philomene. She wrote of concerns that her husband, Emmanuel, and Thaddeus, his business partner and neighbor, had a secret club. She referred to it as, let me get this right, a *so-called* collaborative, I believe. Anyway, she had serious doubts about it. Lucretia wanted her daughter to understand that just because men had money, it didn't mean they'd necessarily earned it, or *came by it honestly*, is how she worded it."

"And what does that have to do with the root cellar?" Dan asked.

"Give me a minute, Dan," Harriett said, clearly flustered. She closed her eyes. "Let me think. Going back to that club thing, Lucretia said something about not trusting the men, but she'd never met any of them. She often heard voices from Emmanuel's office, men talking, but none of them had come through the front door. Her husband was adamant about his office being off limits and she respected his wishes, but she was skeptical. Lucretia also mentioned another man, but I can't remember his name for the life of me. It was Cajun or Acadian—I can't, nope, can't remember it. Anyway, Emmanuel kept dreaming about him, having nightmares, and saying something about the biggest one yet, yep, that's it! *The biggest one yet.* Lucretia said he was going mad."

"So, the tunnel was used for illegal business," Ben said. "I knew it!"

"Where was the tunnel?" Paloma asked.

"It was behind the root cellar. They'd used the cellar as a guise," Horace said. "It was close to the bayou, which makes a great deal of sense now. They'd hidden the entrance to the tunnel behind shelves. It was quite elaborate, wasn't it, Dan?"

"You aren't kidding," Dan agreed. "It was one hell of a tunnel and won't be going anywhere for another century, that's for sure. I can guarantee you we were the first people in there since that Emmanuel fellow snuck in his buddies."

"His office hasn't been entered since his death," Paloma said. "At least that's what I've been told. It was permanently secured the day he was buried."

"He hung himself from the top of the staircase," Harriett said. "How creepy."

"He did no such thing, child," Paloma said. "If that had happened, we'd surely have heard about it."

"But Lucretia wrote about it in her letters. She told her daughter and said she was the only other person to know. The letters! Where are they? I just assumed Tink was coming back down the stairs when she fell."

"Did anyone see them on the stairs?" Paloma asked. "I didn't notice any."

They looked at one another and shook their heads.

"Where could they be?" Harriett asked. "That's weird."

"So maybe there was a big heist of some kind," Ben suggested. "Maybe it went wrong and somehow led to Emmanuel's suicide."

"Lucretia said he was going mad. I think I already said that, but she also said that man's wife was going mad, too. The man with the hard-to-remember surname. His wife was beating on Lucretia and

Emmanuel's door, screaming about her husband's hand with the wedding ring on it. A man named George had to keep her away."

"Wasn't George Prudence's husband, Paloma?" Horace asked.

"Yes, he was. Hand. Harriett, you said *hand*. What all do you remember about the hand?" Paloma asked intently.

"Umm, I don't know. Just what I said. The lady was going crazy like Emmanuel, almost as if it were contagious. The way Lucretia put it, the woman beat on the door repeatedly, or at least, on more than one occasion. She just kept saying things about her husband's hand with the wedding band. That was it. Lucretia said she was mad, which is crazy, right?"

"Yes," Paloma confirmed. "We need to find those letters."

"We'll look for them when we go back to the house," Ben said. "But for now, let's concentrate on Tink surviving her surgery."

THE HOURS SEEMED to drag while the six of them dozed on and off in the uncomfortable chairs of the hospital waiting room. Isaac finally stood up and declared they were long overdue a strong cup of coffee. He dug through his pockets and pulled out some coins. "Anyone else have any to contribute? The machine down the hall only takes change."

Ben stood to check his pockets when a tall, angry man filled the doorframe.

"Are you people here for Catherine Mabrey?" he demanded.

A silence settled over the group. Finally, the sheriff answered. "Yes sir, we are. How may I help you?"

"I'm Augustus Mabrey, her father," he barked. "The woman at the nurses' station told me you all were down here. No one has any information other than Catherine's in surgery."

"Yes, Mr. Mabrey. I'm Isaac Broussard—we spoke earlier. I'm very sorry about your daughter's accident."

"I want her out of this...this *place* immediately," Augustus insisted. "She needs to be medevacked to a real hospital."

Paloma's eyes filled with tears as she stood to make her way to Augustus. She took both of his large hands in her own. "I prayed I would see you again one day, Augustus. I am much older than when we last saw one another."

Isaac reached out to brace one of Augustus's arms. Augustus ignored the effort as he stepped in the waiting room and sat. He was still holding one of Paloma's hands, which he raised to his lips and softly kissed.

"Yes, Paloma. I've thought of you many times through the years. You were so kind to Olivia and me," Augustus said. "What has happened to my Catherine?"

"She took a fall down the stairs," Paloma began. "Harriett and I realized she'd been gone too long and went to check on her. We found her on the landing. Catherine was brought here as soon as she was found."

"What has the doctor said?"

"Catherine was bleeding internally when she arrived. Isaac, the sheriff," Paloma said, pointing to him, "has the same rare blood type and was able to donate enough blood to enable Catherine to go into surgery. He saved her life, Augustus."

Augustus looked up and nodded at Isaac. "Has there been an update?"

"A nurse came in a while back to let us know she'd had a CT scan. The purpose of the surgery was to locate where the bleeding was coming from and to repair it. It's taken quite a while. Surely..."

A sudden shift from the group caused Paloma to look up. The doctor had returned. "I understand Catherine's father has arrived," he began.

Augustus was instantly on his feet. "Yes, Augustus Mabrey. How is she?"

"Dr. Hightower," he began, reaching for Augustus's hand. "May I speak freely in front of everyone or do you prefer we go into another room?"

Augustus looked around, but before he could speak, Paloma had taken the floor. "Everyone here cares about your daughter,

Augustus. They have been waiting for hours. But we respect your wishes."

"You may speak freely," Augustus told the doctor.

"Please, let's sit," the doctor said, taking his own advice and sitting across from Paloma and Augustus. "I won't sugarcoat it. Your daughter had a rough go of things. She was in hypovolemic shock when she arrived due to the blood loss from the internal bleeding. Our neurosurgeon performed a craniotomy to relieve the pressure on the brain."

"A craniotomy?" Augustus blurted out. "Is there brain damage?"

"No, we don't have any reason to believe so at this time. The procedure is not as bad as it sounds. It is a small hole in the skull that takes the pressure off the brain and reduces any further damage from swelling or hemorrhaging. I did an exploratory laparotomy in the abdomen to seal any leaking vessels. Her spleen was damaged too severely and had to be removed."

"Oh my God," Augustus gasped. "What is her prognosis?"

"She'll remain in ICU a few days so we can monitor her, but ulti-mately, she should fully recover."

"I want her transferred to a major hospital right away," Augustus said flatly.

"I understand your concerns," Dr. Hightower said kindly. "But she's been in surgery for over six hours and moving her now would be very high risk. I wouldn't recommend it."

"It's not your call," Augustus replied.

"Mr. Mabrey, she is receiving extremely good care here. Although we're a small facility, we have state-of-the-art equipment and outstanding specialists. Moving her would only prolong her recovery. I would be happy to send her CT scan results to any doctor you choose. I'm certain they would agree with me."

Augustus bowed his head, his shoulders rising and falling with his nervous breaths. "When can I see her?"

"Catherine's in recovery now and will be sedated for several hours. You're welcome to see her when she's moved to ICU, although it'll be sometime tomorrow before she's coherent enough to know you're here. I'd recommend a good night's sleep in a motel nearby."

Augustus turned to Paloma. "You all have been here a long time. Please, go get some rest. I want—*need*—to be here with Catherine." He turned to Dr. Hightower. "Please have a nurse come get me when she's moved from recovery. I'll be right here."

65

PALOMA REMOVED the key from a folded handkerchief in her purse and inserted it in the lock, but the door swung open freely.

"That's odd," she said, looking back at the others who had been dropped off with her. "I could have sworn we locked it."

"We most certainly locked it," Horace said, glancing back at Ben and Dan.

"Someone is messing with us," Ben said.

"We can't be certain," Paloma assured him. "These old locks have a mind of their own."

"Which is even more unsettling," Dan said. "Let's check out Emmanuel's office. If it's been locked up since his death, there's no telling what we'll find there."

"There was something in the family Bible that contradicted what was written in the letters," Harriett blurted before the group headed up the stairs. "Maybe Paloma and I should stay down here and look through it."

"We need Paloma upstairs," Horace said. "She'll understand much more than I will when it comes to the history of this family."

"I have to agree with him," Paloma said to Harriett. "But what stood out to you in the Bible?"

"It was about the death of Philomene Sinclair," Harriett answered, her voice shaking.

Paloma frowned and waved at the others to quiet. "Tell us, dear. What was the conflict?"

"Philomene was Lucretia's firstborn and died soon after her birth. The reason stated for her death was severe facial deformities which prevented her from breathing."

"Birth defects happen quite often," Paloma assured her.

"But Lucretia wrote repeatedly about how perfect and beautiful she was."

"I haven't had children, but I'd think every mother would find their child perfect, despite their imperfections."

"No, Ms. Paloma, there's more. Lucretia wrote only she and Prudence saw the infant and she spoke of how the world wasn't ready for her yet. I understand how that could be construed since medicine hadn't advanced enough to help a child such as hers. But this was different. She wrote to the deceased infant about Emmanuel, but she never referred to him as her father."

"What are you trying to say, Harriett?" Ben asked.

Harriett paused briefly. "Ah, I think, I *believe*, Lucretia killed her daughter. I also think Thaddeus Jackson was the baby's father, not Emmanuel."

"Whoa!" Dan exclaimed, taking a few steps back. "That's a big assumption. There's no way to prove that and I'm sure it's better if we don't revisit it. It wouldn't serve any purpose to put it out there."

"If we only had the letters," Harriett said defensively. "If you'd read them, you'd feel the same as I do."

"We'll bear that in mind, Harriett," Paloma said. "I think we should go through Emmanuel's office now. Horace and I have to visit the funeral home tonight to approve Jericho for viewing."

"I'm sorry," Ben said. "You two go on home. I'm sure we'll be fine. You should rest before you go."

"No," Horace said. "It's best we're here for this. Paloma has a great deal of knowledge of this family and it helps to keep my mind busy. Feel up to staying for an hour, Paloma?"

Paloma nodded as the group made their way up the staircase. As one, they paused at the place where Tink had been found.

"I can't believe it," Ben said solemnly. "Do you think she'll be okay?"

"Yes, I do," Paloma said. "She's a strong, young woman. If she weren't, she'd have left this pile of rubble as soon as she saw it. But not Catherine, she's a resilient one, for sure. And she'd want nothing more than for us to discover whatever's been hidden and bring it to light."

"You're right, Ms. Paloma," Ben agreed.

The group continued up the stairs and paused to gawk at the alcoves leading to Emmanuel's office. "This is crazy," Dan commented. "I didn't even notice any of this when we passed it earlier."

"Our minds were on the women," Horace said as he rubbed his hand across one of the mantels. "Unbelievable workmanship."

"Let's get to the office," Ben said. "Paloma needs to rest. It's been a difficult few days."

Their steps became more precarious as they got closer. The wood lay splintered on the ground after the three of them had forced themselves through. They stepped over the pile of lumber before helping Paloma and Harriett across.

"Would you look at this?" Harriett whispered. "I'd say Dracula's Castle would be a fitting description."

"Could certainly use a thorough cleaning. Goodness, it is so cold in here." Paloma pulled her cardigan sweater together and folded her arms across her mid-section.

"Look over here," Dan said, reaching for her hand to lead her. "This fireplace was used to hide the tunnel leading to the root cellar and bayou. Let me close it back if I can. We're getting the cool outside air."

Horace, Ben, and Dan concentrated their efforts on discovering how the false fireplace worked and how to get it back in place to seal off the tunnel. It had, in fact, been an impressive, state-of-the-art gadget. With the men occupied, Paloma and Harriett began looking around.

Harriett was opening a cabinet when she heard Paloma gasp. Startled, she turned around to find Paloma in a trance-like state. "Oh, my Lord, it cannot be, it simply cannot be," Paloma whispered. Her low, guttural voice caused the men to turn from their work. "'Tis *La Main de Gloire*," she rasped. "Hail Mary, full of grace..."

"Paloma? What is it?" Horace asked as he walked toward her. Horace was at her side when he, too, uttered words to the Mother Mary. "It *is*, Paloma," he stammered. "'Tis the hand of glory, but *whose?*"

By this time, everyone was gathered around the desk with their mouths agape. "What the hell?" Ben asked. "I know that's not a real hand."

Paloma stepped back from the enormous mahogany desk and moved closer to the door. "'Tis," she answered. "'Tis nothing but foolish black magic."

Dan moved closer and inspected the shriveled, severed hand in the glass box. "Surely it's some kind of joke," he said. "It looks real, I give 'em that, but it just can't be. Who in their right mind would want someone else's hand?"

Horace left Paloma's side to lean over the desk and take a closer look. "I'll be damned if it isn't a hand of glory," he said, turning to face her. "But isn't it supposed to be the left hand?"

"What in hell's bells are you two even talking about?" Ben asked. "We have no idea what a hand of glory is."

"What did *you* call it, Paloma?" Harriett asked. "That name in another language."

"*La Main de Gloire*," Paloma answered. "It is derived from the French for the magical mandrake plant. It is otherwise referred to as the hand of glory. 'Tis said to have magical powers for thieves in the night."

"More importantly, is it a *real* hand—as in, was it once attached to a person?" Dan asked, leaning over the desk once again to get a better view.

"Everybody stop, Come over here," Paloma said, taking several steps away from the glass box. "Quit gawking at that disgusting thing and let's think like rational people. First, let's consider that we're looking at a dismembered hand. I'll say it again, dismembered hand. I don't know about you folks, but Kane now has three bodies that are missing their hands."

"Yeah, but this one is like a hundred years old," Ben said. "I hardly think Isaac will consider looking into the culprit of this murder. What would be the point?"

"Are you a complete idiot?" Harriett asked.

"Harriett, please—" Dan began.

"No, Dan!" Harriett shouted. "None of you, except Ms. Paloma, have listened to anything I've said. What are we doing in this office in the first place? Don't answer that, *I* will. We're here to look for clues to three murders and why they're tied to the Sinclair estate. I can't think of a clue more blatant than...than...*that*." She pointed to the hand. "Horace, you said it was supposed to be the left hand, right?"

"Yes," Horace answered. "That is what I believed."

"Typically, it is the left hand," Paloma answered. "The hand was taken from a man hanging from the gallows."

"This one was?" Harriett asked as she swallowed hard.

"No, I don't know where this particular one came from," Paloma made clear. "I am speaking about the origin of the hand of glory."

"Okay, I will start again and maybe the men will listen this time," Harriett said. "I was telling you about the letters—"

"The missing letters," Dan interjected.

"Don't interrupt me," Harriett said. "The lady that was knocking on the door, the mad woman, spoke of her husband's hand, the hand with the wedding ring on it. What hand do we wear our wedding ring on?"

"Our left hand," Dan whispered. "Do you suppose she thought Emmanuel killed her husband and cut his hand off?"

"I have to apologize, Harriett," Ben added. "You're hitting the nail on the head. This hand must somehow relate to those murders because the calling card is the same. But how in the world could we connect something that happened that long ago? Everyone involved in *that*"—he pointed at the mummified hand— "is long since dead. There's no one left to tell us what happened."

"You're right," Harriett said, sounding defeated. "There's no one left in the Sinclair family to tell us how this is tied together."

"There's *one* Sinclair left," Dan said flatly. "Are we forgetting about her?"

66

Ben contacted the hospital as soon as he got home. There wasn't anything new to report other than Tink had been moved from recovery into a room. The nurse answering the phone wasn't allowed to give out any medical information, but did allude to a successful surgery. She also didn't recommend disturbing Tink's father with a phone call.

After lifting his arm to see just how bad he smelled, Ben decided a long shower was in order. As he stripped down and stood under the steaming water, he thought back over his day. He, Dan, and Horace had wrestled with the brush covering the root cellar, made their way down the tunnel that'd been uninhabited for over a century, and broken through the barricade for Emmanuel's office. He'd ridden in the ambulance with Tink and waited for hours in the hospital before topping everything off by going back to the previously sealed office. Yep, he had more cooties than one could count, therefore necessitating an extra-long shower. He lathered and scrubbed before repeating the process two more times. Convinced the filth of the many places he'd visited was now washed down the drain, Ben turned off the water and stepped out of the shower.

He grabbed a pair of lounge pants and walked into the kitchen for a beer.

"Got any hot water left?" Cassius asked casually from the comfort of Ben's recliner.

"Shit, Cassius," Ben shouted. "You scared the hell out of me. But why am I surprised? You need to start contributing to the rent."

"Geez, take it easy," Cassius said as he sipped from one of the beers he'd taken from Ben's fridge. "You left the door open."

"Oh, so it's my fault you're here because I leave my house unlocked. I guess it's also my fault you're always sitting in my recliner because I bought it."

"Now you're getting it," Cassius said with a nod.

"I don't even know why I—"

Ben was interrupted by Cassius's cell phone ringing. "Yeah?" Cassius said in way of a greeting.

Ben could hear a woman on the other end of the line, but couldn't make out the conversation.

"Yep," Cassius said. "Nope." The woman continued as Cassius responded with curt, one-word answers, before ending the call without a goodbye.

"Who was that?" Ben asked.

"It was Betty Biggs," Cassius answered.

"What was that all about?"

"She's working on the program for Opal's funeral."

"And?" Ben pressed.

"She wanted to know if I had a decent suit to wear, and if I wanted to say a few words, and if I had a particular song I'd like to have sung at the service. Stuff like that."

"You weren't very nice to her," Ben said.

"She's been a real bitch since I started hanging out at Syd's. I don't know what her problem is, but I have enough people riding my back, I don't need her on it, too."

"All righty, then," Ben said, putting an end to any further conversation about Betty Biggs. "I assume Opal has been released to the funeral home."

"Yeah, earlier today. Thomas is still in the hospital. He's in bad shape."

"I can only imagine," Ben said. "Listen, Cassius, I don't mean to be rude, but I'm exhausted, man. Make yourself at home, not that you don't already, but I'm going to bed."

"Thanks, Ben. I don't feel like going back to the apartment. It just doesn't feel right to be there alone."

"I get it. Stay as long as you want."

67

AUGUSTUS WAS EXHAUSTED but had refused to allow himself to drift to sleep.

If only he'd been here with her, this never would've happened. It was too much for Tink to handle alone. There was the house, the questions about her mother, a small town in a state unlike any she'd ever visited. If only he'd shared more of his feelings with her instead of trying to make her strong, if only...

The sheets rustled as Tink tossed in the bed. Augustus was at her side in an instant. The doctors had expected her to awaken sometime throughout the night but weren't concerned that she hadn't. Her body had been through a great deal and needed rest.

Tink's eyelids flickered several times before her eyes opened fully. She seemed to struggle for a moment, but then looked at her father, tears spilling down her cheeks.

"No, don't cry, Tink," Augustus said, wanting to weep with relief himself. "You're okay, everything's okay. I'm here now, shh, shh, it's okay."

Tink opened her mouth. "Fa...Father..." she rasped.

"Wait just a minute," Augustus said. "I'm going to get the nurse. Wait right there, I'll be back." He almost laughed aloud at himself.

Of course, she'd be there when he got back.

The nurse was with a patient in the next room and quickly followed Augustus into Tink's room. "You're awake, aren't you, young lady?" the male nurse asked playfully. "Are you hurting anywhere?"

Tink shook her head and pointed toward her mouth and throat.

"Need some water?" he asked, reaching for the pitcher as if it were a rhetorical question. He poured some in a foam cup, replaced the lid, and added a straw. "Small sips for now. Just enough to wet your whistle. You don't want to get nauseous." He checked her vitals, ran a penlight over her eyes to ensure she was following it, and took her temperature. "I'll let the doctor know she's awake," he said to Augustus. "She looks good."

"You're doing fantastic," Augustus told her. "The lengths you'll go to get out of work."

"What happened?" Tink whispered, looking around. "Where are we?"

"Everything is fine," he assured her. "We're at a hospital in Louisiana. You took a little tumble down the stairs, but you're going to be fine."

Her expression went from confused to panicked in an instant. "Oh no," she whispered in the raspy voice. "How'd you get here? How'd you get off work?"

"Shh, none of that, Tinkerbéll," Augustus said as he bent down to kiss her forehead. "I'm just grateful you're okay. Don't try to talk."

"Who are you and where is my father?" Tink said before snickering.

"So, you've become a comedian since I've last seen you?"

"I see our patient has awakened," Dr. Hightower said as he entered the room.

"Yes, sir," Augustus answered. "Thank you for everything you did, Doctor. And my apologies for suggesting—"

"No need for apologies," Dr. Hightower insisted. "We all want what's best for our children. Now let me see how Ms. Catherine is doing today."

68

Blaine Biggs sat at his desk, looking at the mound of boxes on the floor of his office. His sister, Betty, was good at organizing and keeping outdated files put away in the attic, but beyond that, her skills were limited. He'd only hired her because he couldn't afford anybody with more adequate skills.

He'd regretted his decision many times. Betty was beginning to be more trouble than she was worth, often leaving without letting him know and coming in at her convenience. Blaine had repeatedly stressed the importance of a professional environment, but it'd fallen on deaf ears.

However, Betty Biggs couldn't be blamed for today's absence and Blaine wouldn't have traded places with her for anything. With Thomas in the hospital, and Esther falling apart at home, Betty had stepped up to take care of things at the funeral home. Blaine was grateful for the time alone at the office.

As the disarray began to close in on him, he decided to put the boxes in the attic himself. The old house had been a bear to remodel, but ultimately worth the effort. The amount spent to restore it was nothing compared to purchasing a building or even renting one.

He glanced through a couple of containers to make sure he

wouldn't need the contents anytime soon. After stacking one on top of the other, Blaine went up the steps to the attic. He'd expected a dark and dusty space, but it was anything but. The high wattage bulb put off more than ample light, so after placing his boxes in the corner, Blaine looked around.

The attic was about the only storage the old place offered. It'd been built before closets had been put in bedrooms, so storage in the old house was limited to a small linen closet and the kitchen cabinets. The attic, however, was unlike newly constructed homes where the roof space was simply to house the furnace.

Newer homes provided pull-down ladders if one needed to get to the furnace. This home had a well-built, sturdy staircase leading to a large room with plank flooring and a high-pitched roof overhead. It appeared Betty had done more than carry up old boxes. She'd made quite the getaway for herself. There was a table and two chairs in the far corner, a large piece of wood with documents tacked to it, and various baskets with notecards and scrap paper.

"What is *this*?" Blaine whispered. "Of all the nerve!" He walked past the table and over to the wooden board where she'd secured her notes with thumbtacks. After wiping his glasses clean, Blaine put them back on and leaned in to look at the items. He started reading a sheet of legal paper with a list printed neatly in his sister's handwriting.

First order of business

- Stall Blaine as much as possible about contacting Catherine Mabrey (Sinclair). Continue to remind him Baron was firm about her not attending his funeral. The longer she's away, the more time there is to search.
- Meet with the two cons from the extended-stay hotel. Definitely not at Syd's. (Both are proving impossible, not trustworthy, getting frustrated).
- **New meeting place established for Wayne and Dusty. Don't know why I haven't thought of it before, and Blaine

thinks he's the smart one. Set up office in attic, away from town, no one will notice lights on at night and no one will ever go up there. Screw Blaine with all his to-do lists and demanding organization. I, too, can be organized and it's enough that only I know about it. I don't have to wave my intelligence around for everyone to see like that crazy brother of mine.

- **Wayne looks high but we don't have anybody else. So far, they haven't been seen at the estate, but Paloma keeps checking on the house.
- The con artists are coming up empty handed, and Wayne is running his mouth. I'm not so sure he hasn't found something and kept it for himself. He's a punk and I'm not going to listen to his mouth anymore. I've *got* this. Goodbye Wayne.
- Pay off supervisor at hotel with five hundred bucks and driver with confiscated oxycodone. Have Dusty deliver payment to both before they arrive at work.
- **(Botched! Damn father intercepted. Must come up with new plan to scare her off. Catherine may be tougher than we thought, but I doubt it. If we can't scare her, there's more than one way to skin a cat).
- Got uglier than anticipated so I had to ask for help. It was time to make a big decision so went with a double header. Scare that stuck-up Sinclair woman off and if that doesn't work, this will be the beginning of framing her. Either way, she's going to be out of the loop.
- Dusty won't remain silent, I'm sure of it. Stupid Cassius is at Syd's every night trying to get her attention. She's got to go. He's not going to like this, but I can't worry about it. He's stupid and weak, that piece of trash wouldn't ever be interested in him.
- Ah, but how two murders will get a town talking. Too much attention on the estate now. Must be very careful. If the Sinclair woman has half a brain in that head of hers,

she'll get the hell out of town. I'll try scaring her off, but if that doesn't work, she'll be hanging from a hook in the bayou, too.

Blaine collapsed in the nearest chair, unable to read anymore. It had to be some sick joke, something Betty had done to tease him. His head began to swim, making it necessary to reach for the table to stabilize himself. Perhaps it was all a dream and he'd wake up. He and Betty would laugh about it later.

Blaine remained still while the world continued to spin around him. He closed his eyes to allow the feeling to subside, the drunkenness that had come on from such sudden emotion.

Unsure of how much time had passed, Blaine slowly opened his eyes. He was drawn to a crowded shelf a few feet away. He walked over to it, moving several items to reach the blue towel covering a large vase or jar. As soon as he lifted the cloth, bile rose in his parched throat. Stepping away from the shelf too quickly, he lost his footing, and landed on the plank floor. He tried to roll over before he threw up but couldn't in time. The vomit covered the front of his shirt before he could gather the strength to sit up. "It can't be, no it's not, there's no fucking way."

I've got to get out of here, Blaine thought. *Oh, dear God, this isn't really happening.* He glanced at his watch and struggled to recall when Betty had left for the funeral home. His first thought was making sure he hadn't moved anything. Blaine returned the items on the shelf back where they'd been and ensured he hadn't touched anything on the table. *What if I've dreamed this? What if it never happened at all? What if Betty destroys the evidence?*

He reached for the cell phone hooked onto the belt of his slacks. His hands were shaking so badly that it was difficult for him to pull up the camera icon. He took several pictures of the list written in Betty's hand before hurrying back down the stairs. Blaine couldn't stomach pulling the towel off the gallon jar again.

Sweating profusely, he wet a bath cloth in the kitchen and rubbed it across his face and the back of his neck. Blaine figured the sheriff was still at Jericho's funeral, so he quickly dialed Cassius. It rang twice before he answered.

"What's up, Blaine?"

"Cassius, I...I..."

"You all right, man?"

"Yeah, I mean, no. Where are you?" Blaine stammered.

"I was about to grab something at Reggie's for lunch. Want to meet me there?" Cassius asked.

"No, how fast can you get here?"

"Be there in five," Cassius said, ending the conversation.

BLAINE QUICKLY REMOVED his shirt and replaced it with one hanging on the back of his office door then waited outside until he saw Cassius pull up in his cruiser. It was all he could do not to run out to the car to meet him.

"Everything okay?" Cassius asked. "You sounded pretty worked up."

"Cassius, you won't believe it, you have to see this. I'm going to send the pictures I took to your phone in case something happens. It's crazy."

While Blaine was trying to calm down enough to forward the pictures, Cassius's phone rang.

"It's Roxie," Cassius said. "Give me a sec." He pointed toward the door, following Blaine back in the office. "Hey, Roxie."

Blaine could hear Roxie's friendly voice but wasn't concentrating on the conversation. His mind was far from any trivial chitchat.

"I'll be fine," Cassius assured her. "Thanks for checking on me though. The sheriff keeps telling me I need this time off, but I'm better off at work. Feel free to pass that tidbit on to him." He laughed. "He's still in the hospital," he continued. "I'm at Blaine's office now, but I'm going to visit him later. I'll tell him you asked about him."

Roxie offered more words of encouragement before Cassius finally ended the call.

Blaine was alternating between pacing the floor and swaying nervously in place. "Damn, you didn't rush that conversation, did you?"

"What are you *talking* about?" Cassius asked. "It was a two-minute conversation. Anyway, cut to the chase. What's this all about, Blaine? You're acting like someone just pulled an armed robbery on your law office."

"I'd welcome an armed robbery over what I found," Blaine said. "Come upstairs. You're not going to believe it. But wait—let me put the deadbolt on just in case Betty comes back. We'll hear her unlocking that. It's really loud."

"Betty? When did you get scared of your sister? Doesn't she work with you?"

Cassius's phone dinged and he looked down.

"It's just the pic I sent," Blaine said. "Let's go up to the attic and I'll show you the real thing."

Cassius followed behind as Blaine hurried up the stairs. "It's over here," he insisted. "Look! Betty made her own place up here. I never knew. Imagine that. And I thought she was being thoughtful to bring all of my outdated files up here."

"What is this?" Cassius asked, looking at the long sheet of paper Blaine was pointing to.

"It's been her. It has been *Betty* all along. She was killing those people! I know you won't believe it until you read all this."

"Betty can't be the killer," Cassius said. "She isn't strong enough. Leave it alone, Blaine, seriously. She's just messing with you."

"No, I'm not kidding. I'll show you more." He pulled a different piece of paper from the board. "Listen to this," Blaine said, his voice rising an octave.

- Big problem. Cassius was really pissed about Dusty. Even madder that I didn't have the nerve to cut her hands off. He had to do it.

Blaine stopped and looked up at Cassius, who now had his hand on his gun.

"Told you to leave it alone. Damn it," Cassius spat. "Why couldn't you keep your educated ass downstairs and behind your desk?"

"What?" Blaine muttered. "I...I..."

"Stop. You can't wiggle your way out now, it's too late. You were set, your own law office, no student loan. But it wasn't enough, was it? You had to get into our shit, too."

"I have no idea what you're even talking about, Cassius," Blaine insisted. "Why would you...?"

"Hey, don't *put* this on me," Cassius seethed. "Blame your client's family for this shit. I take it you didn't read the letters from your great-great-great-great grandmother, or whatever she was. Probably should've started at the beginning."

"Why don't you just give me the short version?" Blaine asked nervously.

"It all started when Betty was cleaning up the attic for you. You never knew she was going to surprise you with it. She worked a hell of a lot harder than you gave her credit for. But she was always beneath you, wasn't she? Not smart enough to get into college, much less law school. But Betty was smart enough to find the letters, wasn't she?"

"You know, I really don't care," Blaine said flippantly. "In fact, don't even tell me."

Cassius pulled his gun from the holster on his belt. He always carried it, even if he wasn't on duty. "You see, Blaine, it's a little too late for that. You put your nose where it shouldn't have been, and you can't turn back. Betty was right not to trust you. You wouldn't have ever gone along with this."

"With what?" Blaine asked. "If you're going to shoot me, at least let me know why. What was in the letters?"

"Your grandmother, way down the line, wrote some letters to the original Sinclair who built the Sinclair mansion. Emmanuel was his name. He was a crazy son-of-a-bitch. Your great-great-great-great—"

"I get it," Blaine said. "Grandparents down the line."

"Yeah, well the grandfather and the Emmanuel guy were into some shady business together—pirating ships and shit."

"Pirating ships? Betty's pulling your chain, Cassius. I can't believe you fell for that."

"It's in black and white. The letters are so old that they're brittle, man. Samuel, that's your great, great—"

"Stop with that," Blaine said. "I'm not an idiot."

"Oh, I forgot for a second. You're an attorney. Anyway, Samuel and Emmanuel were in cahoots, but Emmanuel thought he was better than your folks. Treated your great—well, you get it—treated him bad, like he was beneath him. They had a big heist planned, so big there were people involved from several states. Your grandfather took all the chances, but Emmanuel got all the loot and divvied it up among the rich folk."

"Doesn't add up," Blaine interrupted.

"*What* doesn't add up?"

"Why would he pirate ships and not get anything out of it? That's bullshit."

Cassius was getting agitated and pointed his gun at Blaine's chest, then his face.

"Calm down, just playing devil's advocate here," Blaine assured him.

"It's legit, man, I'm telling you!" Cassius's phone rang and he looked down. "It's Isaac. I've got to answer it. Say one word and I'll shoot you, got it?"

Blaine nodded. Cassius swiped to answer the phone and cursed loudly. "It's that damn picture you sent me, shit." He messed with the phone briefly before he was able to answer. "Yeah, Sheriff, how's it going?"

"Just left Jericho's funeral. What's your twenty?"

"I...uh...I...uh," Cassius stammered.

"Cassius? You all right?" Isaac asked.

"Uh...yea...I...uh...I'm headed to Reggie's to get a burger."

"Just seeing how you're doing," Isaac said. "Sorry to bother you."

"That's your *last* reprieve," Cassius said to Blaine as he ended his call with the sheriff.

"Humor me," Blaine insisted. "Tell me the rest of the story."

"The pirate story you don't believe?"

"Finish telling me," Blaine urged. "Maybe I'll believe it if you get a little further into it."

Cassius considered it briefly and apparently decided it was a story worth repeating. "This is from the letters written by your great grandmother times two or three. I didn't make this shit up. She was pretty bitter at old Emmanuel Sinclair. You see, her husband, your—"

"I get it, go on," Blaine said.

"He stopped by their house on the way to take the loot to the Sinclair estate, thought it'd impress her if he showed it off a bit. Gave her an inside look at all them jewels and so forth, then went on his way. It was the last she saw of him. Well, so to speak."

"So to speak?" Blaine asked. "Either it was, or it wasn't."

"You have a bold attitude for a dead guy," Cassius said.

Blaine didn't allow his words to deter him. *Surely Cassius won't actually kill me. This is all a dream. I'll wake up soon enough.* "So, was it the last she saw of her husband or not?"

"It was the last she *spoke* with him," Cassius said, wickedly. "The last time she saw him was when Emmanuel Sinclair tossed his left hand, with his wedding band still on it, I might add, on their front porch."

"Okay, let me get this straight," Blaine said. "You know this from letters that my, whatever, wrote to Emmanuel Sinclair. First, *why* would he keep such inflammatory and incriminating letters and second, *how* were they found by you two crazies at the Sinclair estate?"

"They weren't at the Sinclairs', she never mailed them."

"I...I just really don't know what to say. Betty's done a number on you, bro."

"It's legit, you dumbass. For someone that's supposedly so smart, you don't have a lick of common sense," Cassius snarled.

"How much is a lick? I mean, just for shits and giggles, how much is a *lick*?"

"The guy died before she had the nerve to send them, okay?"

"Why would Emmanuel Sinclair throw her husband's hand on the porch?" Blaine scoffed. "That's the most absurd thing I've ever heard."

"According to your—the letters... Emmanuel told everybody that your—"

"I *get* it, I fucking *get* it!"

"The Sinclair dude told his partners that he was double-crossed and never got the loot. But he really kept it for himself."

"And yet he died before he could ever do anything with it. Don't you find that a little sketchy?"

"No, I don't, as a matter of fact," Cassius shouted. "It just means the shit's still hidden somewhere!"

"Ahhh! That's what this is all about. You and Betty think you'll find a hidden treasure."

"You're damn right. We aren't lawyers, ya know," Cassius said sarcastically.

"What's with the *lawyer* obsession? I don't know what you think I make in this little run-down town, but I'm willing to bet, after expenses, it's not as much as you do."

The comment brought a chuckle from Cassius.

"But what I don't get is how those drifters got dragged into it," Blaine said, suddenly recalling what he'd seen on the shelf. "The hands! You two cut off their hands, for Christ's sake, and *kept* them."

"We couldn't very well scout out the estate ourselves. Someone had to do the legwork for us and who else but expendable folks?"

"That's disgusting," Blaine spat. "Why keep the hands? Why cut them off to begin with?"

"Haven't you ever heard of a signature? Don't you watch television? First, they had to be killed because dumbass Wayne kept talking down by the rigs. We couldn't have that, could we?"

"Okay, you got me. I'll play the game for a minute. You killed him because he was talking. Makes perfect sense for a psychopath who doesn't want to be caught. But he was a drifter. Sadly, nobody would've noticed him missing, or even cared, for that matter. Why bring so much attention to the murder? Hanging him from a hook and cutting his hands off? Really? That brought more attention than you bargained for, didn't it?" Blaine asked calmly.

"It was all in the cards, Blaine. Our initial plan was to keep that Catherine woman away as long as possible to find the treasure. That clearly didn't pan out. So, the next move was to frame her for murder, so she'd be taken to jail."

"Leaving the mansion empty to continue looking," Blaine said.

"Exactly."

"And you say that as though it makes sense," Blaine said, more to himself than to Cassius.

"Don't you *get* it? The treasure rightfully belongs to your family," Cassius insisted.

"You mean it belongs to you and Betty," Blaine added. "Don't put me in this shit."

"Look, that woman rolls into Kane, inheriting a mansion she's never even worked for, and then, *boom*, finds the treasure that's been *stolen* from your family. Not only was the double-cross a lie, but Emmanuel Sinclair killed your great, blah, blah, blah, grandfather to boot."

"So, you murder two people and try to justify it as though it's perfectly logical." A lightbulb went off in Blaine's head and he bent over to vomit once again. "Oh my God! Why? Opal raised you when your parents died. Why kill her?"

"We never meant for that to happen," Cassius choked, his voice cracking at last. "She went back to the storage shed to get some cleaning supplies for the gas station and found where Betty had stashed the hands. Opal called here and Betty answered the phone. She was frantic and—"

"Frantic?" Blaine echoed. "I can only imagine."

"Betty went to try to reason with her, but Opal wouldn't listen. She was reaching for her phone to call Isaac when Betty had to kill her. She hit her over the head and called me. We tried to make it look like a foiled robbery but knew nobody would buy it. The only way to cover our tracks was to cut her..." Cassius broke into a brief sobbing fit, pausing to regroup, his eyes taking on a maddening glaze.

"Cut her hands off," Blaine interrupted, seething.

Before Blaine could comprehend the magnitude of what had been done, Cassius's phone rang once again. He glanced down but ignored it.

"That nosy ass, Roxie," Cassius said. "Always trying to stay on top of shit."

"Oh, is she acting like someone in law enforcement?" Blaine asked. "Imagine that."

The ringing stopped and started up again. "Damn her," Cassius said, his anger growing.

"Did you ever find the treasure?" Blaine asked. "I take it you didn't since you're still in Kane."

69

TINK HAD FALLEN into a deep sleep after her brief minutes of consciousness.

"That's to be expected," the doctor had told Augustus. "Her body is reenergizing."

Augustus had grabbed some breakfast in the hospital cafeteria. He dozed off for a couple of hours, but it'd felt like a full night's sleep. When Augustus adjusted the blinds, Tink opened her eyes to the sunlight filtering in.

"You're still here," she whispered.

"Of course, I'm still here," her father answered. "There's no place I'd rather be. Well, anywhere with you, outside of a hospital, obviously."

"I'm so glad you're here," Tink said, turning to look at him. "*Kane, Louisiana*. Can you believe it?"

"It's pretty unbelievable," he answered with a chuckle. "Kane, Louisiana."

"I know it's strange, but for some reason I sorta like it here."

"Sorta? Is that somewhere between liking it and hating it, or between liking it and loving it?"

"Somewhere between it's kind of cool, but I'm not giving up my loft, *sorta*," Tink said, smiling.

"I'm happy to see you smiling," Augustus said, reaching for her hand. "You scared me, Tink."

"I'm sorry, Father."

"Don't be," he continued. "I'm sorry about so many things, especially not sharing more about your mother. It was always difficult, painful actually, to remember her. She was such a bright light, just as you are. I should have realized memories are made to share and fondly recall again and again."

"Father, are you okay? Don't worry. I'm going to be fine."

"I know you are, Tink. I could've been a much better father. It was easier to keep you at arm's length, so it wouldn't hurt so badly if I lost you. But I'm *not* going to lose you, sweetheart."

Tink opened her mouth to speak but nothing came out, her eyes filling with tears.

"Don't cry," Augustus said. "I don't think I could handle it right now." He laughed to ease the lingering awkwardness. "I'm glad you came," he continued. "I never thought I'd say that, but it was important for you. And apparently, you've found some pretty nice friends. They care a lot about you, Tink. They sat here for hours while you were in surgery. *Ben*. Is that his name?"

"Ben? What about Ben? Is he all right?"

"Aside from being sick with worry over you? I suppose. He's got a look in his eye that I don't particularly like."

"What kind of look? He's a nice man," Tink responded defensively.

"It's the same look I had when I saw Olivia. He may be a nice fellow, but he has to pass the Augustus Test."

"You have a test named after yourself?" Tink asked, her eyes sparkling.

"And there you have it, folks, my daughter is officially smitten. I don't need to pull out my Augustus Test to confirm *that* one."

Tink laughed. "Thank you, thank you for being here and understanding."

"Understanding what?"

"Understanding the things that I don't," Tink answered. "Is Paloma okay? Does she know I'm here?"

"Yes, Paloma was here, too," Augustus said fondly, looking away for a moment.

"Did you know her?" Tink asked excitedly.

"Indeed, I did. She was the one bright spot in Olivia's life. Paloma was very kind to her and to me, as well. I regret not ever reaching out to her after I left with you. I'm sure she'd have welcomed hearing about you."

"She's been so good to me, Father, almost like the mother I never knew."

"I'm so glad. It would've been a loss had you not met her. I never dreamed she'd still be here. Tell me about the sheriff," Augustus said. "What's his name?"

"Sheriff Broussard. I believe his first name is Isaac. He's been extremely nice, too," Tink answered.

"There's something familiar about him," Augustus said. "I can't quite put my finger on it, but I think I've met him before."

"You may have," Tink said. "I forget about you and my mother living in New Orleans. I'm sure you visited the estate a few times."

"Yes, I did. Unfortunately, it wasn't ever a positive experience. Olivia's parents were very unkind to her. She could never do anything right in their eyes. If she hadn't been a strong person, she'd have never survived the negativity they pushed on her daily."

"That makes me so sad," Tink said. "I'm grateful she had you."

"She had many friends," Augustus said. "Paloma was a surrogate mother to her, but unfortunately, had to do so from a distance. Paloma's family was always there for her. Olivia often visited their home and picked out books to read. She loved sharing Jericho's words of wisdom with me."

"Oh, Father, that makes me feel so good. It eases my mind tremendously. They, too, have been like family to me."

A knock on the door interrupted their conversation. "Come in," Augustus said loudly.

The door opened and Isaac entered, followed by Ben and Harriett.

"How are you today, Ms. Mabrey?" Isaac asked kindly as the three made their way to her bedside.

"I'm much better," Tink said, trying to lean on her elbows and sit up.

"Let me help you with that," Augustus said, as he fluffed the pillows behind her and eased Tink up. "I'm sorry if I wasn't very friendly when we met. It was quite a shock to get that phone call, but I appreciate you contacting me, Sheriff."

"That's my job," Isaac said. "But, by far, one of the worst parts of it. I'm sure you were taken off guard and I'm sorry that call had to be made."

"Have we met before?" Augustus asked. "You look so familiar."

"No, I don't believe we have. I was born and raised in Kane, but don't recall meeting either you or your wife."

Augustus nodded and turned to Ben, "Please allow me to introduce myself again. A do-over of sorts, as the young people say." He extended his hand to Ben, who reached out and returned a firm shake. "My daughter thinks a great deal of you, and I trust her judgment."

"Thank you, sir," Ben said, his cheeks turning crimson. He turned his attention to Tink. "How are you? You gave us a scare."

"I have a little headache, but I'm okay."

"What *happened*?" Harriett asked, stepping out from behind the men.

"I don't remember any of it," Tink said.

"I was sitting in the kitchen with Paloma and you'd gone to get the letters from the dressing room. You were gone longer than you should've been, so we went to look for you. That's when we found you on the steps," Harriett said.

"We're grateful for that," Sheriff Broussard said. "But I'm sure it's best that we don't bring it back up today."

"I'm terribly sorry," Harriett said. "Dan wanted to come but he's back at Ben's, taking care of the skins."

"The skins?" Augustus inquired.

Ben's face grew crimson again. "Gator season just ended."

"Ben and his brother Dan are two damn good gator hunters," Isaac said, patting Ben forcefully on the back.

"That's good to hear," Augustus said. "I've never even been out on the bayou. I'm sure it's beautiful out there."

"We should go, Father, ah, *Dad*," Tink said with a sly grin.

Isaac's phone rang and everyone in the room, except for Augustus, held their breath. "It's Roxie," he said. "I'll call her back."

"Go ahead, Sheriff," Augustus said. "Don't let us interrupt your business."

"I'll need to head out shortly. It's been crazy around here. But I'm grateful Blaine Biggs was working when this happened. He gave me your phone number. Otherwise, we'd have had a hard time." He looked over at Tink, then at Harriett. "You ladies need to have emergency contacts in your wallets, preferably near your driver's licenses. Most people put them in their cell phone, but fail to understand law enforcement personnel don't have access to their passwords."

"That's a very good point," Augustus said. "Blaine Biggs. Is that the attorney who handled the will?"

"Yes, it is. I knew he had. So, I phoned him for your contact information. He's having a hard time right now, just lost his grandmother."

"Grandmother?" Tink asked. "Did she live in Kane?"

All three of Tink's visitors looked at her as though she'd lost her mind. "What's wrong?" Tink asked.

"Opal Bailey-Blanchard was Blaine's grandmother," Ben said. "Thomas is his grandfather. I thought you knew."

"What?" Tink asked. "I had no idea. How sad."

"I'm sorry to hear that," Augustus said. "He was very helpful with Baron's will."

"He's a nice kid, excuse me—young man. It's hard for me to adjust to the younger generation now being our professionals. He's had a slow go of things but I'm sure it'll pick up. He renovated the old Thibodeaux place outside of town which took most of his savings and—"

"Wait," Harriett almost shouted. "Say that name again!"

"Thibodeaux?" Isaac asked.

"Yes! That's it! Remember, Tink?"

"Not really," Tink answered. "But it must be important so tell us more."

"The letters we found, the ones I was telling you and Dan and Paloma about," Harriett said to Ben. "The one about the man's wife who was upset that his hand was thrown on the front porch with the wedding ring on it. She kept causing problems and—"

"Let's discuss this later, Harriett. That was a century ago and we don't need to rehash all of that while Tink is recovering in the hospital," the sheriff insisted.

"But—"

"Damn," Isaac said as his phone rang. "It's Roxie again." He fiddled with his phone until he swiped across and answered it. "What is it, Roxie?" he asked. "I'm at the hospital." The sheriff paused briefly. The whole room could hear Roxie as she shouted into the phone, but couldn't make out what she was saying. "I'm confused," Isaac said. "Slow down, have you tried to call him? Where is he? What? When I called him, he was acting very vague and..." Isaac's face lost all color as he pushed himself to a chair. "I'm on my way with Ben," he said, motioning for Ben to listen. "No, hell no, don't you dare head out there. I mean it, Roxie. I'll have your job. If there are any units in that area, even from surrounding jurisdictions, have them head over. No radio traffic. Use landlines only. And Roxie, lock the office, don't open the door, and don't leave!"

"What's that about?" Harriett asked frantically. "It has something to do with Thibodeaux, doesn't it?"

"Nothing for any of you to worry about," Isaac said, his hands shaking. "Stay here, Harriett, I'll have Dan call you."

70

"HELL NO, we haven't found the treasure!" Cassius screamed. "You had to rush and call that damn Mabrey girl about inheriting the house. Just couldn't wait to let her know she'd inherited it, could you?"

"You have some serious issues," Blaine seethed. "That house belongs to Catherine Mabrey; it was left to her by her family. Forgive me for not giving you and my sick sister more time to ramble through it for some fabricated treasure from a hundred years ago. No, wait! You didn't have the balls to ramble through it yourselves—you had to hire some piece of shit drifters to do it. Then, ironically, ya'll killed them both to keep your hands clean. Oh, what tangled webs we weave!"

"Shut up, Blaine. It rightfully belongs to us!"

"Yes, per your logic. It belongs to you and Betty because one of mine and Betty's ancestors, not yours, may have robbed a ship for treasure that didn't belong to him. Then another crook stole it from him but died before our ancestor's letters could get to him. I'm sure those letters would've convinced him to give back the supposed loot and make all things right."

"Listen to yourself," Cassius said. "Standing there all high and mighty! You're set for life, but what about Betty and me? We'll never have anything. We deserve that treasure."

"You sound like a little kid watching *The Goonies*, Cassius. I've already told you I'm struggling financially, but do you even know how hard I worked to become a lawyer? Talk about deserving something!" Blaine shouted, his face hot with fury. "Were you there the weeks and months I made it on an hour of sleep a night because I had to study? Were you there when all I could afford to eat was rice and dried beans? Hell no, you weren't! Yet here you are, acting like you went through it with me! You sicken me. You and Betty will both end up in hell for what you've done. I'll make sure neither of you ever get that treasure, if there even is one. Mark my words, you ungrateful son-of-a-bitch!"

Blaine was blind with rage. The magnitude of all that Cassius and Betty had done was finally sinking in and he could no longer contain himself.

"Step back now," Cassius said, raising his gun to Blaine's chest. "Don't take another step toward me or I'll shoot."

"No, you won't, Cassius, you don't have the nerve. Where's Betty to do your dirty work? I forgot, she's busy planning our grandmother's funeral, isn't that nice?"

The sheer anger coursing through Blaine's body was causing his head to pound so loudly he never even heard the shot.

SHERIFF BROUSSARD and Ben heard the shot as they got out of the police cruiser. Isaac kicked in the door of Blaine's law office and both men ran toward the wailing sobs.

"I think it's coming from the attic," Isaac said softly, holding out his weapon. "Stay behind me, Ben."

The two took the stairs as fast as they could, while making as little noise as possible. The sobs grew louder as they got closer. "Sounds like a guy," Ben whispered to Isaac. The sheriff nodded in acknowledgment.

As they reached the top of the stairs, Isaac turned to Ben, motioning for him to stay put. Ben thought of defying him but reconsidered. It wouldn't have been right for him to question the sheriff's judgment.

When Isaac was out of sight, Ben listened intently. It seemed an eternity before he heard the sheriff speak. "What's going on, son?" he asked calmly as he scanned the room. "Listen, Cassius, Biggs is injured. He needs an ambulance now. Does he have a pulse?"

Ben leaned closer to the top of the stairs, listening for a response.

"Cassius, do you hear me?" Isaac asked much louder. "Damn it, Holder, does the man have a pulse? Is he alive?"

"I don't...I... I'm not sure," Cassius finally whimpered.

"Where's your weapon, Cassius?"

Cassius pointed about five feet away where his weapon had landed after the shot.

"Ben! Ben, can you hear me?" Isaac shouted.

"Yes, I'm here, Sheriff," Ben answered from the top of the stairs.

"Grab Cassius's gun from over there and go back downstairs. Call Roxie and have an ambulance sent out ASAP, and for fuck's sake, tell her to call the state police."

❀

Sheriff Isaac Broussard wasted no time getting to the funeral home where Opal Bailey-Blanchard's body lay lifeless in her finest dress.

"Good afternoon, Sheriff," Betty Biggs said as she gathered her purse and prepared to leave. "We weren't expecting visitors today. The public viewing isn't until tomorrow. I just came to view her before poor Grandfather did, to make sure the funeral home had done their job. I'm sure you understand. So sad, really. I hope my poor mother is able to live through this tragedy."

"Yes, I was hoping the same thing," Sheriff Broussard said. "Your poor, poor mother."

"And my grandfather, and Blaine, as well as myself. It's a terrible loss," Betty said solemnly.

KIM CARTER

"Don't force those tears too hard, Betty," Isaac said. "You'll be shedding plenty here shortly."

"Pardon me?"

"Put your hands behind your back, Betty Biggs. You're under arrest for two counts of first-degree murder and one count of second-degree murder. I pray you never see the light of day."

71

THE SHOCK of Betty and Cassius's confession to triple murders, the attempted murder of Blaine Biggs, and aggravated assault against her, delayed Tink's release from the hospital. With Jericho laid to rest, Paloma, Ben, and Horace decided to make the estate as inviting as possible for Tink and her father. Augustus had decided to stay for a few days to help Tink fully recover and secure a home inspector.

Paloma busied herself in the kitchen while Ben and Horace cleaned the blood left behind from Tink's injury. As they dabbed it lightly with damp sponges, Horace whispered to Ben, "I have something to show you."

"Why are you whispering, Horace?" Ben asked. Looking around playfully, he turned back to him. "See anybody up here?"

"No," Horace answered a little louder. "But we sure don't want Paloma to hear this."

"Do tell," Ben encouraged, leaning forward.

"Papa gave me a key before he died. We believe it could be to Emmanuel's desk."

Ben looked down the stairs for any signs of Paloma. "What are we waiting for?"

Stepping over the remaining debris, they quickly entered the office. Horace removed the key from his pocket and nervously handed it to Ben. Both men kept their eyes off the mummified hand on the desk and Ben tried the key. He jiggled it in the largest drawers with no results. Finally, Ben sat in Emmanuel's chair behind the desk and slid the old skeleton key in the middle drawer. It opened easily.

Both men remained silent as Ben looked inside. "It looks like a will of some kind," Ben said, pulling it from the drawer. "Let's look at it over there, away from...*that*." He glanced away from the hand of glory.

They walked back in the hallway and sat in the first alcove. "You read it, Horace," Ben encouraged. "I'll listen. I can't read that fancy handwriting."

"Here goes," Horace began.

Last Will and Testament

I, Emmanuel H. Sinclair, of Louisiana and La'Reau Parish, being of sound and disposing mind and memory, do hereby make this my Last Will and Testament, hereby revoking and annulling all other wills and codicils thereto heretofore made by me.

Horace stopped there. "It's a bunch of legal rhetoric, Ben, leaving everything to Lucretia, it appears." He turned through several pages before stopping on the last one. "This might be something of importance. It's an addendum added later. Listen to this."

To My Unborn Heir:

You are my legacy. One day my estate and all my fortune will be yours. Realize I have taken great risks to secure the Sinclair name and your future. Oh, the things I have seen and done! Your mother would be so disappointed in me, but you, my firstborn son, you will understand. There was no other way!

You see, my partner betrayed me! He tempted your mother in my absence AND he sided with thieves plotting against me! Nevertheless, I found them out and foiled their plans. I had no choice. They had to pay for their sins.

Not to worry, my son, the hand of glory protects us and all that is ours. For now, my good fortune must be our secret and ours alone—not even your mother can know. For Lucretia will never comprehend the necessity of all I have done for you. But you, you will be the best part of me. You will carry on my dreams and take the Sinclair name to new heights. Always remember who you are; you are the Sinclair Legacy.

These clues I leave you:

Keep in mind, as one great author once said, "the solution to our... problem is more rain."

My treasures await you. They glimmer and shine like the water beneath which they lie.

Each piece like a raindrop clearing a unique path for you as it meets the Sinclair soil.

Ponder my thoughts and my treasures you will find. These treasures will be your lifeblood my son, the soul of the Sinclair estate and the heart of your own legacy to come. Now make me proud.

With all my heart and hopes,

Your loving Father, Emmanuel

When Horace finished reading, they sat silently for several minutes before turning to each other instantaneously. Both men mouthed the only place the clues could've led...the cistern.

Wide eyed, they remained seated for a few more minutes before Ben spoke. "Horace, I like to think I know your family well. I believe Tink is much like you. LeBlanc blood runs through her veins just as the Sinclair blood does, not literally, of course, but you know what I mean. This treasure has caused generations of heartache and destroyed so many people."

"I think I know where you're going with this," Horace said as he stood. The men walked down the stairs and toward the kitchen where Paloma was preparing lunch. They stopped by the parlor, pausing briefly in front of the fireplace.

Horace tossed the will in the roaring fire, and both men watched until there was nothing left but ashes.

EPILOGUE

THE LINGERING QUESTION of what to do with the hand of glory remained. Harriett thought it should be buried in the Thibodeaux family plot since they all believed it to be the hand of Samuel Thibodeaux. Dan suggested they simply throw it in the bayou and let bygones be bygones. It couldn't remain in the Sinclair home—that was certain.

Ben and Westmoreland had made amends, even forming a strange friendship of sorts. With opinions differing, Ben remained steadfast that, one, the hand had to go, and two, it needed to draw as little attention as possible. He conferred with Westmoreland, who volunteered to throw it in the Bureau's incinerator. For some strange reason, it gave Ben peace. It would no longer be on the premises and would be incinerated far from the estate. Not normally one to believe in ghosts, Ben wasn't willing to take any chances of even a remnant of the hand remaining on the property. He couldn't get the glass case to Westmoreland fast enough.

❧

THE BEAUTIFUL PORTRAIT of Olivia that had once frightened Tink now brought her peace. She had taken her father to see it when she'd decided the painting should be moved downstairs. "Don't you think it should be somewhere that everyone could enjoy it?" Tink asked.

"Yes, your mother would've liked that," Augustus said. "I've never seen this portrait, it's outstanding."

Tink looked at her father and realized for the first time he was able to remember her mother without sadness. "I'm going to get Ben to bring the ladder so we can take it down," Tink said. Leaving her father with his memories, she went to find Ben.

"I wonder who the artist was," Augustus asked after the portrait had been removed and brought downstairs. "They did a remarkable job. They didn't sign the front. Perhaps they left a signature on the back. It'd be amazing to find them and have them paint your portrait, Tink."

"I don't know about that," she commented.

Augustus got down on his knee and turned the painting around in search of the artist's name. "I'll be damned," Augustus said. "I *know* these aren't what I *think* they are!"

Ben and Tink walked over to see what he'd found. There were several roughly shaped round coins taped to the back of the portrait. Augustus removed one and studied it intensely. "Catherine Mabrey," he began, "you will never want for another thing as long as you live."

"Father, what are you talking about?" Tink removed the tape from one of the coins and looked at it. "This looks like one of those wax seals embossed on the back of old letters." She handed it to Ben to look over.

"Is this a gold doubloon?" Ben asked, his eyes widening as he glanced over at Augustus.

Augustus was immersed in analyzing every detail of the old coin. He sat on the floor with his back against the wall. "Neither of you are going to believe this. This is what is known as the Brasher Doubloon." He held the coin in between his thumb and index finger. "I know all about it because I followed the recent sale of one at Sotheby's. If I told you what it sold for, you'd both have a heart attack. To give you a history, a fellow named Ephraim Brasher was a goldsmith in the late

1700s. At one point, he was even the next-door neighbor to George Washington. Long story short, if possible, he submitted a request to produce copper coins to the New York State assembly in 1787. They had no interest in dealing with coins, but Brasher produced them anyway. They became popular as souvenirs and among coin collectors. There was never a stated value on the coin. But looking at this, it has all the signatures including the EB hallmark."

"So, do tell, Father, what did the last one sell for?" Tink asked.

"Over ten million dollars."

Both Ben and Tink stood dumbfounded, unable to speak.

"I knew you would find them, Catherine," Paloma interrupted, as she walked into the room.

"You knew about these?" Tink asked incredulously.

"Your great-grandfather found them in a box of old ledgers. He wasn't sure if they had any value, but he was ill by then, and not willing to chance passing them on to Baron. He entrusted them with Uncle Jericho, who quickly gave them to me to keep up with. For years they sat in a rusted coffee tin at my place."

"You can't be serious, Paloma," Augustus said, shaking his head in disbelief.

"Apparently they were safe there," Paloma said with a laugh. "When Isaac came by to tell me you were inheriting the place, I figured Olivia's portrait would be the perfect place for them."

"I don't understand," Tink said.

"If they were valuable, Corbin would've wanted someone in the family to have them, someone who cared about Olivia. I knew, even if you sold the place, you'd take the portrait with you if it had any meaning at all. If you kept the estate, and you valued Olivia's memory, you'd never leave it in this back room."

"So only if I removed the portrait, would I find the doubloons," Tink said, processing Paloma's reasoning.

"Exactly," Paloma answered tenderly.

Five Years Later

With the Sinclair estate fully renovated, it was once again a breathtaking sight. The structure remained very much the same as it had when Emmanuel Sinclair constructed it. However, that was where the similarities ended.

The first floor housed the offices for Ben Norwood's construction company. Four of the second-floor bedrooms had been transformed into a legal aid center run by Catherine Mabrey and Blaine Biggs. The ballroom housed the Prudence Lambert Library and Literacy Foundation, run by Paloma and Horace LeBlanc.

Candace Ramsey reluctantly agreed to serve as receptionist and host to all three businesses. She also agreed to stay in one of the guest bedrooms until a cottage could be built for her on-site. Augustus started working three months at his firm then spending one month with Tink and Ben in Kane.

DNA results confirmed Isaac was indeed Baron and Ruby's first-born, but he decided not to make the information public. Isaac was delighted to have a niece but felt no need to change his identity. Out of respect for the sheriff, Paloma, Tink, and Augustus would keep his secret.

Ben and Tink Norwood's twin sons were proof the Sinclair curse never existed. Garrison and Augustus, known as Garri and Gus, lived with their parents on the third floor. They spent most of their time under Paloma's strict and loving supervision. Tink would often see the three of them assembled at the bottom of the stairs as Paloma read the plaque they'd had installed there.

In honor of Monroe Burke, who designed and constructed this magnificent staircase. Having never received any accolades during his life, may it now represent the unwavering dedication and faithfulness to his craft, and may future generations recall him by name each time they're awed by his creation.

Dan and Harriett had another daughter, Lombardi, named after another famous coach. Harriett volunteered part time at the literacy center and Dan joined forces with Ben at his construction company.

Ben's old place remained a bayou getaway for the growing family on weekends.

It seemed that the sheriff's prayer would indeed come true. Betty Biggs wouldn't live to see another day outside of prison walls. Cassius Holder would be up for parole in thirty years.

ABOUT THE AUTHOR

Kim is an author of suspense, mystery and thriller novels. She was a finalist in the 2018 Killer Nashville Silver Falchion Award and recipient of the 2017 Readers' Choice Award for her book *Murder Among The Tombstones*. This is the first book in her Clara and Iris Mystery series. The characters in this series are a couple of overly curious widows who become private investigators and were inspired by Kim's mother and her mom's best friend.

Her other titles include: *When Dawn Never Comes, Deadly Odds, No Second Chances, And The Forecast Called For Rain,* and *Sweet Dreams, Baby Belle.*

Kim's writing career started after she suffered an illness that made her housebound for a couple of years. An avid reader of mystery novels, she embarked on writing as a means of filling her time. Kim shared those early writings with friends and family who encouraged her to pursue writing professionally. Her health struggles and successes have been chronicled on The Lifetime Television in early 2000, *The Atlanta-Journal Constitution, Women's Day Magazine,* and *Guidepost.*

Prior to her illness, Kim worked in many different capacities in county government ranging from Park Director with Parks and Recreation to the Grant Department with Human Services. But, ultimately, it was her job as a correctional officer that provided her the opportunity to interact with a variety of people from all walks of life. Her experiences ran the gamete of inspiring success stories to tragic endings, much like her mysteries.

She self-published her first book *No Second Chances.* One of the guest speakers at the launch party she had at the Performing Arts Center in Newnan, Georgia included her close friend retired Atlanta Police Chief, Eldrin Bell. This connection would become helpful as she started doing more research for other books, this time working with a small publishing house.

Kim started networking and made connections with the Fulton County Medical Examiner's Office. Her research has taken her many places including morgues, death row, and the occasional midnight visit to cemeteries.

She is a college graduate of Saint Leo University and has a Bachelor Degree of Arts in Sociology. Kim has four grown children and lives just outside of Atlanta, Georgia.

Visit Kim Online
www.kimcarterauthor.com

ALSO BY KIM CARTER